FISH
&
CHIPS

CUT & RUN SERIES BOOK 3

BY ABIGAIL ROUX

RIPTIDE PUBLISHING

Riptide Publishing
PO Box 1537
Burnsville, NC 28714
www.riptidepublishing.com

Fish & Chips

Cover art: L.C. Chase, lcchase.com
Layout: L.C. Chase, /lcchase.com

ISBN: 978-1-963773-07-1

Second edition
June, 2024

Also available in ebook:
ISBN: 978-1-963773-06-4

FISH & CHIPS

CUT & RUN SERIES BOOK 3

BY ABIGAIL ROUX

RIPTIDE
PUBLISHING

For everyone who asked for more.

TABLE OF CONTENTS

Chapter One

"Hey, Freddy, Scott, you got to check this out," Special Agent Michelle Clancy said as she trotted into the free weights room of the FBI's Baltimore field office gym.

"Busy," Special Agent Fred Perrimore grunted as he strained with the barbell. His biceps bulged as he pressed up; sweat dotted the black skin along his closely shaved hairline.

"Believe me. It's worth it," Clancy told them in a singsong voice. Her ponytail bobbed along behind her as she bounced on the tips of her toes excitedly, the bright red hair clashing with her freckles and the flushed pink of her face.

Special Agent Scott Alston looked up from where he stood spotting Perrimore. "What is it?" he asked impatiently. Clancy was too easily worked up for a five-year veteran, and Perrimore always took too much weight. If he dropped the bar when Alston wasn't paying attention, there would be shit tons of paperwork to fill out.

"Garrett and Grady are beating the shit out of each other," Clancy answered with something resembling relish.

"So?" Perrimore asked in a strained voice. His large arms trembled with the effort to raise the bar and plates. "They're always doing that."

He was right, but Alston's eyes widened with the news. He began to grin even as he helped pull the bar up and hastily settle it into its cradle with a clank. No way did he want to miss this.

"What the hell, man?" Perrimore complained as he sat up and gave them both an exasperated glare. Alston was already following Clancy out of the room when he heard Perrimore protest, "But what's the big deal? They're always doing that!"

Clancy and Alston emerged into the main gym, where several small groups of agents had dropped what they were doing to gather around the center boxing ring. As Clancy and Alston hurried to watch through the ropes, a chorus of groans and cheers went up as one of the men slammed to the mat with an impact that actually shook the entire ring.

"Get up, Grady! You can't take that shit from him!" one of the watching agents called out in amusement.

Alston shook his head and folded his arms, listening as someone nearby filled him in on the events that had led up to this.

The fight had started out as a simple sparring match between partners. Nothing special. Nothing for anyone to pay much attention to. Several people in the main gym had been initially impressed that the newly arrived Special Agent Zane Garrett could hold his own with his temperamental, extremely well-trained partner, but that was about it. Today's event appeared to have started as a training session, with Ty giving Zane pointers and lessons in some particular technique.

If Zane was trying to learn from Ty, he'd gone to the right place. Unfortunately, Ty wasn't exactly mentor material. Everyone in the Baltimore office knew that Special Agent Ty Grady was good for one thing in the ring: embarrassing the hotshot rookies. If you really wanted to spar with him, you had to handicap him somehow. Alston personally preferred the knee-to-the-nuts-in-the-locker-room-prior-to-sparring method. That usually evened up the odds a little. Usually.

Heads began to turn when the gentle sparring, quips, and teasing between partners had become slightly more heated and the jabs had become true punches that caused the combatants to stagger back with each blow. It was common knowledge how difficult it was to work with Ty Grady. It had come as no surprise to anyone when Zane Garrett arrived that they were always at each other's throats, especially when it turned out Zane was about as headstrong as Ty, which was really saying something. There was already a pool on how long the partnership would last.

"Now, come on, Grady. You taught me that move yourself," Zane said as he backed away a couple steps, his wrapped fists still up and ready. His plain gray cotton T-shirt was soaked through with sweat and pulled across well-defined muscles as he shifted his shoulders.

Alston had to admit Zane was a big dude and saw how he could be sort of intimidating. Not that it would matter a bit to Ty.

Ty rolled to his side and pushed himself up with a low groan. He wasn't quite as tall or broad-shouldered as his partner, but he was solid from head to toe, still a big man in his own right. Alston was of the opinion that his attitude gave him a more imposing air than his bulk. Every agent here knew Ty Grady through one avenue or another. And everyone knew he was just one twist short of a slinky.

He was wearing a white shirt with a picture of a scarecrow on it accompanied by the words Out standing in his field. Not one of the watching agents gave it a second glance. It was, they all knew, his favorite shirt.

Ty looked up at his partner and snarled at him, seemingly unaware of the people watching and now placing bets on who would be the winner. He rolled his shoulders and began to circle again, taped fists up and close to his face. Zane moved in a mirror image, watching Ty intently.

"There's no way Garrett can stay in too long with Grady," Alston predicted. It wasn't that he didn't like Zane. He seemed like an okay guy. Maybe a little dull and straitlaced. But it was Ty he was fighting. The former Marine was on a short fuse on the best of days. When he lost his temper, there was never any telling what would be rigged to blow by the end of the workday.

"He's been in there twenty minutes already," Clancy said, arms crossed as she watched.

"Yeah, but it didn't get serious until a few minutes ago," another agent told them.

"Garrett may surprise you," Fred Perrimore said as he joined them. While he was built heavy and barrel-chested, Alston stood three inches taller than him at six feet, and they both towered over Clancy's petite frame. "He's got some moves."

"Having 'moves' and being trained to kill by the government are not the same thing," Alston said with a derisive laugh.

As if to emphasize his point, Ty moved in a graceful series of feints, jabs, and an arcing roundhouse kick to send Zane to the mat with a resounding thump. He danced away lightly before Zane could touch him.

"Hands ain't the only things that hit, Garrett," Ty said in a low voice, a slight smirk curling his lips.

Zane rolled into a crouch and twisted as he stood, his heel connecting with the back of Ty's knee, forcing it to collapse as he punched Ty in the kidney.

Clancy winced. "I'm thinking Garrett can kick ass just fine," she murmured.

They watched as Ty fell to his knees with a grunt of anger and pain, and then he just as quickly rolled and struck out, taking Zane's legs out from under him, catching Zane's knees between his two calves like a pair of scissors. The crowd groaned when Zane hit the mat a second time, and Ty pounced on him, getting an arm around his neck and rolling him up between his knees, trying to immobilize him.

"Should we stop this before Ty snaps his neck?" Clancy asked in morbid amusement. She and Alston shared a look, Alston privately thinking that he wouldn't put it past Ty to do it. They shrugged at each other negligently, but then both winced when Zane somehow rocked forward and pulled Ty half over his shoulder before shoving him off to one side. Ty rolled away nimbly and sprang to his feet almost instantly.

"We need walls, partner," Zane sniped as he got to his feet. "Something for you to splat against."

Ty shook his head and reached up to the strap of the protective headgear required in the ring. He yanked at it and ripped the padded helmet off, tossing it over the ropes to land at the feet of several of the agents watching. He didn't say anything to Zane, just held out one taped hand and gestured for him to bring it.

"Oh fuck, we're going to have to fill out paperwork about this too," Alston muttered to himself.

Zane's eyes narrowed, and he cocked his head to one side before doing the same, pulling off his own helmet and sending it skidding off the mat to thunk to the floor. "What's wrong, Grady?" he asked ruefully, raising his fists. "Cat got your tongue?"

Everyone watching groaned at the verbal jab. They'd all heard the story of what had happened to Ty and Zane in the mountains of West Virginia. Ty merely smirked without attacking. One of the fists he held up and ready was badly scarred from the cougar bite he'd received several weeks ago and the two subsequent surgeries he'd undergone to fix the damage. Zane's taunt was a low blow.

Without warning, Zane lunged, leading with his left shoulder to shove all his weight into Ty, propelling him toward the ropes. It seemed to be what Ty had been waiting for, though, because he planted a foot and used Zane's momentum to lift him completely off his feet and slam him down into the mat. The entire ring shook again, and a loud groan rippled through the audience.

This time when Zane was down, Ty didn't try to merely immobilize him. He got in four or five rapid punches to the midsection before one wicked left to Zane's unprotected face.

Shouts of protest came from the crowd, but no one moved to stop it. Zane balled up and took the clearly painful hits, and when Ty reared back for a last shot, Zane got one knee pulled back and shoved a foot into Ty's gut, hard, before he started scrambling away from him. Ty stumbled backward, but then he attacked again, too quickly for Zane to get away.

"I think he's getting pissed," Alston observed dryly.

"If Ty was pissed, Garrett'd be dead already," Perrimore pointed out in a flat voice.

Another round of pained groans went up from the small crowd of watching agents as Ty tackled Zane and straddled him, pinning him with his knees.

"That hurt, damn it!" Ty growled at his partner as he held him to the mat by his neck.

"Fuck you, Meow Mix," Zane hissed back as he got one hand on Ty's shoulder—the arm holding him down—having just enough arm length to keep Ty from totally throttling him. He balled up his other fist and punched Ty in the gut. Everyone heard the thump of fist hitting solid muscle, but it didn't dislodge him.

Ty turned his shoulder, slamming his elbow against the side of Zane's head before grabbing him by the neck again with one hand and using the other hand to fend off Zane's attempts at retaliation.

Anyone who knew Ty knew that he wasn't trying to kill his partner, though. Cause brain damage, maybe. But not kill him.

"Guys, this is too much," Clancy finally objected as she raised both her hands.

"You gonna get in there to separate them?" Alston asked incredulously as he watched Zane continue to fight off Ty's other hand while bucking under him, trying to throw him off.

Clancy shook her head, and they watched in morbid amusement as Zane finally, somehow, got some leverage. The two men rolled across the mat in a badly orchestrated tumble, each man too stubborn to release the other as they grappled.

"What the hell is going on here?" an irritated voice bellowed from the doorway of the main gym.

The crowd of agents scattered. Ty and Zane stopped mid-throttle, looking up at their superior like two kids caught roughhousing in the living room.

Alston edged away toward the weight room, stopping just behind the doorway to peer around the corner with Clancy and two other curious agents.

In the middle of the ring, Ty turned his head to look at Special Agent in Charge Dan McCoy, who was glowering at them from several yards away. "Hey, Mac," Ty greeted innocently as he straddled his bleeding partner. "Come down to work the glutes?" he asked with a sincere cock of his head.

Zane gasped for air and rapped his knuckles hard against Ty's chest as he finally pried Ty's fingers from his throat.

"You two, my office, now," McCoy ordered as he pointed his finger at them. "If you can kick the shit out of each other, then you're ready for your next assignment," he muttered as he turned and stalked away.

As soon as McCoy was gone, someone from somewhere in the cavernous workout room wolf-whistled at Ty and Zane and proceeded to applaud the performance they'd given.

Ty stood and took a bow as Zane stalked off toward the locker rooms. Alston snorted and looked down at Perrimore with a shrug. "Better them than us."

"I hear that," Perrimore muttered as he returned to the weights.

Zane let his head loll back and lifted one hand to gently prod his split lip. "Ow."

"Whine about it. It'll make it better," Ty offered as he stood in front of his locker, his back to Zane, and unwrapped the tape from his hands with jerky, irritated movements.

"Bite me," Zane muttered as he dug into his locker for a towel before starting in on the tape on his own hands. He spared an evil glance for Ty. "Teaching me to advance in a fight is a bad idea."

"Teaching you to fight at all is an exercise in futility," Ty responded in a matter-of-fact tone. "Luckily for you, I enjoy things like banging my head against a wall."

"I enjoy banging your head against a wall too," Zane replied as he tossed the balled-up tape at a nearby trash can. He let a small smile quirk his lips as he sat on the bench to unlace his shoes.

"Shut up," Ty grunted at him. But even though his back was still turned to him, Zane could hear the smile in his voice. "And cut it out with the damn cat jokes, huh? They're starting to catch on."

"Fine, fine. No reason to get catty about it," Zane told his partner with a barely concealed grin.

"A for effort," Ty conceded charitably.

Zane kicked his shoes into his locker before pulling his T-shirt over his head and inspecting his abs and ribs. "You had to go for the ribs, didn't you?" he said, his voice pained. He'd had his ribs cracked so many times he figured they might as well be superglued at this point. "Bastard," he tacked on before shucking his socks and standing with his towel in hand.

"You leave them open," Ty informed him. "Because you cover your head and cry like a little girl."

Zane huffed. This was one of the problems with being Ty's partner. While they were trying to learn to live with each other without significant personal injury, that didn't necessarily carry over to their sparring sessions. "I didn't cover once today," he asserted. "Backed off, hell yes. Covered, no."

Ty glanced over his bare shoulder and smirked. "Granted," he allowed. "Think I should shower before McCoy hands us our asses, or should I go in smelling like victory?" he posed grandly as he opened up his locker and tossed his sweaty T-shirt into his gym bag.

Zane bit the inside of his lip against the first answer that came to mind as he deliberately looked his lover up and down, and he spent a few seconds revising what he could say without risking another smack upside the head. "I don't believe McCoy would appreciate your . . . expression of 'victory.'" McCoy wouldn't appreciate Ty's finely tuned musculature or his ass either, but Zane was more than happy to pick up the slack in that area.

"Quit ogling me, sidekick," Ty warned without having to turn around. He grabbed for his shower caddy and a towel, and with one last smirk and wink at Zane, he headed for the showers.

Zane spared a moment to wish the locker room weren't so busy this afternoon. He'd reached a point where Ty's attitude and cockiness were more turn-ons than annoyances. They were harbingers of Ty's playful good mood, which more often than not led to copious amounts of rough, passionate sex.

Zane decided he'd wait to shower until Ty was done. He could only deal with so much bodily temptation in one day.

They sat at McCoy's conference table, behaving themselves and attempting to appear abashed.

Ty figured Dan McCoy knew him better than that, though. He was probably still getting a read on Zane, though, just like everyone else in the Baltimore office. They'd only been actively assigned to Baltimore for a few weeks now. Ty was at home. Zane was still an unknown to most everyone, despite the stories that had filtered through about their past escapades.

McCoy knew enough to know they were up to no good, anyway.

"I hope you got it out of your systems," McCoy finally said to them in annoyance.

"We were just putting on a demonstration," Ty explained easily. "Zane calls it 'How to Get Your Ass Kicked.' It goes over real well with the rookies," he drawled, overly pleased with himself.

Zane just sat there looking cool and comfortable in his well-fitted suit. He had a small smile on his face as he shook his head slightly at his partner.

"Shut up, Grady," McCoy requested flatly.

"Right," Ty muttered. He shifted in his seat and leaned forward. "You said you had an assignment for us?" he asked eagerly. He would take anything over the "getting up to speed" deskwork they'd been doing the last three weeks. Despite one blip up in the mountains of West Virginia, the last eight weeks of Ty's life had been god-awful boring. Even Zane couldn't keep Ty's wavering attention for very long unless he had something shiny to wave around. Ty needed to be doing something or he began to go stir-crazy.

McCoy's lips curved into a slow, slightly malicious smile. "I do," he answered. "Corbin and Del Porter," he said as he retrieved a file.

"Who?" Ty asked, unimpressed.

McCoy smiled and reached to the middle of the table for a little white remote. He turned slightly and pushed a button, causing a small flat screen to flick on. A picture of a large cruise ship appeared on the screen bolted to the wall.

"Oh shit," Ty found himself blurting before he could stop himself.

"This," McCoy continued as if he hadn't heard Ty, "is the Queen of the Mediterranean," he told them with a wave of his fingers at the ship. "It is currently docked in Baltimore, preparing for a fifteen-day cruise to the Caribbean."

"You're not making us take a vacation, are you?" Ty asked in something close to panic.

Zane's chin snapped up in alarm. "Jesus, Grady, we agreed not to even think that word, much less say it."

"Corbin and Del Porter," McCoy said loudly to curtail any more conversation, "were supposed to be on that ship tomorrow. But we finally got enough on these two to detain them." He slid a file toward Ty and leaned back in his seat with a grin. "There's a laundry list of no-nos we can pin on them with a little more evidence, and we'll get it soon enough. What we want from you is something concrete on a few of their contacts."

Ty scratched his head absently as he looked over the file. The two men were implicated in numerous high-dollar thefts: art, antiquities, rare gems. All stuff that was hard to steal and harder to fence. It was difficult to tell whether they were collectors or middlemen, but either way, if the FBI leaned on them, it could produce a lot of information on a lot of different high-end thieves and dealers.

But Ty and Zane weren't leaners. They didn't interrogate suspects who weren't part of their own investigations. They didn't know anything about this case and would be lost if they were asked to do the interrogation. Information wasn't why they were here. He glanced to his side, where Zane shrugged one shoulder, having obviously come to the same conclusion.

"I'm not sure I understand why we're here," Ty said in confusion as he gestured between himself and Zane, still looking down at the file.

"You are here because you two roughly match the physical description of the two men we now have in custody," McCoy answered with a wide grin.

Ty looked up at him suspiciously. McCoy seemed to be enjoying himself too much for this to be good news for Ty or Zane. Zane leaned forward in his seat, frowning, though he didn't speak up.

"We look like them," Ty reiterated flatly.

"Vaguely," McCoy agreed. "Same build, mostly. Zane's coloring."

Ty glared at the man. "I'm not following," he said slowly. "You want us to assume their identities? How's that gonna work?" he asked.

"Corbin and Del Porter were booked to leave on that cruise tomorrow," McCoy said again. "We have it on good authority they plan to meet several of their buyers and sellers while on this cruise, taking advantage of somewhat lax security and customs and what have you in the Caribbean. And since this will be the first instance of the two of them ever showing themselves physically in their business dealings, their contacts only have virtual interactions to go on. They won't know you're imposters. We can get a lot of information out of this if you two take their places and play your cards right."

"I'm not sure I like the sound of this," Zane said. "We've not got word one on the case until today, and now we're supposed to impersonate these guys?"

"You'll be given a crash course. And you're both professional bullshit artists; you're perfect for it," McCoy replied carelessly. Zane frowned at him.

Ty scratched slowly at his cheek. "Okay," he said carefully. He still didn't understand why McCoy seemed to be enjoying the prospect so much. There was a catch coming.

"You leave at nine in the morning. The rest of your team has already been put in place," McCoy told them as he pushed another stack of files toward the center of the table.

"Our team?" Zane repeated. Ty sighed heavily and closed his eyes. There was the catch.

"You know the drill, Garrett, a team. Team leader, two more field agents, and tech support. Read the files so you don't end up shooting one of them when you meet them. And Grady, we'll be needing you to make just a few . . . alterations . . . to your appearance before you go," he said as he studied Ty critically.

"What the hell are you talking about, McCoy? It's not like he can gain fifty pounds overnight," Zane said crossly.

"Nothing like that. Some hot wax and a little bleach, and he'll be set," McCoy continued, barely keeping himself from laughing now.

"Hot wax?" Ty asked in alarm. He heard Zane stifle a snort.

"Del Porter is what you would call . . . arm candy," McCoy drawled with a smirk.

"Oh hell," Zane muttered, leaning back, rubbing his hand over his face, and shifting in his chair uncomfortably. Ty glanced at him, not following.

"I see that Garrett has figured it out," McCoy said, his voice nearly bubbly. Ty shook his head in confusion.

"I didn't mention that?" McCoy asked in feigned innocence as he flipped through his notes as if he needed to check his information. "Corbin and Del Porter aren't brothers, gentlemen. They're lovers. Legally married, in fact." He reached out and placed two silver rings on the desk in front of them. "Go ahead and put those on," he instructed.

Zane went totally still, his eyes locked on the jewelry. Then his chin rose as his gaze shifted to McCoy. "Are you sure this is necessary?" he asked flatly.

Ty very carefully didn't say anything in response as he stared at the shiny rings. He'd worn a wedding ring before as part of a cover. But this was different.

"The Porters are a very out gay couple," McCoy continued, ignoring their reactions to the news. "The fact is well-known to all their contacts. It would be an alarm bell if you weren't wearing the rings," he said to Zane. "Corbin is what you'd call the brains of the operation. Del is . . . pretty."

Ty still sat motionless, staring at McCoy with a churning in his gut as he realized what they were being thrown into. A very out gay couple amongst people who would expect them to act as such—including a team of their own people. He slowly reached out and picked up one of the rings, turning it over in his hand. It was a simple silver band, flat and wide. He glanced at Zane apprehensively. Zane still wore his own gold wedding ring on his finger. Ty didn't know how his partner would react to replacing it, even temporarily. But Zane didn't move a muscle, didn't even twitch as he stared at the single ring still there in front of McCoy.

"Now understand: this may put you both in a few uncomfortable situations," McCoy went on sincerely. "But you've both got UC experience, and I'm sure you'd both rather have to kiss each other than be shot at," he joked. Ty cleared his throat and tried to restrain a smile. McCoy had no idea how right he was. "Those rings are all we're going to provide you for this one," he continued. "We've appropriated the bags they'd already packed for their cruise, so you're set on being clothed and otherwise outfitted. Lucky for us, you two are even roughly the same sizes," McCoy rambled as he stood. "Everything they needed for the deals they were making is in that luggage. You'll have to smuggle weapons on board; we'll come up with some sort of concealment for them in the luggage. The captain and head of security on board have been informed of your involvement, but you are not to break cover even with them unless absolutely necessary. Ty, if you find yourself in the brig, you stay there until they make port. You'll have the rest of your team there if you get in trouble, but when you make land, you're shit out of luck."

McCoy stood at the end of his little speech, looking down at them with a raised eyebrow and a smile. Ty and Zane sat staring at him, their mouths hanging open as they listened.

Dan McCoy had been a good field agent, and he was a good Special Agent in Charge. Ty had even worked on a few cases with him before McCoy had been promoted, and they'd gotten on well—which was probably why McCoy was enjoying this so much and letting it show. Ty sort of wanted to hit him.

"Come with me," McCoy invited with relish as he swept out the door.

A few moments after he disappeared, Zane stood abruptly with a sniff and straightened his jacket. Ty saw that he was grinding his teeth. He lowered his head and looked at the ring in his hand, not sure what to do or say about it. He supposed he would just put his on and let Zane work it out himself. He slipped it on his finger discreetly as he stood up. It was a little tight; he had to force it over the knuckle that was still a little swollen from the surgery he'd had to remove a piece of cougar tooth, but once it got on, it fit well. Ty very carefully didn't give it any extra attention after that.

Zane reached out and plucked up the other ring, closing it into the fist of his right hand before turning on his heel to leave the room. Ty followed them out silently, dreading the hissy fit that would come soon enough.

They followed McCoy down a few floors to an interrogation room and filed into the observation half of one of the suites where an agent, Harry Lassiter, already stood at the glass. Ty and Zane nodded to the man as McCoy pointed through the two-way mirror. "Gentlemen, meet Del Porter."

The man sitting at the table was handsome, probably about Ty's height and build, just a little slimmer. He had short, spiky hair bleached an unnatural platinum blond that contrasted oddly with his dark tan. He wore a sleeveless vest that tied with a simple cord of leather at the crest of his ripped chest, and his entire upper body was well-muscled and toned. He was also clean-shaven and completely devoid of body hair.

He looked to Ty like he should be standing under a waterfall in a gay porno.

Zane paused in place, eyes a little wide, looking from Del to Ty to Del and back.

Ty blinked rapidly at the guy. "I'm supposed to be . . . him?" he finally asked in a stricken voice.

"Good thing you're a hell of an actor," Zane murmured as he continued comparing them.

Ty glared at him briefly and looked back at the man behind the glass. "I'll never pull this off," he said to the other men in the room.

Zane tipped his head to one side, openly appraising Ty's body. "I don't know," he said distractedly. Ty looked back at him hatefully, feeling himself blushing under the scrutiny.

"He's not what I'd call stupid. But he sure as hell isn't the brightest bulb in the pack," McCoy informed them. "He knows just enough to keep his mouth shut. But that and the fact that he's pretty and got himself a rich husband are about all he's got going for him."

"Holy fuck, man," Ty finally muttered. "I'm gonna be this dude for how long?"

"Relax, Grady. You have the easy end of this," McCoy assured him. "Garrett's guy is the real brains here, and no one who's familiar with them will expect you to do anything but lay in the sun and work on your tan. Garrett? In the field, you're the lead on this one. You're calling the shots. Grady is just there as scenery and backup."

Zane snorted as Ty turned to look at McCoy in outrage. Backup? They were partners; there was no lead and backup!

"Ty, we've booked you an appointment at some spa with a name I can't pronounce," McCoy went on as he handed Ty a slip of paper.

Ty reached out woodenly and took the certificate. "I'll get on board with the hair color," he bargained pleadingly. "You're seriously gonna make me wax my chest?"

"You see that guy in there?" McCoy countered with a point of his finger at the man in the interrogation room.

Ty swallowed hard. He had done a lot of things he wasn't proud of in order to assume identities that weren't his. He'd changed his appearance, changed his behavior, treated decent people horribly to make an impression on a scumbag, prepared crack cocaine for others to smoke, taken lives, and any number of other things he didn't care to remember. He knew how important a part the smallest thing could play when trying to convince a stranger that you were someone they thought they already knew. He looked down at the silver ring on his finger and back up at the man behind the glass with a heavy sigh.

"There's a good man," McCoy said with a pat to Ty's shoulder.

Ty glanced at Zane as he felt himself blushing slowly. Though Zane's face was composed, Ty could see the laughter in his eyes.

"I don't know how they'll get rid of the tattoo, but they've assured me they can," McCoy added with another pat to Ty's shoulder.

"What?" Ty cried as he looked at McCoy in outrage.

McCoy just smiled at him. "This guy was obviously never a Marine," he reasoned. "Now, Grady, you get going," he ordered before Ty could have a meltdown. "You're getting the works, so you'll probably be there all fucking day. Garrett, come with me," McCoy said as he gestured for Zane to follow him. "I'll introduce you to yourself," he said wryly as they headed out the door.

Ty felt the sudden urge to beg Zane not to leave him there. He could feel the raised writing on the slip of thick, cream-colored paper in his hand. He looked down at it, thinking of all the procedures the makeover would entail. Salon Láurie . . . waxing, tanning, bleaching, manicures, lotions, scented mud . . .

Del Porter said something suddenly, complaining about being left in the room for so long. Ty turned to look at him in shock. He pointed his finger in outrage and turned to the other agent in the room. "He's British?" Ty cried.

Special Agent Lassiter, who'd been standing there silently the whole time, covered his mouth with his hand and merely nodded in answer, unable to keep from laughing any longer.

"Do you realize what kind of shit-fit Grady's going to have over this when this is all done?" Zane asked McCoy as they walked down the nondescript hallway of holding and interrogation rooms.

"Oh, I'm looking forward to it," McCoy said with relish. "I want pictures, Garrett. They'll be great for the newsletter."

Zane rolled his eyes. "I hope your insurance is up-to-date," he said as they stopped at another door. "Grady doesn't forget people who fuck around with him."

"He gives as good as he gets," McCoy said good-naturedly as he opened a door. Zane grunted and walked in.

The man on the other side of the two-way glass was as different from Del Porter as night was from day. And McCoy was right. Zane did have a general resemblance in height, build, and coloring. But Corbin Porter was definitely high-class. Or he thought he was: finely cut hair slicked back, a ruby stud in one ear, an expensive designer suit with a high-collared shirt rather than a tie, custom cuff links, manicured hands, and Italian leather on his feet. He held himself like a man accustomed to receiving respect, or possibly groveling.

"I didn't say anything to Grady because I didn't want to mitigate his horror. You're going for a haircut and manicure too," McCoy said with a twist to his lips.

Zane nodded distractedly as he studied Corbin Porter. The man was . . . arrogant. That was the word Zane was looking for. Arrogant. And possibly vain as well, but only to the point of knowing he was a fine-looking man.

He was also confident and controlled. He had propped one ankle over the opposite knee as he sat casually at the table, one forearm resting on the edge. He wasn't fidgeting or twitching. He was simply waiting. What gave him away was the anger sparking in his eyes and the tightness around his mouth.

"Do you want to talk to him?" McCoy asked Zane.

Zane slowly shook his head. "I've met his type before."

"He's hardly a drug runner or a computer hacker," McCoy pointed out.

"He's a thug," Zane murmured. "He's dressed up pretty, but he's still just a thug."

"Explains the tattoo they'll be giving you, then."

Zane blinked and turned his chin toward McCoy, who was grinning.

When Zane and McCoy stepped back into the observation room of Del Porter's interrogation suite, Zane had almost expected Ty to still be there, tying himself to the table and begging not to be taken to the salon.

But it was just Special Agent Lassiter, who had been joined by Special Agent Perrimore. They were standing at the glass, looking in at the prisoner with their heads cocked to the sides, like they were studying an animal in the zoo.

Zane peered through the glass as well. Ty was in there, sitting opposite Del, relaxed into the seat with his back to them, his legs crossed and his elbow resting on the table, almost like Corbin Porter had been. But Ty made it seem casual and easy, where Corbin had given off nothing but contempt and hostility. There was something different in Ty's manner, too, but Zane couldn't put a finger on it. He was too surprised to see Ty in there at all. He wasn't the only one.

"What the hell is he doing?" McCoy asked in alarm. "He said he wanted to talk to him," Lassiter answered. McCoy reached over and flipped the speaker switch. "He told us not to listen in," Lassiter told McCoy.

"Fuck that," McCoy responded unthinkingly. "The guy's actually talking—we might get something from him."

"Not like we can use it in court," Lassiter murmured under his breath, and he and Perrimore murmured quietly before snickering over the circumstances of the undercover case again. Zane ignored them in favor of watching Ty as the speakers tuned in.

"How long have you been married?" Ty was asking Del, who sat hunched and defensive, looking at Ty suspiciously.

Del didn't answer; he merely looked down at his hands, probably studying his wedding ring. Zane resisted the urge to look down at his own. He knew, without a doubt, what sort of thoughts were running through Del's mind. Zane squeezed his eyes shut for a moment before focusing on the scene again.

"Did you do it here in the States or did you go somewhere else?" Ty asked, his voice conveying what sounded like genuine interest.

"What the hell does Ty care?" Perrimore asked incredulously.

"He doesn't. He's building rapport, idiot," Lassiter answered idly as he watched Ty closely. "We used to use him to prep suspects all the time. He's charming."

"You two will make a cute couple," Perrimore drawled.

"Shut up. He also has a knack for giving off that dumb-as-a-brick vibe, leaves them off guard."

"Yeah, yeah."

Ty continued, undeterred when Del still didn't answer his queries. "My husband and I, we went to Boston," Ty went on, picking up his hand and flashing the silver ring on his finger casually. The lie came shockingly easily to him. Del's eyes flickered up to him, obviously surprised.

Everyone in the room turned to look at Zane.

"Ah, yes," he drawled wryly as he felt their eyes on him. "He's a sucker for red roses and opera."

Perrimore and Lassiter snorted at him while McCoy chuckled and shook his head. "If there was baseball and Guinness involved, I'd half believe it," McCoy muttered.

Zane rolled his eyes and turned his attention back to the window.

"Lots of history up there," Ty was saying with a tilt of his head.

In the room, Del sat up straighter. "I didn't think they liked that sort of thing in the FBI," he said with a slight curl of his lip. Zane was surprised to hear him speak with a British accent.

Ty shrugged. "You're thinking military. Feds don't have any problems with it. I do my job like anyone else," he said with another wave of his hand. Zane couldn't place what Ty was doing differently with his body, but it made him look . . . gentler. Not feminine, but . . . not as masculine as he was apt to be. Zane couldn't really describe the effect other than to think that Ty looked less alpha. He realized suddenly, as Ty rolled his shoulders, that he was subtly mimicking the man sitting across from him.

It hit Zane right then what Ty was really doing in there. He had no intention of interrogating Del Porter. He was studying him.

Del nodded carefully. "How long have you been with him?" he asked, his tone tentative.

"Long enough to know better," Ty answered with a smile. All of his answers were vague. White lies that wouldn't test Ty's conscience, Zane knew.

Del gave him a half smile and nodded, then looked back down at his hands.

Ty was silent, watching him. From his vantage point behind the glass, Zane could see what Ty was seeing. Fading bruises around the man's wrists, a few on his upper arms.

"He treat you right?" Ty asked suddenly.

Del glanced up at him almost defiantly and nodded again. He held up his hands to display his wrists. "I like it rough," he told Ty with a smirk.

McCoy had to clear his throat, and Zane turned a glare on him.

Ty chuckled and nodded. "I hear ya," he responded neutrally. He continued to examine Del Porter, and the man watched him and waited almost curiously. He looked as if he wanted to say more, but he was still wary.

Zane shook his head as he watched through the glass.

"The little hamster in Ty's head is probably bored," Perrimore observed.

"Thank you for your time, Mr. Porter," Ty said abruptly as he nodded, as if having satisfied himself. He unfolded his legs and stood, heading for the door.

Del watched him go in surprise. "That's it?" he asked in confusion. "You're leaving?"

Ty stopped at the door and turned to look back at the man, his hand on the door handle. "I'm sorry. Did you need something else?" he asked with what seemed like honest surprise.

"You didn't even ask me anything."

Ty laughed and shook his head. "That ain't my job, man," he told Del dismissively before stepping out of the interrogation room and shutting the door firmly behind him.

Del Porter stared at the door and then looked at the mirrored glass incredulously.

"Somebody get Grady to the damn spa," McCoy ordered under his breath as he stalked out of the room.

CHAPTER TWO

Looking over his reflection in the mirror, Zane wondered how such little changes could make him look so different. When he'd gone undercover before, he'd either been in tailored suits in Wall Street financial company offices, or he'd gone messier and dirtier in denim, leather, and sweat. This high-class pizzazz was new.

McCoy had scheduled him for a "gentleman's" treatment at a spa, where he'd been soaked and massaged, had his unruly hair cut in a more refined style so he could use this funky paste to slick it back, had his eyebrows waxed and plucked, of all things, and even had a deep-cleansing facial, where the woman had poked and prodded at his skin with a little metal tool for what had seemed like hours. It had been one of the weirdest and most painful things Zane could have imagined. It would be, he figured, a great interrogation tool.

And the ear piercing had stung like a bitch.

Now he was sleek. Polished. He'd had a manicure, so his hands looked neater, less experienced in brawling. And a pedicure, which had actually felt pretty damn good. But the biggest change wasn't immediately visible. Zane turned around so his back was to the mirror and looked over his shoulder, lifting his shirttails and pushing down the waistband of his dress pants to expose skin.

A graceful twisted vine tattoo spread across his lower back from hip to hip, just below his waist, dipping down to the crack of his ass in an inverted triangle of stark black, simple, striking lines. It wasn't real, of course, but the effect was still the same. He wondered what Ty would think about it. Ty seemed to love his own tattoo, but the leering Marine bulldog with its smoking guns was definitely more Ty's style than this more graceful design.

Sighing, Zane let his shirt fall. It was already open down the front, unbuttoned, exposing his chest. He hadn't bothered to put his undershirt back on after the massage at the spa. He'd been in the process of getting ready for bed when he'd been arrested by the strange sight of himself in the mirror. He started to pull the shirt off his shoulders, but he heard a key in the front door and moved out into the hallway on bare feet, listening as someone entered the apartment. It could only be Ty; he was the only person Zane had ever given a key, and Zane never left a door unlocked. When Zane peered around the corner, though, a stranger stood there. It took him a little too long to realize it was Ty after all, and Zane was glad he didn't have his gun in hand.

"Don't shoot me," Ty said in a flat, tired voice, obviously thinking exactly the same thing Zane had been. He began to loosen his tie and unbutton his shirt as he walked closer, tossing pieces of his clothing haphazardly to the floor and furniture as he approached Zane.

"Are you just getting done with the—"

"Yes," Ty muttered as he yanked his tie off. His shirt fell open as he bent and pulled off his shoes.

Zane looked over the long, tan body before him, his brows rising slowly the more he took in. The people at the spa had done the works on his normally scruffy partner. He was Ty, but . . . not. He was clean-shaven for the first time in months, and his short hair had been bleached an unnatural white-blond. It stood straight up, as if offended by its new color. Ty's entire body looked retouched, his tanned skin shinier, smoother—and likely softer—than it had ever been. His well-defined chest was devoid of its usual dusting of dark hair, and the effect made him sleeker.

Zane wasn't sure what he thought of the hair, but the rest of Ty was a walking wet dream.

Which was . . . hysterical, really. Zane blinked several times and pressed his lips together hard.

"Go ahead. Get it out of your system," Ty invited as he tossed his dress shirt at the couch. He waved his hand at his newly waxed chest.

Zane let the smile loose. "You look . . ." He crossed his arms and shook his head. "Different," he settled on, trying to not laugh outright.

"Yeah? Well, you look sleazy," Ty told him with a smirk as he looked Zane up and down critically. He took a few slow steps, circling Zane as he sized him up.

Tipping his head to one side as Ty walked around him, Zane lifted one shoulder in a defensive shrug. "It's the gel they put in my hair."

Ty shook his head, pursing his lips thoughtfully as he tried not to smirk. "No," he drew out. "Something else."

Zane waited, sure that Ty would enlighten him. "You look airbrushed," he observed once Ty stopped in front of him. "Like in a skin mag."

Ty lifted his chin and squared his shoulders, looking Zane in the eye as he mulled over a response. "Yeah," he finally said slowly. His lips curved into a wicked grin. His hazel eyes seemed almost neon-green with the platinum-blond hair accenting them. "But I make this shit look good."

Zane raised an eyebrow as he pointed at Ty and twirled his finger. Ty clucked his tongue. He raised both arms to the sides, holding them out as he turned in a slow half-circle. The muscles of his shoulders and back were, as always, well-defined as he stood with his arms raised. The flex of Ty's bicep drew Zane's attention to the unblemished skin. It was odd not seeing the tattoo on Ty's shoulder, but Zane was too distracted by the rest of him to ask about it. Ty turned his chin to look over his shoulder at Zane, and Zane could see a smirk on his lips. Ty never flaunted himself, not that Zane had ever seen anyway, but the man had a mirror. He wasn't immune to a little cockiness, not when it was well-deserved.

"The word that comes to mind is 'beefcake,'" Zane drawled, looking Ty over, appreciating the view.

"Mission accomplished, then!" Ty said happily as he turned to face Zane again. He frowned suddenly. "Is 'beefcake' one word or two?"

Zane laughed. "Who cares when you've got a great ass?"

Ty narrowed his eyes. "I'm not used to you being the brains of the operation," he murmured. "You know what I think we need? I think we need some practice."

"I wonder if I should be insulted," Zane posed, narrowing his eyes as he set his hands on his hips. "I'm the one with a degree in statistics," he reminded.

"You'd seriously rather argue credentials than fuck me?" Ty asked with an incredulous laugh.

"Well, if you'd said that," Zane said as he took a couple of steps closer to Ty.

Ty took a step back and put his hand on Zane's chest, raising one eyebrow playfully as he used the other hand to point at himself. Zane now saw that Ty's usually calloused hands and fingers were now well-manicured and relatively smooth, making the newest scar on his hand even more noticeable. "Hold your horses, Lone Star. Are you calling me stupid?"

"No way. I have a sense of self-preservation," Zane said as he set his hands on Ty's hips, their chests brushing.

Ty bit his lip and sucked air through his teeth, raising his chin as if considering what Zane had just said. "Since when?" he finally asked softly.

Surprised, Zane straightened, reviewing his words. He inhaled slowly, pushing away a slight dizzy feeling. Ty made him feel like that more and more lately. "Since I got a partner I trust," he answered.

Ty looked at him seriously as he stepped closer, letting Zane's arms encircle his hips. He put one hand on Zane's upper arm, fingers digging into his bicep. He reached up with the other hand to touch Zane's face, gliding his fingertips along Zane's lips as he looked him over. It was an odd gesture from his normally undemonstrative partner, one that struck Zane silent as he waited for Ty's next move. He had expected Ty to make another comment or wisecrack, but Ty said nothing, letting his fingers slide down Zane's neck, over his chest, down to his waist to disappear under the unbuttoned shirt Zane still wore. Zane shivered.

"Care to help me get into character?" Ty whispered with a mischievous smile.

Zane hummed slightly and pulled Ty flush against him. "What kind of help do you need?"

Ty pushed up on the tips of his toes, brushing his parted lips against Zane's. They were warm and moist, and Zane slipped his tongue out to wet his lower lip practically as soon as Ty pulled back and moved both hands over Ty's body in slow, deliberate motions, coasting across that incredible-looking amazingly silken skin.

Ty slid his hands up and down Zane's chest and arms and then wrapped his arms around Zane's neck—something Zane didn't think he'd ever done before—and kissed him again. It was a soft, tantalizing kiss, one that begged for Zane to come and get more.

Zane's body reacted in a hurry: his pulse picked up, and he could feel his cock swelling in his pants. With a soft growl, he wrapped one arm around Ty and trapped him against his chest as Ty tried to take a step away. Ty laughed softly, and Zane answered the teasing kiss with a firmer, wetter one.

Ty gave him a low moan as he arched his back just enough to press closer against Zane. The sound was something else wholly unlike him, at least at this stage in their fondling. He seemed to be trying his best to make Zane drag him to bed. If this was what he meant by getting into character . . . then damn. The passive-aggressive seduction was a hell of a turn-on and a successful enough tactic that Zane wasn't going to worry about being manipulated right now. Instead, he slipped his hand into the back waistband of Ty's suit pants and dragged his fingers around to the front, where he pulled at the button.

Ty didn't move to help like he usually did, just ran the fingers of both hands through Zane's hair as he waited patiently for Zane to get his clothes off. It was so odd, Zane couldn't help but chuckle. It was obvious Ty was enjoying the teasing. It probably wasn't a role he'd ever had much opportunity to play. When Zane paused, Ty moved closer, pressing into him again as he nipped at Zane's ear.

"Doesn't seem like you need much practice. What's gotten into you?" Zane murmured as he dragged his lips along Ty's exposed throat. He unfastened Ty's pants and started pushing them down over his hips.

"Nothing, yet," Ty answered with a slow grin. "That's your job," he said softly, his breath gusting across Zane's cheek.

Zane groaned as he moved his hands to squeeze Ty's ass and captured Ty's lips with his own, this kiss hungrier as Zane shifted to grind himself against Ty's thigh. It was a good thing Ty wasn't this agreeable more often, he thought distantly. It was blowing Zane's mind with how sexy it was. Ty would have him eating out of his hand if he behaved like this more often.

He'd probably be better off not mentioning that.

"Come on, beautiful," Ty coaxed as he began to gently pull at him with the hand he had tangled in Zane's hair. He steered him toward the bedroom door, kissing at him with those same soft, enticing kisses as he did so.

Zane lifted his brows in silent comment, but he wasn't about to speak and ruin the moment. He wasn't willing to release Ty for one second as he let himself be drawn along. But he did stop them long enough to push Ty against the doorjamb and suck and nip along Ty's shoulder. Ty raised his chin and closed his eyes, moaning wantonly again as he let his fingertips slide down Zane's neck.

"Fuck," Zane groaned as he arched into Ty's body and got them moving again into the bedroom. He wasn't having any luck remembering if they'd done anything resembling foreplay before now. They each knew what the other wanted, and that was the release. But this new side of Ty was hot and seriously, almost painfully, arousing.

Ty let his hands slide across the fronts of Zane's shoulders, pushing Zane's shirt back and down off his shoulders, and he wrapped his arms around Zane and kissed at his neck, his jaw, and his ear, all slow, sensual touches of his lips to Zane's skin as he caressed him. He pulled the shirt down and off Zane's arms as he pressed their bare skin together and nipped at Zane's ear again.

Zane shivered, let out a harsh breath, and shook his shirt loose before gripping Ty's hips inside the open pants and dragging him the last few feet to the foot of the bed. His head fell back to allow Ty more access to his neck as he spread his stance and gathered Ty right up against him.

"Zane," Ty murmured breathlessly as he pulled away just enough to push his own briefs down and tug at Zane's pants. Fumbling as he reached between them to unfasten his belt and pants, Zane cursed under his breath as he finally got the button undone and the zipper down so Ty's hands could snake inside to touch him. Zane was erect in his underwear, the soft cotton boxer-briefs doing nothing to rein him in. Ty's hands began sliding against his skin, trying to push the pants down and pull Zane closer at the same time. His lips just barely brushed Zane's, tempting him, enticing him to dive down for the contact. Zane's tongue slid along Ty's lower lip as he chased those full, wet lips, and he nipped at Ty's tongue when Ty's hand closed over his erection.

"Fuck," Zane hissed. "You're driving me insane."

Ty smiled against his cheek. "You're the one in the driver's seat. Do something about it," he invited in a silky voice as he let his lips move against Zane's as he spoke.

Zane pulled back with a gasp and shoved Ty down to the bed. Holding onto his aching cock, Zane pushed his pants down with his other hand and kicked them aside, staring down at his lover. He craved him; it was crazy how turned on Zane was.

Ty turned his head slightly to look up at him, and he smiled again, clearly pleased with himself. He kicked off his briefs and pushed himself back into the middle of the bed, laying himself out invitingly. The ease with which he was submitting was all still very suspicious. Narrowing his eyes, Zane looked over Ty's nude body as he pushed off his own briefs, wondering just how amenable his lover was feeling tonight. After a moment's consideration—and admiration—Zane pointed at him and rotated his finger in a silent "roll over" order.

To Zane's increasing surprise, Ty's smile widened, and he obediently rolled over onto his stomach and pressed his face against the sheets, pushing his hips up in a slow, sensual motion.

Now Zane knew something was up. But damn if he was passing on an opportunity like this one. If he had to pay for it later, so be it. Crawling over Ty's thighs, Zane rubbed his groin against Ty's firm ass. Humming slightly, he bent to bite hard at Ty's neck as one hand slid down Ty's spine.

Ty gave a soft, plaintive gasp when he was bitten, but he pushed his hips up to meet Zane without further complaint. He groaned softly as their bodies touched and Zane's weight settled over him, the sound muffled by the much-washed cotton.

Zane grabbed for the drawer next to the bed and yanked it open, pulled out a condom and a tube of lubricant, and slicked his fingers. He reached down and tugged Ty's hip up, holding him firmly as he dragged one finger down Ty's cleft, leaving a thin trail of lubricant behind. He could see Ty shudder and clench, and it made his gut cramp in sympathy. He knew very well that moment of anticipation, waiting for Ty's fingers.

Ty sighed loudly as he lowered his head and spread his knees wider, practically begging Zane to fuck him. "I don't need that," he told Zane with certainty. Zane sucked in a breath as he spread out his hand over one ass cheek, squeezing greedily. He knew Ty hadn't been drinking this evening to mentally prepare himself for his less-substantial role on this cruise, but beer or drugs never made him this easy to handle, even when they were in the midst of fucking. Was this Ty's interpretation of Del Porter? Was this the Ty he'd be seeing for the next two weeks?

Ty reached back and dragged his fingers over Zane's hip, his fingertips just barely able to reach. Despite Ty's words, Zane slid a finger inside him and ran his free hand across Ty's skin, skimming up and down his back, wanting that tactile sensation as he rubbed Ty inside.

"I don't need it, Zane," Ty breathed pleadingly, pressing his face into the bed and groaning impatiently. "Come on," he urged as he tried to push his hips higher.

Heat flooded Zane. He could feel his cheeks flaming, and it certainly wasn't from embarrassment. Wondering how far he could push Ty before he'd start pushing back, Zane instead pushed another finger inside Ty and, spur of the moment, smacked Ty's ass.

Ty didn't even flinch, but he did growl in frustration as Zane took his sweet time. He pushed back on Zane's fingers and spread his knees just a little wider, begging Zane to fuck him. Zane groaned and moved his free hand to close his fingers around the thick cock bobbing below Ty's belly. He stroked a few more times and pushed in more fingers, twisting as he added pressure. The crack of that slap was echoing in his ears, just like the blood throbbing in his cock.

"Dammit, Garrett!" Ty called out through gritted teeth. He pushed his hips back demandingly as he reached to drag his fingers against the skin of Zane's hip, as if he desperately wanted the contact.

The lingering touch felt like trails of fire against Zane's skin, and he had to draw a slow, deep breath to try to pull together some measure of control. He didn't want this to be over anytime soon. "What do you need, baby?" he breathed against Ty's ear.

Ty turned his head, trying to brush his cheek against Zane's face. "You know what I want, Zane."

Christ, the sound of his name in that desperate voice. It was impossible to ignore. Zane slid his lips along Ty's cheekbone before he pulled free and grabbed for the condom, rolling it on and slicking up hastily. One hand pressing on Ty's lower back gave Zane the right angle, and he pushed, holding his breath, gasping when he slid inside, where it was so tight he thought he'd lose it right then and there. So much for control. He stretched out over Ty's body and pinned him to the bed.

Ty gave a short shout of pleasure, and a shudder ran through him as Zane settled on him. "Baby," he groaned. He slid his hands out to the sides, flexing his fingers against the sheets, silently inviting Zane to hold him down. He so rarely allowed that, and Zane almost didn't know what to make of it. Zane licked his lips, shifted his weight, and moved each shaking hand to cover Ty's before bearing down to keep him in place. His extra few inches of height on Ty were coming in handy. Then he started to move slowly, rocking in and out, working his cock in deeper, and he ignored the sound, suspiciously like a whimper, that tore from his own throat.

"Fuck yes," Ty whimpered, sounding relieved as he placed his cheek against the sheets and closed his eyes. He gave a slow moan as he tried to push his hips back to meet Zane's rocking.

Zane squeezed his eyes shut and ducked his head to slide his lips and tongue along Ty's spine as he reveled in the slow, thorough attention he was giving Ty's incredible ass. As he gasped for a breath between kisses, Zane decided he'd have to try this again—slow and steady—because it sure as hell felt just as incredible as their usual hard but satisfying fucks.

Ty writhed under him, struggling against the pressure on his body and the hands that held his wrists but not actually trying to get away. He seemed to be enjoying the sudden submissive role.

"You said you needed practice," Zane said on a groan, not really able to work up any accusation.

"Christ, Zane, stop talking," Ty gasped out, lifting his head off the bed just enough to try and look over his shoulder before he gave up and pushed his face against the sheets again.

Zane scoffed but snapped his hips twice, hard, before returning to the slow rhythm. He might have suspected Ty of "practicing" this submissive act elsewhere if he didn't know better. They'd not spent a night apart since Zane had moved into his new apartment in Baltimore three weeks ago, and almost every time they'd been together recently, Ty had topped. Zane sure as hell didn't mind. But this was addictive, too, and he leaned more of his weight onto Ty's back, focusing on steadily thrusting into the welcoming body under his.

Ty tried to speak, but he was obviously incapable of forming words. He merely moaned long and loud, digging his fingers into the sheets and still trying desperately to push his hips up against Zane's thrusts, if his trembling was any indication.

The sounds sent pangs through Zane's gut, and he had to stop again to take a couple of deep, slow breaths. He pushed himself up to his knees and looked down at his hips, seeing his cock slide and disappear into Ty's tight ass. He pushed himself in, moving painfully slow, then pulled back out just for the pleasure of watching. He groaned as Ty tried to shove back against him, and the urge to fuck Ty into the mattress almost took him over.

"You want to walk tomorrow?" Zane asked hoarsely, gripping Ty's hips to hold himself still. Ty shook his head mutely, his entire body tensing as he rolled his hips. "Fine," Zane growled. He reached down, grabbed Ty's hand, and twisted that arm behind Ty's back, as if getting ready to handcuff a suspect. He gripped Ty's forearm hard and held him down by the other shoulder, and Zane swore under his breath and thrust in with some strength the first time before pulling back until it felt like he might slip out completely. Then he thrust in again, out, and in again, his breathing tense and harsh as he tried to contort enough to watch himself. "Well-fucked looks good on you anyway."

"Everything looks good on me," Ty told him, managing to laugh breathlessly before he gasped and moaned. "Harder, baby."

Gritting his teeth, Zane lowered himself until he was holding Ty down with his weight once more and did as Ty demanded, speeding the shifting of his hips and starting to really fuck Ty in earnest. He jerked Ty back every time he pushed roughly in, and he hissed and moaned each time he sank deep as their bodies slammed together.

Rather than the violent battle for control this sort of brutal fucking usually caused, Ty merely writhed and moaned with each thrust, rolling his hips to help Zane sink deeper, sliding his glistening skin and hard muscles against Zane, occasionally calling out Zane's name or begging for more and harder. He never even tried to loosen his hands from Zane's grip or pull his arm out from behind his back.

"Ty—" Zane choked out as he started to bend over Ty's back, feeling the tension inside him about to snap, the few minutes of hard fucking unraveling his control.

"Not yet, baby, please," Ty begged, his voice hoarse and desperate.

Zane pushed himself back up, releasing Ty's arm and tugging him until his ass was in the air, his knees spread wide in a vulnerable position Ty rarely tolerated for long. Zane gripped his hips and eased back, watching himself again as he tried to slow his thrusts. He gave Ty three or four sensual slides, carefully pulling the head of his cock almost completely out, forcing those tight muscles to spread. Ty clenched hard around him, grasping for the sheets to hold onto as Zane snapped his hips and shoved in hard after each slow pull. Zane pulled back one last time, rocking there on the edge.

Ty couldn't even manage a response other than to cry out sharply and bury his face in the tangled sheets below him. To Zane's increasing shock and pleasure, he didn't move his hips to force Zane back into him; he was taking all the punishment Zane offered happily, begging for it, and the thought nearly drove Zane crazy. He snapped his hips again, driving into Ty hard and not slowing this time. Zane huffed for breath and reached around Ty to wrap his slicked hand around Ty's cock, pumping it with the rhythm of the pummeling.

Ty curled in on himself, his body taut and incredibly tight, moaning helplessly as he spilled over Zane's fingers. Zane choked for a breath and cried out hoarsely as Ty's body clenched around him. The sounds Ty made when Zane fucked him, desperate and needy and uninhibited, were always too much for Zane. His control snapped and he pushed in hard once, twice, countless more times as he came hard and fast, using and abusing Ty's willing body before collapsing onto Ty's back with an aching groan.

It was a long minute before Zane found the will to carefully pull out of Ty and drop to lie beside him on his back. He was still sucking in deep breaths when he turned his head to look at Ty closely.

Ty smirked at him as he lay unmoving, his hazel eyes dancing merrily. "Good?" he asked, his usual teasing tone now back in his voice.

Zane stared at him as his pulse still throbbed. "Yeah," he agreed. "That was ... unusual."

Ty's lips twitched in amusement, and he smiled wider. "Wanted to see if I could pull off the sex kitten vibe," he explained blithely as he pushed himself from his belly onto his elbows. "Turns out I can!"

"Great," Zane muttered, rubbing at his eyes. "We are supposed to leave the cabin, you know."

"Just getting into character," Ty said with a half shrug of his shoulder. Then, in a voice eerily like the man Zane had seen behind the glass today, complete with the British accent, he said, "You must have had fun; you missed a chance for a cat joke. Love the earring, by the way."

The accent surprised Zane. He knew from Ty's dossier that his partner was an accomplished mimic. He could pull off a number of accents and varying pitches and tenors, and he was competent, if not fluent, in several languages, Farsi and French among them. Several times since being moved to Baltimore, Zane had witnessed one of their colleagues come to Ty and request he make a phone call or recording in a particular accent for a case they were working.

Zane had just never had occasion to see him—hear him—in action. This case would be interesting for that aspect alone, to see if Ty could pull off the British accent for an extended length of time.

Zane huffed his annoyance and leaned away as Ty tried to poke at the ruby earring. "Trust me, I've got enough holes in my body. I wasn't too thrilled about this one. But I guess it's better than another bullet hole."

Ty reached out to run his finger down Zane's cheek, one eyebrow raised in amusement. "It's too shiny not to mess with. You do realize I'm going to yank it at some point just to see you scream."

Zane narrowed his eyes. "Try it and I'll yank on something sensitive of yours, jerk," he said with a light smack to Ty's flank.

Ty's palm flattened against Zane's cheek, and he scooted closer, pressing his nose to Zane's with an impish grin. Zane harrumphed quietly at the gesture. Ty was rarely playful; it was both fun and exasperating to see him this way. He ran his fingers through Ty's now-blond hair. "Not too sure what I think about this," he said with a slight frown. It didn't look right at all, and he knew, despite what he just said, that he'd already decided he didn't like it.

Ty grunted and pulled his head back, losing the playfulness. "Yeah, well don't get used to it. As soon as this shit's over, I'm buzzing it all off," he muttered as he turned his face away and pressed his nose into the pillow. He rolled and pushed his back against Zane as he burrowed under the pillow. He was like a very large puppy trying to take over a very small bed.

Zane shifted to his side and slid his arms around him, noting how his fingers caught on the bare flesh of Ty's chest. He hadn't noticed it when he'd been focused on fucking Ty's brains out. "Good," he murmured in agreement, happy to settle down and hold him close. As his palm cupped Ty's shoulder, Zane remembered the missing tattoo. He was almost afraid to ask. "How'd they get rid of the bulldog?"

Ty grunted and raised his head, pushing the pillow aside as he rolled in Zane's arms and tossed a leg over his hip. He rotated his shoulder forward to inspect his bicep. "Some sort of synthetic cover-up. Like movie makeup. They said it should be okay for about a week. And they taught me how to do it in case something happens to it." He patted his arm consolingly. "Poor puppy."

Zane laughed softly, but Ty didn't seem to notice.

"I'm not sure what was more unpleasant. The waxing, the bleaching, or the manicure," he told Zane in a disgruntled voice. He laid his head back down. "They used things on my fingers I haven't seen since Afghanistan," he muttered thoughtfully as he slid his arm under Zane's and then looked at his fingertips, tangling their limbs together further. "And holy shit, did you get a massage? Brunnhilde went a little overboard with the deep tissue thing. My shoulders are killing me."

The word Afghanistan caught Zane's attention, but the mention of muscles hurting almost diverted it. Yeah, now that he thought about it, he was a little achy. The masseuse had told him he would be. But he'd also just done all the work in their little romp. "Yeah, I'm a little sore," he said quietly, thinking about how little he knew of Ty's past, especially things like tours in hostile Middle Eastern countries, a Marine Recon team being a family, and why he spoke Farsi like a native.

"I feel like I got picked up by a pterodactyl," Ty muttered. He either didn't realize his slip or was thankful Zane had ignored it. Either way, he was silent for a long time, looking at Zane with a slight smile. Finally, he took Zane's hand and kissed the tips of his fingers before rolling to his back.

Zane remained pressed against his side, settling his free hand on Ty's belly. "I don't see any bite marks but mine and the cat's," he teased. Ty groaned and rolled his eyes, looking at Zane sideways as he tried not to smile. "It's okay. Nothing will show . . . as long as you wear a tie to the office tomorrow," Zane added cheekily.

"I'm not worried," Ty muttered. "We're supposed to be at the office early so they can go over all our technical shit," he informed Zane softly, falling back on the topic of work to avoid the subject of ties and getting caught fucking a coworker. He gave a deep sigh of resignation. "We're so screwed, Garrett."

"Why do you say that?" Zane murmured as their legs easily settled together. They were both still sticky and sweaty and so were the sheets, but Zane didn't care.

Ty shrugged. "It's one thing to play a part. It's another to play a real person," he said with emphasis. "Our marks know the people we're supposed to be better than we do. And we'll be flying solo. That backup team will be a last resort. Our only weapons are whatever we can sneak through security on the HMS Sinkytowne." His nose wrinkled, and he sneered slightly. "It's like a floating death trap. And my Manchester English is pretty damn rusty."

Zane wasn't too sure a high-class cruise liner could be called a death trap, per se, but he got the idea. Ty had probably had enough of boats for one lifetime after being deployed so many times. "McCoy also said these people haven't ever met, and it's not that likely they really know that much about each other. The less we try to act like someone else, the better off we'll be," Zane said, knowing from past experience that being yourself as much as possible while undercover made it easier to act your way out of trouble.

"Right," Ty murmured, humming as his fingers slid across Zane's.

Zane poked him gently in the ribs. "Is that a 'right' as in agreement or a 'right' as in humoring me?"

"A little of both," Ty drawled with a smile.

"I told McCoy that we wouldn't back down from a challenge."

Ty turned his head and blinked at him, nonplussed. "Okay," he said slowly, as if expecting a caveat to the statement.

Zane frowned slightly. "Do you disagree?"

"No," Ty answered in the same tone. "I'm just saying . . . we're screwed." He gave a laugh. "But hey, I get to work on my tan. And my accent."

"Where did you pick up a British accent? If I didn't know better, I'd think French Foreign Legion."

Ty snorted and laughed. "I would look good in the hat thingy." He smiled warmly at Zane, but Zane knew him well enough now to see through the warmth in his eyes to the gears turning behind them. Ty was trying to find the shortest distance between two lies. "We trained with an SAS team. British Special Forces. Special task force preparedness deal. We taught each other more than battle tactics." He began to laugh again. "Somewhere in the south of England there is a guy with a still in his cellar making Grandpa's moonshine."

Zane grinned, almost believing the story. Knowing Ty, it was probably somewhat true. Ty likely had trained with an SAS team and gotten them all drunk on Chester Grady's moonshine. But Zane also had no doubt that the SAS team was not where Ty had perfected that accent. He decided to let that drop too. It wasn't really important. "Ah, the power of a little liquor for loosening tongues. In more ways than one."

"Just trading cultural treasures," Ty said, tongue-in-cheek.

Zane turned his face into Ty's bicep as he chuckled. "Did they know what they were getting when you handed around the flask? Or did you just give them the recipe and say good luck?"

"Mm. In retrospect, it's not a good idea to get an Englishman drunk if he's not quite unarmed yet."

"I don't want to know," Zane mumbled.

"Probably not," Ty agreed as he stared up at the ceiling, smiling faintly.

Zane relaxed further against Ty's body and inhaled. Then he frowned and sniffed again. Ty smelled like . . . lavender and vanilla. "Did they bathe you in lotion? Or rub you with cookie dough or something?" Because there was also a whiff of cinnamon, now that he actually tried to figure out the odd scents that definitely weren't Ty. Maybe coconut too.

"Kinky," Ty commented. He held up his hand and smelled his bicep, shaking his head. "It's from the massage and . . . whatever it was."

"Is this that spray-on tan stuff?" Zane asked, curious, as he prodded at Ty's bare belly and the wide expanse of skin.

"No," Ty answered in a slightly insulted voice. He swiped at Zane's hand and rubbed at his belly like it tickled. "I'm always this color, they just . . . buffed me a little," he explained, voice shaking with laughter.

"You are not always this color," Zane objected, sending his wiggling fingers right back to the hollows along Ty's ribs for a moment. "You weren't tan up to here." His palm skimmed up Ty's inner thigh.

Ty turned and grabbed for Zane's hand, pushing it back to the mattress and rolling toward him. "Quit it."

Zane chuckled and evaded Ty's grasp, sliding his hand instead over Ty's hip to pull him closer. "No, they did something. It looks weird. You look like—" He shut his mouth with a snap.

Ty raised an eyebrow. "Like what?"

"Ah . . ." Zane cleared his throat and muttered a soft curse. He was going to get shit for this. "You look like a Ken doll."

Ty barked a surprised laugh, pressing his mouth against Zane's shoulder to snicker quietly. He closed his eyes and shook his head finally. "I know," he moaned as he rolled onto his back and slung his arm over his eyes.

"So, doll, what are you packing for the cruise?" Zane drawled, figuring he might as well play it.

Ty grunted and glanced sideways at Zane with a crooked grin. "Nothing."

Zane smirked and deliberately dragged his gaze up and down the long, tanned, nude length of Ty's body, and he felt fresh interest curl in his belly and thought about how he would expect a man like Corbin Porter to act if the incredible man in bed with him was his and his alone. "Hmmm. I'll have to lock you up in the cabin, then. No way am I sharing this"—he ran his hand familiarly over Ty's body—"with just anyone. Doll."

"Oh God, you're getting into character now, aren't you?" Ty groaned, laughing as he stretched under Zane's hand.

Zane groped him a bit before lifting that hand to cover Ty's left hand and lace their fingers together. The two rings rapped together lightly, reminding him of what was coming. "You're mine, Del," Zane drawled, more than a hint of arrogance sharpening his tone as he took the opportunity to look over Ty possessively, not hiding it one bit. And damn if it didn't feel good. "Just you remember that when you go showing off that fine ass around that ship in those nonexistent swim shorts of yours." Now he could feel the laugh threatening, caused by his outrageous playacting, and he knew it had to be showing in his eyes.

Ty was watching him, biting his lip against a smile. "He's that much of an asshole, huh?" he finally asked, his voice wavering with amusement.

"Oh doll, you have no idea," Zane continued, one eyebrow pointing up officiously as he forced the amusement out of his demeanor, curling up his lip ever so slightly as his dark eyes took on a rapacious glint. He tightened his grip on Ty's hand, the rings cutting in just a bit, which helped stave off the laughter. He knew he was a damn good actor, but if anyone could see through it, it would be Ty. Might as well test it now.

Ty smiled, barely restraining a laugh before he composed himself with remarkable speed. But he only managed to look at Zane seriously for mere seconds before his lips twitched into another smile and he snorted, trying not to laugh. He slapped his hand over his mouth and struggled to stay quiet. Finally, he regained control and looked at Zane once more with a somber nod.

Zane frowned at him for a long moment before rolling his eyes, because all he wanted to do was laugh too. "You're right. We're totally screwed."

Ty began to laugh softly, the sound low and warm. His thumb slid across the metal of Zane's wedding ring, and he lifted their hands and looked at the rings, one gold and scuffed from years of constant wear, one bright and silver and new. The laughter ebbed. Ty licked his lips as he examined them, and then he lowered their hands and slowly rolled into Zane, his body languid and pliable once more as he draped over him. It was a subtle but immediate change in his demeanor. Zane knew Ty was a damn good UC, which required a lot of acting. But he hadn't known Ty had the ability to literally become someone else with just a shift of his body. He was impressed. Very impressed. And a little disturbed.

Ty nudged Zane's nose with his and then kissed him slowly. "We'll be just fine," he assured Zane in the British accent, his voice pitched just a little higher than normal. He smiled against Zane's lips. "You just have to own it. Believe that I'm yours and you're mine," he whispered slowly before dragging his teeth along Zane's bottom lip.

Zane's chest felt tight, more than it should even with Ty's weight upon him. His entire body tingled with the words. He let his eyes half close, not wanting to examine the feeling too closely, and exhaled shakily as Ty's words echoed in his ears.

"Make me believe it, darling," Ty coaxed in the fake accent, his voice a bare whisper.

Zane closed his arms around Ty to hold him in place and tried to find the mindset he'd been cultivating all day. Corbin Porter was a self-serving, arrogant, possessive bastard who believed life was his way or the highway. It hadn't taken Zane the whole twenty minutes of listening to him during questioning to figure that one out. What Zane worried about was how Corbin's predictably selfish hold on Del all too easily translated to Zane's own silent craving to keep Ty to himself . . . and how his very headstrong and independent lover would react to it.

He clenched his fingers into Ty's warm skin. "You are mine," he asserted in that sharpened, confident-sounding drawl. "I know it; you know it. And so will anyone else who looks at you."

"There you go," Ty murmured approvingly, draping his leg over Zane's hip and kissing him again languidly, the simple action simultaneously more submissive and seductive than anything Ty had ever done to him before. The effect was intoxicating, and Zane found both his body and his mind responding in just the way he figured Ty intended.

His partner had just reached new levels of manipulative evil, damn him.

When he pulled back, Ty allowed just enough room to pull Zane's hand up and look at it. "You waiting till morning to switch them out?" he asked softly, the accent and assumed seductive identity gone just as suddenly as they had come.

Zane's gaze flickered to their entwined fingers, and he stared at the rings for a long moment. Then he closed his eyes. Of all the details this case entailed, this was the one thing Zane truly resented. Yes, it was for a job, and a lot of time—years—had passed since Becky died, and it didn't hurt like it used to, but it still . . . ached and felt very unfair. He drew in a painful breath and let it out slowly before reopening his eyes. "Remind me?"

Ty looked down at the ring expressionlessly. Then he met Zane's eyes and nodded without a word. They both knew there was nothing he could say to make it better, and it was impossible to decipher what Ty was thinking. Ty always avoided the subject of Zane's wedding ring just as devotedly as Zane did. He gave Zane's hand one last squeeze and then let go and rolled away, groaning softly as he got to the edge of the bed and sat up.

Zane watched him, silently grateful for how Ty handled his request. The rings were a bigger deal to him than he wanted to admit, and Ty knew that. In fact, Zane was surprised to see that Ty was still wearing his after putting it on this morning after McCoy's order. "Are you trying to get used to wearing it?" he asked carefully. Ty would know what he was referring to.

Ty turned his head so he was looking at Zane out of the corner of his eye, still sitting on the edge of the bed. "Guess you could say that," he answered in a low, gruff voice that made Zane shiver. He looked down at his hand. "I put it on, and I guess my finger's swollen. Haven't been able to get it off."

"Not even with the massage oil?" Zane asked with a frown. Ty just shook his head. Zane grinned slowly. "Try the lube."

Ty snorted. "If it starts hurting or I get desperate. May as well leave it on till then." He was nearly mumbling as he spun the ring around his finger.

Zane wondered, not for the first time, what was going through Ty's mind as he looked at it.

"Mind if I use your shower?" Ty asked sedately.

"You don't have to ask," Zane murmured, watching his back.

Ty stood, groaning again as he stretched. He glanced back at Zane and gave him a slight smile. "Got a little carried away, huh?" he said as he walked toward the door. "You're so easy," he added in a pleased voice as he disappeared into the hallway.

Zane snorted as he rolled onto his back and smiled at the ceiling. Ty Grady was such an egotistical bastard, yet somehow he turned Zane on like no one else ever had. He mused over that, rubbing his ring idly, until he heard the water start in the shower. With a soft grunt, he pushed himself up and out of bed. That egotistical bastard was naked and wet. No way was he letting that pass without taking advantage of it.

CHAPTER THREE

Ty led the way out of the elevator, walking into the tech lab with a shift of his eyes toward his partner. Zane didn't look much different outwardly. New haircut, new earring, manicure, but he was still himself under the pricey tailored clothes. Ty couldn't help but feel slightly self-conscious about the changes he had undergone, but he was too good at his job to show that outwardly. He hoped. Luckily, there wasn't much of anyone at the office at seven in the morning on a Saturday. They planned to board the ship by eleven.

"Good morning, gentlemen," Stacy Knight greeted as he came over to them, trailed by a lackey whose name Ty couldn't remember carrying a plastic storage box. Knight held two files in his hand, one of which he handed to Ty.

"Good morning, Q," Ty drawled, smirking as he took the file. Knight handled most of the briefing and debriefing of agents when new or unusual technology was being used in a job. Ty didn't know why he needed to see them before they left for the cruise ship, but he sort of dreaded what Knight was going to show them.

"I don't have time for you to think you're clever this morning, Grady," Knight returned dryly. "Both of you give Terry your guns, knives, garrotes, crossbows, and any other unusual weapons you might be carrying, please."

"What? Why?" Ty demanded.

"You and your baggage will go through security just like at the airports for X-ray and random search. We have to figure out how to hide the weapons and other equipment in your luggage, and we'll have to be creative, since the bags will go with a valet. So fork it all over."

Ty and Zane both grudgingly pulled out their service weapons, followed by their backups and any other weaponry they had hidden on them. They placed each piece into the plastic box. When Ty was done, he smoothed a hand over his jacket and nodded to Knight, but Knight merely sighed impatiently as he watched them. Ty shook his head and watched with a hint of amusement as Zane continued piling hidden knives into the bucket.

There was a moment of silence after the last thin throwing knife was placed inside. "Is that all?" Knight drawled, unimpressed.

Zane rolled his eyes and crossed his arms. He always carried those knives when he was working out of the office; it was an odd quirk Ty hadn't seen in any other civilian agents. The skill and habit came courtesy of some extra training Zane had lucked into at the academy to make up for his lack of police or military experience. Ty approved, though he wouldn't tell Zane that.

"Well. Now that we've established dominance, follow me," Knight said with a roll of his eyes.

"I feel naked now," Zane muttered.

Ty glanced at Zane and winked at him. Zane hadn't really had a chance to meet many of the support staff in the Baltimore office yet, and Ty probably wasn't the best person to introduce him around, not with the reputation Ty had garnered.

"You look like you had a rough night," Knight commented over his shoulder as they trailed along behind him.

"Just doing some research for the case," Ty responded with a shrug of one shoulder.

"Sure you were," Knight muttered with a smile.

They followed Knight to a small conference room, where Special Agent in Charge Dan McCoy sat waiting for them. McCoy stood when they walked in, looking them both over critically.

"I almost didn't you recognize you myself," he finally said with an approving nod. "Let me see the arm," he said as he held his hand out to Ty.

Ty shrugged out of his jacket and rolled his sleeve up, turning his bicep toward McCoy. His tattoo was no longer there. It was odd looking down at his arm and seeing nothing but skin.

"How'd they do it?" McCoy asked in real interest.

"Some sort of synthetic," Ty answered unhappily. "They glued it down."

"Looks pretty good if you don't know you're looking for it. We'll make certain to have spare parts in your luggage somewhere," Knight commented as he leaned closer and peered at Ty's arm. Ty put his hand on Knight's forehead and pushed him away.

"Personal space, man," Ty told him with a good-natured smirk. He heard Zane stifle a snort.

"Speaking of personal space, let's get right down to your toys for this one," McCoy said as he nodded to Knight.

Knight turned to a rolling table much like the kind on which surgeons kept their instruments and picked through an array of devices sitting there. He lifted a pair of sunglasses and turned to hand them to Zane. He handed another to Ty. They were unusually heavy as he hefted them in his palm.

"Stylish," Ty commented dryly.

"Shut up. They're embedded with a video feed here," Knight told Ty as he pointed to the upper left portion of the frames. "The other side holds a battery with enough juice for about an hour of recording or three hours of transmission. Use it sparingly. There's no recharging it."

"Okay," Ty mumbled as he turned the glasses over and frowned at them.

"I'm not sure what good these will be," Zane murmured, setting them aside.

"One of your goals is to take pictures of the men involved. We figured a Nikon might raise suspicion," McCoy told them. Ty and Zane both nodded slowly.

"And this is your document scanner," Knight said as he cradled a long device in both palms. It was roughly the size of a ruler, just slightly thicker. "You know how to use one of these, right?" Knight asked Ty dubiously.

"Push the button, scan the document," Ty answered obediently.

"And no using it as a club. It's not built for violence," Knight admonished.

"I only did that one time!" Ty argued. "And to be fair I'm pretty sure it was already—"

"Can it, Grady. No more using sensitive tech gear to maim, understood?" McCoy interrupted.

"Yes, sir," Ty said in a disgruntled voice. Zane wasn't even trying to stifle his quiet laughter.

Knight continued. "We tried to devise some way for the two of you to communicate by radio, but we have nothing inconspicuous enough on such short notice. You'll be on your own as far as that goes."

"Cell phones?" Zane asked dubiously.

"They're not reliable at sea, even if the cruise line claims they are. Not worth the risk of issuing you any, and you can't take your own. You'll have the Porters' phones, with all their contacts. But I'd be careful answering them if I were you," Knight rambled.

Ty looked between the two men. No reliable way to communicate with his partner or with the rest of the team while aboard ship. Great. Zane didn't look too happy either.

"You'll be reporting back to us by secure server, but the only access will be on the public terminals. You will go by the codenames Punch and Judy."

"Punch and Judy," Zane repeated, voice devoid of emotion.

"Hilarious," Ty commented acerbically.

"I amuse myself. Get over it," McCoy shot back. "The computers are public, so remember you'll have to be careful and clever when accessing the server."

Ty pointed at Zane. "His job." Zane shrugged.

"Right." McCoy handed them both thick folders. "And these are your itineraries."

"Our what?" Ty blurted in alarm. They hadn't been told about any itineraries yesterday. That was pretty high up on the list of shit they needed to know about.

"How heavily are we scheduled?" Zane asked, not sounding surprised. Ty looked at him sideways, but Zane was studying the papers and paying him no attention.

"They're pretty firm," McCoy told them apologetically. "They found them in one of the Porters' bags as they were searching them for intel."

"How much planning have you put into this case, exactly?" Ty asked critically.

"The ink is still drying," McCoy told him wryly. He held up a hand to curtail any further protests. "Listen, this opportunity practically dropped into our laps. We've managed to keep a lid on the arrest of the Porters. There are half a dozen agencies that should be notified that haven't been. Interpol, Europol, Scotland Yard, and the Italian Guardia di Finanza, to name a few. Every one of those will be screaming to get their fingers in the pot, and you both know what happens when a case becomes a jurisdictional war. The only way to keep that lid on is to go in silent and go in fast."

"Which also means there's a very real chance of you being arrested for trading in stolen antiquities if you run into an agent of any of those organizations," Knight told them with a hint of childish glee.

Ty shot him a dirty look, and Zane sat forward as he asked, "And if we run into one of those other agencies—"

McCoy cut him off loudly, calling their attention back to him. "Your goal is to gather intel, understood? Do not attempt to apprehend, detain, capture, curtail, restrict, inhibit, or otherwise prevent the activities of any of the criminals. Understood?"

"Yes, sir," Ty and Zane answered in unison, Ty not bothering to hide how unimpressed he was with the inventory.

"Porter has two partners: an Italian by the name of Lorenzo Bianchi and a Turk named Vartan Armen. Bianchi is the face of the ring, the only one who surfaces. He does the buying. Stolen antiquities, art, priceless relics, you name it."

"Where's this intel coming from?" Ty asked.

"Italy. They've had a bead on Bianchi for a few years now but no way to get a foot in the door. Everything about him on paper is legit. That's where Armen and Porter come in. Armen targets and handles acquisitions; Porter arranges transport and storage. There is absolutely no information in the wind about Armen. We don't even have a picture of him. Yet."

Ty lifted the camera glasses and cheekily saluted his boss with them.

"How'd you catch up to Porter?" Zane asked curiously.

"Traffic violation," McCoy said with a pleased smirk.

"And you're damn sure these men have never met in person?" Ty demanded.

"Sure enough to risk your lives on it," McCoy assured them. "Each man has a carefully planned itinerary meant to coincide at intervals with the others'. That's how they plan to do their communicating. Or so we understand."

"So we have to stick to these like glue," Ty concluded as he waved the file in his hand.

"Yes. Your objectives are simple. Get pictures of Vartan Armen. Glean as much information as you can about their operations. And don't get killed."

Zane stood at the foot of the circular California king with its fancy linen and coverlet, hands on his hips, looking down at the three open suitcases: one his, two Ty's. Correction: One Corbin's, two Del's. There were already clothes hanging in the closet that had arrived in garment bags. He wrinkled his nose and looked down at all the stuff and shook his head.

They'd been greeted by a note from the maid on the foot of their bed, telling them the room had been cleaned by Stella and they could be assured there were no bugs in it. Apparently someone on their team was posing as a maid and had swept the room for electronic listening devices. It gave them a little freedom, anyway, and considering the entire ship was closed-circuit recorded, they'd take what small amount of privacy they could get.

Ty stood not far away, beyond the partitions that divided the lavishly decorated Owner's Suite into bedroom and living areas, contemplating their surroundings. Their suite was one of only six like it on the entire ship, with over five hundred square feet of space. It had to have cost the Porters a pretty penny.

It was also completely decked out for the holidays. A miniature Christmas tree stood in one corner near the balcony doors, and a fruit basket of festive treats sat on the dresser opposite the bed. The entire ship was decorated in similar fashion. Much of the crew wore red Santa hats and ridiculous smiles. Christmas trees in pots and sprigs of mistletoe and white twinkle lights bedecked every area of the ship.

Zane had been sort of shocked to find that Ty loved the holiday theme. He'd complained all morning about missing Christmas with his family, but he'd been distracted by the luxurious appointments they'd found when they entered the cabin.

"Well, it's better than the berth on the last cruise I took," Ty told Zane with a slight smirk as he turned to face him.

Zane chuckled. "Bunks aboard an LST?" he joked.

"We had to share, sleep in shifts," Ty answered wryly. He waved at the cabin full of ebony wood and Persian rugs on the floor. His eyes were shining as he moved toward Zane. "Now I get an upgrade, and I still have to share a bed. A freaking round one."

"If you're uncomfortable, there's plenty of room on that huge couch to stretch out," Zane teased, turning to face him with one hand on his hip. Ty looked so strange with that blond hair, but Zane was seeing past it now. He focused on how Ty moved, on the color of his eyes, the timbre of his voice, and how it all still made his pulse speed up a little.

"You'd cry if I really did that," Ty told him with a laugh. He turned away from Zane again, heading for the light streaming through the balcony doors.

"Well, pout maybe," Zane drawled, following along behind him through the stateroom. It was almost the same size as his apartment, actually. He shook his head over the extravagance. While certainly entertaining to have one of the largest staterooms on the entire cruise ship, it was a hell of a waste of money when all they'd be doing was sleeping there. But it wasn't their money, so Zane shrugged it off.

"If you're over four, you're not allowed to pout," Ty claimed absently. He pushed through the double glass doors that led to their private balcony and let in a rush of cold ocean air. It was the middle of December on the eastern seaboard. It was cold. But Ty inhaled deeply, putting his head back and smiling as he did so.

Zane leaned against the doorframe and just watched. While the dark ocean was gorgeous in the crisp December air, it was Ty who held his attention. Zane didn't even want a cigarette, which was a normal craving that hit him courtesy of fresh air and stress. Ty was distracting like that, diverting in thought, word, and deed for better or for worse, and that had made it easier for Zane to altogether quit smoking—

again—a few weeks ago. Zane sighed silently. For better or for worse. Being "married" again was making him . . . sappy.

For a couple of months now, he'd been content to have Ty near, but Zane was waiting for Ty to get antsy. Ty wasn't the type of guy you were supposed to get attached to, because Ty couldn't, or wouldn't, settle down. In fact, Zane was in awe of the fact that their fooling around was still holding Ty's interest at all.

Ty must have sensed his eyes on him, and he turned to look over at Zane as his smile faded. "What?" he asked with a flop of his hand. "We're not ten minutes into this, and you've already got that look like you left the stove on."

Zane smiled slightly and shook his head, lifting one hand to absently rub at the new earring. "Just wondering what we're in for."

Ty met his eyes for a long moment, his expression telegraphing his desire to perhaps say something with sincerity. The look faded though, and Ty smiled slowly. "We'll be in for the night," he quipped suggestively.

Zane wondered what he'd been about to say, but what had come out was interesting enough. "There is room service," Zane drawled. It was an all-inclusive high-dollar cruise ship program, so they could have literally anything they wanted, as long as it was available. They'd taken the five-cent tour upon their arrival and had a quick-service lunch, but they'd wanted to get to their suite quickly to head off anyone who might try to get there first and bug the place. It was just past one, and their first scheduled event wasn't for twenty-four hours.

"At least with room service I don't have to eat with a British accent," Ty said, tongue-in-cheek as he tried not to smile. He leaned against the doorframe as the wind brushed at his thin cotton shirt.

Zane watched goose bumps rise on Ty's skin and took the two small steps to stand right before him, their chests practically brushing as Zane ran his hands up Ty's arms. "Aren't you cold out here in the wind?"

"That's the worst come-on line I've ever heard, Zane," Ty admonished blandly. He hooked a finger into one of Zane's belt loops. "It's a good thing you're pretty or you'd never get laid."

"Pretty?" Zane echoed in surprise. Ty merely laughed, the wide smile highlighting the laugh lines around his eyes and mouth, lines

Zane saw all too rarely. He shook his head and said, "I have never in my life been called 'pretty.' And come to think of it, I don't think I've ever had to use a come-on line, either."

"The latter is because you're pretty," Ty claimed with a huff of air that brushed Zane's cheek. Zane had to chuckle as he bowed his head. It was just too silly to think of himself that way, with a twice-broken nose healed a little crooked, wrinkles at the corners of his eyes, and a hell of a lot of scars. Ty turned his head and pressed a kiss to Zane's cheek, and then he put both hands on Zane's chest and pushed him away. "Let's get those bags straightened out. I want to see how many weapons they managed to slip in with us."

Zane reluctantly let go and followed him over to the ridiculous round bed. Choosing one of the suitcases, he picked up a heavy, zipped dopp kit. "I'm almost afraid to look," Zane murmured before opening it. It was an old-fashioned shaving kit with a marble bowl, horsehair brush, and two straight-edge razors. Among other toiletries, there were also two long whetstones with elastic around them, and when Zane turned them over, he found one of his knives strapped to each heavy stone. "Resourceful," he said with a raised brow. "Although I'm not sure how I'll wear them with walking shorts and a polo."

Ty glanced over to see what Zane was doing and nodded when he looked at the shaving kit. "Hopefully they got more than just your pig stickers in," he muttered as he poked his finger through one of the neatly packed suitcases. "What the hell are walking shorts? You're such a geek, man. I guess we can use the straight-edge razors if we want to make a horror show of it."

He pulled out a plain leather toiletry bag and unzipped it, peering in for a second before merely letting it go.

It dropped to the mattress with a clatter of its contents as Ty stood frozen, his head turned away, eyes closed, his hands still out in front of him like he might be traumatized.

Zane glanced up, and when he saw the mess, he choked on a laugh. "Ah . . ." He cleared his throat as he looked at the variety of sex toys spilled across the duvet: three different dildos, a set of metal cock rings, a scattering of clamps, a bottle of toy cleaner, a few silk scarves, and a couple of long boxes with clasps. He picked one of the boxes up and opened it. Inside was an implement even Zane wasn't familiar with displayed on a slide of velvet. When he pulled up the small board, Zane found pieces of a disassembled gun inside.

"Like I said," Zane continued, though now he was trying not to laugh, "resourceful. I wonder who laughed their asses off while packing this up."

"That's my gun," Ty said in an offended voice. "They hid my gun in the sex toys? That's not right, man." He shook his head and continued muttering to himself as he began pulling out pieces of clothing and toiletries, carefully examining them for anything else that might have been hidden for them.

"Good hiding place, if you ask me," Zane said as he picked up a jeweled dog collar and glanced toward Ty's neck, visually estimating the possibility of a fit and deciding it just wouldn't look right. "What security guy is going to take apart a vibrator to check for a slide barrel?"

Ty didn't respond, merely looking askance at the collar and the appraising look in Zane's eyes. He snorted at him and then pulled another small bag toward him, Del's designer satchel, unzipping it with a hint of dread. He looked in warily, like more rubber dongs might jump out at him, but then dumped the contents onto the bed. There was an iPod, a set of headphones, a few puzzle books, two ear wigs, and three wireless listening devices. Ty looked up at Zane and shrugged.

"My question would be 'Are they theirs or ours?'" Zane said as he opened a small drawstring bag and looked down into it. After a moment, he simply pulled the strings to close it and dropped it on the bed. The fabric didn't muffle the soft clinking noise.

"What's that?" Ty asked as he nodded at the bag.

Zane picked the bag back up and pulled out a set of heavy-duty handcuffs. "These may be useful if I can't get you to sit still," he said, dangling them on one finger.

Ty shook his head and pointed one long finger at Zane warningly.

"You try it and I'll freak out," he said seriously.

"Freak out?" Zane asked, brow furrowing. "Why?" He didn't think he'd ever seen Ty tied up, except for when Zane had found him in that dark catacomb in New York City, almost suffocated . . . "Oh. Okay." He dropped the cuffs back into the bag and tossed it aside.

Ty pressed his lips tightly together and looked down at the bag again. "Maybe we can use them if we make an arrest," he finally decided wryly before pulling more clothing out of the suitcase. There was a small stack of briefs and soft T-shirts, and he set them aside, in front of Zane. They'd been allowed to bring their own underwear, at least.

"I've not really thought about buying stuff like this," Zane said slowly, dropping another small box labeled Vacheron Constantin after opening it and finding a very expensive watch. Other boxes held cuff links, old-fashioned tie clips, and various other high-dollar accouterments.

"On our salary, you can't afford to look at stuff like this." Ty licked his lips and looked over at Zane with a frown. "These guys are way out of my league," he declared as he looked back down at everything they'd spread across the bed.

Zane turned and sat down on the edge of the thick mattress so he could look at Ty. Money wasn't something they'd ever talked about, and considering how Ty was reacting to their pricey surroundings, Zane wasn't sure if now was a good time to broach the subject, even in jest. "It's just for show. Having expensive things doesn't determine who you are."

Ty shrugged. "Not unless you're an ass," he answered carelessly. He looked around the luxuriously appointed cabin. "I've just never known anyone who lived like this. Not sure if I can pull it off."

Zane looked around and shrugged. He'd had pricey clothes with designer labels once upon a time, and he'd lived in ritzy places before. He preferred his ratty sweats and apartment, or better, Ty's row house. "It's no big deal. Just window dressing. Nobody needs to live like this. They just want to be pampered. Money makes it easy to be lazy." Ty looked at him with a tiny frown, and Zane sighed inwardly and shrugged. "Personal experience," he murmured, leaning back on one elbow.

"With being lazy?" Ty asked with a slight smile.

Zane shook his head slowly. "You know me better than that."

Ty smiled wider, but then it faded back into a confused frown. He clearly wanted to inquire further, but they were still at a stage where asking about each other's pasts was an uncomfortable venture.

Zane watched the emotions cross Ty's face and decided an answer was in order. "My family has money," he admitted. "Ranching operations for several generations now."

Ty's only reaction was to arch an eyebrow. Zane knew his normally expressive partner well enough to know that an expression of so little emotion was hiding a more natural response. Ty's poker face was impressive unless you knew him well. "How much?" Ty finally asked, exposing his curiosity.

"In my opinion, they've got more money than sense," Zane said with a small shrug. "I don't really know."

"That's probably a lot, then," Ty concluded, a hint of ill-concealed discomfort in his voice.

"Probably," Zane allowed. "I'm not exactly much a part of the family anymore." The old pain of it twinged a little, and he pushed himself to sit up again. "So it's not something I deal with."

Ty turned his head to watch Zane, but he didn't take a step back or move away to give him space. It was an oddly intimate inaction. "So . . . what, you got cut off?"

Zane shook his head. "We just don't get along." He didn't really want to get into a rehash of Dallas—too much potential for messy emotions he tried to keep buried with the rest of his past, not to mention the dreaded wailing violin section. He forced a smile and looked up at Ty. "I like your family a lot better."

"They're that bad?" Ty asked disbelievingly.

Zane had to laugh. "There's no way to compare, really. You've got your family baggage, right? Well, I've got mine. And you know me and baggage," he tried to joke, but it came out flat to his ear.

Ty's eyes strayed to the array of bags and belongings on the bed; then he looked back at Zane and nodded somberly. "If you ever want to talk about it," he offered slowly, a smile forming as he finished, "you've got Deacon's number, right?"

Warmth stole through Zane's chest, and it was easy to return the smile. Comments like that did a lot to remind Zane that Ty really did care about him. Even if Ty was shoving him off on his psychiatrist brother. "Yeah." Then he looked down at the mess littering the bed. "So. Don't worry about this shit. It doesn't mean anything. And you don't need to act any differently to deal with it."

"Yeah, yeah," Ty muttered as he turned away and ran a hand through his bleached-blond hair. He moved away from Zane and the bed and began walking toward the balcony again. He stared out the open door for a long moment, apparently trying to settle himself and find the right mentality to be Del Porter instead of Ty Grady.

As Zane watched him, he saw the set of Ty's shoulders change, saw the tension melt off him, saw his gait alter as he paced toward the doors, and by the time his partner got to the balcony and turned around, Ty seemed comfortable in his surroundings and in his new skin. It was a subtle change, just like the one in Zane's bed last night. Ty seemed to be able to slide into a new persona quickly; he just didn't seem to be able to maintain it for very long.

He gave Zane a crooked smile. "I still need some practice," he said, assuming Del Porter's lyrical accent. It changed the tone of his voice, the pitch. Even the hint of mountain gravel and growling quality Zane had grown fond of was gone, replaced by the smooth British tones.

The ability again impressed Zane, though he immediately missed Ty's natural voice. But if Ty wanted to play the game here in the cabin from time to time to help them stay in character, he'd go along with it. It couldn't hurt. The best way to stay safely undercover was to live it, but he seriously doubted they needed to go that far on this case, and Zane would much rather be with Ty than Del.

"And just what do you suggest?" he asked in the haughty tone he used for Corbin.

Ty moved toward him, smiling as he walked up to stand in front of him and put one finger on Zane's shoulder. He let it slide up to Zane's neck teasingly and gave him a chaste kiss. Then he said in his normal voice, "I want a nap. And then food."

"Easy enough. Shove this crap off the bed, and we have nap time. Then there are six full-service restaurants on board, two on the luxury level," Zane pointed out as he settled his hands on Ty's hips. "That doesn't count room service and all the other buffet and counter-service places."

"Room service. We'll go over our game plan. But first, let's 'shove all this crap off the bed,'" Ty parroted with a smirk as he stood and hauled Zane off the bed, then hooked a foot around Zane's ankle and shoved him ever-so-gently to the floor.

"Hey!" Zane objected, but he laughed as he thumped lightly on the carpet. He drew his knees up and balanced his forearms on them as he looked up at his partner. "Gee, I feel so loved. Thrown on the floor with the rest of the crap," he teased.

Ty nodded, pleased with himself. He reached over and swept the rest of the stuff off the bed as well, sending it off the edge to land behind Zane on the floor. Then he climbed into the round bed, and Zane heard him flop down heavily. Zane huffed and shifted to his knees so he could crawl up onto the bed and right over top of Ty. "You're lucky you're pretty."

"Damn right," Ty agreed with a cocky smirk as he stretched like a cat and made himself comfortable on his back.

Zane chuckled before shifting and lying down next to Ty. He looked from side to side. For such a big bed, it was actually pretty narrow once you took into account the round mattress and how tall and broad they both were. He shrugged slightly and folded his hands over his waist. "I don't know if I'll sleep," Zane murmured, although he was a little tired. While he slept much better now than a couple months ago, a late night, a really early morning, and new stress didn't necessarily offset his edginess on the job and strange surroundings.

Ty didn't respond, and when Zane glanced over at him, he saw that his partner was already asleep, face relaxed, breathing evenly. Zane sighed in exasperation. Ty had the same ability as a lot of people who'd ever served in the military: he could sleep on command whenever and wherever. Zane envied the ability. He carefully turned onto his side and scooted up against him, slid his arm over Ty's waist, and laid his head on the pillow, bracing his cheekbone on Ty's shoulder. It was easy to let his eyes close, and he briefly entertained the thought of Ty as his own personal teddy bear as he fell asleep.

Their personalized itineraries for each day, printed and slid under the door the night before, came in a fussy green folder tied with a red ribbon and supposedly matched the more general overviews McCoy had given them that morning. Although they had reviewed the summary documents briefly, Ty intended to go through them again as they ate dinner, just to assure himself there weren't any surprises.

He sat at the small marble-topped dining table in their cabin, knee bouncing as he perused Del Porter's scheduled activities. "I swear to God, if they have me down for another massage I'm diving overboard," he mumbled as he rubbed at his sore shoulder. The masseuse had warned him he'd be achy for a few days, but this was ridiculous. He'd fallen out of helicopters and not been this sore afterward.

Zane forked up some salad as he looked at Corbin's list. "Some vacation," he commented. "Two scheduled activities a day plus meals, some extra excursions while in ports. Although evenings are pretty clear, looks like."

Ty nodded. It was easy to build a profile of the two men they were impersonating just by the activities they'd paid for. Rock climbing, waterskiing, cliff diving, scuba diving, a fairly tame "zip-line adventure over the jungles of Puerto Rico," and several other activities in the same vein. Adrenaline junkies. Or suicidal, depending. Ty raised one eyebrow and smiled slightly. "I'm beginning to like these guys."

"I'm going to guess that Corbin's the adventurer and Del tags along. Although he did look like he worked out," Zane commented. "Are there any differences in the itineraries?"

Ty slid his folder closer and peered at Zane's, comparing them side-by-side. "Looks like Corbin has a few nights reserved at the private-game poker tables. High stakes." Ty whistled low. "A hundred thousand buy-in? Hope you're not playing with government money, partner," he teased.

Zane pointed at a note starred to one side of his itinerary. "The Porters' account has been preloaded with the ship's bursar. It doesn't say how much, though."

"Do you play poker?" Ty asked as he sat back and studied Zane. He had a feeling Zane would be good at it. He had one hell of a poker face.

"Yes," Zane said absently, taking another bite of salad as he read through the activities list. "Did a lot of gambling in Miami." He glanced up with a smile. "Poker is all about statistics and luck."

"Uh-huh," Ty responded dubiously. "But I'm talking gambling with money, papi, not your life," he said with a pat of Zane's knee. He knew all he wanted to know about what Zane had done in Miami.

Zane's smile widened as he set down his fork. "I'm good at both. But I'll stick to money this time. Especially since it's not mine."

"I appreciate the assurance," Ty mumbled, privately thinking he'd believe that when he saw it.

"I don't diss you and your guns. Don't diss me and my numbers," Zane said mildly as he went back to his dinner.

Ty glanced up at him and narrowed his eyes. He'd been thinking more along the lines of Zane sticking to gambling with money and not life and limb, but apparently Zane was still self-conscious when it came to his what bordered on idiot savant levels of number-crunching ability.

Ty didn't really envy the ability, but he did respect it. Ty saw things in a jumbled mess, like a jigsaw puzzle that had been tossed onto a table. He could piece that puzzle together without turning over the pieces to see what was on the other side, simply going on instinct and what felt right. But Zane's mind instead took those jumbled pieces and categorized them, turned them all right side up, top to bottom, labeled them by category ranging from color to the name of the dude who cut them out at the factory, and then methodically snapped them into place.

The differences in methods made them a mostly compatible, daunting team, if not occasionally at odds.

Zane glanced up from his plate and raised an eyebrow, apparently waiting on Ty's retort that hadn't come. Ty frowned at him, looking to turn the conversation another direction. "What's wrong with my guns?"

Zane chuckled. "There's nothing wrong with your guns. And speaking of, we'll have to see if they got mine in the luggage too. I don't like being unarmed." He reached for the breadbasket, then took a fluffy yeast roll and offered it to Ty.

Ty shook his head, smiling slightly. It was so easy to distract Zane sometimes it was shameful. "You're going to have to carry mine most of the time anyway," he said. "The only thing I have to wear that's thick enough to conceal a gun is that tux." He nodded toward the garment bags in the closet. He plucked at the shirt he was wearing. Aside from the shirts being just a little tight at the seams around his shoulders, he found that he kind of liked Del Porter's wardrobe. Most of the clothing was made of fine linen or light muslin or cotton, appropriate for tropical locales. But there was no hiding a .38 in the clinging folds.

"There is that, at least. Corbin's got high-fashion taste, and that means long sleeves, even if they are silk shirts. I might get away with one blade." Zane shrugged. "Silk is hot," he tacked on.

Ty nodded and looked back down at his folder before Zane could see the smile on his lips. Silk also stuck to skin like glue. He'd spent a few very sweaty nights on silk sheets that he didn't remember fondly. Mainly because the owner of those silk sheets had tried to kill him later . . .

Anyway, he also didn't consider silk shirts high fashion, unless you were a guido and liked lots of bling, too, but he wasn't going to get into that with Mr. Walking Shorts.

"Corbin has a manicure five days in," Zane said as he pushed his plate slightly away, most of the food he'd spooned onto it gone. "Does Del have any salon appointments?"

Ty flipped through the itinerary quickly, wincing as he caught sight of the hot stone massage. He rolled his shoulders unconsciously, trying to ease the throbbing ache in them.

"If you're already hurting, just tell them you want something different," Zane said.

"It's just up around my shoulders. I guess that's where all the knots were," Ty muttered as he jerked his thumb over his shoulder. He flipped the page. The massage and sauna time on day five were the only spa treatments scheduled. Thank Christ. "Are you dive certified?" he asked abruptly as he looked over the details of their scuba diving session.

"No. I've never been scuba diving. Doesn't matter, though. Corbin's certified. Where is that?" Zane pulled his itinerary closer and ran his finger down the list.

"St. Maarten," Ty grumbled. He was watching Zane thoughtfully, unhappy with the fact that even after all the months they'd been partnered, he'd had to ask Zane about so small a fact. How well did he really know his partner, a man he was fairly sure he was falling in love with? He'd been pondering that ever since Zane revealed his family was apparently very wealthy. Ty had never suspected, never even been particularly curious about Zane's family or why he never spoke of them. Could he really be in love with someone he was afraid to ask about his past?

Zane flipped through the folder of materials and pulled out the activities booklet. Ty had already glanced at it, but he'd set it aside in favor of what they actually had scheduled. The booklet included descriptions of all the events, event length, how much exercise it included, and prices. Zane paged through the booklet before stopping and reading. "Says beginner to advanced level can be accommodated. I should be okay, right?" His nose wrinkled. "Scuba diving," he said in a speculative tone.

Ty sat back in his chair, bottle of water in hand, as he continued to watch Zane while his partner was distracted. It had taken him a while, but he'd finally overcome the embarrassment when Zane occasionally caught him watching. He still preferred to be covert about it merely because it was more entertaining. Zane was intriguing when he wasn't aware of it. Such as now. His attention appeared to be completely focused on the booklet as he looked up their various activities. He murmured to himself, sometimes frowning, his long fingers wrapped around a slim ink pen as he made notes. Brow furrowed, black eyes intent.

Ty kind of wanted to jump him. He smiled and took a long drink of water to curtail the urge. He cocked his head to one side as he watched Zane go still and frown deeply. Now he wanted to jump him ever more. But instead he made himself ask, "What's wrong?"

Zane's facial expression morphed into one of disbelief. "Cliff diving?"

"I gather you've never been cliff diving either?" Ty asked wryly.

"Or waterskiing." Zane turned up his nose. "Maybe I'll be sick on cliff diving day."

"Maybe we won't have to keep it up that long," Ty offered kindly.

"If we're done early, think the Bureau will have us go back before the end of the cruise?" Zane asked as he leaned back in his chair.

Ty shrugged negligently. "Probably not. Too costly to come get us. Why, you looking for another vacation so soon?" he asked with a wicked glint to his eyes.

Zane's eyes widened. "You bite your tongue or—"

Ty laughed at Zane's predictably horrified reaction. He pushed his chair back to balance on its back legs, grinning widely. "That never gets old."

Zane made an aggrieved sound as he tossed the itinerary back on the table. "We're not close enough to a decent hospital for any nonsense like a . . . stretch of several days with no work," he improvised awkwardly. "There's no telling what kind of medical facilities these islands have."

Ty let his chair thump back down and stood in one graceful motion. He bent and kissed Zane soundly, smiling even as their lips met. He felt Zane relax under his touch, and his lips opened under Ty's. Ty lingered over the kiss, enjoying the down time while they had the opportunity. When he finally pulled away, he pressed his nose to Zane's cheek, still grinning as he mumbled, "You're so easy to rile."

Zane turned his head, seeking Ty's lips again as he lifted his hands to hold on to Ty rather than the chair. "I could start hiding it again, but you seem to enjoy seeing it so much," he said between kisses.

"I do," Ty allowed, dragging his lips over Zane's before kissing him one last time and standing.

A long sigh preceded Zane's words. "So, if Corbin and Del are doing all this stuff, it's a good bet the others are doing some of it. And according to the ship's map, all the staterooms at this level are right on the end of this deck. There's not too many of them, though I don't know what it matters. This entire ship is high-class."

"Six of them, in fact," Ty said as he sat down heavily. "Plus a few family suites and one big-ass Royal Suite, all of which are crowded here at the stern on Deck Eight. It's a damn good bet our quarry is across the hall or next door."

Zane glanced toward the bedroom area with a frown. "I wonder how well soundproofed these walls are," he muttered.

"I haven't heard any idle conversation through them since we've been here," Ty offered. And he had indeed been listening, paying attention for that very reason. He smiled slowly. "It wouldn't hurt to give them a passionate scream or two at night, though. To sell our cover, of course," he said with false sincerity.

"Hope you brought cough drops, then, 'cause you're gonna be hoarse," Zane drawled.

Ty's smile warmed, and he winked at Zane cheekily. His little experiment last night had obviously gone over very well with the guinea pig. Ty had liked it as well, though it had definitely been a step out of his comfort zone. "Don't know if I could handle that every night," he admitted with unusual candor. He was still sore from what Zane had done to him, but mostly in pleasant ways. Ty didn't bottom often, for reasons he had never actually contemplated. He enjoyed it quite a bit.

"I don't think it will matter which of us is yelling," Zane said as he shifted in his chair.

Ty cocked his head playfully. "Statements like that make me wonder if you've been doing it right," he teased.

Zane groaned and let his head fall back so he was looking at the ceiling. "Don't tempt me with that challenge. We have work to do."

"Okay," Ty murmured, holding up both hands apologetically. He pulled his folder back toward him and flipped the page over, trying to concentrate again. "What the hell is the Queen of the Mediterranean doing cruising the Caribbean, anyway?"

"Billy Ocean owns the rights to the other name."

"Why would they name the ship Billy?" Ty asked with a sidelong look at Zane.

Zane ignored him, though the corner of his mouth curled up slightly. "Are there any of these activities that we seriously don't need to be doing, regardless of the schedule? I really don't think cliff diving is a good idea," he said, the reluctance clear in his voice.

"Why?" Ty asked as he looked up at Zane curiously. He looked uncomfortable. It was an odd look on a man who'd gone through the things Ty knew Zane had gone through. "What?" Ty insisted after another silent moment.

"It's scary, okay?" Zane muttered. "Unnerving. I hate free fall."

Ty fought hard not to smile or let any amusement show in his eyes, although he knew he could rarely hide emotions from Zane anymore. He nodded and reached out to pet Zane's knee. "Me too," he said simply.

Zane let out a slow breath and nodded before returning his attention to the papers. "Anyway," he started, but he didn't say any more than that.

"It helps if someone shoves you over the edge," Ty told him seriously, thinking Zane's fear of falling might go beyond simply falling off a cliff. It was the loss of control. It was just one more reason Ty knew that falling in love with his partner was a solo endeavor.

"I'll pass, thanks," Zane answered immediately. "I can handle this kind of stuff as long as I'm attached to a line. But diving off a cliff is just like losing my grip on a knotted rope."

The knotted climbing rope at the FBI Academy represented Zane's physical washout his first time through. He'd graduated the second time, but Ty knew he still thought of the academy and its rope as hell. "There's always rock climbing," Ty offered, but he couldn't put much effort behind it. The conversation had struck a tender nerve, and he'd lost the relatively good mood he'd been in. He perused his itinerary silently, not really seeing it anymore.

"I was hoping for a break from dangerous situations," Zane explained after a quiet moment. "We're on a goddamn cruise ship, you know? What could happen? Who would go on a nice, relaxing cruise to take a fucking zip-line ride through the jungle treetops?"

Ty hummed thoughtfully, focusing on the question. "I'd be really interested to see the other guys' itineraries, see which outings match up with all three," he said suddenly. "What if these adventures have a purpose? Like, they're going scuba diving, but they're really collecting some antiquity off the ocean floor they mean to sell?"

"There's a shopping extravaganza planned on Tortola, British Virgin Islands," Zane said. "Maybe a meeting off-ship to make a sale?"

"Or a buy," Ty said with a nod. He stood with his folder and began moving toward the balcony again, unconsciously drawn to the fresh air and light despite the frigid temperature outside. He reached over one shoulder and began rubbing the sore muscle at the base of his neck, his frown growing, his mood gone sour as he grew restless. This was why he tried to avoid any topics that evoked the thought of being in love. It always ended with the depressing knowledge that it was very much a free fall. A solo one.

"How about we take a break and go walk around while it's still light out?" Zane suggested from behind him.

"Sounds good to me," Ty muttered. He threw the folder onto the small sofa in the sitting area.

"Well, let's go, then, doll," Zane drew out in Corbin's voice.

Ty winced and made a derogatory sound as he turned and looked at Zane. "Hold on, I have to put on my British," he said with a long-suffering sigh.

Zane's smile reappeared. "I'll wait."

Ty snorted. He'd been struggling with the persona of Del Porter, flitting in and out of it when he attempted to sink himself into it, worrying about the accent and his ability to maintain it when around other passengers. He slid his feet into a comfortable pair of loafers and waved Zane toward the door. "I'll get it," he told Zane with false confidence.

Zane appeared at his side rather than walking away, and he reached to curl his fingers around each of Ty's wrists, capturing them firmly and slowly pulling them down and around Ty's back as he leaned in close.

Ty raised one eyebrow, flexing his fingers against Zane's grasp. He didn't try to get loose though, and he didn't feel the edge of panic threatening that he once would have, if his hands had been restrained. The handcuffs he knew he couldn't handle.

But he trusted Zane.

"Maybe you should change into something nice," Zane suggested smoothly. "Give me something gorgeous to look at while we walk around." He kissed the soft skin under Ty's chin.

Ty lifted his chin for the kiss, then looked back down his nose at Zane carefully, trying to decide if he was helping him become Del or making fun of him. Then Ty's expression warmed, and he smiled wryly. There was a part of him that was almost enjoying the idea of the roles they were supposed to play, even though he'd spent most of the morning griping. It was certainly a far cry from who he really was.

"What would you like to see, darling?" he asked, the British accent back in full force.

A gentle tug on Ty's arms had him arching back enough that Zane could nip at his throat. "Something that will get you noticed," Zane murmured before he bit down and then licked over the abused skin. "You know how much I like that."

Ty laughed even as he tried not to lose his balance and take them both down. "You hate that," he corrected wryly.

Pursing his lips, Zane made a noise of agreement. "I suppose what I really like is seeing people covet you and knowing you're mine." He nipped at Ty's earlobe before he released Ty's wrists. "Go on, then."

Ty snorted, smiling almost sadly as he met Zane's eyes. He sort of wished Zane meant it, rather than saying it as part of the character he was supposed to be playing. But wishing would get him nothing but heartbroken, and they had a case to concentrate on.

"We can do this," he assured them both in a low voice.

The itineraries told them which classy restaurant they were expected at for which meals, so picking a place for lunch the next day was a decision they didn't have to make. Zane made a quick study of the finely appointed dining room—also decorated in greens and golds for the holidays—as the hostess led them to a table seating four other diners. That would leave two empty seats besides them, and they'd be able to socialize with relative ease. Zane pulled out a chair and nodded for Ty to sit down. His lips twitched as he watched Ty and waited for the show to start. Zane didn't intend to stay quiet, but he definitely imagined "Del" as the bigger talker of the two.

Ty glanced at him and gave him a wicked grin, silently saying watch this as he sat down in the seat Zane had picked for him. Zane wouldn't consider Ty an attention whore, but he definitely didn't mind having the spotlight either. In another life, he probably would have made a great actor.

Ty greeted the other diners happily, smiling widely at them and receiving the same sort of warm response Ty always got when he turned on the charm. This was a whole new level of charisma, though, uninhibited and unfettered by Ty's usual tough-guy image. Zane didn't try to hold in the amusement or the smile—no reason to. He sat down, a bit back from the table so he could prop one arm on the edge and casually cross his long legs, and rubbed his hands together a bit. They were dry from the bit of ubiquitous hand sanitizer he'd gotten from a dispenser when they got out of the elevator.

Ty made a production of introducing them to the rest of the people at the table, receiving the names of their fellow diners in return. It was, after all, part of their job to identify the short list of names they'd been given. Two names, to be precise: Vartan Armen and Lorenzo Bianchi, the other two major players of the smuggling ring besides Corbin Porter. Zane certainly didn't expect to go through the list of a few thousand passengers one by one, but they had to start somewhere. Lunch was as good a place as any.

"And how is everyone this afternoon?" Ty asked them grandly as he reached over and took Zane's hand in his beneath the table. They weren't being overly obvious with public displays, simply because Ty had claimed it lacked class to be all over each other all the time. So far they had managed to exude merely a subtle closeness that was all too familiar, the same kind they shared when in private. If Zane's eyes happened to linger a little longer while watching his "husband" . . . well, who would blame him? Even with the garish blond hair, Ty was striking.

Ty continued to chat idly with the others, asking about their favorite things to do on board, including the Christmas parties throughout the cruise, and places to visit when they made port. Zane tried not to smile too much. It really was funny, if not somewhat shocking, listening to "Del" chatter. Ty was not what one would classify as a chatterbox. On the contrary he was—and Zane should have known better than to be surprised—a very competent conversationalist.

Zane turned his attention to the room at large, acting content to take in the scenery as he studied their surroundings: emergency exits, windows, safety measures, hidden cameras, other vacationers, loads and loads of decorations. He listened with half an ear until a waiter of Hispanic extraction, dressed neatly in the khaki-colored pants, white button-down Oxford, and navy blue sweater that was the crew uniform, approached and started taking drink orders after handing out a single sheet luncheon menu.

After hearing a variety of requests rattled off by the other passengers, the waiter stopped and looked at Ty expectantly. Ty looked up at him and hesitated, obviously having forgotten to peruse the menu.

"Anything you like, doll," Zane spoke up smoothly, his low voice carrying.

Ty glanced to him and back at the waiter, quickly ordering a three-course meal from the menu that included a beverage meant to complement the meal. Zane wasn't sure if Ty had actually looked at it or just pointed.

Zane skimmed the choices, picked a simple entrée and salad, and asked specifically for Evian rather than a cocktail. The waiter nodded, completed the other orders, and left. The conversation still went on around them, Ty speaking in the accent he'd almost perfected. Zane wasn't hearing as many slips now as when they'd left the cabin. Ty even had the colloquialisms down when he used them. He might not have fooled a native, but he could have fooled Zane.

When Ty let his fingers slide over Zane's palm as he smiled at one of their tablemates, Zane predicted that by the time this lunch was over, Ty's face was going to hurt from smiling so much.

A member of the wait staff appeared with their beverages, placing a frozen, pale pink drink in front of Ty before moving on. Ty blinked at it, his nearly flawless façade wavering just slightly, but then he smiled and thanked the waiter as he reached for the peach Bellini.

Zane leaned toward him and practically purred, "Enjoy it, doll, we're here to celebrate, right?" He laid his hand on Ty's forearm and squeezed gently. He figured they were doing pretty well assuming these identities, even if they were making it up left and right. They were playing off each other well. Like a real married couple. Something about that made Zane feel better than he thought he should.

Ty squeezed his hand under the table, as if he knew what Zane had been thinking. A few moments later, Ty leaned toward him and said, "These pink things are actually pretty good."

Zane laughed quietly, and Ty leaned away again. From then on, Zane relaxed and smiled as he talked with the gentleman nearby about recent politics, assuming what he thought of as Corbin's cocksure drawl. When he shifted his gaze to look toward Ty some minutes later, Zane found himself wondering where this charming talker had come from and how he'd be able to keep him after the case. And that surprised him enough that he didn't hear the waiter speak to him.

Zane blinked and realized he'd been staring when Ty nudged his knee expectantly under the table to prompt him. Then one of the women at the table tittered behind her hand, and instinct took over. Zane reached out to brush his knuckles lightly across Ty's cheek as he smiled warmly and then turned his attention to the waiter, who was confirming his order before setting down his plate. Ty shivered involuntarily and shook his head, leaning away from Zane as the woman next to him asked him a question.

Zane could hear the two other couples at the table murmuring, but he didn't acknowledge it. He had gotten caught, after all. It seemed to him from his quick study that Corbin wouldn't care about what other people thought. Only Del—Ty—mattered, and his hand stayed in Zane's, his thumb rubbing Zane's fingers gently, sliding over the smooth metal of his fake wedding ring. It was oddly soothing.

It was easy to watch Ty's masterful performance for the rest of lunch, and Zane let himself enjoy it.

CHAPTER FOUR

Ty lay on one of the teak deck chairs, stretched out with his hands behind his head and his eyes closed against the bright winter sun filtering through the protective glass that housed the indoor pool. Just after lunch he and Zane had decided to show their faces and actually try to enjoy themselves before they got deeper into the case. Ty had opted for the pool before remembering the piece of synthetic skin covering his tattoo. He wasn't sure if it could be submerged, and he wanted to test that in private before he dove in.

He'd been lying still for far too long, though. He kept telling himself it was part of the cover. This was the only thing anyone expected him to do. They figured being in plain sight the first afternoon would be a good plan, and the pool area under the dome meant it was plenty warm, especially with the sun shining through the glass.

Ty wasn't sure where Zane had gotten off to. He knew he couldn't dog his partner's steps for fear of looking too suspicious, but it made him nervous nonetheless, letting Zane out of his sight. He knew there were agents on the ship somewhere, no doubt looking out for them. But he had yet to make any of them, and that alone disturbed him.

No one was so good that they could consistently hide when a trained eye knew to look for them. Ty told himself they were probably keeping a low profile and not to worry about it.

Finally, he couldn't take the relaxation any longer, and he raised his head, squinting as he looked around to see if Zane was anywhere near, searching for a dark head somewhere. He passed over the first three almost immediately. Then he caught sight of a man surfacing in the pool amidst a gathering of women in various amounts of swimsuit.

Ty cocked his head, allowing himself to examine the tightening of his chest in reaction to spotting his partner. It had been happening more frequently lately. Ty didn't know if it was because he just had more opportunities to spot Zane in a crowd now, or if it was due to the more obvious possibilities. He had stopped trying to deny the fact that he was in love some weeks ago. The fact that they were not only able to show each other some attention here on the cruise ship, but that they were encouraged to do so, was only adding to the weight of the feelings he'd realized in the mountains of West Virginia.

He still had his doubts, of course, and the thought still unnerved him, but he had pretty much come to terms with it. It was almost amusing. If he'd been a betting man, he would never have picked himself from the two of them to be the sap who fell in love.

Ty sighed slightly and shielded his eyes, watching Zane idly.

It was clear that several of the women were flirting with him, and it was crystal clear that Zane—Corbin—was vastly amused. Zane slicked his wet hair back with one hand as he spoke with a couple of them before the group laughed and Zane gave that full-of-it smile Ty had quickly come to associate with Corbin. The real Corbin Porter was obviously a dick, if Zane's impression of him was anything to go by.

But Zane, with the self-assured addition to his attitude, was hitting buttons Ty hadn't even known he possessed. He sighed, looking down at the silver ring on his finger. It was still odd to see it there. And it was unnerving that he still couldn't seem to get it off. He tugged at it like he had been all morning. It was just a little too tight, and it didn't budge over the still-swollen, scarred knuckle. Tonight he intended to take some soap to it. Or if that failed, Astroglide.

He looked back up, sighing as he continued trying to spin it around on his finger. It took a long moment for it to register that Zane was wading toward him, a couple of the women trailing along, still talking as they entered into shallower water.

Ty watched him appreciatively, not worried that anyone could see like he normally did. Hell, it would be odd if people saw him not watching now, right? He stretched back out on his deck chair, crossing one ankle over the other and putting his hands behind his head again.

It gave him a comfortable vantage point to see the water stream over Zane's skin as he climbed the shallow steps out of the pool. Ty's eyebrow climbed as he took in the bright red European swim shorts that stuck to Zane's skin like crepe paper, well below the navel, a streak of scarlet across his lean hips and muscled abdomen.

Ty crossed his ankles the other way and looked up at the sky briefly, fighting his natural reaction to the view. His own swim trunks were similar, but in black. He hoped he pulled the look off as well as his partner did.

Then Zane lifted the towel to wipe his face and turned his back to Ty. Ty did a double-take when he caught sight of the ink on the lowest part of Zane's back, under the mishmash of thin white scars he knew were there. It looked like a twisted vine with small leaves and thorns—a simple but striking set of black lines that wrapped and twisted around, reaching from hip to hip along Zane's lower back before dipping down to a point just inside those very brief red shorts, forming an inverted triangle that stood out against Zane's tanned skin.

How the hell had he missed that?

Ty slapped his hand over his mouth to muffle the laugh that threatened. Finally, Zane was getting a little of the same treatment Ty had been dealing with. Ty supposed being forced to wear white linen and platinum hair was better than a henna tramp stamp.

He snorted as he lay there alone, and he had to look away before he began laughing harder and made a scene. Once he'd regained control, he looked back as one of the women stepped closer to Zane, her face clear to Ty since she faced him, and she very deliberately placed a hand on the bare skin of Zane's hip to brush her fingers near the tattoo. Ty whistled softly, hoping the henna or whatever they'd used to put the tattoo on wouldn't rub off when it was wet.

He couldn't have heard the proposition any clearer if he'd been standing right there next to them. He lowered his head, watching idly as he let his hand fall to his side. He'd never really seen Zane flirt, other than his playfully pitiful attempts at trying to seduce Ty into bed. And during their first week together in New York when they'd met with Serena Scott.

She was the type who ate her bedmates afterward. Zane had seemed to like it.

The woman's mouth formed a surprised O before a slight frown crinkled her brow. Zane turned enough that Ty could see the smile curving his lips, tipping his head in Ty's direction as he placed his hand on hers and removed it from his hip, though he kissed her fingers before releasing it to ease the rejection. The flustered woman stepped back and nodded, offering him an embarrassed smile, and Zane turned to walk toward Ty, Corbin's smile still in place.

Ty didn't move as he watched Zane approach. He merely kept his eyes on him, a smile quirking his lips as Zane got closer. Then Zane stopped at the foot of the lounger and openly looked him up and down. "Enjoying yourself?" he asked before wiping at his face again with the towel he carried.

Ty couldn't help but stretch under the frank appraisal. He gave Zane a content smile. "I am now," he answered wryly, the accent coming easier to him. The accent, he'd found, actually made it easier to be Del Porter. When he stopped using it in private, it was much more difficult to find the headspace. He couldn't commit himself to using it all the time, though. It sounded too damn silly.

Zane's smile turned into a smirk. "Sit up, doll," he said as he rubbed the towel over his chest and abs.

Ty raised an eyebrow. Zane really seemed to be enjoying his role. He pushed himself up onto his elbows, gave Zane a crooked smile, and sat up as requested. Zane straddled the lounger, sat, and slid in behind him, then leaned back, Ty neatly between his sprawled legs. "Ah. Much better vantage point for tracking interesting people," Zane murmured pleasantly, dropping Corbin's oily drawl.

Ty reached over to the table beside the chair and retrieved his sunglasses. He rested an elbow on Zane's knee, looking around as he let his fingers coast along the damp skin of Zane's calf. The dark shades masked his perusal of the crowd. Several people were watching them, some deliberately, some surreptitiously. One man in particular observed them from across the deck and had been doing so ever since Ty had caught sight of him more than thirty minutes ago.

"I think I've made one of our contacts," Ty told Zane as he let his hand travel to the back of Zane's knee and along his thigh. He resisted mentioning the tattoo. He didn't think he could without laughing yet.

Zane grunted in acknowledgment. "Only one? Spot any of the team?" He laid his hand over Ty's shoulder, stroking lightly with this thumb.

Ty's lips twitched. "Not yet. You're enjoying this, aren't you?" he declared in amusement, turning to glance back at Zane briefly. His fingertips just barely brushed Zane's skin. It was a chaste, tantalizing gesture.

Zane's look edged toward a leer. "Hell yes," he said.

Ty smiled and turned his head to fully look at Zane, one eyebrow raised behind the designer sunglasses. It was rare to catch Zane in this mood. Ty wanted nothing more right then than to head back to the luxury stateroom, lock the door, and get on his knees. And he was okay with that.

He took his sunglasses off and met Zane's eyes, knowing his partner would read him like a book.

That leer was firmly in place in Zane's flashing eyes as Zane reached out, wrapped one hand around Ty's neck to pull him close, and kissed him hard. Ty flailed slightly when he was yanked, having to contort a little and lean far backward to meet the kiss. But he relaxed into it quickly, letting the odd feeling settle over him.

It was an entirely new sensation for him, kissing another man in public. Something he had never done. Something he was really enjoying. He reached up to drag his fingers through Zane's wet hair. He hummed along with the kiss, letting his body react and not trying to fight it. They had two weeks of this on their cake surveillance assignment. They might as well enjoy it. It seemed like forever before Zane pulled back, though it couldn't possibly have been more than eight or ten seconds.

"Let's go," Zane rasped. "I've had enough sun for one afternoon, and I'm sure you've had your fill of people-watching."

Ty smiled and turned his head to glance around the pool again. His entire body buzzed after the kiss, another new thing for him, and he didn't want to move and ruin it just yet. The man across the pool still watched them casually from behind his own sunglasses.

Ty cocked his head at him. He was tall and thin, his hair a deep black and his complexion what Ty might have called swarthy. They couldn't approach him. He would come to them at the specified time, whenever the hell that was. Until then, all he and Zane had to do was . . . be married.

Ty grinned and deliberately leaned his body back against Zane's chest. He rested his head on the front of Zane's shoulder and turned his face until his nose brushed under Zane's chin. "I'd rather stay here a while longer," he said in a low voice. His hand slid up Zane's inner thigh, disappearing between their bodies.

The low rumble of an amused chuckle shook Ty slightly as Zane dropped his chin to steal a kiss, quicker this time, before curling his arm around Ty to rest his hand on Ty's belly. He was now pretty much serving as the back of the deck chair, and Ty was lounging against him. "If you want. You'll make it up to me later," Zane teased.

"Oh, I know it," Ty responded as his fingers found what they'd been seeking. He smiled mischievously, lowering his voice as he let his fingers glide over the bulge in Zane's swim trunks. "I look forward to being bent over the balcony railing," he told Zane with certainty, his voice low.

That got a reaction that wasn't smooth, cocky Corbin. Both Zane's hands tightened as he sucked in a quick breath, and his cock jumped against Ty's hand. When Zane spoke, his voice was thick and rough. "Whatever makes you happy, doll."

Ty grinned triumphantly. His fingers continued to move teasingly, hidden behind his back. The exotic-looking man still watched them. Ty found it odd and slightly disconcerting. He laid his head against Zane's chest again, brow furrowing as he fondled his lover, hidden in plain sight.

Zane slid his fingers through Ty's hair, and Ty thought he just might have felt those fingers shaking. Then Zane tugged gently after a particularly firm caress. "You are skating on thin ice."

Ty smiled and looked around again. He was being fairly discreet. No one around them seemed any the wiser. He moved his other hand to glide idly along Zane's thigh as he used it as an armrest. He could see how some enjoyed this game of passive seduction. The thrill was in Zane's reaction. How far could he go before Zane lost his control?

"You plan to punish me somehow?" he asked in the most innocent voice he could muster. The accent actually helped with that.

"Oh, I think I can come up with something suitably chastising," Zane said darkly. His voice was dropping closer toward a growl.

"If it doesn't involve me on my knees in some fashion I shall be wildly disappointed," Ty drawled as he gave a squeeze of his hand in emphasis. He was pleased with himself for remembering the intricacies of the dialect.

Zane laughed aloud, and Ty could see clear interest on a few other faces. Zane was drawing a lot of attention, and well he should be. Hell, probably half the people up here—women and men—would want Zane to bend them over a balcony railing.

Ty turned his head to nuzzle against Zane's chin again. "You didn't tell me about the tattoo."

"I figured you'd noticed," Zane murmured. "It's not exactly subtle."

Ty laughed and shook his head. "Haven't had occasion to see that side of you lately."

Zane chuckled, and it shook both of them this time. "So what do you think?"

"I'm more impressed with the rest of you," Ty assured him with another smirk. He gave Zane a few slow strokes. He wanted Zane in him, and now. But more than that, he wanted Zane to want it enough to make a move.

Zane hissed quietly. "Doll . . ." His voice carried a warning tone. "You'll make me forget we're supposed to be working."

"We are working, remember?" Ty drawled as he continued to slide the tips of his fingers against Zane's swimsuit.

Zane splayed his hand over Ty's chest and started stroking up and down his sun-warmed skin, going a little lower each time. "And I'm wondering just how Corbin would decide between being smug and showing you off or being jealous and dragging you to bed away from prying eyes," he said throatily.

Ty shifted his body against Zane suggestively. If they were getting up to head to the cabin anytime soon, he wanted Zane just as turned on as he was. He might even be able to push him over the edge and get him to go rough on him. God, that was fun, watching Zane battle between control and wild passion. His fingers stroked along the hard ridge in Zane's shorts.

"I vote for the bed," Ty murmured with a smirk.

Without warning, Zane surged up out of the deck chair, practically lifting Ty to set him on his feet. He grabbed a towel in one hand and Ty's wrist in the other and started stalking for the doors that would lead into the concourse of luxury cabins. Ty nearly stumbled, barely grabbing his sunglasses, and Zane's grasp on his wrist was the only thing that kept him on his feet as he was dragged away from the pool. He bit his lip in anticipation of what might be coming and tried to look suitably chastised as he followed.

Zane pulled him inside, and the forced air spilled over them as they moved through the entryway and into the wide stairwell. Once they were around the corner, Zane swung Ty around with a growl and pinned him to the wall, his head narrowly missing a sprig of holiday cheer taped to the bulkhead. "You have any idea how close I was to tipping you back on that chair?" he growled, grinding his obvious hard-on against Ty's thigh.

Ty tangled both hands in Zane's hair and bit his lip again against the smile that threatened. "God, I love it when you do this," he told Zane with relish, his voice a bare whisper as he tried to catch his breath.

"This?" Zane purred against Ty's ear as he pressed his body against Ty's from chest to thigh, heated bare skin catching and skipping instead of sliding. He deliberately dragged one hand down Ty's side toward his shorts.

Ty shook his head, fighting the grin as he let his fingers slide down Zane's face. "I believe you were growling," he corrected. He wrapped his arms loosely around his lover's neck and tilted his head up, silently requesting a kiss.

Zane's response started as a hum in his chest and built to the requested growl as he dipped his chin and pushed his lips firmly against Ty's just as his palm cupped behind Ty's thigh to hitch him closer. If Ty didn't know better, he'd think Zane planned to fuck him right there in the hallway. When Zane growled again, dropped the towel, and slid his other hand under the fabric of Ty's shorts to cup his ass, Ty suddenly wasn't so sure he really did know better.

Zane had just dragged his tongue along Ty's lower lip when Ty heard someone very close by clear his throat. He jerked back in alarm as Zane's hands abruptly tightened on him, and Ty banged the back of his head against the wall. It was a knee-jerk reaction to being caught Ty was pretty sure he'd never get over. He didn't like being surprised.

A man stood in the middle of the corridor looking into the stairwell, watching them passively. It was the same man Ty had seen observing them outside. He was quite striking up close. His hair was dark and curly at the ends, cut just above his shoulders and slicked back, with hints of gray at the temples and along his hairline. His stylish goatee was carefully maintained, hiding the hard lines of his lips. He held his expensive sunglasses in his hand now as he looked at Ty and Zane in bemusement. His eyes were a deep mahogany, a beautiful color, but cold and emotionless. The steel gray bathing shorts he wore just intensified that effect.

Zane straightened to his full height, curled his arm around Ty's shoulders, and subtly pulled him closer, splaying his hand across Ty's collarbone possessively. Ty bit back the annoyance the protective stance caused.

"Can I help you?" Zane said, the sounds rumbling between put out and wary.

"Mr. Porter?" the man asked in heavily accented English. Ty couldn't quite place the origin. Turkey, maybe. He wasn't sure. What was obvious was that this had to be one of Corbin Porter's contacts aboard the ship. And he definitely wasn't Italian. That left Vartan Armen, the acquisitions specialist.

"I'm Corbin Porter," Zane acknowledged. "You must be—"

"Vartan Armen, yes," the man broke in. "Only the one telephone conversation more than a year ago does not give one much with which to draw a conclusion, I know." Armen paused and looked Ty up and down. "I must admit, your . . . husband gave you away."

Ty had to fight not to bristle at the man. He felt like a pit bull, his hackles rising because he didn't like the scent of the man. He snorted at him as if amused. Zane must have picked up on the tension, though, because the hand on Ty's shoulder began to rub soothingly.

"He does attract attention, doesn't he?" Zane said.

Armen gave Ty a polite look and nod. "Quite striking, indeed. I am aware we are not to meet until some days hence, but I feel all this cloak-and-dagger is quite cumbersome. We're not here to hide from one another," he said with a smile that seemed genuine. "My stateroom is 8520, if you wish to contact me before our scheduled activities coincide. I feel dinner and drinks would put us all more at ease before we convene any business."

"I agree," Zane answered as he nodded. "I'm sure it won't throw our itinerary off too much to make a change."

Armen gave a courteous nod. "Very good. I shall be in touch."

Ty remained silent, practically vibrating with the desire to jump in and say something, dig for information, anything before the man left them. He remained silent though, feigning boredom as he looked away with a long sigh. He slid his sunglasses on as if preparing to return to the pool, and he looked back at Armen. With one push of his thumbnail to the inside of the frame, he activated the tiny camera inside the designer sunglasses. He stared at Armen just long enough to hope the camera got a clear shot, then pushed the button again and looked away.

"We'll see you soon, Mr. Armen," Zane said, a slight hint of closure clear in his tone.

"Until then, Mr. Porter," Armen said. He nodded to Ty. "Mr. Porter." And then he was gone, through the doors to the promenade.

Ty stepped back slightly, letting his hands slide down and away from Zane's body as he watched the man disappear. "He's kind of slimy, huh?" he said, still using his accent for fear of losing it.

"Yes." Zane watched the doors with narrowed eyes. "That's a good description."

"So much for sticking to our itineraries," Ty murmured. But if Armen was advancing the schedule, perhaps this job would go faster than they'd anticipated. "But hey, now we know where he's staying," he added brightly. "Right the fuck next door."

Zane finally turned his chin and refocused his full attention on Ty. "And we don't need to worry about any meetings for the rest of the day," he said with a ghost of a smile.

"Good, gives us time to contact the backup team, get some eyes and ears on this guy. I think I got a good picture, which means we're already halfway done," Ty answered distractedly as he peered at the doors and reached out for Zane again almost unconsciously. His hand met warm, firm skin as Zane took a step closer.

"Is that all?"

Ty looked at him with a twist of mischief on his lips. "And my accent is slipping," he claimed as he moved closer to his partner, his fingers dragging against Zane's skin as he wrapped his arms around his waist. "I think I'm going to need a little more practice before dinner." He pressed a kiss to Zane's chin.

Zane's lips quirked as his arms slid around Ty's waist. "Who are you and what did you do with Ty Grady?" he asked under his breath.

Ty smiled and pulled himself closer, brushing his lips against Zane's. "Don't get used to it, darling," he drawled, kissing Zane again languidly.

Zane's low chuckle was practically a purr. "Then I'll enjoy it while I've got it. C'mon, baby. Finish what you started out by the pool."

They were in foul moods by the time their scheduled dinner came around, mostly because they'd discovered after getting to their cabin that their luggage included a whole lot of lubricant—flavored, scented, warming, desensitizing, stimulating, silicone, gel, and one tiny tube that Ty suspected had glow-in-the-dark and/or explosive properties—but not a single condom to be found.

Ty cursed himself again for not having foreseen that. Zane had gone to take a shower, muttering darkly after watching Ty go through all the luggage. Now Ty could hear things clinking and sliding and thumping on the marble vanity in the bathroom. When Zane stepped into the doorway, his hair was all slicked back, and he wore tailored black pants that rode low on his hips and a braided gold chain around his neck. Nothing else.

"Dinner had better be good," he said in resignation. His mood had taken a hit with Armen's appearance and had deteriorated all afternoon, capped off by them losing track of time. Now they didn't even have time to make the evening interesting before dinner and let off some steam.

Ty looked at Zane blankly and shook his head, trying to see the humorous side of the situation. He failed miserably and grunted at his equally cranky partner. "I know the guy's all kinds of classy, but you're putting a shirt on, right, papi?" he asked wryly.

Zane stalked over to the wardrobe to riffle through the choices with an aggrieved sigh. He looked to be visibly wrangling with making himself relax.

Ty grunted in sympathy and scratched at his chin idly as he watched. "We'll stop by one of the pharmacies and get some after dinner."

"Oh, that will go over well. Are you worried about getting pregnant?"

Ty cocked his head and narrowed his eyes at his belligerent partner. He deserved to be cranky, but Ty didn't deserve to be the target. Ty waffled between responding in kind and trying to defuse a possible argument. Fuck it. "Maybe you're just not a good enough lay, and I'm cheating on you," he posed finally.

Zane yanked a shirt off its hanger and turned around. "If I found you cheating on me, I'd beat you black and blue. And you'd get off on it," he growled in Corbin's voice.

Ty narrowed his eyes further and leaned forward. There had been a couple times now that he actually believed Zane as Corbin. This instance especially qualified. The line between them was easily blurred. Ty didn't particularly like this element of Zane's transformation, possibly because it didn't actually feel like a transformation. It was like there was a part of Zane somewhere in there really meant the things he said.

Now Zane steadily held his gaze as he pulled a shirt on. Zane's eyes were deep brown, almost black, and not at all warm. Ty wasn't at all intimidated, but he was annoyed just enough to want to deny Zane the fight he was angling for.

He smiled slyly. "You're probably right."

The icy scowl on Zane's face thawed a little, as did the chill in his eyes, and one corner of his mouth curled up as he gave Ty a wink. "Of course I am."

Ty rolled his eyes and stood. "You ready, cupcake?" he asked drolly.

"I'd feel better if I knew where our damn backup was," Zane groused as he tucked in the black silk shirt. He'd left two buttons undone at the collar, and he looked slimmer, almost wiry, in the all-black ensemble, despite his six-foot-five frame and broad shoulders.

"What about weapons?" he asked as he strapped a narrow stiletto inside one wrist and buttoned the cuff.

"Well," Ty started with a heavy sigh as he looked down at himself, "I don't have anywhere to hide mine. But we can stash one or two more on you maybe." He looked Zane up and down critically. It was relatively easy for a trained eye to spot a concealed weapon, and their main concern was being discovered as frauds. "I guess the real question is, would Corbin go packing, or should we hide it good enough to make it hard to get to?"

"Porter's a thug. A smug one who's careful, but he's not paranoid. Too proud for that. I think he'd carry but have it well concealed for use in a pinch," Zane said.

Ty couldn't help the gleam that entered his eyes. "That means we have to be creative," he said with a certain relish as he scanned over Zane's body again.

"Creative," Zane repeated, and he looked down at himself as he watched Ty study him. "Like . . . what? I already wear concealed knives."

Ty smirked and cocked his head. "Inner thighs are good, right at the groin. Material's always roomy, so it doesn't show, but it's uncomfortable as hell. Also hard to get to unless you feel like shooting off a round right next to your johnson. Lower back is probably the best place. Won't impede movement, less noticeable, especially if you don't take off the jacket," he surmised as Zane pulled a black suit jacket out of the wardrobe. "We just need something to secure it. Other than stuffing it into your belt, of course."

"Because that's so comfortable," Zane said with a sigh. "But it'll do unless you have another idea." He walked over to the small satchel on the bedside table and pulled out Ty's gun from where it was hidden in a large box of jewelry that consisted mostly of leather and chains. They hadn't found Zane's Glock hidden anywhere.

"I do," Ty said haughtily as he headed for the only bag he'd been allowed to pack of his own things. There was a single Ace bandage in there, brought along out of habit. He held it up to Zane with a raised eyebrow. "Okay, so it's not a MOLLE system, but you make do."

Zane cracked a smile and started pulling his shirt back out of the waistband. "Fix me up, then."

Ty bit his tongue on any possible response and unraveled the bandage. They used Zane's belt to make sure the gun stayed in place, and Ty made quick work of wrapping the bandage around Zane's torso to secure it. It served to hide the telltale form of the gun's pommel, but that was about it. Ty pushed Zane's shirt down and stood back with his hands on his hips, surveying his handiwork.

"It'll do," Ty told him, realizing belatedly the dubious tone to his voice.

"As long as it doesn't clatter to the floor, it'll be fine," Zane said as he tucked his shirt back in and picked up the jacket. "I feel better, anyway."

"Oh, what a relief," Ty muttered sarcastically.

Zane just smiled and walked to open the door for him. "Let's go, doll."

Ty merely rolled his eyes as he walked past him. Give the man a weapon and suddenly he was all smiles again.

Come to think of it, that was probably one of the traits that kept Ty interested.

They walked down the corridor together, Ty glancing surreptitiously at Zane as they moved. He cleared his throat and reached out to slide his fingers into Zane's, taking pleasure in the ability to do so without fear of being spotted. "At least you make frustrated and cranky look good," he commented, tongue-in-cheek.

Zane took up Ty's hand and kissed his knuckles, offering a rueful look of apology before lacing their fingers together as they walked out into the several-stories-high, glass-walled promenade. "So you think Del is as proud to show off Corbin as Corbin is Del?"

"No, he's just after his money," Ty answered blithely, trying not to smile as he watched Zane out of the corner of his eye for his reaction.

Zane's lips twitched. "Corbin can probably afford whatever eye candy strikes his fancy." He leaned slightly toward Ty as they walked. "But I'm thinking my version of Del is easier on the eyes."

"Flattery will not get you laid any faster," Ty told him with a frown. He was aware of his own good looks and not too modest to use them occasionally, but Zane rarely offered a compliment when they weren't half-naked already, and Ty didn't think he'd ever noticed so many eyes lingering on him as he had the past day or so. It was unsettling for a man who'd spent most of his life trying not to be noticed.

"Somehow I don't think you keep me around for my seduction skills," Zane said dryly.

Ty barked a laugh before he could stop himself. He glanced at Zane and smiled affectionately at him. Zane's goofy lines and occasional unabashedly cheesy attempts at seduction were just part of his charm. Cheesy, goofy, thank-God-he's-pretty charm. "I think I can safely concur."

Zane staggered slightly and clapped a hand over his heart in mock-surprise.

"Just take comfort in the fact that I keep you around for the amazing sex," Ty murmured to appease him.

"How amazing?" Zane wheedled.

"Don't push it."

CHAPTER FIVE

They walked into the swanky restaurant indicated on their ever-demanding itineraries, and a cheerful hostess wearing the ship's colors and a green Santa hat asked them to follow her through the candlelit dining room. Zane glanced around casually: it was your typical fancy sit-down place with painted cream wallpaper, glittery chandeliers, china, crystal, and linen on the tables, and one bank of floor-to-ceiling windows. Nothing surprising. The hostess led them to a raised dais that ran along one side of the room next to the wide windows that displayed the dying sunset and stopped by a table.

After a moment's pause, Zane walked to the far side and pulled the chair closest to the wall out, indicating for Ty to sit. Not that he was trying to be extra suave, but he figured he'd go ahead and give Ty the seat that would put his back to the wall. Zane didn't like people walking up behind him either, but he wasn't likely to react violently out of instinct. And besides, Ty would warn him long before anyone suspicious got close enough to do damage.

Ty raised one eyebrow at him in warning despite his good intentions. Too much gallantry on Zane's part might cause Ty to lose it. Which might be fun to watch. Tonight, though, Ty sat obediently in the proffered chair and laid the linen napkin across his lap as he watched Zane step around the table to sit down across from him.

The hostess wished them a pleasant dinner and disappeared with surprisingly little fanfare. Considering how staff members had been consistently tripping over themselves and each other to help the guests, Zane was mildly impressed.

"At least we have a view," Ty mumbled as he looked out the windows at the setting sun. The fading sunlight fought with the candlelight, casting odd shadows across his face.

Zane did glance outside, but he preferred to watch his partner instead, still studying the odd contrast of Ty versus Del. He opened his mouth to comment on it when a waiter stopped at the table, left them menus, a wine list, and a specials card, and whisked away after promising to return post haste.

"Well," Zane said, leaning back comfortably. "Isn't this schmanzy."

"You're such a cynic," Ty accused under his breath.

"Why do you say that?" Zane asked curiously as he looked around them again. He had to admit that the decor was tasteful. Just upscale, which he'd learned a long time ago didn't necessarily mean you were getting your money's worth.

Ty pointed out the window at the last brilliant rays of sun as it faded below the horizon. The pale blue sky was streaked with pinks and oranges and one splash of brilliant crimson. "That is free," Ty said quietly.

Zane nodded slowly. Every once in a while, Ty came out with one of these comments that really made Zane step back and appreciate what he had. Right now, he definitely included Ty in that tally. "It's gorgeous. We should see about eating dinner on our balcony sometime." Their suite was on the starboard side, so they could get some sunsets all to themselves, if they wanted.

Ty smiled, but it was a melancholy one wholly uncharacteristic of him. Zane watched him for a long moment, and then he reached out to cover Ty's hand on the table with his own. "You okay?" he asked quietly.

"Just trying to remind myself not to get too comfortable."

"It's okay to enjoy yourself," Zane answered, phrasing his words carefully. "We've got two weeks here. Busy and eventful weeks, but two of them. To ourselves, mostly."

"We don't have anything to ourselves until we've done our job," Ty reminded softly. His voice was even, not at all bitter or resigned like it might have been. But there was something beneath it that was hard to identify.

"We're together," was Zane's simple answer.

Ty's lips compressed as he continued to hold Zane's gaze across the table, and his eyes warmed like he was trying to hide his amusement. It was enough. Zane would rather see humor at his expense in Ty's eyes than any kind of pain.

"So. Want to look at the specials?" he asked as he held up the card. Ty snorted and snatched the card out of Zane's hand, flipping it over to peruse it with pursed lips. The melancholy was gone, replaced by his usual unique style of bravado. Zane pulled one of the full menus closer. "Anything look good?"

Ty didn't respond for a moment, and when he did, his voice was totally devoid of inflection. "I see fish. And more fish. And oh look, shrimp. With fish."

Zane opened the menu and skimmed the entrée list. "It appears this would be a seafood restaurant. Besides salad. Although we're paying enough that I'm sure they'd hoof a steak up here from somewhere for you if you asked."

"I like fish," Ty muttered as he reviewed his own menu. He sounded almost insulted.

"I know that. But you like steak better," Zane pointed out with a smile.

"Shut up," Ty muttered with a shake of his head. "Maybe I can order fish and chips and feel like I'm at home," in said a falsely wistful voice.

The waiter appeared at his elbow, and they made their orders, Zane passing when the man offered wine with the meal. Again, Ty hesitated when the drinks were brought up, as if not sure whether he should order one.

"I highly recommend the Verdicchio," a hearty, accented voice said, interrupting the waiter's explanation of the wine choices. "They'd do well to have an Orvieto, but alas, we must make do."

Zane turned his attention to the man sitting at a nearby table who had spoken. He had dark Italian coloring and features to match his accent, and Zane guessed him to be in his early to mid-fifties by the depth of the voice and the gray at his temples. "Sounds like good advice. Doll? Want to try that?"

"Perhaps another time," Ty answered softly, watching Zane with narrowed eyes.

"The wine list is not so extended, but I would call it sufficient, I suppose, considering the surrounds," the man said, his deep voice easily carrying across the aisle between their tables.

Zane glanced over to observe a statuesque brunette sitting with the man who had just spoken, and she was commenting in what sounded like Italian, her sentence ending with a name: Lorenzo. And by the tone of her voice, she was chiding him.

"Ah, yes, excuse me. I do tend to go on," the man told Zane in apology.

Zane smiled in response and checked to see if Ty had caught that exchange. A probably-Italian man named Lorenzo eating in the same rotation as they were. Chances were really good that this was their other main contact, Lorenzo Bianchi.

Ty was looking devotedly at his menu, his head cocked in a manner that said he was indeed listening intently to the couple at the neighboring table. As Zane looked at him, Ty glanced up at him from under his lashes. He had heard.

Zane ordered the first dish that caught his eye. Then the waiter turned to Ty and took his order before making himself scarce.

"Ah, and you will feel the want for the Orvieto, choosing such an exquisite and light grilled fish without sauce," Bianchi said, wagging a finger in the air at Zane expansively.

"I'm sure there will be plenty of opportunity for wine during the cruise," Zane said smoothly, turning his body slightly in the chair so he was more open to the Bianchis.

"Ah, champagne with breakfast, mixed drinks at lunch, cocktails with the appetizers, wine with dinner, and cognac with my cigar. I do indeed like that," Bianchi said with a smile as he laid his napkin on the table next to his plate.

Zane had to ignore how dry his mouth had just gotten. That laundry list of drinks was appealing in its own scary way. "Well, it is vacation, after all," he commented.

"Bah, vacation. Life is all about love and liquor," Bianchi said with a grand gesture to the woman with him. "Isn't that right, Norina?" She smiled indulgently and nodded, and Zane saw the light of it sparkle in her dark eyes. She matched Bianchi for coloring, though Zane would place her as younger than Ty, early thirties at the most. "Ah, to beautiful women in love!" Bianchi proposed, holding up his nearly empty flute before finishing it in two swallows.

Zane let out a chuckle and nodded. "I'm sure we would join you in some variation of your toast if we had glasses."

Bianchi narrowed his eyes, looking between Zane and Ty curiously, when Norina spoke up in a spate of Italian, and his eyes widened in surprise for a moment before he broke into a full laugh as he stood and offered his hand. "Well, then to beautiful people in love. I am Lorenzo Bianchi, and it is a pleasure to meet you finally. You are Mr. Porter, no?"

Zane smiled as he stood and shook hands with Bianchi. "I agree with both those sentiments. Corbin Porter, yes."

Bianchi continued to chuckle as he pumped Zane's hand. "Well, well, Mr. Porter, it is as Norina supposed. Perhaps we meet earlier than planned, but it was indeed a good first discussion, don't you agree?"

"Yes, I think so, Signor Bianchi." Zane turned partway toward Ty. "This is my husband, Del Porter."

"Very nice to meet you, Mr. Porter and Mr. Porter," Bianchi said as he offered his hand to Ty as he gestured with his other arm for Norina to stand. "And this is my gioia, Norina."

To all three men's shock, the Italian beauty stood and threw her arms around Ty enthusiastically, talking rapidly in elated Italian as she hugged him. Zane caught himself before responding with anything more than a laugh, but that certainly wasn't something he'd expected to see. He was sure Ty hadn't been expecting it, either, and glad Ty had been able to repress the Instakill.

"Ah, they spent so much time on the computer planning this and that," Bianchi said with a wave of his hand. "That will be why you and I sit in peace at the poker tables."

Zane rubbed at his chin as he suppressed the reaction to frown. So Norina and Del were email pals. That could be good. Or not. "I'm looking forward to it."

"Come, Norina, you and Mr. Porter can catch up tomorrow," Bianchi said pleasantly. "We have that concert to see."

Norina chattered a little more as she hugged Ty one last time before giving Zane a brilliant smile. Zane really hoped what she was saying wasn't something Del was supposed to be understanding and answering, because it was obvious Norina expected Del to understand Italian. They all said their goodbyes just as the waiter appeared with the appetizer and salads, and Zane sat down in his chair to take a deep breath and process.

Ty remained standing, watching them go with a smile firmly in place. He waved one last time as Norina Bianchi turned and waved back at them excitedly. As soon as they were out of sight, Ty turned to Zane, smile gone and face expressionless, and he sat heavily in his chair. He looked like he desperately wanted to say something, rail against McCoy and God and Donald Duck for putting them on this cruise ship in this position. But he remained silent.

Zane couldn't think of a single thing to say, so he started on his salad as he reviewed the conversation, committing details to memory, and watched Ty poke at his bowl of vinaigrette-covered greens. Zane could almost physically feel Ty restraining himself. He knew his partner's temper well, having seen Ty lose it on various occasions. Ty's mood was what one might call mercurial. Depending on the subject of his ire, it was oftentimes amusing to watch him go off. Other times, like on a mountaintop in West Virginia where he'd started lecturing men on the best way he could kill them, it could get a little iffy.

Tonight could probably be considered iffy, too, if Zane couldn't figure out how to get Ty to let off some of that steam he could see slowly building.

Finally, Ty looked up from his salad and narrowed his eyes at Zane. "Do you speak Italian?" he asked calmly.

"No," Zane said in apology.

Ty just nodded jerkily, as if he had already known that. "Crap," he muttered under his breath as he went back to his salad.

Zane understood Ty's concern. Any little thing could break an undercover assignment, much less a big problem like not speaking a language. Maybe . . . maybe Corbin could be feeling a little possessive and decide he didn't want Del going off on his own, even if it were with the lovely Norina, who, in theory, would be less of a threat to Corbin than her manly Italian husband. "She didn't act like she expected a reply as she went on at you in Italian," Zane reasoned. "She just seemed excited to meet you."

"God, I hope she speaks English," Ty murmured as he put down his fork and pinched the bridge of his nose. "If she realizes I'm not Del, she goes to her husband, and we're royally fucked."

Zane decided to throw his idea out there. "I could decide I don't want to spend even an hour without you, and you could blame it all on your jealous husband."

Ty sighed and looked up at Zane seriously. "That won't really move things along. And you don't come across as the outrageously jealous type, anyway. No, you handle your end, I'll deal with mine."

"Corbin struck me as a very possessive man. I've not pushed the idea," Zane said as he pushed his empty salad bowl aside.

Ty cocked his head, the Italian dilemma momentarily forgotten as he looked at Zane curiously.

Zane shrugged slightly to play it off. "I don't know how you'll react. I didn't want to risk it in a public meeting only to face your wrath after," he said with a half smile. If he had his choice, he'd be a lot closer to his "husband" a lot of the time. But he was struggling to find that line they were supposed to be walking on this assignment, and he didn't want to confuse what was coming from his interpretation of Corbin and what was truly coming from his own desires.

Ty was silent for a moment, and then he gave a derogatory snort and said, "Face my wrath?"

Zane leaned forward on his elbows and spoke seriously. "You haven't seen me jealous."

Ty laughed and shook his head as if he thought Zane was joking. That was what Zane expected. He was getting better at predicting how Ty would react, at least in relation to the personal side of their partnership. He didn't join in the laugh, instead picking up his water glass and leaning back in his seat to wait.

Ty was still smiling when he stopped laughing, watching Zane in a mixture of amusement and wary confusion. After a moment when Zane still didn't speak, Ty's brow furrowed, and he cocked his head. "Seriously?" he asked, forgetting the accent he'd managed to keep up until that point.

Zane glanced out the window at the now-dark sky, wishing he'd just let it drop. This wasn't really public dinner conversation. "We'll talk about it later. Let's just say I'm sure I feel quite possessive of my very handsome husband."

Ty looked at him speculatively, the silence hanging heavy between them. It was an awkwardness they had rarely experienced. Zane waited for some sort of response. He couldn't read Ty's face, but he hoped Ty could recognize the honesty in his. Yes, under the right circumstances, Zane could see himself being very jealous. But he honestly wasn't sure if he had that right, as much as he suddenly wanted it.

Finally Ty shook his head decisively. "You get laid too often to be jealous," he announced flippantly as he reached for his glass.

Zane thought about arguing but instead gave Ty a smile and let it go. It was all semantics anyway, jealousy versus possessiveness. Dropping the topic now meant he could chew on the idea plenty himself later without Ty blowing him off with a joke.

It only hurt a little bit.

After dinner and almost an hour of browsing and shopping, Zane was still preoccupied by Ty's dismissive comment in the restaurant. "You get laid too often to be jealous." Zane wasn't too sure. Even before playing Corbin Porter, he'd been fighting thinking He's mine about his partner, because the implications were just too big to get his head around.

Not too many weeks ago, he'd stood next to Ty's hospital bed and admitted to himself that he didn't ever want to let Ty go. But he hadn't yet found a way to reconcile that with the reality of their complicated lives. And now, because this crazy case completely warped their "reality," he could be as possessive as he thought Corbin would be, and Ty—or Del—wouldn't complain. Not in public, anyway.

But what about when the case was over?

Before dinner, he'd assumed Ty wouldn't want him staking any sort of claim, physical or emotional, except as part of their cover, and then only grudgingly. Zane hadn't heard anything to change that assumption, but he hadn't exactly asked, either. He'd put it off, shying away from a topic that felt like a trip-wired land mine settling in the center of his chest.

Zane turned in place where he stood outside a ritzy accessory store and watched Ty finger through a display of sunglasses. Ty turned to look at him, wearing a pair of aviator sunglasses just like the ones he'd left at home, the tag sticking out sideways at his temple. Zane smiled despite his mixed feelings. "Don't you have a pair like that already?" A legitimate question, Ty or Del.

Ty took them off and looked at them, smirking. "You can never have too much awesome," he claimed. He set them back down and slid his hands down his sides, where his pockets should have been. He grumbled about the soft linen pants and searched for something else to do with his hands as they continued to stroll. He was getting twitchy, and his mood had steadily declined since dinner.

Whether the cause was the prospect of dealing with Norina Bianchi or the conversation they'd had regarding jealousy was anyone's guess. Zane had started casting around for something shiny, sweet, or sticky to throw in Ty's path as an emotional diversion.

"If we want dessert later, there's no lack of places for snacks," Zane said as they passed by a bakery kiosk and a soda shoppe. It was just one floor of three on the impressive, very brightly decorated promenade, sort of a high-class carpeted mini-mall and food court with anything from an Orange Julius to a Godiva Chocolatier and a cheap T-shirt shop to a Tiffany & Co. store. All complete with a twenty-foot-tall glittering Christmas tree in the center of it.

"I would kill you for some gummy bears right now," Ty muttered. He reached out and laced his fingers into Zane's, apparently deciding that it was the best thing to do with his otherwise idle hands.

"You should have looked when we were in the store," Zane said, moving them along the walkway. They'd found condoms in a remarkably discreet corner of a mini-grocery, but instead of risking exposure by purchasing them, Ty had palmed a box. When they'd stepped outside the store again, Zane had discovered the box safety tucked away inside his suit jacket. One day Zane was going to find out how Ty did that and how he always managed to nab his cigarettes without him knowing. Tonight, though, he was just grateful for his partner's loose morals. "You want to go back and get some?"

Ty sighed unhappily and turned his head from side to side, cracking his neck. "Let's go back to the computers and see if there's news from home. That shot I took of Armen has to have produced something."

"No," Zane decided, reaching out to take Ty's elbow and pull him closer. "We told them we'd check in every morning. We have to stay predictable. And before you suggest it, we're not sitting in that cabin for days while we wait for some predetermined time to arrive. We need to be out and about, and there's got to be stuff here to keep us amused."

He started pulling Ty along, though his "husband" was reluctant.

"I hate you a little bit right now," Ty claimed, though he was conceding to the logic by not fighting with him.

"And that's different than usual how? Stop pouting, doll," Zane drawled as he squeezed Ty's hand. He glanced at his partner. "Surely we can find something to make you smile."

Ty stepped closer, squeezing Zane's hand back as he lowered his voice, losing the fake accent. "If you keep patronizing me, I'm going to kick your ass when we're alone. And you won't have sex for two weeks, just remember that."

Annoyed, Zane stopped in place, turned Ty toward him, and put one hand on Ty's face, thumb under his chin to make him look up. "I'm teasing, and you know it. There's no reason for you to be this cranky," Zane said, injecting a tinge of warning into his voice, and it wasn't Corbin's influence.

Ty narrowed his eyes, his head tilting slightly in the way it usually did in the ring before Zane ended up on the mat. But he seemed to remain aware of the other passengers on the promenade and the fact that they could always be observed. He said nothing, just exhaling heavily in response. Playing his role, whether he liked it or not. Zane frowned. It wasn't like Ty to be this difficult, even if he wasn't thrilled with his part in the case.

Conscious of the people walking around them, he released Ty's chin, and when Zane spoke, he kept his voice very low, deliberately dropping Corbin's drawl. "Is there something really wrong I need to know about?"

"Look at me!" Ty hissed. "Do I look like I'm having a good time here? Stop enjoying yourself so much, you prick."

It was difficult to decide between a huff and a laugh, but regardless, Zane rolled his eyes. "Suck it up," he answered. "You've had a hell of a lot worse." He slid his arm around Ty's waist and got him walking again. "What you need is a drink," he announced.

"Damn straight," Ty said almost angrily. "But I can't drink because who's an alcoholic?" he asked sarcastically. He was obviously frustrated, both by the role he had to play and by the lack of outlet for that frustration. He was tense despite all the "relaxing" he'd been doing, and Zane knew he'd be spoiling for a fight that was not of the good by the time they got to the cabin if he didn't find something for him to get into first.

But this Ty not drinking thing? Zane needed to put a stop to that thought right now. He caught Ty by both shoulders, met his eyes, and spoke clearly but quietly. "Listen to me. You don't have to quit drinking just because I have. Seriously."

"I'm not that cruel," Ty told him frankly. "I've seen the look in your eyes when alcohol is mentioned. It's the same look you give me, so I know what you're thinking."

"It's not cruel. And what do you mean, the same look I give you?" Zane asked, frowning a little. "Whatever look you're seeing in my eyes isn't anything other than me wondering if you're wondering if I'm gonna ditch the wagon and drink up."

Ty shook his head patiently. "It's the look of an addict seeing something he wants," he said without malice. He spoke with an almost-kind frankness that was rare for Ty, made even more surreal by the British accent he was again employing. He held up three fingers. "Alcohol, drugs, me. You think of all of those things in the same way. I'm the only one that won't hurt you to indulge, and I'm not cruel enough to combine two of them in front of you."

The surprise kept Zane quiet for a few moments, and he had to gather his thoughts before he could reply. Why he was constantly surprised by how observant and insightful Ty could be, he didn't know. "I do appreciate the thought. But really, I can honestly tell you that as long as you're around, it's no contest."

Ty snorted and looked away, his eyes darting back and forth over the crowd of passengers shopping along the promenade. He came to some sort of decision, though, and he nodded and glanced back at Zane uncomfortably. "I'll keep that in mind."

Zane nodded slowly and decided that was the best he could do for now, at least on that topic. He still had a cranky and worked-up partner who needed some kind of outlet. "C'mon."

He pulled Ty along to a map of the promenade and looked at the entertainment choices while Ty fidgeted impatiently. It was past nine, and the dance clubs were rocking—Zane could hear the muffled music—but he wasn't sure something more soothing might not be a better choice. Still, they'd walk past the clubs, check them out. He made note of a couple places and then steered Ty in the direction of the music.

"What?" Ty finally asked as Zane led him.

"Distraction for you and entertainment for me, coming right up," Zane announced as they descended a wide double staircase.

"What do you mean, 'entertainment'?" Ty asked suspiciously as he looked back at the steps. "Are we headed down to the clubs?"

"Yes," Zane answered as he glanced to his side to look at Ty. He still caught himself double-taking most of the time. That obscene bleached-blond hair.

"I don't know, man," Ty said apprehensively as he pulled Zane closer and lowered his voice. He was having trouble maintaining the nuances of the accent. Zane was surprised he'd managed to do it this long. "It's usually all crowds and strobe lights and people touching you where your gun's supposed to be in these places. I don't go out dancing unless I know no one's going to come out of the woodwork with a knife at my back."

"Considering everyone had to go through a metal detector and X-ray to get on board, chances of that happening are lower than usual, despite me skewing the curve," Zane said. He squeezed Ty close and smiled at a couple walking by. "And I'll be watching your back," he added quietly.

"You went through security, and you're packing," Ty reminded him distractedly. "You like dancing?" he added in a surprised voice.

Zane smiled genuinely as they reached the bottom of the staircase. "No," he corrected, leaning over to bump Ty's shoulder with his own. "I love dancing."

He didn't get to go nearly as often as he used to, and not at all since moving to Baltimore; he hadn't had a chance to scope out the clubs since he was spending his evenings with Ty. When Zane had worked in Miami, he'd gone out almost every night, although he'd also had the excuse of working. Clubs in Miami were notorious for criminal wheeling and dealing.

"I didn't know that," Ty murmured, sounding oddly disturbed by the fact.

Zane shrugged. "I did tell you about the square-dancing," he said under his breath. "Who in their right mind would square-dance if they didn't love dancing?"

"That's entirely different!" Ty laughed as they got closer to the pounding beat of the music.

Zane grinned, glad that he'd gotten a smile out of his partner. He felt the music reverberate through him as they neared the entrance of one of the clubs. The name Neptune was scribbled in purple neon over the double door, and velvet ropes blocked the entrance. The crowd beyond writhed in the dim room.

"So your plan is to liquor me up, get me all sweaty and worked up, then take me back to the cabin?" Ty asked him, his tone placid.

"Oh, it may not have been my plan before, but it sure as hell is now," Zane agreed wholeheartedly. If he had a choice in his night's companion, he'd much rather have the aroused and pliable Ty from this afternoon than the cranky, fractious man of this evening.

"I like it," Ty said approvingly. He led Zane into the club, the bouncers letting them pass by the waiting line without a moment's pause. Ty might argue differently, but he knew how to use his looks when he needed to.

He'd also been right about the strobe lights, but it wasn't too bad. The club was on the small side but remarkably full. There were tiered dance floors on three different levels and tables surrounding them. For once, there was no sign of holiday decorations. The bar was with them on the ground floor, and Zane pointed Ty in that direction, hoping he'd get something, even if it wasn't alcohol.

Ty didn't hesitate, apparently having made his decision after his brief discussion with Zane earlier. He let go of Zane and cut his way through the crowd. As Zane watched him go, he could see people in the club, both men and women, turning to take a second look at Ty as he moved past them. It was difficult to suppress the urge to preen as people noticed, but then he remembered he didn't have to stop himself—Corbin would flaunt his husband for all he was worth. So he just slid a hand into his pocket to wait, knowing full well Ty was coming back to him and only him. Oh yes, smug was a good word for it, Zane figured. And as he saw Ty making his way back toward him, he really couldn't have cared less about being called possessive, either.

Despite his protests about the dangers of the crowd, Ty was already smirking, a drink in one hand as he moved through the mass of people. In order to do it, a person had to shift with the rhythm of the music or be knocked around for their efforts. Ty did this expertly. Zane suspected he'd spent his fair share of time in places like this. Only Zane imagined the type of place Ty would haunt would have fewer strobe lights and more peanuts on the floor.

Ty moving fluidly through the throng, shifting his hips or rolling his shoulders, was a beautiful thing, Zane reflected, and his body agreed. Ty would look even better dancing. His streamlined body was practically made for it.

When Ty reached him, he was grinning widely, holding his drink up out of the throng. Bodies moved around them in time with the beat of the music. It had no words that Zane could discern, drowned out by the bass. It was just as well. It made it easier to concentrate on the thump under his feet and deep in his chest, driving up his heart rate, and for now, that was what Zane was interested in. He jerked his head in the direction of the center of the dance floor and raised an eyebrow in question.

Ty took a long drink from the cup in his hand and moved closer, wrapping an arm around Zane's neck to pull him close enough to speak to him. It was impossible for them to remain still in the sea of dancing bodies, with the music pumping through the room, and they were moving by default. They didn't actually have to move closer to the dance floor in order to dance because the mob absorbed them.

"This is a first for me," Ty practically shouted in his ear. "Never danced with a guy before. On purpose, anyway."

Zane smirked and slid his hands down Ty's back to spread across his ass and subtly pull him nearer, not that anyone would see it for the crowd. Zane wasn't missing out on this opportunity. He'd never thought he'd have a chance to dance with Ty at all; he didn't exactly seem the type for a moonlit sway on the aft deck with the small jazz band they'd seen the night before.

And they certainly couldn't do this in Baltimore.

Ty moved closer, as close as he could get, pressing his body against Zane's as they moved together. People shifted around them, strangers touching and writhing indiscriminately along with the beat. But Ty's eyes and hands stayed on Zane and Zane alone.

CHAPTER SIX

The line for the rock-climbing wall was a long one, and the wait even longer since there was a necessity to watch and linger for the intended victims. The cold was not a problem, but impatience was. He did not like doing what he considered such menial tasks as wet work.

The good weather and party-like atmosphere of the ship made his job somewhat easier, though. People were happy and oblivious, and he was able to subtly insert himself just in front of the two men when they arrived. It was a masterpiece of malevolence, making certain he was the one climbing just before them without anyone noticing what he'd done or what he was about to do.

He carried a small ceramic knife in a bag on his hip, one he'd been able to carry past the low-tech metal detectors, and it was innocuous enough if by some bad luck he was searched by security. It was also easy to ditch if necessary; all he had to do was throw it hard against something solid and it would shatter into a million pieces. On the cruise ship, though, that wasn't really a problem with weapons. If he was close enough to the edge, he could simply toss it overboard and watch it sink into the dark blue depths.

He didn't foresee needing to do that.

As he climbed the fake wall, he carefully pulled the belay line to him, collecting it at his belly so no one below or above would see what he was doing. When he came to the spot on the rope he thought would do the most damage, he slid the palm-sized knife from his fanny pack and quickly made a cut, almost a third of the way through the nylon line. It wasn't much, barely noticeable to the naked eye since the knife was so sharp. When given a cursory examination, it wouldn't be seen.

Only when it reached the carabiner above and the weight of a human body was pulling on it would it become apparent.

After tucking the knife away, he waved to the attendant about three meters above him and slowly began to make his descent. He took care with the rope, mindful not to put too much weight on it and to let it play out at what seemed a natural rate. When his feet touched the padded ground at the base of the wall, he was content in the knowledge that when the rope broke because of too much weight on the compromised line, his quarry would be the one in the harness.

Zane shook his head and sighed as he stood in the bright sun and crisp winter air, looking up the gray rock wall toward the clear blue sky. He was starting to wish Corbin was a supergeek weasel or an old, portly man who walked with a cane. These things were hell on his nerves.

He brought his attention to ground level, where Ty stood next to him, trying to stay still as a short and rather stout staff member named Manny checked over his harness. Their turn on the rock wall had been by appointment, another demand of their itineraries. The line was lengthy, and it wound around the platform and down the ramp passengers had to climb to get up to this point. The deck level made the lofty rock wall, perched near the stern of the large cruise ship, seem just that much higher.

Zane was now doubting his decision to eat a hearty breakfast. It wasn't that he was scared, per se. He knew he could climb the damn wall and that he'd be fine, especially in a harness strung on a thick, anchored nylon rope. He wasn't afraid of heights. It was just the whole falling thing that sort of scared him shitless.

Jingling caught his attention, and Zane watched Ty shake his shoulders out as he tried to buckle the strap of his helmet under his chin. He had fallen victim to one of the Santa hats and was wearing it over his helmet. Zane snorted and reached over to pluck it off and toss it to the side.

"Ready to go?" Zane asked gamely. He was glad he'd lost the rock-paper-scissors game for who would climb first.

"You look a little green," Ty responded wryly, although the teasing of his voice lost something with the fake accent. His chin was lifted as he messed with the strap, and he was looking down his nose at Zane with a smile. With the helmet covering his platinum-blond hair, he looked like himself again, even if he didn't sound like it.

Zane wrinkled his nose and stepped close enough to push Ty's hands away from the buckle, flipping over the twisted strap on one side so it buckled easily. "We'll be hooked up to something. I can deal. I'm sure it's a hell of a view from forty feet up."

"Yeah," Ty said with a laugh. His voice was full of sadistic glee. "You don't get seasick, do you? Even on a ship this size, I'm pretty sure you'll feel the roll up there."

"I have no idea," Zane said honestly, setting his hands on his hips.

"I guess we'll find out."

Even though they'd been settling into their roles on board quite comfortably for the last two days, it was still a slight surprise when Ty stepped closer and gave him a quick, chaste kiss on the lips before turning toward the gray wall covered with red, yellow, green, and black handholds, marking the varying degrees of climbing difficulty.

Zane stood there smiling like an idiot as Manny made certain the belay device attached to Zane's harness was operating properly, telling Zane that he was Ty's counterweight and instructing him how to use the simple device the rope passed through. It could be easily secured in case of a fall, using Zane's weight to counter Ty's if he slipped. Zane looked up the length of the rope to the anchor at the top of the wall and figured he'd need to keep the rope close to taut, just in case. Knowing Ty, he'd fall and swing free like an acrobat just to make Zane's harness abuse his fun parts.

"Okay, Extreme Sports Ken, go for it," Zane said after resettling his sunglasses.

Ty looked back at him in exasperation, one hand on a notch in the rock wall. "Here's where I ask, 'On belay?' and if you're prepared to catch me if and when I fall to my possible doom, you reply, 'Belay on,'" Ty told him.

"Belay on," Zane reported dutifully, a few of his academy memories filtering back. He'd had a short course in rappelling way back when, but it hadn't stuck with him, and it wasn't quite the same as rock climbing. The commands sounded familiar, though.

Ty cleared his throat against a laugh and said, "Climbing," before hefting himself up onto the wall. Manny leaned over and murmured to Zane, and Zane obediently announced, "Climb on," as he watched Ty's every move.

Ty wore a pair of green athletic shorts and a navy blue sleeveless shirt this morning, both relatively tight to avoid loose clothing getting caught in the ropes or snagging on the wall, and it was easy to see his defined muscles flexing as he deftly moved from one grip to the next. It was obvious he had done this before, and not just on the odd weekend excursion. Force Recon probably got pretty familiar with this kind of thing.

Ty climbed with efficiency and precision of movement, making decisions about which handhold or foothold he would move to quickly and scaling the wall like a spider monkey. It was common sense: the longer he stayed clinging to one spot, the more fatigued his muscles would be and the more difficult it would be to continue upward.

Ty didn't dally. He was heading steadily toward the middle of the wall and the large outcropping there.

"Great," Zane muttered. "He would decide to take the toughest route." As the rope grew taut in Zane's hands, he carefully let loose some length so Ty could keep moving diagonally. The higher Ty got, the more Zane wished he'd been more insistent about staying in bed this morning, although he knew it was silly. Ty was a highly trained Marine, and a little rock wall like this was amateur hour to him. The thought really didn't help Zane feel any better, though. Again he thought of Ty swinging around like a circus clown, and he pulled at his harness uncomfortably.

"Your friend's a good climber," Manny said appreciatively as he watched Ty's agile ascent.

Ty slowed to a stop, briefly fussing with the line that had gotten tangled. "Tension!" he called down.

Zane pulled carefully on the line to tighten it up. "Yeah, he loves this kind of stuff," he replied absently, not taking his eyes off his partner.

As soon as the slack was taken up, Ty started up and over again. He was definitely moving toward the outcropping because it offered a more difficult climb. The outward incline meant the rope would take less of his weight as he went, and it was more taxing on his limbs as he pulled himself higher. Even from twenty-five to thirty feet below, Zane could see the muscles of Ty's shoulders and forearms bulging as he neared the tip of the outcrop. It then occurred to Zane that he hadn't even thought about Ty's fingers. The surgery on Ty's hand hadn't been all that long ago, and Zane hadn't asked if Ty had regained the strength and flexibility he was used to.

As if in answer to his question, Ty gave a short shout of frustration from above as he tried to grip one of the outermost notches with that hand. He pulled it back and shook it, looking down at them as he clung to the underside of the outcropping. He leaned much of his weight on the harness, more hanging in mid-air as he kept his hand on the wall than relying on the holds. Zane thought he might be grinning.

"Fingers!" Ty called down, shaking them.

Zane snorted. "Try using them!" he yelled back up, just to be annoying.

"I did! They didn't like it!" Ty called down.

Zane could see him searching for a different hold, probably one that wouldn't tax those weak fingers quite so much. Ty looked down at his harness suddenly, and at the same time Zane felt the rope lose tension in his hand. Zane pulled down on the rope to take up the slack, figuring Ty was preoccupied enough with his fingers not to call out.

Ty looked down at them in consternation. "Tension!" he shouted down, even as the rope grew slack once again in Zane's hands. If Ty's end was slack, Zane's should have been getting tauter, not the other way around.

"What's with the rope?" Zane asked Manny as he kept pulling on it without finding any resistance. He saw Ty glance down at him and then look up sharply, his entire body jerking in alarm at some warning that Zane couldn't hear or see. Ty's free hand scrabbled at his harness, almost in a panic that was highly uncharacteristic of him.

"Rock!" Ty called out, his voice just as panicked as his actions. The warning that an object was falling confused Zane just as much as realizing Ty was trying to untie the securing knot that bound the rope to his harness. The rope in Zane's hand suddenly thumped to the ground at his feet, and there was a whipping noise as dozens of feet of the heavy blue nylon rope fell from the heights of the rock wall.

"Hold on!" Zane yelled as he realized the anchor rope had just snapped. There was nothing he could do but watch, shocked and sick and scared as Ty fought to find purchase on the wall more than thirty feet above him.

As the rope fell, Ty was still trying to free himself from it. People waiting in line for their turn at the wall began to scream as they saw the two halves of the rope falling. The shorter end of the broken rope, the one still attached to Ty, fell past him just as he whipped the knot loose and threw it away from his body. But the weight of the heavy, falling rope was enough to pull at him even as he let it go, and Zane watched in horror as it dragged his body away from the outcropping.

Ty gave a wordless shout as his legs and one arm swung free from the wall. The rope landed with an anticlimactic thud several yards away from where Zane stood. Thirty feet above, Ty dangled from the outcropping by one hand, body twisting as if buffeted by the ocean breeze.

"Throw down another rope," Zane demanded of Manny, who was on a two-way radio, waving at someone at the top of the wall. "Inflatable cushion? Anything?" Frustrated beyond belief, Zane moved to try to stay where Ty could see him, close enough that he might be able to do . . . something. His heart was in his throat and blood was rushing in his ears. It was one thing to be in trouble and stay calm. It was another to be stuck watching it, helpless.

Ty hung there motionless for an eternity. He didn't kick his feet in a panic or even try to reach for an extra handhold with his free hand.

The only things keeping him from falling to the doom he'd joked about not ten minutes before were five white-knuckled fingers.

He looked down at Zane as everyone on the platform scrambled.

"That sucked, man," Ty called down in a frustratingly calm voice. There was a jitter of nervous laughter and gasps from the watching crowd.

Zane shaded his eyes as he looked up at his partner and swallowed hard before answering. "Will you quit showing off!" he yelled, trying to play off the fear buzzing in the air around them.

"Don't panic, sir!" Manny called up, sounding frantic himself. Losing a wealthy passenger in a freak climbing wall accident probably wouldn't look good on him or the cruise line. Neither would the blood smear.

Ty twisted and reached out slowly for the wall. He was hanging from the very tip of the outcropping, possibly the worst place for him to have been stranded. He couldn't get his feet under him for purchase until he moved. And moving would be hard with only one hand. On the plus side, if he'd been anywhere else on the wall, he probably would have fallen when the rope did.

Ty gripped another hold, and Zane saw the muscles in his shoulders and back bunch as he tried to pull himself further up. When his hand slipped away from the wall again, Zane heard a very un-British curse drift down.

Zane clamped down on the urge to yell at Ty, instead turning to Manny. "Is there anyone up top to drop a secure line?"

"They're working on it, sir," Manny said shakily, holding up the two-way.

Zane grabbed it out of his hand and pressed the talk button as he returned his attention to Ty. "Who's up there?" he snapped. But there was no answer. The attendants who had been up there when Ty started the climb were gone, hopefully in search of another rope.

Above, Ty had regained his hold on the wall with both hands and was merely hanging limp. "It's this damn ring," he called down. "My fingers," he continued, not actually finishing any of the sentences he started as he looked up and around him. It was harder to hear what he said when he looked up, but when he looked back down the people below could hear him say, "The pessimist says, 'It can't get any worse!' And the optimist replies, 'Oh yes it can!'"

The crowd tittered nervously, not sure whether to laugh.

Ty released one hand and made a swipe for a handhold further away, but he missed and swayed precariously before securing himself to the original one again.

"Jokes. He's cracking jokes," Zane said under his breath, deciding that once Ty had both feet on the ground he was going to smack him. Hard. Right after he kissed him unconscious.

Ty had sense enough to remain quiet after that as he continued struggling to find a way up or down, left or right. He made several more failed attempts at swinging himself around the edge of the narrow outcropping, during the last of which he lost his grip with both hands and very nearly plummeted the thirty or so feet to the platform. He slid several inches, scrabbling at the wall with both hands: a split-second of honest-to-God free fall. Zane thought his heart was going to stop on the spot before Ty was able to catch another hold and stop himself.

Ty didn't shout or scream or even curse, which to Zane meant either Ty truly was beginning to panic or his fatigued muscles were about to give out and he was expending all his energy on holding on. Either way, they had to get him down.

The fall, however, proved fortuitous. Now farther below the outcropping with his good hand in a different position, Ty had more options. As two men at the top of the wall finally came to the edge with a new rope and shouted down frantically, Ty was able to pull himself over, slide his toes onto something solid, and press close to the wall. He practically sagged in relief as he rested his arms.

The attendants tossed two new ropes down, both ends landing a few feet away from where Zane stood. Manny rushed to grab one end and attach it to the belay device on his own harness, the other to another staffer, who shouted wordlessly up once they were both hooked up. One of the attendants above swung over the edge, slowly making his way down toward Ty with the other end of the new rope.

Despite the relief of this imminent rescue, the man was still a good fifteen feet above Ty, and his progress down was slow. There was a ripple of gasps and murmurs as Ty began to slowly climb up toward the man who was descending.

"No, sir! Stay where you are!" one of the staffers called out.

"Calm down, kid," Ty called back in annoyance as he continued to climb slowly. It was obvious to Zane's eyes that Ty was tired and being far more careful than he had been when attached to the ropes. He was going slowly but making the same pace as the man attempting the difficult descent.

"Hey, Lone Star!" Ty called down again.

Zane snorted and rubbed his hand over his face. "What?" he yelled back.

"A rope walks into a bar," Ty announced. He paused dramatically as he struggled with finding a foothold. Then he went on, his voice strained with the physical effort. "Orders a beer. Bartender tells him, 'We don't serve ropes in here.' So the rope leaves the bar and goes outside, asks a guy passing to fray him at both ends and tie him in a knot. The guy does what the rope asks, and then the rope goes back inside and orders a beer. The bartender looks at him and asks, 'Aren't you that rope that was just in here?' And the rope says, 'I'm a frayed knot!'"

Another ripple of nervous laughter and a smattering of clapping met his words. The crowd had grown considerably larger since news of possible death and dismemberment had spread.

Zane stared up at Ty, at a loss for a long moment. Then he called out, "How long have you been saving that one?" He knew his voice was bordering on strident, but Zane didn't care. He was mad, upset, and scared, damn it! And all Ty could do was tell jokes!

"Been waiting until it was relevant," Ty called down with a short laugh. He sounded winded from trying to talk and climb at the same time. He steadied himself where he had his feet on two solid holds and then pressed his forehead to the wall, flattened like a bug on a windshield. Zane growled in frustration. At least Ty had enough sense to know when he'd reached his limit.

Luckily the man climbing to him was only feet from him, and soon he reached him with the rope and began looping it through the carabiner rings on Ty's harness. For a short moment, Zane was so light-headed with relief that he thought he might fall over. Instead he turned to Manny and asked, "Where are the stairs to get up there?"

"Stairs?" Manny echoed. He looked shell-shocked.

"To the top of the wall. Where are they?" Zane said insistently, glancing up to see Ty moving again, now safety anchored and getting closer to the top. He would be determined to reach the top rather than just pushing away from the wall and letting them lower him down.

Manny pointed to the side of the fake rock façade, and with one more look to check on Ty's progress, Zane took off at a run to get up there. He rushed the steps and made it to the top just in time to see two men helping Ty over the edge of the wall. Ty crawled away from the edge and immediately flattened to the floor, looking like he was trying to hug the solid ground. Zane dropped to his knees right next to him, reaching down to touch and reassure himself that Ty was okay.

"Baby?" Zane whispered, the panic echoing through him again now that it was over.

Ty looked up at him in surprise, and this close Zane could see that despite the jokes he'd been cracking, Ty's entire body was shaking, and he was covered with a fine sheen of sweat. "Did you fly up here?" Ty asked incredulously as he pushed himself up.

Zane didn't answer, didn't even think; he just pulled Ty into his arms and held him close, letting the fear rush through him and slowly start to dissipate.

Ty hugged him back hard, one arm around Zane's neck as he twisted awkwardly, still on his knees.

"Are you okay?" Zane asked shakily.

"I'm afraid not," Ty whispered against Zane's neck, his voice barely audible. He began to shake silently, his body trembling with nervous laughter. Zane huffed and hugged him closer, but he didn't think it was too damn funny.

After a long minute of being unable to let go, Zane finally pulled back enough to fumble with the buckle of Ty's helmet and yank it off. He tossed the thing to the side so he could kiss Ty gently and pull him close again. It was a struggle to hold himself together, and Zane really didn't want to make a scene, but . . . "Jesus, baby," he said brokenly. That moment of watching Ty slipping and falling was burned into his mind, and he couldn't wipe it away.

"It's okay," Ty murmured gently. He patted Zane's face awkwardly. "Let's unhook me so I can go throw up somewhere," he joked weakly as he sat back on his haunches and began pulling at the harness. The two attendants helped him get loose, offering mumbled apologies and expressions of admiration for how he'd managed not to fall, but Ty merely nodded to them as he pushed at the harness. He probably wasn't hearing them. His mouth was set in a hard line, and he was still trembling as the adrenaline burned off. He looked up at Zane and met his eyes, giving a shaky exhalation after he stepped out of the harness and kicked it away.

Zane held out his hand. "C'mon, baby. I think that's enough for this morning."

Ty took his hand and squeezed it hard, pulling himself toward Zane as if he were one of the ropes Ty had just been harnessed to. He wrapped an arm around Zane's waist and hugged him close for a moment before sliding under Zane's arm and letting it encircle his shoulders. It was the first time Zane could remember Ty initiating such a display of physical comfort after something traumatic. He wondered if it was for show or if it was real.

Zane hated that this case was forcing him to ask himself that over and over.

As they started walking, the slight difference in their heights made it easy to move without stumbling, even while descending the narrow stairs. By the time they got to the deck, Zane thought he might be calming down, but then a mob of staff surrounded them with bodies and babble.

"Mr. Porter!—"

"Please let us apologize—"

"Mr. Porter, are you okay?"

"Can we get you anything? Mr. Porter, we'll do whatever—"

"Enough," Zane snapped firmly above the noise, silencing them, anger finally rising over all the other welling emotions. "We just want to get back to our room. You can be sure I will let you know if we need anything and just exactly what I think about this accident."

The cowed staff melted out of their way, and Zane got them moving again.

"Hold on," Ty murmured as he patted at Zane's belly to stop him from trampling anyone in their way. He began to pull away, still looking dazed. "I want to see the rope."

Zane frowned at Ty briefly, thinking Ty might actually be in shock, but then his brain caught up to Ty's. "It's out on the platform."

Ty moved toward where the rope lay in a messy pile of coils at the base of the wall. Manny stopped him, asking him if he needed a doctor and once again barraging him with offers of assistance and comps and everything else under the sun. Ty waved him off, shaking his head and giving the man an easygoing grin. Though he must have been shaken,

Zane had to give him credit for maintaining the winning smile that seemed able to charm just about anyone.

"Could you cut the end off that rope for me?" Ty asked Manny grandly, his accent back in place. "I'd love to add it to my collection of things that have almost killed me."

Ty laughed and patted Manny on the back as if he was making light, and the workers who could hear him seemed to attribute it to either the carefree attitude of a daredevil or a British stiff upper lip. Either way, they weren't about to refuse anything Ty asked at that point. Soon Ty was moving back toward Zane with six inches of rope clutched in his hand and a forced, charismatic smile firmly in place.

Zane slid his arm around him again. "Let's go," he suggested. "I don't know if you need a break, but I sure as hell do." The staff members around them laughed in weak relief.

As they passed by the large crowd of milling passengers, many of whom called out to them in congratulations or sympathetic relief, Zane had a hard time simultaneously shaking a few hands and nodding at people while trying to keep Ty's head down so no one got a very good look at him. They were trying to stay under the radar; this was not exactly the best way to do it.

Ty finally cleared his throat and glanced sideways at Zane. "I wouldn't recommend the rock wall to you. Very high."

"Get the insults in now while I'm still too thankful to have you here safe to mind," Zane warned.

"I'll pass," Ty muttered. He held up the rope as soon as they were far enough from the crowd not to draw attention. Half of the thick rope was frayed horribly, almost fuzzy from the trauma inflicted by its separation from the other end. But roughly a third of the failed end was clean and straight, with nary a ruined strand to be seen. Ty turned it around grimly. "It was cut."

As soon as the door to their stateroom was closed and locked behind them, Ty felt his knees go weak. He reached out to the wall nearest him and closed his eyes as he let the weakness seep into him while he had the chance to let it. He hung his head and sank toward the carpet without further warning, just thankful to be on solid ground and in private.

"Whoa, baby, c'mon, not on the floor," Zane murmured as he caught Ty partway down. The worry was clear in his voice, which wavered enough that Ty took note of it and tried to man up a little. He attempted to gather himself with a deep breath. "Much more comfortable on the bed," Zane continued.

When Ty sat on the end of the bed—or what he assumed was the end of the bed, since the damn thing was round—he simply hung his head and leaned over. No matter how many times a person almost died, it never got to the point that it was easy to shrug off. After a moment of composing himself, he raised his head and dejectedly looked at Zane. "Even when I'm someone else, people try to kill me," he joked.

Zane sighed and sat down next to him. "Must be your charming personality showing through all the bleach." He reached out to run his fingers through Ty's abused hair.

Ty closed his eyes and leaned into the touch. "I may have given us away out there," he said ruefully. "Someone is apparently trying to kill or at least injure one of the Porters. If they were watching, they heard me cussing without my accent."

"I really can't bring myself to care about that right now," Zane murmured, rubbing Ty's back in slow, soothing motions.

Ty looked at him more closely, surprised by the statement. Zane didn't meet his eyes, and his face was set with what looked like pain.

"Hey," Ty said softly as he placed a hand on Zane's knee. "Look on the bright side, right? At least it wasn't you," he tried with a laugh as he patted Zane's thigh.

Zane shook his head slowly as his eyes tracked to meet Ty's. "No. That would have been easier to handle," he said baldly.

"All right then, next time you dangle over the ocean," Ty offered as he unconsciously rubbed at his abused fingers. He understood what Zane meant, though. Ty knew from a previous, ill-advised discussion about their deepest fears that Zane's was not being there to save the day when the proverbial shit hit the fan. Zane had been much more eloquent in his wording, of course. It was one fear Ty had no idea how to assuage. And it was a legitimate one, since it probably happened a lot and Zane just didn't know it.

"No problem," Zane whispered as he caressed Ty's cheek with a slightly trembling finger. "I didn't realize I'd be so—" His voice actually broke, and he looked away, out into the room, his hand falling away.

"Zane," Ty prompted gently. He was beginning to worry. In all fairness, it really should still be him falling apart at the seams, not his partner. It almost made him angry that he had to be the one to narrowly escape death or injury and console his partner about it. For a brief second, he allowed himself the suspicion that Zane might be putting on just to give Ty something to focus on. He let that fancy pass when he saw the real emotion in Zane's eyes.

Zane drew a sharp breath and cleared his throat. "Sorry, he said. I think it's sort of hitting me now. What could have happened. I don't know why. It's not like I wasn't standing there scared out of my mind."

He offered Ty a smile that didn't make it to his eyes.

"You damn well better have been!" Ty blurted indignantly.

"I was," Zane said fervently, taking Ty's hand again. "I couldn't do anything."

Ty exhaled sharply and stood. "Let's not linger over it, Garrett," he said with forced nonchalance. No matter what he said to Zane just now, he knew he'd be dreaming about falling tonight. Discussing it in detail might help ease Zane's mind, but it wouldn't do Ty a damn bit of good.

Zane's hand tightened to keep Ty from moving away. "You scared me. You didn't cut your own rope, but how could you literally be hanging by your fingertips and still be joking?"

Ty looked down at him in surprise and gave an insulted huff. "Cut my own rope?" he repeated.

"Ty. Please," Zane said, his voice carrying a hint of that dismay. He shook his head a little as he tried to hold Ty's gaze.

Ty tilted his head and petted Zane's hand. "One thing I've learned is, if you're too focused on the falling and how horribly it's going to hurt, you don't see what's around you. You might miss the very thing you can hang on to, something that could stop the fall altogether. So if you stay calm . . ." He shrugged. It wasn't a lesson he'd necessarily learned while literally hanging in the air, but it served for many of life's difficulties. Including literally hanging in the air.

Zane still didn't look happy. "Not one man in a thousand could have done what you did today. I couldn't have."

Ty didn't disagree. He'd had extensive training in order to do exactly what he'd done today. Not to mention a healthy dose of pure dumb luck. Zane knew that, and Ty didn't understand why he was so upset. He was silent, frowning in confusion as he watched the play of emotions over Zane's face. But none of them stayed in place long enough for Ty to really interpret them.

"I told you what I think about free fall," Zane finally said. "And staying calm isn't enough. You up there joking? You weren't doing it for yourself, were you?" It wasn't so much a question as a conclusion.

"Well, you know how amusing I find myself."

"Yeah, right. You were about to fall thirty feet, and you were more worried about me than you were about yourself." Zane stood and reached to place a hand on each side of Ty's face, holding him still. "Are you okay? I couldn't do anything but stand and watch before, but I could do something to help now."

"Yeah, you can," Ty murmured somberly, his eyes darting back and forth as he looked over Zane's sincere face. "You can get me some Tylenol. And ice. And a drink. And possibly a nice gentle massage, 'cause I'm not going to be able to move my arms in an hour."

Zane leaned to kiss him, just a soft press of the lips, probably to halt Ty's litany of demands. "You can have anything you want, baby."

Ty almost gave in to the gentle sentiment, but he closed his eyes and shook his head obstinately. "Quit it!" he demanded, barely keeping himself from stomping his foot in a petulant fit. He wanted Zane back to being his normal indignant self, not this weird quixotic version of his lover and partner. "Snap out of it and ... I don't know ... yell at me for almost dying or something!"

"All right, all right," Zane said, smiling a little and straightening his shoulders, giving himself a slight shake. "Next time you do something like that, I'm going to smack the hell out of you, okay?" He stole one more kiss and sighed, then padded over to the phone. In the next moment, he was talking to the butler service. "What do you want to drink?" he directed at Ty, his hand over the mouthpiece of the phone.

"A lot," Ty answered grimly.

Zane ordered a six-pack of Guinness and large pitcher of iced tea, a shot of their best whiskey, a bucket of ice, some cold sandwiches and chips, and a cookie platter in quick succession before hanging up.

"Cookies?" Ty asked with a smile he didn't try to restrain.

"Comfort food. You get beer; I get cookies," Zane explained as he kicked off his cross trainers and walked back over to the bed.

Ty watched him move, seriously considering tackling him and relieving some stress in a more favorable manner than a shower or cookies. But he decided against such a tack, considering how distressed Zane seemed and how important the morning's events might be to the grand scheme of things. "So," he said quietly. "Do we think someone is trying to kill Del, or do we think someone's figured out we're not the Porters and they're trying to kill me? Or us, I guess, since there was no way of knowing which of us would go first."

He watched as Zane studied him silently for a moment and then advanced on him. "There's not been enough exposure for our cover to be blown unless there's a wild card in play who actually knows the Porters. We have no reason to think that," Zane said. He stopped right in front of Ty, looking down at him. "Take off those shoes."

The firm tone of voice alone made Ty shiver slightly, and it took him a moment to realize he was still wearing the climbing shoes supplied by the staff at the rock wall. Ty looked down at them in surprise. He felt himself flush at the absentmindedness, and he yanked them off one at a time, tossing them toward the sofa. "So why try to hurt one of the Porters?" he posed as he did so. "A fall like that wouldn't necessarily kill. Especially since cutting halfway through a rope isn't exactly a precise method. Whoever did it had no idea when it would rip. And since I doubt Del or Corbin are better climbers than me, it's likely they'd have been lower when it did go."

Zane grunted in comment as he walked around the edge of the bed. He sat and pulled up his legs, leaning against the headboard and crossing his legs at the ankle. "It's awfully imprecise. We could have skipped our appointment or been late and it could have been someone else up there." His voice was steadier now, almost back to normal.

"Which proves two things," Ty said with a frown. "Whoever did it isn't in a hurry to kill us—them—whoever they're trying to kill.

And they're not afraid to hurt innocent bystanders doing it. My bet's on Armen. Anyone who likes to drink as much as the Italian can't be sober often enough to plan ahead."

"Not necessarily. If you've got tolerance, alcohol might sharpen your attention, not blunt it."

The comment brought Ty up short. He'd been joking about Lorenzo Bianchi and his love of wine, an off-handed comment he probably shouldn't have made. But Zane's sincere belief in the words he'd just uttered disturbed Ty enough that he wasn't able to keep the surprise and concern out of his expression. Zane just offered a shrug and a rueful smile.

"Is that really what you think?" Ty asked, unable to help himself.

Zane's brow creased a little. "Yes. Everyone reacts to alcohol differently, just like drugs, just like injuries. Depends on how you handle it, what you let it do to you. Why?"

Ty realized he was staring at Zane slightly agape, and he quickly pressed his lips together. He shook his head sadly. The reasoning seemed very . . . self-serving for an alcoholic. He didn't want to argue with Zane just then, so he nodded and looked away, determined to let the thread of conversation die a natural death. He moved toward the bed, pulling his damp shirt over his head and casting it aside as he sat in the general location of the end of the bed. He examined the scar on his hand. His ring finger was beginning to swell even more. He was never going to get the damn ring off. He might actually need to have it cut off soon.

"I'm sitting here trying to think of a creative way to yell at you for scaring the shit out of me, and nothing's really coming to mind other than fucking you against the shower wall until we both feel better," Zane said from behind him, his tone calm and conversational.

Ty nodded distractedly. "I do need a shower," he commented in a voice to match.

Zane shifted his weight to climb off the bed and moved toward him, reaching out one hand. When he glanced up, Ty was surprised to see the intense look in Zane's eyes. His fingers brushed over Ty's skin, but they flinched after a firm rap on the stateroom door.

Ty looked up at Zane and smiled gamely. Zane glanced to the door and back to Ty, clearly considering ignoring it until there was a second knock, louder than the first. Zane huffed and stalked across the room to unbolt the door and open it just enough to look out.

Ty watched tensely, hands loose near the gun he'd stashed under the mattress earlier, and hunched over so he could grab it quickly. He couldn't see or hear their guest, but he wouldn't put it past Zane to growl at them to go away so they could proceed to the shower as planned.

"Unless you're hiding a cart with cold beer and cookies, go away," Zane growled at whoever was out there.

Ty laughed softly and shook his head. He lay back, leaving the gun safely under the mattress, rolled on the bed, and stretched out on his stomach, surprised by the adrenaline still coursing through him. He hadn't almost died in a while. He wasn't handling it well.

Zane exchanged a few more words with the person on the other side of the door before shutting it firmly and shooting the bolt. "We are now top of the treat list," he said wryly as he walked back to the bed. "The ship, if not the world, is ours on a platter."

"Great," Ty replied without enthusiasm. "What else is on that damned itinerary?"

"Too many other extreme sports for my liking," Zane muttered as he sat on the edge of the mattress and started rubbing Ty's neck with one hand.

"What would be the point in disabling Del or Corbin at this stage?" Ty posed as he stared listlessly at the balcony doors.

"Nothing other than removing them from the equation," Zane answered, twisting a little to use both hands to knead Ty's shoulders carefully.

"Thank you, Sherlock," Ty said with a small smile. "I meant why. Have we stumbled into a business takeover, do you think?"

Zane stayed quiet for a minute as he massaged, his fingers firm on Ty's skin. "You mean Armen trying to take over."

"Or Bianchi," Ty said with a nod.

"I suppose it could be us—the Porters—trying to take over, and one of the others is simply striking first," Zane suggested as he kept up the massage, moving more to Ty's shoulders and upper arms.

"You're much better at that than the last lady," Ty mumbled distractedly.

The warm hands squeezing and rubbing kept moving in smooth circles and slides. "Porter does seem the type to try a takeover," Zane mentioned, continuing the conversation as if Ty hadn't said anything. "An enterprising thug. Bianchi . . . well, my first impression isn't one of aggression. Armen is dangerous."

"Right." Ty sighed heavily, closing his eyes and concentrating more on Zane's hands. He had long fingers on big hands, and he spread them across Ty's skin expertly as he massaged the muscles bunching with tension. First the fingers would dig in and knead until it was almost painful, but then Zane would let up and start soothing the area with long swipes of the heels of his hands, gently shooing the discomfort away.

Ty realized he was letting Zane divert him from the slightly more important issue they now faced. He raised his head and turned it, resting it again so he was facing Zane. "You're getting distracted," he accused.

The corners of Zane's mouth pulled up slowly, and the smile echoed in his eyes. "Am I, now?" he drawled, dragging his fingertips down Ty's back.

Ty shivered violently, then rolled and reached up to knock Zane's hand away. He miscalculated where he was on the circular bed, though, and his shoulder hit the edge of the mattress and he went toppling over the edge with a flail of his arms and an abbreviated yip.

There was silence for a brief moment, and then Zane's head appeared to look down at him.

"Haven't you had enough of that for one day?" He didn't sound particularly amused. Ty sat up, rubbing the back of his head and glaring up at his lover balefully, as if it had been Zane's doing. "Don't look at me," Zane said as he shifted in place, still up on the bed. "This one you did to yourself, dumbass."

"I hate this bed," Ty muttered as he sat on the floor dejectedly and examined his abused hands. He couldn't be bothered to get off the floor.

"Come back up—" Another knock interrupted Zane. He climbed off the bed with a grunt, trudged to the door, and opened it much the same as before.

Only this time he immediately pulled the door further open so the room service cart could be pushed in to their table. The staffer made herself scarce—no telling if she'd heard about the crazy morning—and Zane locked the door behind her.

Ty had to stretch his neck to watch him over the edge of the bed. Zane busied himself with the tray, smiling down at the plates he uncovered. "Hey, get your Tylenol and come eat," he said. "Then I have liquid relaxation for you."

"Garrett, come over here," Ty requested quietly.

Zane turned his chin to look at him, his brow furrowing slightly, but he walked over to where Ty still sat on the floor and stopped, waiting with a questioning look.

"This floor is surprisingly clean," Ty told him pointedly as he gestured to the lush carpet at Zane's feet.

"Should I interpret that as 'bring me a sandwich and a beer,' or as 'get down here and kiss me'?" Zane asked as he crossed his arms and looked down at his partner.

Ty just smiled wistfully, a part of him wishing he didn't have to beg Zane to get down there and kiss him. He held out a hand. "Help me up," he muttered instead. Zane took his hand and pulled him up obligingly. Ty patted him on the arm and moved past him, toward the cart and the array of food and drinks. He'd only just picked up a bottle of beer when they heard another knock on the door.

"Oh, this is just getting ridiculous," Zane muttered.

Ty shook his head and popped the top on the beer anyway. "I got it," he said as he waved Zane off and shuffled barefoot to the door. He opened the door wide, assuming that whoever had tried to kill Del was sneakier than a gun to the face in the doorway of his suite.

He was right, but what greeted him was almost as alarming. Norina Bianchi flung herself into Ty's arms as soon as he'd opened the door, accompanied by a rush of foreign babble and her smiling husband. After a tight hug, she leaned back, patted both his cheeks, and then hugged him again. She sounded worried, and Ty gathered the pair had learned of his mishap on the rock wall.

"Yes, I'm fine. Come in," he invited, flustered as he tried to gently extricate himself from the woman's arms without spilling beer on her.

He heard Zane's voice from behind them. "Signor Bianchi, please come in. I'm going to guess your lovely wife heard about Del's grand adventure this morning."

"Ah, yes," Bianchi said as he shooed Norina out of the doorway so they could all get inside and shut the door. "Here she comes, flying into the cabin to go on about a big excitement in the sporting center."

Norina was still talking rapidly to Ty, her beautiful face undergoing a dramatic series of frowns and worried expressions. Ty was pretty good with languages and could upon occasion pick up what someone was saying from knowledge of similar languages or even the meanings of root words he recognized. But trying to decipher any of what she said when she spoke it at Mach 7 was impossible.

He smiled in amusement, suddenly finding the situation incredibly funny. He reached out and took one of her delicate hands in both of his and patted it. "Slowly please," he requested with a glance at Zane and a wink. "Corbin doesn't speak the language nearly so well as he pretends."

"Oh!" Norina exclaimed as she looked at Zane with wide, dark eyes. "I must apologize! In my excitement I forget myself."

Ty practically sighed in relief. She spoke English. Now he just needed to convince her to continue to do so even when his fake husband wasn't around.

"No apology needed, Signora," Zane said pleasantly. "Won't you come in and sit down? We just ordered refreshments for the afternoon."

"I told my Norina you would be . . . comforting each other," Bianchi said knowingly. "After such a harrowing experience. But no, she needed to see your Del for herself."

"They said you had fallen," she told Ty as she put both hands on his chest and gazed up at him. Ty didn't know if it was because she was Italian, because she knew he was gay and therefore "safe" to grope, or if she was just the touchy-feely type, but he really wished she'd stop touching him quite so freely.

"It was a minor accident, not nearly as bad as the rumors, I'm sure," Ty assured her as he plucked her hands off his chest and steered her toward the sitting area and the other two men.

"As you see," Zane said as he filled glasses from the bar with ice, "Del is up and about, doing just fine."

"Yes," Bianchi commented, looking over the cart from room service. "And you ordered a drink from room service to settle your own heart, no?" he said, indicating the shot of whiskey.

Ty raised one eyebrow at Zane. He'd forgotten about the glass. He wasn't fond of whiskey, but he didn't think Zane knew that. However, Ty didn't know if Zane had ordered the shot for Ty or for himself.

Zane waved a nonchalant hand at it as he poured tea. "Would you like some tea? Or there's beer, and I believe we have a selection of sodas in the bar fridge and a couple bottles of wine besides."

"We had wine with lunch," Norina said, stepping back from Ty slightly but moving to hold his arm as they walked to join Bianchi and Zane at the table. "I will have tea, please."

"Tea. Bah. I will have the beer if it is not American," Bianchi said as he pulled out a chair, looking ready to make himself at home.

Ty had to hold back a sigh. No more massage for him. But this was why they were here, he told himself, to get information from these people. Not to get laid repeatedly by his partner in a luxury suite. No matter how much that appealed.

CHAPTER SEVEN

Bianchi was in high spirits when he joined Zane, Armen, and a few other players in the private lounge. He also carried high spirits—literally. He had a hinged wooden box, and once he set it down, he pulled out an ornate blue and silver bottle and cradled it in the crook of his arm.

"Gentlemen!" Bianchi greeted expansively. "I come bearing a gift, bought specially with our American friend here in mind."

Zane looked from Bianchi to the bottle and back, and his stomach turned. "A gift for me?" he asked, forcing pleasant surprise into his voice.

"You have told me how you so enjoy the premium Chivas, yes? So I have brought you your own bottle of Regal Royal Salute—although I shall insist you share," Bianchi said, clearly very pleased with himself.

Zane silently swallowed on the upset welling in his throat, trying hard to deny he was feeling even the slightest bit panicked. Apparently Corbin Porter had a penchant for fine Scotch whiskey, and damn, Chivas Regal Royal Salute? That was fifty-fucking-year-old Scotch, and only a seriously limited number of bottles had even been made. Bianchi had to have paid a fortune for it . . . or he'd acquired it in another style of business transaction altogether. "That is such a kind gesture, Signor Bianchi. But I can't possibly—"

"Of course you can, and you will! I insist. We are here to enjoy ourselves and celebrate our acquaintance," Bianchi said. The look in Bianchi's eyes told Zane that Corbin Porter would never decline such an offer. The sinking feeling intensified as Zane mentally flailed for an exit. There had to be a gracious way to bow out, but as he looked at the other players, all smiling and appreciative, Zane knew there wasn't.

A waiter arrived a few moments later with empty tumblers for all the players at the table. Bianchi filled the glasses generously, and when he personally held one out to Zane, Zane knew he was trapped. There was no way to avoid this, short blowing his cover—and Ty's—over a glass of whiskey.

He gave Bianchi Corbin's best full-of-shit grin and raised his glass for the toast to their health even as his stomach roiled.

Zane hadn't had a drink, any drink, in almost ten months.

The first taste of the very expensive Chivas was, well, intoxicating.

Ty sat on the balcony of their suite staring out at the rolling ocean, feet twitching as he hummed a tune he was pretty sure was actually two or three different songs. He was bored. It was only the fourth day of cruising, but other than almost falling off the rock wall the morning before, nothing had happened, and Ty wasn't in a position to make anything happen.

He'd spent almost the entire day doing nothing. He supposed that was what some considered a vacation, but it just made him twitchy and nervous.

He understood the necessity for following the itineraries, but he was really beginning to hate those damn things. After dinner last night, Zane had gone off to a high-stakes poker game with Bianchi, Armen, and several other high rollers, hoping to glean information that could prove useful. Ty wasn't needed there, and his presence probably would have made the other men wonder. They'd decided it wasn't worth the risk for him to tag along, and the same applied tonight. And even if they'd been able to contact them, none of the other AWOL team members could be there for backup, either, since it was a private game. Which was another thing that made Ty restless as hell.

It sort of reminded him of his last float before he'd left the Corps. Knowing there was action elsewhere but stuck in sick bay, useless, with a bullet hole in his shoulder. Then, at least, his chest hadn't itched where all the hair had been ripped out by organic scented wax.

He knew it was a self-imposed boredom this time, of course. They were on a cruise ship. It was, by definition, a floating fun house.

Only Ty wasn't having fun, and he wasn't willing to go too far where he couldn't be found if there was trouble. The four-man support team that was supposedly out there somewhere wasn't really a lot of help. Ty hadn't seen hide or hair of any of them. He knew it was out of necessity; they were merely there as a fallback, a last-ditch emergency response team if everything went tits up. Still, Ty would have felt better if they'd been given some way to contact them other than going out on the deck and waving their arms, hoping one of them was watching.

None of that would have made him feel better anyway. He didn't know any of the other agents, and he didn't trust what he didn't know.

He sat there for barely five more minutes before he lost the will to be bored. He hefted himself out of the lounger and turned to head back into the cabin, determined to find something to keep his mind busy that didn't involve disaster scenarios.

He went to Del Porter's leather satchel, opened it, and peered inside with a twinge of guilt. He didn't like going through Del's personal belongings any more than he liked being Del. Granted, they'd already made a cursory search of all the luggage, including this bag, but Ty had tried not to delve too deep.

Now, though, he was desperate.

Inside the satchel were a few Sudoku and crossword puzzle books, which shocked Ty, since the guy wasn't exactly supposed to be the intellectual type. He reached in and pulled a few of the books out, flipping through them to find them almost entirely filled in. He groaned in disappointment. That would have given him something to do, anyway.

He'd been avoiding the ship's fitness areas simply because he didn't like the crowds, but he would do a few laps around the designated jogging track if all else failed. If he could find music, he'd be better off. He remembered seeing an MP3 player in one of these bags.

He set the books beside him on the bed and looked back into the satchel. There was a small, pale green iPod and a set of matching earphones, a stick of deodorant, a pair of reading glasses in a Gucci case, and not much else.

Ty picked up the iPod with a pleased smile. He plugged in the earphones and put one bud in his ear as he turned the device on to make sure it would work before he got ready for a run. He set it to shuffle and put it on his knee as he reached for the Gucci eyeglass case.

He opened the case out of curiosity, wondering if they really were reading glasses. He was almost surprised when he found they were, and he held the stylish frames up to look them over. They were rectangular wire frames with thick, flat legs. Not exactly what Ty would have chosen if he had to wear glasses, and they had probably cost more than he made in a month.

The most interesting thing about these reading glasses was that when he held them up and looked through them, they didn't alter his vision at all. Ty frowned at them and slid them on as the iPod began to play a spoken word track in a language Ty wasn't sure of.

The reading glasses were merely glass, and they were heavier than they should have been, slightly reminiscent of the sunglasses he'd been given to take pictures. He took them off and turned them over, bending the legs experimentally. He couldn't concentrate with the foreign words in his ear, though, and he picked up the iPod to peer at the track name. He'd thought it was an audiobook track, but it was labeled as a song he'd never heard of. Ty huffed and thumbed over to the next song, but it, too, was a spoken word track that was labeled incorrectly.

Ty stared at it, listening to the words in his ear. He could catch certain words and phrases of the garbled recording, enough to pinpoint the language as Italian and enough to recognize it as a conversation, not a lecture or book being read. He also recognized that it wasn't a studio recording. It sounded very much like the result of a bug placed close to a person speaking.

Ty's body went cold as he realized what he'd found.

"Shit," he drew out slowly. He stopped the track and pulled the earbud out of his ear. These were wiretaps. These were professional-grade wiretaps on Del Porter's iPod. How did the office miss this? He turned the glasses over in his hand again and snapped one of the legs off, not really surprised when he found a thin wire snaking through the plastic. He shook the hollow arm and a flat receiver roughly the size of a dime fell into his palm.

"Shit," he said again.

He squinted at the mechanism. He didn't recognize the model, which meant it wasn't American, Russian, or British.

"Shit, shit, shit."

Del Porter wasn't who they thought he was. The Bureau had nabbed somebody else's informant. And whoever was behind Del Porter's spying probably knew Ty and Zane's secret as well.

Ty stepped into the ornate casino room and looked around quickly, searching out Zane or any of the other members of the team who might have been hanging around. Where the hell were all the nosy support personnel when they were needed? Ty still hadn't spotted a single one of them.

He moved through the crowd slowly, seeking his partner amid the throng of gamblers, but he knew the poker game wouldn't be out here. The ship-run games and tables were a joke, so the high rollers who had come to play had claimed a private room for hosting their own evening "tournaments." Ty scanned the back walls over the gaming tables, finally seeing a door behind a strategically placed decorative screen. It was possibly a staff entrance, but more than likely it was the private room that played host to all the whales.

He made his way toward it, the little iPod held tightly in his hand, hidden inside his pocket. Zane had their only gun, and Ty hadn't even grabbed a knife for fear of not being able to conceal the weapon well, and he felt naked as he moved through the crowd.

He stepped behind the screen to find an intimate, richly decorated room with a private bar and six draped tables. He stopped at the entrance, looking for Zane eagerly. If they could get what was on that iPod to someone who could speak the language, it might be enough for them to end this assignment tonight. Not only that, but the possibility that Del was an informant might be enough to make the FBI pull him and Zane completely off this goat rope. They could be screwing around in a foreign entity's investigation, and the Bureau hated sticky political messes.

Most of all, though, Ty was concerned that whoever Del was reporting to might be on board with them and may have already made him and Zane as frauds.

He spotted Zane, sitting with his back to the entrance at one of the closer tables. Ty shook his head. Zane must have been the last one to arrive to settle for sitting there, facing the wall. Ty moved slowly, circling around a little so Zane would see him approach in his peripheral vision.

Zane was sitting back, relaxed in his chair, mostly sideways to the table, legs crossed primly as he'd taken to doing when acting as Corbin. There was the faintest of cold smiles on his lips, but his dark eyes were hooded and blank. The look was intensified by his now standard all-black suit ensemble. He held a snifter of something that was a rich caramel color in the hand away from the table—the other men had glasses as well, and the bottle was there on the table. There was a decent amount of chips stacked in front of him. If he saw Ty, Zane gave no sign of it as he watched Vartan Armen, who was considering his own cards.

Ty slowed, looking around the table. He'd never had occasion to play poker with Zane, but he could imagine his partner was good at it. He was a hard man to read and almost obsessively observant of small details. He continued to move closer, carefully coming up on Zane, hoping he looked suitably embarrassed to be interrupting.

He put a hand on Zane's shoulder, letting it slide up to his neck as he bent next to him. Both Armen and Bianchi looked up at him, as did the two other men at the table, but Zane didn't acknowledge him.

Ty waited a moment, watching the other players. Armen frowned a bit under Zane's scrutiny and looked at the stacks of chips in the center of the table. Each chip was labeled as $1,000—and there were a lot of chips out there. Armen smiled, set down his cards, and added two more even stacks of chips to the pile.

Ty watched the game briefly. If it had been Zane's money, he might have waited, but it wasn't, and Ty's hair was blond until they could get out of here. He put his mouth closer to Zane's ear and whispered, "I need to talk to you."

Zane's attention had transferred to the next man around the table, who had just as much a poker face as Zane. "Not now, doll," Zane drawled as he set down his glass in front of him.

Ty blinked at him in surprise. He looked down at the cards in his hand and then over at the other men at the table. He had a fair hand, but nothing worth writing home about. His eyes strayed to the glass on the table near Zane's chips. It was nearly empty, and Zane certainly smelled of alcohol. Ty let his hand slide over the back of Zane's neck, looking up at him as he put his other hand on Zane's thigh and squeezed.

"It's important," he insisted, the accent feeling strange on his tongue as he tried to convey just how important this might be.

"I'm sure it's not," Zane replied easily, nodding as the man across the table folded. The next gentleman, an older man wearing a finely tailored smoking jacket, tapped his chips on the table idly as he considered his cards. Zane would be next, if he hadn't started the betting.

Ty didn't care about the game, though. He stared at Zane, willing him to look up. In his pocket was possibly their plane ticket home, or more probably a bull's-eye painted on Ty's back, and Zane wouldn't even look at him? Ty fought not to grit his teeth as he dug his fingers harder into Zane's thigh.

"Darling," he said pointedly, hating the polite accent and the fact that even cursing made him sound like he was sitting at tea with the Queen.

Zane's head tipped to one side, and he laid his cards on the table face down. "Excuse me, gentlemen. I'll be right back," he said pleasantly. And he was out of the chair, yanking Ty up by his upper arm and marching him the fifteen feet over to the door.

"Don't tell me you've run across something you can't handle," Zane growled, a clear note of annoyance in his voice.

"Not exactly, but—"

"Then go handle it. Armen, Bianchi, and I are talking business between rounds, and I won't be distracted. I'll deal with you later." With that, he gave Ty's arm a slight shove, turned his back, straightened his jacket, and strolled back to the table, retaking his seat smoothly without a glance back. The men at his table similarly ignored Ty.

Ty watched his partner go, struck speechless by his careless dismissal. He thought briefly about following him back to the table and kicking his ass, or at least announcing the cards Zane held in his hand, but the urge passed as he convinced himself their cover was more important.

As he stared at the table, he saw Armen throw down his cards with a sniff and Zane rake in the chips, stacking them as he toasted the table with his glass before taking a drink. Bianchi laughed merrily, wagging his finger at Armen before lifting the bottle and starting to refill the glasses.

Ty clenched his jaw, anger welling inside him at the sight of the expensive bottle of Scotch. He turned on his heel to leave the room before he got any angrier. He didn't need his partner's help to get something done on this fucking ship. All he had to do was head to the computer center and a nice private corner to tap into the secure server, call it in, and inform someone back home of what he'd found. He'd have a translation of the wiretaps by morning, and when Zane came stumbling in from his poker party, Ty would tell him all about it then.

He stalked through the casino, pushing through the crowd as he muttered to himself in the British accent he was beginning to hate. He'd just barely stepped out of the casino into the causeway when he was grabbed from the side and pushed with a hand that gripped his elbow tightly.

Another man came up on his other side as the two strangers flanked him, marching him toward one of the doors that would lead to an outside deck.

Ty didn't protest. He remained calm and forced himself to wait until the situation clarified itself. The moment he saw a weapon he'd be breaking bones, though.

"Taci e vieni con noi," one of the men said to him under his breath.

More Italian. Ty didn't understand it, but he was fairly certain the man had just told him to keep his mouth shut and move. The tone was pretty much universal.

They pushed through the exit doors and out onto the deck, where the spray from the sea and the wind assaulted their senses and blew their ties into their faces. Ty almost took the opportunity to break away from them. He even flinched in preparation of the attempt, but he stopped himself. Whatever this was, it had to do with Del Porter, and that was who Ty was right then. Del Porter wouldn't leave these men bleeding on the decks, and Ty wouldn't either, if he could help it.

The grip on his arms tightened, and the two men led him to the left, toward one of the lesser-traveled causeways on that deck.

They finally released him once there was really nowhere to run, shoving him toward the railing. Ty stumbled toward it, gripping the slick wood before turning around to look at them warily.

"Che cazzo stai facendo?" one of them demanded.

Ty leaned forward slightly, as if listening closer might actually make him understand the foreign language. It was definitely Italian. Which was fucking awesome, because Ty still didn't speak Italian. Dolce and Gabbana here could threaten him all day long. He still wouldn't understand what they were saying.

"I don't . . ." Ty shook his head helplessly, just barely remembering his own fake accent.

"Do not play stupid with us," the second man said irritably. He had thin brown hair and a sickly complexion, as if the sea didn't agree with him. Ty had seen it before. "Why did you miss the meeting?" Gabbana demanded.

Ty blinked at him rapidly, his mind whirring as he tried to decide how to play this. He had no idea who they were or what they were talking about, and sometimes the best thing to do was just . . . play dumb.

The first man rolled his eyes and reached into his cheap suit, extracting a small Beretta and stepping forward to shove it into Ty's stomach. His other hand held Ty's shoulder as he spoke to him in low tones. "You will not fuck around with us, chiaro?"

"I understand," Ty answered hoarsely with a jerky nod. The muzzle of the gun dug further into his rib cage, and he winced as his hands gripped the railing behind him. The wind was much stronger here by the edge, and it whipped at Dolce's black hair and tugged at the sleeves of Ty's thin shirt.

"Where is the information you were to bring us?" Gabbana asked in a bored voice.

"Information," Ty repeated as he shook his head. Of course they wanted information. This was exactly what Ty had been worried about: Del's handlers coming to collect. At least they didn't seem to know Del Porter personally. Ty wasn't sure if that was a good thing or a bad thing for him.

The man with the gun pushed into Ty hard, using the leverage and the height of the railing to lift Ty's feet off the deck and push him backward. Ty gasped and gripped the railing harder, reaching with his other to grab onto the lapel of Dolce's suit.

He was beginning to think his cover wasn't worth the effort.

"The tapes, frocio," Dolce whispered into his ear. Whatever that word meant, Ty knew he didn't like the connotation.

"Tapes," Ty repeated breathlessly. His toes just barely brushed the wood of the deck, and his fingers wound into Dolce's tie. If he went over the edge, he wouldn't go alone. He briefly wondered if Italian loafers could be used as flotation devices, but then the man put more pressure against his ribs, shoving him even farther backward, and Ty gripped the polyester tie tightly. "Tapes," he said again quickly. They had to be talking about the recordings he'd heard on the iPod. "They're in our cabin," he told them quickly. If he didn't get his feet on the ground soon, he was going to tear them both apart, cover be damned. He was getting seasick.

Gabbana reached out and backhanded him, hard enough that Ty felt blood trickle down his chin from his newly split lip, and then the man pulled a gun and blatantly shoved it at Ty's face. Ty felt his heart rate pick up even more, the adrenaline making him a little lightheaded as his upper body hung out over the open sea below. Of course, if the guy shot him in the face, it wouldn't really matter how far the drop was.

Gabbana's gun pressed against his cheek, and Ty didn't try to regulate his reaction, his breathing becoming harsher. Del Porter would be scared shitless, right? Well, Ty figured he was doing that pretty well right about now. Two guns were hard to contest no matter how much ass you could kick.

"You had better hope they are closer than your cabin," Gabbana said quietly. His gun moved until it was in Ty's mouth, scraping against his teeth and sending a horrible shiver up and down his spine, like nails on a chalkboard. The man's dead fish eyes didn't give much away, and Ty believed he just might pull that trigger. He nodded against the gun, and the man pulled it back just enough for Ty to speak.

"In my pocket," he said, cursing himself for handing over the one piece of information that might have been worth anything to them so far.

Dolce released his shoulder, and Ty felt himself waver. The railing was thick enough to stop him, though, and his feet hit the deck with a thump as the man dug into his pocket for the iPod. When Dolce pulled it out, the two men backed away, letting Ty's knees go weak. Again.

"Do not forget who you are working for," Gabbana said as he slid his weapon back into the folds of his coat. Ty resisted the urge to ask the man to remind him.

"We shall be in touch," Dolce said almost cordially, and then the two men turned and left him alone, slumped at the railing and breathing hard. He put his hand to his lip, wiped blood away from it, and looked down at it on his fingers.

"I hate this fucking case," he murmured to himself.

A good two hours after Ty's interruption, Zane tucked a credit slip for a modest amount of money into the inside pocket of his suit jacket. He'd pretty much broken even at the table with Armen, Bianchi, and two other high rollers on vacation, staying enough to the positive that he'd not been able to shoehorn in an excuse to leave until now.

He'd used the time to study his supposed business partners, looking for tells and nervous twitches, tracking how much they won and how much they lost. Bianchi was eternally jovial and content, a personality quirk that almost took its toll on Zane's patience. Armen was quite the opposite, approaching somber, even after winning a hand. He was not delightful company.

Zane knew Armen had been watching him carefully; he'd been particularly attentive when Ty had shown up. Zane had been on a roll at the point, having won three hands in a row, and a whining spouse seeking attention simply wouldn't register as important to a high roller.

Despite his show otherwise, the problem had registered with Zane after the fact. Ty just didn't get that agitated without reason. But Zane had not been concerned until after he'd summarily dismissed Ty. At the time, he'd been more focused on the job, on getting Bianchi or

Armen to talk about themselves or their mutual business than he had been on his partner's state of mind.

So now he walked out of the casino, forcing himself to make his way casually back to their cabin as he grew more and more worried. The warmth of the expensive Scotch lapped through him, making everything around him false and bright. Zane had nursed the first glass as long as he could, but there had been a second, and a third, and then it had been too late. He could still taste it now, the burn of the ultra-premium liquor on his tongue and at the back of his throat.

Seeing Ty had gotten Zane's attention, and he'd consciously stopped emptying his glass. But it had been long enough since his last fall from grace that his tolerance had suffered. He knew how to operate under the influence in the line of duty; it just couldn't be avoided in the alcohol-soaked underworld. He'd already slipped into that cold and detached state of mind before Ty had arrived, and Zane hadn't even recognized it. It was like sliding on an old, comfortable disguise, and remembering Ty's earlier words about his drinking, Zane was worried now.

Even through the worry, Zane felt the relief and succor of the alcohol, the allure that welcomed him, called to him. In the past, alcohol had given him an edge, and it still burned in him, allowed him to slough off the nerves and distractions and brought the most important things into focus. Zane knew himself when he was deep into the drink while undercover. He'd spent too many years living it not to appreciate it. He'd also learned how destructive it could be. How destructive he could be under the influence.

The concern for Ty ate at him as he left the promenade, rode up the elevator, and entered the hallway leading to their stateroom. Zane had thought at the time he was handling the situation the right way; now he wasn't so sure.

When Zane entered their cabin, he found the place entirely upended. His heart skipped a few beats, and instinctively he dug under his shirt at the small of his back and drew his gun. He shut the door without a sound and silently made his way into the dimly lit room. Suitcases lay turned upside down and emptied, their possessions scattered all over the floor. The mattress was hanging off the bed and still cocked sideways, the bedcovers a shambles. The pillows of the couches littered the floor, and the doors to the balcony stood open. Either Ty had thrown a temper tantrum, or they had a problem they hadn't expected. Zane was inclined to choose option A, remembering the look on Ty's face when Zane had turned his back on him.

Zane winced.

He moved on through the bedroom to check the balcony and then walked to the bathroom, where the door was ajar and one of the sinks was running.

Ty was bent over the sink, shirtless, letting the water run into the palm of his hand and then repeatedly splashing his face. Relieved, Zane looked him over: Ty's face was pale and drawn, and the shirt he'd been wearing when he'd come to see Zane at the poker table was on the marble counter beside him, a single drop of blood on the collar clearly visible.

Ty abruptly jumped back, his hand going to the knife on the countertop. He jerked to a stop, his back against the marble tile of the bathroom wall, weapon in hand, breathing hard as he stared at Zane.

Zane let out the breath he'd been holding and looked Ty over while slowly lowering his gun. He felt his focus snap into place: on Ty now, rather than Bianchi and Armen like before. "What happened? Are you all right?"

Ty lowered his head slightly, glaring at Zane as his hazel eyes flashed with anger. "Had a party," he answered in a deceptively calm voice as he straightened up and stepped back over to the sink to turn off the water. "Sorry you missed it," he added as he set down the knife, picked up a washrag, and dabbed at his lip gingerly.

"I should have been here," Zane said as he reached out to lightly touch Ty's chin and turn his head so he could look at the split lip.

Ty flinched away from him and smacked his hand away, snarling wordlessly at him. The calm façade was gone just as quickly as it had come. He shoved Zane away from him and followed to shove him again, right out of the bathroom. He balled his fist as if preparing to take a swing, but then he gritted his teeth and flexed his fingers, snorting loudly. It always took Ty a lot of effort to rein in his temper once he'd lost it, and he visibly struggled with it now.

Now Zane knew what had happened was serious. He tried to study Ty more closely to see if he was hiding an injury. He appeared to be unharmed aside from the bloody lip. "What happened?" Zane asked him again.

"Fucking Italians!" Ty blurted with a wave of his hands, launching into another threatening temper tantrum, and Zane actually leaned back in surprise. Ty's next words were shouted. "They tried to toss me over the railing! I don't speak Italian, Garrett!"

"The railing," Zane repeated blankly. Then it clicked. "The railing? As in into the ocean railing? What did they want?" Scenarios began playing out in Zane's head, every one of them ending badly . . . because he wasn't there. Zane felt ill, all that lovely Scotch suddenly threatening to make an appearance.

Ty just seemed to grow angrier in the face of Zane's belated concern. He stood fairly trembling as he balled his fists at his sides, trying to calm himself. That was an exercise in futility, in Zane's learned opinion, but no way was he voicing that now.

"They didn't say anything to give you an idea of who they were?" Zane asked carefully.

"I think they were Guardia di Finanza," Ty said through clenched teeth, the Italian words rolling off his tongue as if he did speak the language. "Even Italian cops wear cheap suits. Del was supposed to meet with them, and when I missed it, they came looking for me." He waved his rag at the trashed stateroom. "They took the fucking wiretaps I found. I'm guessing they flipped the place, then came after me when they didn't find them here."

"The wiretaps were with you," Zane concluded. He inhaled deeply and nodded, believing Ty must have had a hell of a scare for him to be this livid. Staying in character would have made him fairly helpless, and Zane felt a stronger pang of worry that he tried to quash. "That was what you came to tell me about," he said, though he wasn't sure what he'd have been able to do about it.

"Not that it matters now," Ty snarled.

"It's done, Grady. Let it go. We'll find the wiretaps," Zane said as he walked over to the desk, put down the gun, and started to pick through the contents scattered across the top of it. He was having enough trouble focusing on anything besides his partner to worry about the past now. Ty was silent, and when Zane glanced over at him, he found Ty still standing in the doorway to the bathroom, watching him with a mixture of anger and what might have been pain. It was similar to the look he'd given Zane at the poker table.

For a moment, Zane was glad he'd enjoyed so much whiskey. If it weren't for the calm and cool it gave him, he'd either be really upset over Ty's near-death experience, so quickly on the heels of the climbing wall "accident," or he'd be giving Ty a smack upside the head right now, damn the repercussions. Instead, he waited for Ty to continue.

"Do you have any idea what we lost tonight?" Ty asked him in barely controlled anger.

Zane swept the mess of papers into the desk drawer before leaning both hands on the desk and looking at Ty, feeling exasperated. "No. But whatever it was they hung you over a railing for, Ty, it wasn't worth your life," he said, trying to reason with him though he was growing more upset by his partner's lack of control. It was wreaking havoc with his own, and he squeezed his eyes shut for a moment. He wasn't feeling the buzz much anymore, and it was starting to affect him. "So forgive me if I'm a little less concerned about some information than about you standing here."

Ty watched him silently for a moment. "You don't really seem all too concerned about that," he accused finally.

"What do you want me to do? Fall on my knees at your feet and thank God you're still breathing? You'd laugh," Zane retorted with a wave of his hand.

The heated emotion in Ty's eyes finally drained away as Zane watched him. "Yeah, I guess I would," he said finally. He turned and tossed his rag into the bathroom in disgust, then moved into the cabin and bent to begin gathering the scattered contents of their bags without another word.

Zane resisted the urge to roll his eyes. Ty was in a snit and would have to sleep it off, and Zane didn't feel charitable enough to play peacekeeper while coming off a buzz. Maybe he gave in too much as it was. Shaking his head, he took off his jacket and started picking up clothes as well.

They'd thrown most everything in the cases and drawers when Zane decided he didn't want to stay there while Ty was silent and moody. First he considered going back to the casino; odds were good Bianchi and his Scotch whiskey would still be at the table. It was tempting. Very tempting. But after a long minute's thought, Zane instead grabbed his swimsuit and kicked off his shoes. A swim would be just the thing to work off the annoyance crowding his head.

Ty was kneeling beside the bed, going through a pile of jewelry that had been upended. He had picked up one of Corbin's cuff links and was looking at it with a deep frown, turning it over and over like he'd never seen one before. When Zane moved, Ty looked up at him. "You're going for a swim?" he asked incredulously.

"Would you rather we walk the halls looking for the men who attacked you? That would certainly be restful," Zane answered shortly.

Ty stood slowly, looking at him as if he was just seeing him for the first time. "Are you always like this when you're drunk?" he asked with disdain.

Zane frowned. Now Ty sounded like the asshole he'd first met, distrustful and superior, and he was making a judgment call while overemotional. Typical. "Like 'this'?" he asked as he unbuttoned his dress shirt.

"Not giving a shit," Ty provided sadly.

Zane stood and took a few steps toward Ty as real anger sparked his temper. "You think I don't give a shit about you?" he asked with precision. "Just what kind of response are you expecting from me here?"

"I don't know, Zane," Ty answered. His voice was flat and tired. "I expect you to be my partner. I expect to be able to trust you. I expect you to stay at least moderately sober, and I expect you to listen when I tell you it's important," he rattled off, his voice getting sharper.

"If it had been life or death, you'd have gotten your point across," Zane said, the anger flaring in the face of Ty's cold composure, and Zane just let it loose. "I am doing my job, and I am handling the drink just fine."

"Oh yeah?" Ty asked, clearly unimpressed. "All right, then," he said as he looked down at the cuff link in his hand. He held it up. "Tell me about Bianchi's cuff links."

Zane narrowed his eyes, setting his hands on his hips. "What is this, some kind of test?"

"You're a detail guy, right?" Ty asked him in a casual tone. He still held Corbin's cuff link between his thumb and forefinger. "You were doing your job. Playing poker. Examining your opponents. Looking for tells, details that could give you clues to their personalities," he said. "What did Bianchi's cuff links look like?"

Zane opened his mouth to answer and found himself grasping. He could see Bianchi's face. His black tuxedo jacket, the white sleeve fastened by . . . He frowned.

Ty watched him expressionlessly, finally lowering his hand as he pressed his lips together and nodded. "That's what I thought," he muttered, and he tossed the cuff link to Zane.

Zane caught it awkwardly, still preoccupied. He should have known that detail; he was sure he'd seen those cuff links. He looked at the one in his hand, turning it over, feeling a resurgence of annoyance. "So tell me why cuff links are important to notice at a poker game."

"Other than the fact that he rubs his finger over them when he's nervous?" Ty asked quietly. He pointed at the one in Zane's hand. "It's a bug. And from what I learned tonight, I'd bet Bianchi's are too. Armen wasn't wearing any."

Zane glanced down at the jewelry, suspicious, and skimmed his memory for seeing Bianchi do that. Ty couldn't have been there for more than three minutes, and he'd noticed that? Concern Zane didn't want to feel prickled down his spine, and he hated it. "So it's a bug. That's no good to us if we're not the ones listening," he said, tossing the cuff link onto the bed.

Ty shook his head and turned away.

"You're not seriously going to tell me that I'm negligent because I don't remember what his cuff links looked like," Zane said coldly.

"We'll talk about this when you're sober," Ty told him with finality as he knelt back down to continue going through the pile of trinkets on the floor.

"If I've committed such a terrible mistake that you're this upset about it, I should probably know," Zane said, even though he could feel his control over his emotions slipping.

Ty stopped and remained still as he knelt, his head down. When he looked up, his entire body was tense. "I needed your help, Zane," he said softly. He looked over at Zane and stood. "Your partner needed you. I had the key to the case in my fucking pocket," he said in frustration, holding out his hand. "You think I don't know how important what you were doing was? You think I would have interrupted you if it hadn't been something huge?"

Zane struggled to parse Ty's reply, his own annoyance and doubt and now a revived nausea throwing him off-kilter. He swallowed hard, trying to pull it together, trying to refocus and find that cold space again. Ty was great at giving guilt trips. "All right," he said. Fuck, he needed a cigarette and a drink.

"All right," Ty echoed. "That's all you have to say? All right?"

Zane was sick from the mixture of frustration and upset that Ty's accusations caused. It was giving him a headache. "There's no point, is there? I was wrong. You've made your point very clear." He pushed his shirt off his shoulders and dropped it on the bed.

Ty watched the shirt hit the bed, then looked up at Zane. Something in his eyes sparked suddenly, and he moved toward Zane quickly. "You want to go for a swim?" he asked as he moved on Zane and grabbed him, taking his forearm and pulling and turning it, jerking Zane around to face the opposite direction. His fingers dug into Zane's shoulder from behind as he held his other arm and shoved at him, using the twisted arm to guide him toward the door. "Let's go for a fucking swim," Ty snarled as he slammed Zane's chest and face against the cabin's door. He held him there with the weight of his body as he reached for the door handle.

The unexpected sudden spin made Zane dizzy, and he was so shocked by Ty's abrupt manhandling and his head thumping hard against the door that he couldn't even pull himself together to throw him off. Ty wasn't gentle as he pushed him down the corridor that led out to the outer deck. He didn't mind running Zane into walls or doorways anytime Zane gathered himself enough to resist, and Ty kept wrenching the twisted arm painfully to keep Zane from being able to struggle. When they burst outside, the cool evening air hit them; the brisk wind carried the smell of the sea. Even along the Florida coast, it was cool enough on a December night out on the ocean that the decks were virtually empty, save for the bravest or most inebriated of guests. The pool itself was deserted, even under the glass roof, glowing a peaceful blue-green in the night as a low mist of steam hovered over the warm water.

Ty shoved him toward it, muttering about him being a drunken idiot. Something finally clicked as the past half hour flashed through Zane's head. This could be bad. Very bad. As they approached the pool, he started to struggle a little, but he was already off-balance, and Ty just twisted his arm a little more. He'd certainly shed the submissive personality of Del Porter, danger be damned, apparently.

Ty forced him to the edge of the pool, snarling in his ear. "I'll be goddamned if I get killed 'cause you're too drunk to care." And with that, he hooked his foot around the front of Zane's shins and shoved him from behind, pushing him into the pool.

Even with the warning, Zane barely got a breath in before he hit the water in the shallow end of the pool with a noisy splash. His hip and shoulder painfully struck bottom in the four feet of water, stunning him, and he gasped out what breath he had before surfacing to look for Ty. He'd just barely gotten in some air when he realized Ty was in the pool with him, right beside him.

Ty reached for Zane's head and forced him under water again with another sweep of his legs to knock Zane off his feet. Zane reached to cover Ty's hands, to pry them loose, but Ty's fingers twisted in his hair, and Zane couldn't even struggle much. He lashed out at Ty's torso, but the water slowed him too much for it to have any effect.

Despite Zane thrashing on his knees on the bottom of the pool, Ty held him under water until Zane's lungs were on fire, and then he was violently yanked up out of the water. Ty put their faces close together as Zane spluttered, trying to breathe and talk at the same time. Their noses almost brushed as Ty snapped at him.

"You wanna deal with me now, Zane?" he asked through gritted teeth, echoing what Zane had told him as he'd dismissed him from the poker room.

Before Zane had a chance to answer, Ty dunked him under again, holding him there for just a few seconds this time before pulling him back up. Zane coughed out water and choked desperately for breath, one hand gripping Ty's forearm, blinking his eyes hard against the stinging saline. The combination of it all broke Zane out of the alcohol-induced mindset, and he lost what detachment he'd been clinging to.

"Stop," he gasped out between coughs. "Wait—"

Ty shook his head and vehemently forced Zane's face under the water again. A split-second later he pulled him back up, gripping his chin with his other hand as he continued to hold Zane by his hair. Zane choked hard, dizzy now from the lack of air, the dunking up and down, and the buzz burning off. It all brought the whole evening crashing down on him like a leaden weight.

"I'm sorry," he got out in a hoarse, panicky garble. "I'm sorry!"

Ty was breathing hard from the effort of manhandling him, his breaths gusting across Zane's wet face in the cold air. The hand in his hair loosened, sliding down to his neck to keep Zane's head above water. Ty's other hand let go of Zane's chin and wrapped around his waist as Zane tried to get his feet under him. Ty held him up in the water and rested his forehead against Zane's. For the moment, it was all Zane could do to weakly grasp at Ty's arms. Despite the water being relatively warm, they were both shivering as Ty held Zane close to him.

"Damn you, Zane," Ty panted finally as the disturbed water lapped at their bare chests.

Zane coughed and choked again as he tried to get in air, breaths hitching as the delayed panic set in, and his hands shook visibly as he tried to hold on. His legs wouldn't cooperate. It was all he could do to nod.

Ty stood up straight, water streaming off his arms as he pulled Zane up with him. "Come on," Ty muttered, his teeth chattering as he got Zane's arm over his shoulders to help him out of the heated pool. He began leading Zane toward the wide steps. Off-balance, Zane wavered a little even with Ty helping him along, and when they got out, he was shaking hard from the adrenaline and shock and was shivering from the cold.

The cold air outside the pool's dome hit Zane like a sledgehammer, the last straw breaking any buzz, any pride, and any confidence Zane had in himself.

Ty kept his arm around him as he led him toward the entrance that would take them to their cabin. The effort seemed to have taken all the steam out of him as well, because he was sedate and silent until they got back to their stateroom. He made sure the door was locked behind him; then he pushed Zane gently toward the bathroom.

"Get in the shower," Ty ordered tiredly. "Get warm."

Zane nodded and laid a hand on the wall as he took a few wavering steps, but when a wave of dizziness threatened, he considered kneeling down there and being miserable for a while. The arguments he remembered without even the faltering filter of intoxication left him feeling ashamed and unworthy. He felt sick thinking about the very first glass of whiskey.

Ty moved around him, struggling out of his wet trousers and leaving them and his soaked briefs in a puddle on the bathroom floor. He grabbed an artfully rolled towel from the basket on the counter and began wiping himself off. He glanced over at Zane as he finished up, looking him up and down with clear contempt. He tossed the towel at the floor in front of him. "Goodnight, Corbin," he muttered as he walked past him, his shoulder brushing Zane's none too gently as he moved toward the bed.

Zane squeezed his eyes shut for a moment before he walked slowly to the bathroom, stepped inside, and shut the door behind him. He got the shower started, turned it up hot, climbed in, and slumped against the wall. His eyes burned, irritated from the saline used in the pool. Between that and the shower spray, it was easy to explain away the tears scattering down his cheeks.

CHAPTER EIGHT

When Zane woke, it was sudden. His eyes snapped open as he inhaled sharply, and he jerked upright to look around, heart already pounding.

"Morning," Ty greeted dryly from where he sat on the couch. He wore a thin pair of pajama bottoms and fuzzy pair of slippers and had his heels propped on the table in front of him. He was flipping through a book of Sudoku puzzles.

Zane blinked at him several times, trying to process through the adrenaline. He couldn't remember if he'd been dreaming or what had woken him. It had been a long time, weeks, since he'd awoken so abruptly. He was sitting up in the bed, nude under the tangled sheet, and his chest and throat hurt. He needed a drink of water, because he was parched.

Then Zane remembered why.

He drew in a slow breath and lay right back down so he could stare at the ceiling.

"Water and ibuprofen on the table there," Ty offered as he sipped something out of a delicate china cup. The butler service had obviously already been there to deliver breakfast.

Zane tried to swallow and couldn't, so he rolled to his side and reached out a hand that was embarrassingly shaky to pick up the glass. In short order the ibuprofen was down, the glass was empty, and he was again looking at the ceiling. "Thank you." His voice came out very raspy, even after the water.

Ty merely hummed in response, his attention back on the Sudoku book in his hand. He was being surprisingly cordial this morning. Zane really hoped it wasn't to cover serious anger. Ty could still be furious, even after working off some of it during the debacle in the pool. Zane raised both arms and pressed the heels of his hands to his eyes. Not so much because his head hurt—he'd never really suffered classic hangover symptoms—but because remembering how upset Ty had been hurt more than any dunking.

Ty didn't speak again. The only sounds he made were the clink of the china as he set it aside and the shuffling of the pages as he turned them.

Well, drawing out the inevitable would only give them both heartburn. "How much trouble am I in?" Zane asked hoarsely.

"I'm not your keeper, Garrett," Ty responded evenly. "No one died."

Zane sighed. He knew no one had died. He knew exactly what had happened last night. He just didn't have perspective, because when he drank, he focused in on whatever he thought his goal was to the exclusion of everything else. Last night, Ty had been part of "everything else." That was the problem: Ty wasn't his keeper—Ty was his conscience.

Zane sat up and scooted back to lean against the headboard. "Lorenzo Bianchi brought Corbin Porter a present," he rasped. "A sign of goodwill and respect between friends, he said."

The hardness in Ty's eyes didn't fit with the fluffy bedroom slippers. It was almost comical. "I suppose the word 'moderation' isn't in an alcoholic's vocabulary, hmm?" he asked easily. If he was still angry, he was hiding it well.

Despite the lack of outward signs of anger, every comment cut deep. Zane felt hollow as he met Ty's eyes. "I didn't think my tolerance would have dropped so much," he said softly. "I thought I could handle it."

Ty continued to look at him, his face expressionless. The lack of emotion was wholly unlike Ty; usually he couldn't be trusted to hold his temper and his eyes were easy to read. The lack of outward emotion simply meant he was trying very hard to hide whatever he was feeling. Finally, he set the book aside and pulled his feet off the table. "At least you know that for the next time," he observed.

Zane wrapped his arms around himself, knowing he wouldn't get any sympathy or comfort. Ty had never given him any reason to think he suffered addictions like Zane did, and despite making an effort not to drink around his partner, Ty's reactions suggested no small amount of disdain for Zane's substance-abuse problems—ever since his first snarky comment eons ago when they'd first met: "What, you're a recovering alcoholic?"

Ty certainly didn't want to hear Zane boo-hoo about it. Zane wished, though, sometimes, that Ty would at least acknowledge how goddamn hard it was for Zane to say no to so much every single day of his life.

Ty was still watching him. "You do realize you'll probably be expected to drink again, right?" he asked softly.

The thought hurt Zane so badly inside that it had to show on the outside somehow. He could still taste the liquor, and his throat and belly burned for it. He nodded jerkily. It would make everything easier to handle, clearer to see, smoother to swallow. It would cool him off and soothe his nerves. And with every sip he'd damn himself further. Zane knew that when that bottle was back in front of him, he wouldn't be able to handle it.

"You're just going to accept that?" Ty asked him in frustration. He stood up quickly, one of the fuzzy slippers in his hand. He held it up, waved it, then tossed it angrily at the wall. "Why the hell am I the only one that cares about that?" he shouted as he came closer.

"I care about it. There's just nothing I can do about it," Zane answered.

"Bullshit!" Ty snapped, jerking his head as if he'd just bitten a piece out of something.

"Will you listen to me for once! Just once!" Zane yelled angrily.

Ty stopped abruptly, staring at him for a moment before he breathed in quickly and nodded. He looked down and shook his foot, kicking off the other fuzzy slipper with a muttered curse. He looked back up at Zane and nodded again. "I'm listening," he said, sounding sincere and serious.

Zane took a couple moments to pull himself together, because he figured he wouldn't get another chance to try to explain this. When he spoke, it was as raw and honest as he could make it. "You want me to be able to drink and handle it better. To be able to resist what it does to me and push it away when it gets to be too much. But the truth is that just one taste is too much. There is no handling it, no matter how much you care." He stopped for a moment, staring at Ty and willing him to comprehend. "You have to believe me. Even if you don't understand," he begged.

Ty looked at him silently, his eyes darting side to side as he studied Zane's face. He didn't really look like Ty, not with the airbrushed sheen. But they couldn't change his eyes. He took another step toward the bed and knelt beside it, taking Zane's hand in his and looking up at him. "I don't understand what it takes," he admitted, looking up at Zane earnestly. "I don't understand what it does to you. But I do know that you are the most incredibly stubborn human being I've ever met," he went on with a hint of frustration. "You're stronger than last night."

Zane's breath caught. He'd had no idea that was how Ty thought of him. It made him feel ten feet tall . . . and at the same time cut down to size. The unvarnished reality was that he was, and always would be, an alcoholic and drug abuser who hung on by his fingertips every day trying to stay sober and do his job. He squeezed Ty's hand. "I wish I was what you believe," he whispered. "I wish I was what you need me to be."

Ty looked down at his hand and sighed heavily. He seemed to be struggling with what to say or do, and seeing Ty indecisive was another novel experience, though not an entirely enjoyable one. Finally, Ty swallowed hard and looked back up. "Zane," he said hoarsely. Then he stopped and looked down again quickly before meeting Zane's eyes again with determination. "You're everything I need you to be," he whispered.

The quiet words stunned Zane. How could Ty say that after last night? Or rather, how could Ty say such a thing at all? A slight shrug of helplessness was all Zane could manage.

"I know it's hard," Ty murmured. "But you can't leave me hanging like I was last night," he said in a harder voice. He was still on his knees, holding Zane's hand between his. "I had a gun in my mouth, and you were playing a drunk Corbin Porter at the tables."

Zane flinched but met Ty's eyes evenly. "I know," he whispered. "I would never have forgiven myself if something had happened to you."

Ty actually smiled slightly. "Well, at least we agree on that," he said wryly. "Look, I . . . I gather that most of your undercover work was spent drunk, am I right?"

"A big chunk of it, yeah," Zane admitted, his drawn-out words advertising his reluctance. He didn't like giving anyone ammo to shoot him with, even Ty. "It wasn't exactly unusual, considering the locale."

Ty nodded. Zane had told him about being a UC in the seedy underbelly of Miami. But this undercover assignment couldn't be more different. It was like comparing a burnt hamburger to a Kobe filet.

Ty went on, his voice mirroring the reluctance Zane was feeling. "And I'm guessing with your tolerance, it was never really an issue." He held his breath, looking up at Zane as if measuring how much more he wanted to say. It was obvious he was having second thoughts about whatever he'd been getting at.

"Yeah, that's right," Zane answered, willing Ty to keep talking.

"If you tell anyone this, I swear I'll kill you," Ty threatened suddenly, pointing his finger at Zane warningly.

Despite his surprise, Zane immediately shook his head.

Ty cleared his throat and waved his hand. "When I'm working undercover, I can't take any kinds of meds or drugs, mostly because I risk reacting badly to them. You know about that. But I can't drink, either, though not for the same reasons you shouldn't. So I had to learn ways to fake it. I can show you how to get around it, if you want me to."

Zane frowned a little while trying to follow Ty's explanation. It didn't make a lot of sense, but he'd figure it out later. Ty was extending a hell of a peace offering, and that was what was important right now. "Yeah, I want you to."

Ty nodded in apparent relief, and he patted Zane's knee. "I'll show you today, in case we hit it at dinner. Okay? Now help me up."

Zane nodded and leaned over to kiss him gently before Ty could get too far away. "Since we're being so brutally honest, I have to say this is a hell of a lot more difficult than it being just the job."

"What do you mean?" Ty asked with a frown and a shake of his head.

"I care about the job. I do. But I care just as much—if not more—about what you think of me."

Ty opened his mouth as if he were going to respond, then closed it again and pressed his lips into a tight line. "We'll deal with impressions later," he said, and it was painfully obvious that it wasn't what he'd intended to say. "I just want to live through this fucking case and get home and shave my head," he told Zane with a sincerity that was almost amusing.

Zane ran his hand through Ty's hair and wrinkled his nose. "I agree." Then he rubbed his hand fast and hard over Ty's head playfully.

Ty smacked at his wrist and grunted as he pushed himself to his feet. "Quit it. It's worse than dragging your socks on the carpet," he mumbled as he stepped away.

Zane chuckled and leaned back, just enough of the huge weight off his chest to let him breathe again. There was still so, so much that could go wrong. But Ty had listened. And . . . Zane watched as his partner—his lover—moved around the room. And Ty had given him yet another chance. After the danger, the anger, and the hurt, Ty had dragged him out to that pool to sober him up instead of just kicking him out or dismissing him as a lost cause. He had made the effort to help Zane, even if it had seemed like punishment and revenge at the time.

Ty muttered to himself as he walked away. He was fiddling with the ring on his hand, unconsciously trying to get it off. Zane watched the pull of muscle across his shoulders, admiring the way he held himself upright and proud, even here when it was just the two of them. Even as Zane watched him, Ty pushed at the band of his pajama bottoms, kicking out of them so he could change. "I deserve another medal for dealing with you," he told Zane grudgingly as he tossed the pants away, unaware of Zane's intense scrutiny.

Zane sighed and silently acknowledged that Ty was right. Clambering out of the bed, Zane ducked into the bathroom and emerged five minutes later cleaned up and in a pair of loose silk sleeping pants. "Any idea what's next?" he asked.

Ty had changed into a pair of stylishly distressed jeans with holes at the knees of the worn, soft denim. He hadn't bothered to put on a shirt. With nothing but Del Porter's wardrobe at his disposal, Ty had taken to wearing as little as possible. Zane had to admit he selfishly enjoyed it. Ty waved the Sudoku book he'd been looking at earlier. "I found some disturbing things last night," he told Zane. "We have a whole shitload of problems. Del Porter? Ain't as stupid as he looks."

"I didn't talk to him, but it didn't seem like that would take too much," Zane commented as he stopped next to him.

"These puzzle books are full of codes," Ty told him. "I haven't cracked them yet. I found an iPod full of recordings I'm pretty sure he took by using these," he went on, pointing to a pair of cuff links and broken reading glasses. "I'm not sure why or for who, but the Italian authorities have a stake in this too. All I know for sure is the FBI has put their boot up somebody else's ass on this one, and we're fucked, because no matter how much I want to, I still don't speak Italian."

Zane stared at Ty as he took it all in. This was what Ty had tried to tell him last night. Zane rubbed one hand over his face. "We're stuck in someone else's sting," he muttered. "Shit. This assignment has been totally fucked up from the beginning."

"Exactly," Ty muttered. He tossed the books down and threw himself onto the sofa gracelessly. The tired bent to his shoulders was more obvious, and it seemed like maybe he'd been up a lot longer than Zane had suspected. It was possible he'd never gone to sleep.

"So now what?" Zane asked. "You look like you need a nap, but I think we might want to find our team, have them look into the manifest for passports originating from Italy, and call back home to see if McCoy has any clue about this fun little twist."

"I have searched for the team," Ty said with a low, precise growl. "They're apparently Olympic-level stealthy, because I couldn't find any trace of any of them."

Zane frowned. "Something's not right about that. They're supposed to be close enough for us to call for backup. Calling out their names over the bullhorn isn't exactly subtle."

"If they were anywhere near us, they'd have called out the cavalry last night when Dolce and Gabbana were feeding me a gun barrel," Ty muttered as he examined his fingernails critically.

"Did they really do that?" Zane asked carefully.

Ty looked up at him as if he hadn't expected him to have heard and then waved him off with his typical easy attitude. It was frustrating at times, knowing how much trauma Ty could hide behind a smile or a joke. "Dolce and Gabbana took the iPod full of recordings," he told Zane, as if he were somehow up to speed. "But this morning I figured out Del was taking notes with these," he added as he pointed at the array of Sudoku and crossword puzzle books. "I understood some of what they said to me last night before they started with the English," he told Zane. "Pretty sure one of them called me a queer," he added with a wry smile.

"How perceptive of them, Del," Zane said drolly as he reached for one of the books. "What about the Sudoku?"

"Whatever method he was using, I don't follow," Ty admitted as he showed the pages to Zane. "I can't even decide if I think he's brilliant for having a coded backup or stupid for writing shit down," he muttered. He was silent for a moment. "They said it with malice," he finally added, obviously unable to let go of it.

Zane looked up from the squares full of letters to study his partner intently. "I told you you're a damn good actor."

Ty returned his look seriously, his gaze unwavering. "I'm not really acting much anymore, Zane."

Zane swallowed on the nervous flutter that stirred to life in his chest. He sensed there was more to this than just the words. "And you don't like it," he said neutrally, not wanting to influence Ty one way or the other.

Ty held his eyes, appearing to hold his breath too as he considered his answer. "I don't like the way some people look at me," he admitted with difficulty. "But fuck them," he added with certainty. "I'm the one I look at in the mirror at night."

Zane huffed quietly and moved to stand behind Ty, sliding his arms around his waist to gather him close, hoping desperately that Ty didn't push him away. "I don't like the way some people look at you either," he murmured against the side of Ty's neck.

Ty turned his head, his cheek pressing against Zane's nose. "I don't think we're talking about the same people," he said wryly. His voice grew more serious. "The ones who look at us like we offend them. Those are the ones I'd like to deck."

"I understand," Zane said. The us in that sounded pretty damn good, and though Zane could smell a possible discussion there, he'd had enough of serious life topics for the month, much less the day. "Ignore them. They don't know what they're missing out on."

Ty burst out laughing, then clapped his hand over his mouth to stop himself.

Zane chuckled and nipped at Ty's neck before he said, "So they pass on ogling the best-looking ass on the ship. My gain."

Ty snorted, though it was obvious he was trying not to smile. His hand came to rest on Zane's forearm, and he leaned his head back against Zane's shoulder. "Now I think you're just trying to get laid."

"I do watch you, you know," Zane murmured, sliding one hand up and down on Ty's chest and belly. "Did long before this case."

Ty jerked his head to the side and turned in place, giving Zane's chest a half-hearted shove. "You're not getting out of trouble this easily. We have work to do."

Zane started to smile and tightened his arms. "One kiss," he bargained. He wanted to keep Ty's mind off what others thought of him and on what Zane thought of him.

Ty shook his head, but his arms tightened around Zane's waist as Zane pulled him closer, and Ty was smiling. "Make it a good one," he challenged playfully.

Oh, Zane was more than up for the challenge. He raised one hand to grip the back of Ty's skull and claimed his mouth in a torrid rush, literally plundering Ty in a bruising kiss. It went on and on as he expressed the possessiveness and desperation he felt, but then he slowed, appreciating Ty's kiss like he hadn't in a long time, and he smoothed and gentled the movement of his lips as he cajoled Ty's tongue into play. Every touch he got back turned him on more, but since he was getting only one kiss, he wanted to make the most of it. Zane didn't let go as he drew it out, tracing Ty's lips with his tongue and tenderly lapping at Ty's swollen bottom lip before finally surrendering it and pulling back.

When he did, Ty groaned softly and took Zane's face in both hands to keep him from moving away.

"Damn you," he muttered in defeat, pulling Zane closer to kiss him again.

Ty sat on one of the many lounge chairs set up along the wide deck, looking out over the choppy water. He held his sunglasses in his hand, the roiling clouds overhead making it too dark to need them. He'd pulled both feet up into the seat and was resting one elbow on his knee, his eyes on the water but his mind elsewhere.

He probably would have looked like a model waiting for his picture to be taken if it hadn't been for the garish red Santa hat he was wearing. He actually felt less self-conscious with it on because it hid the platinum blond hair.

Zane had gone off to yet another poker game after an early dinner. He had seriously balked at the idea at first, fearing another bottle of Scotch, but when Bianchi had called, there had been hints that business might be conducted at this one. Ty had wanted to accompany him, but again, it was too risky. Plus, Zane needed to know Ty trusted him. Ty wasn't actually sure that he did—at least when it came to the drinking—but now was as good a time as any to find out.

So with Zane gone, he'd come out here to clear his mind and hide from Norina Bianchi, who seemed determined to force him to have another massage. He'd been out here for about half an hour, staring off into nowhere and enjoying simply being there for once.

Everyone else had cleared off the deck soon after his arrival, scrambling inside with their arms full of beach towels and books, expecting the quickly approaching dark clouds to bring rain with them. Ty knew better, though. He'd seen enough on the water to know when a storm was coming. A storm was definitely coming, but it wasn't coming with these clouds.

He sat motionless, enjoying the utter silence of the approaching front and the cool breeze on his salty skin. The ominous clouds reflected off the water, turning the surface silver. It was an otherworldly seascape, one that took Ty to places he hadn't visited in some time. He was so lost in thought that he didn't hear anyone approaching.

"Do you not suppose you should get inside?" a voice asked from behind him.

Ty's expression didn't change even though the sudden appearance of the man had startled him. He merely tilted his head from one side to the other, watching Vartan Armen move in his peripheral vision.

"It's not going to rain," Ty answered slowly, the British accent coming out satisfactorily. He still needed to work on it. And he needed to know why in the fuck Armen was out here when he was supposed to be playing poker inside.

Armen remained silent, and he sat in the chair next to Ty, seemingly content to watch the ocean roll just as Ty was. The clouds passing overhead were moving fast, the reflected light turning the water a deep sea-green now. When Armen did finally speak, his voice was low and serious. "You've taken to your role quite astonishingly well."

Ty felt his body go cold, but again he didn't react outwardly, continuing to stare at the green water without comment. If Armen had found them out as frauds, this was a surprisingly civil way of announcing it.

"I hired you to spy on the man, not fall in love with him," Armen said calmly, though his clipped tones betrayed his annoyance.

Ty turned his head to look at him, forcing himself to skillfully conceal his shock with a blank expression. Armen met his eyes and raised one eyebrow as if expecting Ty to say something. Ty stared at him without any intention of speaking. Anything he said right now would give him away as an imposter.

"Well?" Armen asked expectantly. "Are you merely more capable than I ever supposed, or will it truly be a problem if you're forced to harm him?"

"It won't be a problem," Ty answered immediately.

"Good," Armen said with a pleased sneer that made Ty feel greasy as he looked at it. Armen looked him over critically. "When you told me you'd have to change your appearance I admit I wasn't expecting this," he said with a gesture at Ty's face. "I quite approve."

Ty merely nodded, his mind racing as he looked back at the water again. He found it was slightly more difficult to catch his breath than it had been five minutes ago.

"I have the flash drive you left for me at the hotel. I assume you received your payment promptly? Good. I want the other drive before the cruise is over. The money will be wired to your account as before."

Ty swallowed hard and decided to take a chance on digging for a little more information. "And the Italians?"

"They are none of your concern," Armen said sharply. "Your job is Corbin Porter. Let those blasted, feeble Guardia agents handle the Bianchis."

Ty nodded obediently, his jaw clenching.

"If he catches wind of your plotting, I assume you will take care of things," Armen ordered abruptly as he stood. "Good day, Mr. Porter."

And then he was gone, strolling off down the length of the deck as the wind kicked up and plucked at his tie.

Ty licked his lips, tasting salt as he ruminated over this new development. He waited calmly until Armen was out of sight, and then he pushed out of his chair and sprinted for the doors.

Zane had just tossed a couple $1,000 chips into the pot to call and leaned back in his chair when he saw a familiar face appear at the door to the private lounge where the serious poker players congregated. A glance at his watch confirmed that he'd not even been at the table for thirty minutes, and Zane was starting to wonder if he'd be able to leave Ty alone at all without something disastrous happening.

Ty hesitated at the door, looking around the room as if searching for someone else before he took a single step into the room. Zane frowned slightly but kept his eye on Ty while also watching the cards dealt out in the hand of five card stud on the table. Ty didn't move closer, though. He merely stayed at the entrance and watched. After thirty seconds dragged by, Zane threw in his cards, picked up his half-empty glass, and excused himself, nodding to the dealer who said he'd hold back Zane's chips for the time being. Within another few breaths, Zane joined Ty at the door just as another couple passed by.

"Miss me, doll?" Zane asked casually, staying in character.

"I definitely missed something," Ty murmured as his eyes searched the room again furtively. "We need to get to a computer. Now."

Zane raised one brow and slid his arm around Ty's waist, turning them out to the game room. "By all means, lead the way." Then he lowered his voice. "And who are we looking for?"

"Armen," Ty hissed in answer. "If he sees me here with you right now, we're both in deep shit."

"I've not seen him tonight," Zane said as he dropped his arm and moved to put himself between Ty and the bulk of the game room as they walked, just in case.

"I have," Ty said grimly. He took Zane's hand and began pulling him through the casino faster, barely slowing when someone got in his way.

Zane pressed his lips together hard as they wound their way out of the room and out into the promenade. Ty wouldn't sound so grim if it didn't have to do with a death threat. Del sure was a target. Zane quickly angled Ty off into the next hallway, which was thankfully empty. "We can cut around the back way to the library and avoid the public areas. What's going on?"

Ty stopped and put his back to the nearest wall, looking over Zane's shoulder first and then meeting Zane's eyes. "I was sitting out on the deck watching the storm roll in," he started in a low voice. "Armen found me out there. The short of it is that he hired Del to get close to Corbin, to spy on him. He came to me to make certain I was still up to the job. Wanted to make sure I wasn't too attached to my mark," he spat out.

Zane swallowed on his surprise and cleared his throat. "He hired Del to spy on Corbin—on his own husband? And Del agreed to it? Jesus." He set his hands on his hips. "Can this case get any more fucked up?"

Ty closed his eyes in frustration. "Del is a merc, Zane," he said through gritted teeth. "He's not married to Corbin because he loves him. He married him because he was hired to seduce him. We have to contact Baltimore and let them know he's dangerous."

Zane went absolutely cold as fury threatened. Yes, Corbin Porter was a thief, a thug, and an asshole. But no one should be taken in and played like that. Not with marriage. Zane forced himself to take even breaths and look Ty over. "You're okay?" he checked, just in case. For all they knew, Del turned tricks for Vartan Armen too.

"I'm pissed," Ty answered emphatically. Whether he was angry for the same reason as Zane was anyone's guess, though. "And I'm worried that if Del is able to contact Armen, our cover will be blown all to hell. Which is why we need to get to a computer."

"Let's go. If Del turned on Corbin, he might have weaseled his way out of custody," Zane said as he turned to lead the way to the satellite internet terminals in the library. Then a thought occurred and he stopped still. "Is it possible Armen was playing you? Trying to make you flip cover? That he already knows?"

"Anything's possible at this point," Ty muttered unhappily. "I played it as straight as I could."

"I know you did," Zane said, already trying to think of contingency plans. "Come on."

They were in the library in under ten minutes, and Zane sat down at one of the terminals in the back. He quickly logged in, paid for the account time, and launched an anonymous browser session, and within a couple of minutes had gotten through the umpteen layers of encrypted and password-protected server gateways to launch a secure e-mail on the Bureau's extended system.

As soon as the e-mail was sent off, Ty leaned over the computer desk and banged his head on the table. The little white ball on the tip of his Santa hat flopped over disconsolately. "That's the most anticlimactic SOS I've ever seen sent," he muttered against the table.

Zane chuckled wryly and leaned back in the chair. All they could do was wait here for an answer. "You should have brought your crossword puzzle book."

Ty sighed heavily and sank to his knees, then turned and flopped onto the ground, effectively hiding under the desk so no one could see him there with Zane. He propped his elbows on his knees and looked up at Zane, ready to wait, and Zane reached over and pushed the tip of the hat off the desk.

It didn't matter that they were in what might be a life-threatening situation. Zane's thoughts focused sharply on just exactly what Ty could be doing while on his knees under that desk, if he'd just scoot over between Zane's legs. It took a hell of a lot of willpower to try to banish that thought.

They watched each other silently for a couple of minutes before Zane spoke up, more to distract himself from the urge to get on his knees too. "Want to watch a football game?"

That got Ty's attention. He perked up and leaned forward.

"How?" he asked eagerly.

Zane shrugged and turned back to the terminal. He minimized the e-mail window after making sure it would alert them to a new message and launched a new window. After several clicks, he was scanning through available streaming video from the NFL Network. "We've got Jacksonville versus Buffalo, Atlanta and Cleveland, Broncos at the Ravens, and . . . Arizona at New Orleans. Take your pick."

"Give me Saints," Ty demanded as he got to his knees again and turned to look up at the computer. His arms were folded over the edge of the table, and he stayed on the ground, content to kneel there at Zane's knee.

"Not Baltimore?"

"Ravens are like step-children," Ty answered as he squinted up at the screen. "I love them, but they're still sleeping on the couch when the house is full."

"So what team did you grow up watching? From West Virginia . . . the Steelers?" It only took a few keystrokes to pay for the satellite access, and the game from the past Sunday popped up on the screen, just before kickoff.

"We were sort of a perfect storm," Ty answered as he rested his chin on his hands. "With baseball it was all Braves all the way on TBS. But football, we caught Cincinnati, Washington, Pittsburgh, Philly, Cleveland. Whoever was on network that week. I was partial to the Redskins. But I got attached to the Saints when I was in Louisiana."

Another piece of Ty's life casually revealed. "I never watched any team but the Cowboys before I lived in Miami," Zane commented, storing away the new little bits of information about his partner.

"Well, I've always been a whore," Ty said wryly.

Zane looked down at Ty in surprise, and his comment popped out before he thought about it. "Wow. I am so true to form." Ty still razzed Zane for fucking around with prostitutes-turned-informants on the job, even though it had happened way before they ever met. Zane had been a serious mess at the time, but he sure wasn't now.

Ty glared up at him briefly, but he didn't take exception to the comment. Not vocally, anyway. He just pointed at the screen and wagged his fingers urgently.

Zane turned up the volume as the players lined up. "There you go," he said, happy with himself.

Ty patted Zane's knee, appearing just as pleased, and he left his hand resting there as he watched the screen devotedly. Zane smiled and spent just as much time watching Ty as he did the game and the minimized tab.

They were partway through the second quarter before the little tab started flashing.

"About damn time," Ty said as he pointed at the flashing icon. "Click it, click it!"

Zane paused the video and clicked over to the e-mail. He opened the RE: and started reading:

Thanks for the update. The Punch and Judy show's still on.

"That's it?" Ty asked incredulously. "I'm gonna kill Mac when we get home."

Zane leaned back and rubbed his eyes. "I'm certainly starting to feel like a damn puppet," he muttered.

Ty sighed loudly, and his shoulders slumped. "Well," he drew out reluctantly. He looked up at Zane with a shrug. "I guess we keep going." His fingers tightened against Zane's knee as he pushed himself off the floor.

Zane watched him stand. "Aren't you forgetting something?"

Ty looked down at him with wide eyes and patted his pockets absently, then nodded as if remembering what he was forgetting. He bent over to kiss Zane squarely. When he stood back up, he said, "Saints win it 17-9. Come on." And he turned and started toward the exit.

It took Zane ten keystrokes to shut down the terminal, and he was on Ty's heels out the door.

Ty led the way to a lounge some ways from the promenade. It wasn't as busy as many of the bigger restaurants. Zane glanced around at the low lighting, leather couches, and tiny tables, and he wondered what Ty was thinking.

"Are we having a snack?" Zane asked as Ty walked to a grouping of overstuffed armchairs in an out-of-the-way corner.

"I am keeping away from places I know Armen might be right now," Ty answered as he raised his hand to get the attention of a waiter. "And . . ." He hesitated and looked at Zane worriedly. "I told you I'd go over some tricks with the drinking on duty. I figure now's as good a time as any. Because I sure as hell need a drink."

Zane raised a brow, then shrugged, and sat down. "Sounds good to me."

"What can I get for you, gentlemen?" a waiter asked as he appeared at their chairs.

Ty held up two fingers. "Two glasses, bucket of ice, bottle of water, and a Scotch, please," he rattled off quickly before Zane could even open his mouth. The waiter nodded and moved away.

Ty appeared unsettled, so Zane decided to sit close to him. He settled in the chair next to Ty, crossed his legs easily, and leaned toward his lover. "We're not in view of the door," he pointed out. "You can ease up a little."

Ty glanced at the entryway, then met Zane's eyes. He appeared somber and worried, the odd look in his eyes one that was singularly arresting. Zane held his gaze for a long moment before reaching out to touch Ty's forearm and rub it gently as he waited for Ty to calm. His partner was usually pretty laid back—despite his innate twitchiness—but when Ty got riled up, it could be a difficult proposition to gear him down. Zane was all too aware of how he'd been contributing to Ty's most recent stress.

Ty took a deep breath and leaned closer to him. "You still want to do this?"

Zane frowned a little. "Why wouldn't I?"

Ty smiled slightly. "Okay. We both know you have to drink sometimes to sell a cover. And I think we're in agreement that you shouldn't. At all. A friend of mine taught me some tricks years ago for those situations. I . . . didn't really handle them well at first."

Zane thought that sounded a bit ominous. "Okay," he replied, dragging the word out a bit.

Ty continued to look at him guardedly.

"What?" Zane asked, a bit exasperated. "I'm not going to make fun of you. I've certainly got no place throwing stones about this."

Ty worked his jaw back and forth and then snorted. He was smiling as he looked away. "I'm a goofy drunk," he admitted.

Zane didn't see what was so bad about that. "That would affect work, yeah, but why is that so awful in general?"

Ty laughed. "One day I'll show you," he promised, looking back at Zane with a hint of that old mischievous sparkle in his eyes.

That was promise enough to make Zane smile and relax. "All right. On with the lesson."

"First: always order extra ice. Let it melt in your drink and dilute it." As Ty talked the waiter returned with a tray and the requested items. The tiny table at their knees was more for show than anything, but he managed to fit the three glasses on it. Ty placed the ice bucket and the carafe of water on the ground. Once they were alone again, Ty said, "And order the next round before you're done. The waiter will clear out your old drink when he brings your new one."

"Makes sense," Zane commented as he watched Ty move things around.

Ty took the glass of Scotch and wedged it into the seat beside his leg. Then he moved the remaining two glasses around on the table and poured water into both of them, filling both almost to the brim. He picked one up and mockingly toasted Zane with it.

"The best way to stay sober is to be a sloppy drunk," he said under his breath. He jerked his hand to the side and sat forward suddenly, as if he was excited about what he was about to say. Water sloshed out of his glass onto the floor. His eyes were bigger as he grabbed for Zane with his free hand. "Be very excited when you talk," he said emphatically, waving his hand again.

Zane tried to hold back his smile, because really, this was supposed to be serious. He nodded piously instead. Ty held his glass up to show him that nearly a quarter of the water was gone already.

He drank down a few gulps of the water until only a third of it remained, then he set it on the table. "Best way to drain your glass is to spill," he said as he reached for the glass of Scotch and took a sip of it. He set it on the ground at his feet. Then he looked up at Zane. "Nice to meet you, Mr. Porter," he said suddenly, half standing and sticking his arm out as if he was about to shake Zane's hand. He knocked the water glass over with his hand, sending it skidding off the table into Zane's lap.

Zane could only flinch as the water splashed over his pants and the glass thumped to the floor. "And hope the guy doesn't want you to pay for his dry cleaning," he said wryly as he brushed at his thighs. "Effective, though."

"Sorry about that!" Ty exclaimed, moving closer and grabbing for the nearest napkin and helping Zane dry his lap. Zane noticed he'd even added a slur to his words as he mumbled apologies.

"You can help me like that as long as you want," Zane drawled as Ty dragged the napkin across the front of his pants. "And I'll order you another drink," he pointed out.

"Clumsy, clumsy," Ty muttered with a sad shake of his head. "I've probably had enough," he claimed as he sat back in his seat. He smiled slowly and held up Zane's key card. "It's useful for other ventures as well."

Zane hadn't even noticed. "Well, that's embarrassing," he muttered as he shook his head. But he still smiled.

Ty handed it back to him. "That's a different lesson." He took another sip from his glass of Scotch and then picked up the glass he'd dropped and set it on the table again. He dropped a few ice cubes into it, then poured out some of his Scotch into it. Then he added more ice.

He gestured to the glass. "One drink is two."

"If I let that much ice melt into it, there's no way I'd get even a remote buzz," Zane observed.

"And that's the point," Ty murmured. He gulped down what he'd just poured into the water glass. "Now I've ordered and, in theory, consumed three drinks. Still only half a glass of Scotch is gone. You get the drift?"

Zane nodded. "Yeah, no problem," he said quietly as he studied Ty's face. He still looked worried. It was a simple set of ideas, but Zane figured he could put them into use without much trouble. The poker room was busy enough for him to move drinks around undetected.

"Sometimes, if you get there first, you can get an empty glass. Switch them out somehow, like I just did, or dump drinks under tables or in plants or decorations. A lot of it's situational. Your best friends are extra ice and clumsiness." Ty shot back what remained of the Scotch he had ordered. "Okay, let's go find you some dry pants," he said in a hoarse voice as he set the glass down on the table with a clank.

"I'm thinking you'll feel better behind a locked door," Zane agreed as he stood up. "And then tonight I get to practice my lessons."

Ty stood and stepped over to Zane. He slid his hand around Zane's waist and pulled him closer. "I know it's hard," he whispered. "But next time you think you might need a second glass, just remember that I will kick your ass when you get home." He punctuated the threat with a forceful kiss.

The words flowed over and into Zane and sank in deep as he gave in under Ty's lips. He'd already known he'd answer to Ty, anytime, anywhere. But now Zane believed, for the first time in so long, that he had someone who truly cared about him.

After the climbing wall scare and the Del Porter nonemergency, Zane had been sure they would be plagued by other accidents and loudly insisted they should avoid excursions that involved gravity. But the past three days had been oddly threat-free, enough so that Ty had started wondering if the rope at the rock wall had really been an accident after all. If it hadn't been for that visit from Armen, Ty might have been able to convince himself.

After Armen's little "discussion," though, neither Ty nor Zane could relax. It made what might have been an enjoyable few days tense and frustrating.

Among other activities on their itinerary, they went waterskiing and kayaking off a private island near Haiti, one owned by the cruise line. The first was not to Ty's tastes, but Zane had called it exhilarating and said he wouldn't mind trying it again. The kayaking was enjoyable for no other reason than Ty could begin humming "Dueling Banjos" at Zane whenever he wanted, and Zane couldn't manage to smack him with his paddle without tipping the kayak over.

Zane played poker with Armen, Bianchi, and some other high rollers every evening for an hour or two. He was able to pry a few vague details out of Bianchi about his part of the business, but Armen remained close-lipped. So Zane contented himself with winning modestly, and Ty had been honestly surprised when Zane had handed him a $10,000 poker chip one night. Apparently 10K was modest for the Porters. It wasn't likely they'd get to keep it—the FBI had a way of collecting everything it could get after an assignment—but the money wasn't the point. Ty knew that Zane just liked the rare moments when he succeeded in surprising him. And he had.

On yesterday's excursion, they had hiked for five hours through a rainforest in Puerto Rico to the "Exciting Jungle and Zip-line Adventure," which really wasn't all that exciting or adventurous, since it turned out to be a thirty-minute harness ride through the treetops. The hike itself had been more fun. Ty would have preferred to have kept on into the dense tropical forest, but he'd been assured the jungles weren't safe for going out on his own. Ty had barely restrained a snort when the serious young guide had said those words. Ty was pretty sure he could have shown the kid what an unsafe jungle really looked like.

On today's agenda was the "thrilling cliff diving experience for swimmers young and old," a chance to plunge fifty-five feet from a natural rocky cliff into the protected cove below. Now this Ty could get behind. He seemed to be among the few, though, because there were a lot of people going to the top of the cliff and almost as many walking back down.

Looking up at the height from which the few brave souls were leaping, Ty had doubts that Zane would be able to handle it.

"It's a long hike up there," Ty tried casually, glancing sidelong at his partner. "Been a long day too. We can skip it and head back to the ship if you want."

"I don't mind hiking up there," Zane answered with a shrug. "I know you've been looking forward to this all week."

Ty snorted. He'd known Zane would pass on the easy out if he offered it. "It's a long climb, darling," he said in a low voice, still mindful of those around them who could overhear. "No need for you to make it if you just plan to walk back down."

Zane studied him for a moment before glancing up the cliff. "I'd rather have the company for at least part of the time, doll."

Ty looked him over carefully for a long moment before nodding. "If you insist," he said with a smile, then began making his way toward the narrow trail.

The climb wasn't terribly steep, since the path was cut into switchbacks up the mountainside to preserve the natural flora, so it took a little time to get up there. They walked quietly for a few minutes before Zane spoke up. "It's not the height, you know."

"It's the falling," Ty finished for him with a nod.

"Yeah," Zane murmured. "You know me; always want to be in control." He snorted like he'd made a joke.

Ty watched his footing diligently, smiling to himself while Zane couldn't see his expression. He knew all too well how anything Zane couldn't control, or at least figure out, drove the man to unbearable reaches of crazy. "Yeah," he finally said softly. "But sometimes you miss the best things because you can't control them."

"Like what?" Zane's voice was relaxed and reflected some curiosity.

Ty smiled wider, glancing behind him to get a look at Zane. "If you have to ask . . ."

"There are things I do even though I can't control them," Zane said pointedly as he swatted at Ty's ass. "But choosing free fall? No. I'd rather face . . . snakes in the mountains," he said with a little chuckle at the end.

Ty snorted derogatorily, unappreciative of the attempt at humor. He still found very little about that episode of mountain hiking gone wrong funny.

"Right. It's the difference between something just edgy enough to get a high and something truly scary," Zane said as they slowed near the top of the cliff.

Ty shook his head and sighed. The view up here was beautiful, but it was often depressing for Ty to catch a glimpse into Zane's thought processes. He would much rather stare at the ocean beyond the cliff. "You're all about the high," he said sadly.

Zane edged one shoulder up. "Can't deny that, I guess."

Ty would have had to call bullshit if he'd even tried. Ty turned to look at him. The sun was setting, casting a warm glow over everything, including Zane. Sometimes Ty wished he knew what to say to help Zane, but then he reminded himself he wasn't exactly what one could call stable, either. There was a lot of pot and kettle going on here.

Instead of anything particularly inspiring, he just waved his hand at the cliff's edge. "Endorphin rush is one hell of a high. Sure you don't want to jump?"

Zane raised a brow and walked over to the railing, where he peered over the side and watched another man jump, screaming and flailing all the way down to the dark pool of water far below. He turned, a wry smile in place, and rejoined Ty with a pleasant, "Hell no. You go right ahead."

"Fair enough. Are you going to freak out if I do it?"

The smile stayed, but Ty could see Zane's shoulders tense slightly. "No."

"If you're going to lie, baby, at least do it with flair," Ty said wryly.

Zane rolled his eyes. "Oh doll, if something were to go wrong, how would I ever go on without you?" he drawled in a melodramatic singsong. Then he shook his head. "I won't freak out," he said more seriously. "I don't like it, but I'll deal."

Ty gave him a thorough appraisal, not certain why he wanted Zane to take the chance and jump with him. But he did. He also knew he wouldn't be convincing him to do it. He knew that with the same certainty he knew Zane wasn't in love with him. The comparison dampened the thrill of jumping, that was for sure.

Zane reached out, clasped Ty's wrist, and pulled him gently closer. Then he dipped his head to brush their lips together for a few bare seconds. When he straightened, the smile was Zane's, not the fake smirk he'd been using to play Corbin. "Go on. You'll enjoy it."

Ty found himself smiling wanly, appreciating the effort. "I'd enjoy it more if I could shove you off first," he said in a teasing, coaxing voice.

Zane's physical reaction wasn't one Ty recognized right off. It was almost a wince, barely there, a caught breath that he overcompensated for, eyes blinking hard. It was gone in a couple of seconds, but when Zane's gaze darted to the edge of the cliff and back, Ty realized Zane was truly scared. He hid it well, but not well enough.

"I'll have to see what I can do tonight to make it up to you," Zane said after a little too long of a pause.

"You do that," Ty said softly, regretting the teasing. He stepped discreetly to the side to block Zane's view of the cliff, and he kissed him quickly. "Now head back down so you don't see me jump. I'm not walking back down that freaking hill when there's a faster route."

Zane nodded slowly and backed away a couple steps. He paused, as if he was going to say something, but he managed a pretty convincing smile before he turned and followed the path down.

Ty waited a breath, then turned to find the attendant near the edge of the cliff watching him expectantly. There were a few people still milling about, but they all seemed ready to turn back rather than going through with it.

"My turn?" Ty asked the attendant brightly. The man smiled and nodded.

Ty took one last glance down the path, patting down his pockets to make certain he'd left everything with Zane, spending those last seconds to steel himself.

He'd told Zane once, but he wasn't sure if Zane remembered that Ty was afraid of heights too.

With one last hesitation, Ty turned and sprinted for the cliff's edge, throwing himself over before he could have second thoughts about the jump.

The part Ty both dreaded and loved about falling was the rush of fear itself.

CHAPTER NINE

The assignment was starting to wear on them. The experience of living in a fancy stateroom, eating incredible food, and enjoying the excitement of their daily itineraries had quickly faded into a slightly fearful, somewhat dreadful obligation that was certainly convincing Zane that they were here to work instead of play.

He had hoped yesterday's evening of shopping on St. Thomas would turn up some business, but it had been tense, dull, and disappointing, just like the rest of the week had been. That dangerous amalgam made for a cranky partner but some seriously hot sex at night.

Sex. He and Ty had been all over each other for days now. While Zane had no complaint whatsoever, it was really bizarre trying to remember that they were supposedly working. The waiting was getting to both of them, and the sex was the only outlet they had aside from the rare foray into a carefully planned adventure like that zip line across the treetops. Each night—or day, as the case proved to be more often than occasionally—grew progressively more heated and intense.

Zane's emotions were as well, and he was having a difficult time keeping in mind that the constant proximity and living the lie of being Corbin and Del Porter skewed those emotions. It didn't mean the close, passionate connection between him and Ty was as real as it felt.

Everything would change when they went home. Ty would change.

Zane sighed and resolved not to think about it as he pulled his shirt over his head and tossed it toward the sofa. It was exhausting, having a good time. They'd been here seven extra-long, activity-filled, frightfully boring days, and he was thinking spending most of one in bed sounded like a great idea, especially after Ty and his daredevil diving had strained Zane's nerves yesterday.

Zane's reticence hadn't prevented Ty from running at full speed toward the edge of the cliff and throwing himself off it with the kind of cavalier pleasure only the insane could maintain and live through. Zane hadn't told Ty, but he'd stopped at the railing around the mountainside and watched his lover jump over the edge. Zane's heart had plummeted as if it had been him taking the leap. He had to say one thing: Ty's form was beautiful as he dove toward the placid pool below. He wondered if it was something that came naturally or if it was all Ty's training.

One thing he did know: Ty was fearless.

He laughed slightly, shaking his head and turning around to look through the cabin. He wondered where Ty had gotten to. His partner had mentioned something about needing to run an errand as they left the restaurant after lunch. Zane had already decided to be lazy for a while, so he'd come back to their cabin, kicked off his shoes, and padded across the room to the chaise, where he sat and stretched out with a sigh.

It was only a few minutes later when he heard the door to the stateroom open and close, and then the rustle of a plastic bag as Ty came in and set down whatever he'd bought.

"I'm pretty sure I just got groped while buying toothpaste," Ty told him with a frown as he struggled with the tiny buttons of his shirt. "By a tiny little old lady with dead butterflies on her hat."

Zane had to fight hard not to laugh. He had noticed the past few days that whenever Ty got frustrated, he began pulling off pieces of clothing left and right. It wasn't like Zane didn't mind looking, but the fact that he was doing so now probably meant he didn't think being groped was funny.

"I'm surprised it wasn't more than that, you wearing those pants," Zane murmured, eyeing Ty's ass.

Ty rolled his eyes. Zane wondered how much longer Ty would go before he put a stop to the lecherous comments Zane intended to keep making. He watched his partner, appreciating the view as Ty went to sit on the sofa, propping his feet up on the table in front of him. "I'm bored," he told Zane grumpily. "How do people live like this?"

"I have no idea," Zane murmured sleepily. He was bored too. But at least he could go to the casino and feel like he was doing something worthwhile, even if he hadn't discovered anything useful so far. He'd seen Vartan Armen twice outside of their poker games, but only for the seconds it took for Armen to nod and move on. It obviously wasn't "time" yet.

They'd been dancing, shopping, touring, swimming, and neither really had any interest in shuffleboard. Zane had been only half joking when he suggested the country-Western line dancing lessons, which had set Ty to cackling. Aside from those options, Ty was stuck . . . sunning himself and making nice with Signora Bianchi, whom he desperately avoided every chance he got. It had moved past funny into ridiculous a day ago.

Ty dug the heels of his hands into his eyes and groaned miserably as he rubbed at them. Zane opened one eye to peer at him. "What's wrong?" he asked. The rubbing looked like more than simple tiredness. "Are you that restless?"

"Yes," Ty answered in frustration. "I haven't gone for a run in a week," he grumbled as he sat up, and his knee began to bounce rapidly. "The only thing I've managed to do is climb half a rock wall and then nearly fall off. And paddle lazily around some private island."

"So go for a run," Zane said easily, ignoring the sarcasm. "There's a really nice running track around the upper outside deck. You've got the body of a runner. No one would think anything about it."

"Oh, I have the body of a runner, huh? Zane," Ty said slowly, closing his eyes as he leaned forward, as if he were about to broach a complicated subject with a small child, "I have never been leered at so much in my life," he said with emphasis. "By men or women. There is no way in hell I'm going to any of the gyms or running anywhere unless it's nighttime and everyone's at the clubs trying to get laid."

Zane couldn't hold in the quiet laugh. "Poor baby. You cannot tell me you haven't been ogled a lot in your life."

Ty looked at him with wide eyes, his frustrated expression one of complete sincerity. "No," he insisted. "At least if I was, I never fucking noticed it!"

Zane frowned. "You're serious?" He looked Ty up and down significantly.

"Yes," Ty said in an affronted voice. He shifted uncomfortably under the sudden scrutiny and stood. "Why?" he asked defensively as he began moving toward the balcony.

"Because..." Zane had seen Ty use his good looks to his advantage. He knew that Ty was aware of how he appeared to others. He could turn on the charm and all but the coldest of hearts would melt for him, and half of that battle was physical. But Zane suspected what Ty was talking about now was a different type of ogling, and he thought better of a flippant answer. He studied Ty for a long moment, realizing that blowing off the question wouldn't make his partner feel better. "You're a very handsome man," he settled on, keeping his voice low and serious.

Ty turned and looked at Zane over his shoulder, one eyebrow raised as if he expected there to be a joke following the statement. When he saw that Zane was serious, he gave him a slight jerk of his chin and snorted at him before turning to look out at the ocean that rolled past the ship.

Zane rose to his feet and walked over to stand behind him, curling his arms around his waist. He was getting used to this being-able-to-touch thing. "What's the matter?" he teased gently. "It's all fun and games till somebody pays you a compliment?"

Ty was silent, his head bowing as he looked out the balcony doors diligently. "I guess you catch me off guard when you're being honest," he finally decided with a wry twist to the words.

"I think we're honest with each other," Zane murmured against Ty's cheekbone. "We just don't... volunteer much to be honest about."

Ty turned his head slightly, tensing briefly under Zane's hands before he relaxed again. "Volunteer," he repeated carefully.

"Neither one of us is much for sharing," Zane stated, one of his thumbs beginning to rub Ty's belly.

"I share," Ty argued stubbornly. His hand slid into Zane's hip pocket in an unconscious gesture.

Zane cleared his throat in a disbelieving sound. "Such as?"

Ty was silent, obviously trying to come up with an answer. Finally, he grunted. "What do you want me to share about?" he asked. He sounded uncomfortable.

Zane just shrugged. "It was more of a comment on past information," he said. He wasn't about to push Ty to "volunteer" anything right now. They hadn't seriously argued in two days. He enjoyed the bickering and teasing much more.

Ty was chewing on his bottom lip, one hand in Zane's pocket, the other resting on top of Zane's. "I don't mind questions, you know," he finally said softly. "If I can't tell you what you want to know, I'll just tell you that," he assured Zane. "Just . . . for future reference," he said.

"Like if I asked about the phone calls in the middle of the night that send you off to work without me?"

Ty was silent for a moment, and then he lowered his head slightly and leaned forward. "I can't tell you what you want to know," he answered, voice low and monotone.

Zane nodded. He'd known Ty wouldn't be able to talk about the odd jobs, but he'd asked anyway. He had his suspicions. After a few months of practically living with Ty, little clues had added up. Ty's Force Recon background gave him a special set of skills for wet work, he was a skilled undercover operative, he disappeared "on assignment" unannounced—sometimes for one night, other times for days—and he was unusually close to their boss's boss, Richard Burns, Assistant Director of the Criminal Investigative Division of the FBI. If somebody higher up in the Bureau, like Dick Burns, was going to tap anyone for a little "side job" that needed a special touch, Ty would be a clear choice. Zane's other theory had to do with high-class prostitution rings and a sketchy office fantasy football league.

"In a way, it's a relief to at least hear that," Zane said quietly. He could feel Ty holding his breath, the way he did when he wanted to speak but didn't plan to. "It's okay. I do understand why you can't talk about it."

Ty jerked his head in a nod, but he still hadn't exhaled. "Maybe one day I can tell you about it," he finally said tightly.

"All right," Zane murmured. He cast around for something to distract Ty from the tension. "How about something off the wall? What's your favorite dessert?"

Ty turned his head, and his cheek brushed against Zane's lips. Zane could feel him relaxing as the subject changed. "I don't like chocolate," he answered after a moment's thought. "But turtle pie. You know what that is?"

"Ice cream with caramel and pecans," Zane said. "But it's covered in chocolate."

Ty smiled slightly. "Walking contradiction, ain't I?"

Zane hummed as he squeezed his arms around Ty before loosening them again. "Always have been, always will be," he confirmed. "Drove me nuts when we first met."

"Well, you returned the favor," Ty muttered. He pulled away and turned around. "What do you mean?" he asked as an afterthought.

"Didn't want me as a partner but made sure I wasn't hurt. Hated me but took care of me when I was hurt. Acted like a muscle-bound idiot but displayed intelligence at odd times." Now that he thought of it, Ty still did that. Zane paused, remembering those first days fondly now that they were further removed. "Fought with me the whole time but missed me when I was gone," he added with a smile.

Ty moved in front of him, stepping farther away. Wincing internally, Zane let his hands fall free rather than holding on to him. He feared he'd shared too much; Ty was never comfortable when they started reminiscing or talking about feelings, something Zane tried to keep in mind. Inhaling deeply, he shifted his weight to give Ty some room.

"Odd times, huh?" Ty finally asked in an amused voice.

Zane paused after only moving a step. "Well, at first," he allowed, his lips quirking into a relieved smile. "You were dead set on having me think you were a total asshole."

Ty grinned slowly. He'd obviously enjoyed it at least a little bit. He cleared his throat and looked down at his hands as the smile faded. "I was hoping . . . to keep you at arm's length," he admitted as he looked back up at Zane and winced.

Zane frowned. "What do you mean? Keep the pansy-ass poster boy an arm's length from the case?"

Ty shook his head wordlessly, his eyes serious and slightly sad.

"You mean . . ." Zane shook his head. He didn't need to dwell on the past. "And now?" he asked instead. "I'm closer than an arm's-length away."

Ty smiled slightly. "It wasn't personal, Zane," he offered. "I'd just lost my partner. I didn't want another one."

Zane relaxed. He remembered that now. It had only been a year or so since Ty's partner had been killed when Zane first met him. Nodding, he went back to the chaise and sat, stretching his legs out. "I hated you, but you knew that."

Ty smirked. "That was my goal. You didn't have much choice," he offered flippantly as he turned back toward the balcony.

"No shit. And I hated even more along the way that you forced me to keep revising my opinion."

Ty lowered his head and glanced over at Zane. Zane wondered what he was thinking. He almost always wondered what Ty was thinking when he couldn't read his emotion in his face. Now, though, he thought he just might be comfortable enough to ask. "What?"

Ty shook his head and moved toward him. "Let's let the past stay in the past for now, huh?" he murmured as he sat down next to Zane and sprawled gracelessly.

"Yeah," Zane murmured. Then he shrugged. "Your turn." He leaned back and yawned, arching his back.

Ty looked at him in surprise. "My turn for what?" he asked.

Amused with himself, Zane laughed lightly. "To ask an off-the-wall question. It's a game, baby. Get with the program. I thought you were bored."

Ty snorted and looked over Zane carefully. "Why'd you switch over to guys?" he asked.

Zane's nose wrinkled. That wasn't a question he'd expected, but he didn't mind answering. "It came up during a long-term assignment. Tried it, liked it, stuck with it. And it reminds me less of the past."

Ty nodded and looked away. He seemed like he wanted to ask something more, but he remained silent, idly playing with the ring on his finger that he hadn't been able to get off.

"You can ask, too, you know," Zane said after watching him for a minute.

Ty sighed heavily and looked up at him with a small smile. He held up his hand, displaying the silver ring. "Got any tricks for getting these things off?" he asked. It was painfully obvious that it was not the question he'd wanted to ask.

Zane fought the urge to frown and growl at him to just ask the damn question already. Instead he rubbed a hand over his eyes. "Go soak your hand in cold water and then use some soap under it," he said quietly.

"I already tried that. Tried the Astroglide too. Useless," Ty mumbled as he looked down at it. He sighed and stood again, pacing away from Zane.

After watching him walk back and forth, Zane did finally growl at him. "For fuck's sake," he said tiredly. "Ask the damn question. I'm not going to take your head off for it."

"I know," Ty answered immediately, not at all surprised that Zane knew he had something more to ask. "I just . . . I don't think I want to know the answer," he admitted.

Zane considered that silently and decided there was nothing he could say. He crossed his legs at the ankles and waited. Ty would either ask or move on to something else, and he would have to let it go.

Ty just nodded at him. He ran his hand through his bleached hair in a nervous gesture Zane rarely saw, and then he turned away and moved toward the balcony again. He seemed drawn to it, like it represented freedom or something equally nebulous. Zane kept his head turned to watch him and, after a couple minutes, shifted to pull his legs up on the chaise so he could lie down and still see Ty. It made him wonder: what could the question be that would make Ty so nervous? Something to do with what he'd asked Zane? Maybe he was afraid Zane would ask him the same question. It had crossed Zane's mind.

The muscles of Ty's back and shoulders tensed as he stood there. It was weird to see him without the dark hair and the tattoo on his arm. It was also weird to see him in those clinging linen pants, but Zane would never be complaining about those.

Zane blinked. Tattoo. "Feel like some coloring?" he asked, deciding a change of subject would help Ty relax.

"Huh?" Ty asked as he turned around and looked at Zane like he'd lost his mind.

"Coloring. My tattoo," Zane prompted. He was surprised by how taken aback Ty was. He must have really been lost in thought.

"Oh," Ty murmured as he turned around and moved closer. "Hell, I'll try anything at this point," he agreed easily.

Zane told himself to forget about the unasked questions and focus on what could possibly be coming. If he played his cards right, he might be able to seduce Ty into topping him. Ty hadn't broken character in the entire week they'd been here, and Zane missed being fucked. With Ty it was always an incredible thrill. "The pens are in my dopp kit on the vanity," Zane told him.

Ty moved to get them without another word. Zane got up off the chaise, shrugged out of his shirt, pushed down his pants and briefs, and climbed naked onto the bed, settling comfortably on his belly. He'd hoped Ty would emerge from the bathroom without those nicely fitted linen pants, but Ty either wasn't thinking ahead or Zane would have to try harder.

A moment later Ty ran his fingers up Zane's spine, barely touching the skin as he sat down on the bed next to him. Zane shivered and closed his eyes. He didn't know what it was about Ty's touch, but it was electric every time.

"Better a pen than a pocket knife this time," Ty murmured to him. He pressed a kiss to Zane's shoulder before uncapping the pen. "Ooh, these are the smelly good ones," he said with an obvious grin.

Zane chuckled. "So easy to please," he teased. "Be sure to color inside the black lines, not the white ones, please," he requested, referring to the pale criss-cross of scars and pock marks already decorating his back. Some of those marks had come from said pocket knife when Ty had scraped glass and metal shards from an exploded computer monitor out of Zane's back.

"Hey, I know my ink, okay?" Ty said in an offended voice. "It's got a lot of curly things, huh?" he mumbled as he ran a fingertip over the design. He then put his free hand on Zane's shoulder, letting his fingers slide across Zane's scarred skin as he bent and pressed the tip of the pen to his back. He moved the pen in slow strokes, unconsciously moving his face closer and leaning more of his weight against Zane as he worked.

Closing his eyes, Zane focused his will on not twitching. The pen was almost a tickle, just barely firm enough to keep from triggering an unfortunate reaction of wiggling and helpless laughter. So he tried to think more about Ty's weight on him and how he hadn't been fucked for too long.

Just as he'd started on that line of thought, Ty began to blow on the pieces of the tattoo he'd drawn in already, and God help him, Zane squeaked.

Ty raised his head to look up at him. "Okay?" he asked in confusion. "It doesn't burn, does it?" he asked dubiously.

Zane cleared his throat. "Ah, no, it's okay. Just caught me by surprise."

Ty shifted to his other knee, patted Zane's bare ass, and then continued with the drawing. He moved slower on what Zane assumed were the thinner parts, his hand sliding across Zane's skin in graceful arcs and curls, following the lines of the tattoo. And then he would stop and blow gently. Each time Zane inhaled sharply as his gut clenched and dug his fingers into the duvet.

"Almost done?" Zane asked through gritted teeth. He thanked God that the ink dried in about fifteen seconds—the woman at the spa had likened the pen to a Sharpie—and wouldn't smear when he rolled over on it.

"One more curly thing," Ty muttered. He blew on it carefully and then sat up and put the top on the pen with a snap. Zane almost made it, but that last flicker of breath across his skin sent a tremor through him, and he gasped quietly.

Ty finally took note of his reaction, and he placed his hand over Zane's back, bent to kiss his shoulder, and then moved slowly to lean more of his weight against Zane's body and whisper into his ear. "You're so easy."

Zane groaned and curled his hands into the coverlet. "Guess you've got my number," he said hoarsely.

Ty's hand dragged across his shoulders and down his arm as Ty nuzzled against his neck. He kissed just below Zane's ear, nipping at his earlobe and the ruby stud there. Zane hummed encouragingly and tipped his head to the side, exposing more of his neck as he pushed his ass up against Ty's groin. Ty pulled at his shoulder, urging him to roll onto his back. He ducked his head to brush his lips against Zane's as Zane shifted his weight and moved, his arms wrapping around Ty as he did. Zane bit gently at Ty's lower lip and sighed, happy to feel his lover's weight on top of him.

Ty moved until he was settled over Zane's thighs, leaning into Zane heavily as he kissed him languidly. Both hands tangled in Zane's hair, his elbows resting on Zane's biceps and pinning his arms to the bed. Zane flexed his fingers and let his hands fall limp, investing himself in the kiss and the thrill of having Ty over him. Ty's thigh rubbing against his aroused cock just made it more enjoyable.

The kiss became more heated as Ty moved his body against Zane's, the soft material of Ty's pants the only thing between them. Ty growled suddenly as he pushed up onto his hands and knees, and he hooked his elbows under Zane's arms and dragged him into the center of the oversized round bed. Zane's pulse picked up, thinking about the possibilities. When Ty was truly hot and bothered, it could be an amazing experience, like being mauled by a lion without the fuss of needing stitches after.

Ty kissed him passionately again, rutting against Zane's hip slowly as he worked himself up. Zane met his kiss with more enthusiasm, and he gripped Ty's hips, encouraging him. Hearing Ty, listening to him pant and groan, was setting Zane on edge even faster than feeling Ty rub against him.

Ty pulled away from the kiss abruptly, pushing up onto his hands and knees again. Only this time he didn't try to move Zane. He lowered his head and kissed at Zane's chest as he crawled backward, Zane's fingers dragging up Ty's sides as Ty moved while pressing a tantalizing line of kisses down Zane's stomach to his hip. Zane groaned and spread his legs, propping one knee up as he arched against Ty's lips.

Ty happily moved to let Zane lean his thigh against him. He reached for the other leg, sliding it up until the backs of both Zane's thighs rested against the outsides of Ty's broad shoulders, his head between Zane's legs. He ducked his head to kiss at Zane's inner thigh as his hands wrapped around Zane's hips. The tension heightened along with Zane's catching breath, and he forced himself to keep his eyes open so he could watch the erotic sight. Ty was severely testing his self-control.

Ty looked up at him, his changeable eyes practically shining with mischief, and then he ducked his head once more and took Zane's cock into his mouth. Zane swore under his breath as his body jerked, the hot wet of Ty's mouth surrounding him. Once before—some weeks ago—Ty had done this. He'd gone down on Zane, and Zane hadn't even been able to see it because it had been so damn dark in those mountains. He'd imagined what it would look like, though. But now ... Christ. Now he didn't have to imagine. He could see his cock sliding between those full lips, see Ty's tongue lapping at him. Zane was suddenly sure he didn't have enough control to enjoy this as long as he'd like.

Ty arched his back, practically picking Zane's hips up off the bed as he moved. His hand splayed across Zane's lower belly, his fingers digging into Zane's skin as his head bobbed rhythmically and he took Zane's cock in deeper, sucking and licking and letting the shaft slide between his lips.

Trying to draw out the pleasure was a fight in itself, and watching Ty work didn't help. But Zane wouldn't close his eyes, even as his entire groin tightened dangerously in response to Ty's sucking. Zane was close, so close. He found his hips rocking upward as he tried to thrust himself into Ty's hot, wet mouth. He reached down and pushed at Ty's shoulder in warning, trying to draw the pleasure out at least a little.

Ty let him slide slowly out, looking up at Zane briefly as he let the head of Zane's cock rest against his lips in a tantalizing display.

"Christ, you're good at that," Zane gasped out mindlessly.

Ty laughed almost soundlessly. Then he winked and proceeded to lick Zane's cock from the head all the way down the shaft and back up. He pressed his lips together hard, then forced Zane back between his lips.

A harsh cry ripped out of Zane as his back arched and his hands flailed, trying to catch and push at Ty's arms in warning. But Ty tightened his hold on him, pinning him to the mattress and swirling his tongue around the head of Zane's cock before bobbing his head up and down and sucking on him hard.

"Ty," Zane ground out as he writhed, "I'm—" A rough gasp replaced his words as he lost the fight to hold back his climax. His orgasm swept over him, and he came while still in Ty's mouth, spurting against his tongue, sending warm pulses to the back of Ty's throat.

The very thought and sight of it was driving Zane out of his mind even as he shot his load.

Ty didn't seem to mind, groaning wantonly and continuing to suck him and swallow as Zane came. The pleasure went on and on, building until Zane cried out and jerked in Ty's arms, trying to get loose as his cock turned so sensitive he couldn't help but gasp and shiver.

Ty finally relented, lifting his head and loosening his grip on Zane's hips to let him move. He sat back and watched, grinning as Zane shuddered and groaned and clutched at the bedspread. Ty licked his lips and pressed the back of his hand to his mouth, trying not to smile. "You're too easy," he told Zane again in a pleased voice.

Zane groaned again as he shifted to lay flat on his back again, his legs still spread with Ty between his knees. "You think resisting you doing that is easy?" Zane managed to get out between breaths.

Ty reached out, ran his palm over Zane's knee, then patted his thigh, and crawled up between his legs to kiss him. "It's fun anyway," he murmured before kissing him again.

"Fuck yeah, it is," Zane agreed fervently after their lips parted again. He liked the slight hint of himself on Ty's lips; it caused the possessiveness in him to grow exponentially. He ran his fingers over Ty's swollen lips. "I really wanted to see that up on that mountain."

"Well, there you go," Ty drawled.

"Probably a good thing I didn't. I wouldn't have been able to keep quiet." Zane shivered again and pulled Ty down on top of him.

Ty gave a grunt and fell against him gracelessly. He pushed his face into Zane's neck and growled, the sound low in the back of his throat as he ran his hands down Zane's arms and tightened his grip around his elbows. The sound also sent an anticipatory shiver through Zane's body.

He moved his hands to grip Ty's hips, forcing them down against his own, shifting under them, and feeling Ty's hard cock against him. "C'mon, baby," he whispered in Ty's ear. "I want to feel you."

Ty made another frustrated sound against Zane's skin, pressing his body down into Zane's demandingly. "I've gone a whole fucking week without breaking character," he reminded Zane.

"And you've done a wonderful job," Zane said before licking at Ty's earlobe and sucking it between his lips.

Ty slid his fingers into Zane's hair and gripped it hard, pulling Zane's head back to kiss at his chin. "You're going to make me fuck you, aren't you," he said in a defeated voice, though he didn't really sound too upset about the prospect of falling out of the submissive mindset of the false Del Porter.

Zane practically purred as he arched up into him. "I can't make you do anything," he said before sighing. "But I can't fuck you so soon after you sucked my brains out through my dick."

Ty snorted and pushed up onto his hands and knees to look down at Zane with a crooked grin. "You're so freaking romantic. I don't know how I keep my pants on."

Zane grinned and laughed. He pushed himself up onto his elbows, kissed Ty longingly, and scooted back to lean against the headboard. "Well then," he drawled, injecting the darkness of Corbin's voice into his own as he tried to slip into that hateful character, "give me a show, doll."

Ty shook his head and crawled toward Zane again. "I refuse to do the accent during sex," he claimed stubbornly as he grabbed the backs of Zane's knees and pulled until he lay flat again.

Zane raised an eyebrow as he let Ty move him. He reached up and pressed his palm against Ty's chest, dragging it down to his belly and farther to tease between his legs. "My my, feeling uppity tonight, are you? Two refusals so far. What's next?"

"I didn't say I refused," Ty murmured before kissing him languidly. Zane slid his tongue messily along Ty's bottom lip and cupped one side of his face in his palm, caressing gently. Ty could turn him hot and cold and back inside a minute's time, and that was while fully clothed and often armed. In this situation he didn't have a chance, and his gut cramped pleasantly in recognition of the fact.

Ty's fingers trailed down Zane's chest as he hovered over him. His nose pressed against Zane's cheek, and his lips just barely grazed Zane's as he spoke. "You want a show?" he asked in a whisper.

Most of Zane's brain checked out as he flushed with heat thinking about the many and varied connotations of that offer. "Yeah," he rasped.

Ty remained motionless for a moment, and then he slowly glanced his lower lip against Zane's before pushing up to kneel over him. Now, Ty was not what Zane would ever think of as an exhibitionist. But he had done a lot of things this week Zane never thought he would or could do. Ty slid his hands under the soft material of the cream-colored pants he wore and pushed them down to his knees, exposing himself to Zane's appreciative gaze. Ty didn't attempt to remove them further, though, instead straddling Zane's thighs as he let one hand drift across Zane's belly. His other hand slid slowly up his own thigh as he watched Zane, who had to swallow hard. His eyes darted from Ty's face to his hands and back.

They'd never been like this with each other: just watching, not even really touching. They'd always been satisfied by fucking out the arousal, though that was fast becoming only a temporary fix. Zane didn't think there was a way he'd not want Ty anymore, and the quiet times they lay together were becoming more addictive. At this moment, there was no choice but to watch, and it was so intimate Zane could hardly stand it.

Ty's hand moved slowly at first, his eyes fluttering closed and his head tilting back as he sat over Zane's thighs and stroked himself. His other hand merely rested on Zane's belly. He groaned softly, opening his eyes to look down at Zane again. Zane was riveted by the sight before him. Ty's long fingers curled around his cock as he touched himself in the way that most pleased him. Zane had to remind himself to breathe as he moistened his lips. Ty spared him a knowing smirk before speeding his hand and moaning softly. The fingers on Zane's belly began to curl, dragging against his skin as Ty's head fell back and he pushed his hips forward into his own hand. Zane fought the urge to groan as his body reacted more quickly than he would have expected. Then again, he'd never had this kind of visual, indirect stimulation to help him recover. Ty straddling him, his pants pushed down haphazardly, and his hard cock in his hand was the most debauched show Zane could imagine.

Ty's eyes were closed again, his soft moans almost constant as he stroked himself. He climbed onto his knees and edged forward. The pants cooperated, sliding down his legs to his calves, and he placed his other hand flat on Zane's chest as he lowered himself again to sit and rub against Zane's groin. Zane's hardening cock slid against Ty's ass as he arched his body. His hand moved faster, and every inch of Ty's tight muscles telegraphed his pleasure and how much he wanted Zane inside him as he touched himself.

"Jesus," Zane swore under his breath, his hands moving unconsciously to Ty's thighs and gripping them. He was starting to ache now, the pressure of Ty's weight and movement making it wonderfully worse. His eyes widened as he tried to take in as much of the sight as he could. Ty was moving constantly, writhing, unable to remain still as the pleasure built. His blunt fingernails dragged across Zane's chest as his hips rocked. He groaned wantonly and gasped Zane's name as his shoulders hunched and his body coiled.

Zane was speaking before he realized it. "That's it, baby. Wanna hear you. Wanna see you come all over me. C'mon, baby," he said hoarsely as he lifted his hips up to grind against Ty's rutting.

Ty gasped and rocked down into Zane's body under him, his hand squeezing hard as his entire body tensed. He gave a sudden shout, short and hoarse, and his shoulders snapped back as he began to empty himself onto Zane's belly.

"So goddamn gorgeous," Zane breathed, ignoring how hard he was and how much he wanted to flip Ty onto his back in favor of soaking in the sight of Ty as he climaxed.

Ty panted as he hunched over Zane, barely keeping himself from just flattening out. He breathed hard, his eyes closed and his breath gusting warm against Zane's face. Then he raised his head slightly and kissed Zane passionately, moaning into the kiss as he laid his body out over Zane's.

The wet slide of their skin sent another shock through Zane, and as they kissed he wrapped his arms around Ty and rolled them over, settling on top of him and grabbing his wrists to pin them to the bed. The possessiveness in him flared nearly out of control as he took over the kiss hungrily.

Ty laughed breathily, his body relaxed and pliable under Zane. "Baby," he murmured, the sound so soft Zane wasn't even sure Ty knew he'd said it.

Zane dragged his tongue down the side of Ty's neck. "You ever wanna get fucked, now you know what to do to get it," he growled, biting down on Ty's collarbone and thrusting against his thigh.

Ty laughed harder. "All I have to do to get fucked is look at you," he reminded wryly as he tried to wriggle out of the pants that still clung to his calves.

Zane huffed and climbed off him long enough to grab the bottle of lubricant and a condom off the side table. "Fine," he said as he yanked Ty's pants off and settled back between his knees, cussing as he tore into the box and ripped open a packet so he could roll a condom on. His belly was still sticky, and he ran his hand through it, then gripped his own cock and jacked himself slowly with a hand slicked by Ty's come. "You ever wanna get fucked hard, now you know what to do to get it."

"Oh God, yeah," Ty groaned excitedly as he pulled his knees up and then wrapped his legs around Zane's hips. He looked up at Zane, his eyes glazed and full of desire.

Zane was too wound up; it was tempting to just take Ty right then. But he made himself place one palm on Ty's belly. He'd been fucking Ty every day, sometimes twice a day, for an entire week. Sometimes without any form of preparation. Ty didn't need it or want it, usually. They both liked it rough. But Zane always asked. "You want this without prep?" he rasped, patting Ty's thigh.

"Yes," Ty answered breathlessly. He closed his eyes and nodded, running his hands up Zane's arms, letting his fingers drag over the defined muscles.

Zane shuddered as he grabbed for the little bottle and slathered himself with lubricant. He leaned forward, bracing himself on one arm as he guided his cock with the other. Ty flinched at the cold lubricant, but he lifted his hips and groaned as Zane pushed slowly into him. After a couple slick slides, he settled in and started to rock, but he could tell right away it was going to take a hard push to sink himself fully inside; even though he'd fucked him just that morning, Ty was tight and close around him, so tense and fucking warm. He always was. Hoping to God he didn't hurt him, Zane reached to slide his hand behind Ty's head and lift it so he could capture Ty's lips as he snapped his hips forward with a grunt.

Ty cried out desperately, the sound nearly muffled by Zane's lips but not quite. His fingers dug into the back of Zane's neck, and he shouted hoarsely again as his entire body arched beneath Zane's. Zane gasped for breath, pulled his hips back, and then sank in again, slower this time, though it was almost as difficult to move as Ty clamped down around him. Despite Ty's bucking hips, Zane started to fuck Ty steadily, his breathing heavy, and he growled again as he grabbed Ty's wrists and held him down. "Gonna fuck you till you scream," Zane ground out as he watched Ty's face.

Ty could do little more than whimper and writhe in response. His eyes fluttered open to look up at Zane, but then he pushed his head back and closed them again, squirming beneath Zane and squeezing his knees together at Zane's waist, lifting his hips to meet each of Zane's thrusts. Wanting more room to move, Zane reared back and grasped behind each of Ty's knees, pushing them toward Ty's chest so he could thrust right against his ass, their skin slapping with each push.

Ty cried out again, struggling against Zane's weight and starting up a litany of incoherent begging and cursing. He grasped for something to hold onto besides the sheets. He didn't seem to know what to do with himself or with the pleasure as Zane rammed into him. Zane realized he hadn't seen it before—he'd always had Ty from behind, fucking him on his knees or bent over a table or against the wall of his bedroom. He'd never been between Ty's legs like this, holding him down, feeling his body tense around him, watching him lose control.

Ty may have been acting the submissive this week, but surely he was too far gone to be actively thinking about it now . . . and Zane had done it to him. With a gasp for air, Zane lost his tenuous hold on his control and let loose for a series of brutal thrusts as he started to come again.

Ty threw his head back and cried his name desperately, and even in the midst of his orgasm, Zane could feel Ty's body pulsing around him. Zane ducked his head and tried desperately not to lose that feeling.

Ty held to him tightly, breaths coming in ragged pants. He very nearly whimpered as Zane's movements slowed, and he pressed his lips to Zane's damp temple as his body practically melted, the tension seeping out of him. Zane held on to just enough strength to slowly lower Ty's legs and settle himself down carefully before letting himself relax atop Ty's sweaty body with a long groan, his lips brushing Ty's cheekbone.

Ty lay with his eyes closed, gulping air. "Jesus, Zane," he finally managed to say.

Zane grunted and pressed a kiss to Ty's cheek. His head was still spinning, and he was afraid that if he opened his eyes, the world would tilt. He just wanted to hold Ty close.

All too soon Ty moved beneath him, sighing as he gently tried to urge Zane to roll. The noise out of Zane's throat was something of a protest, but he reached between them and carefully pulled out with a plaintive sigh. Ty groaned with him. Zane shifted so his weight rolled off Ty, and he lay against Ty's side instead. Ty remained on his back, eyes closed and body limp. After a couple minutes of just breathing, Zane's pulse began to settle, and he opened his eyes to look at his lover. Ty's platinum hair was damp with sweat, and he had the back of his forearm resting over his eyes. The silver ring on his finger glinted in the light, catching the imperfections and scuffs Ty had already managed to inflict on it.

Seeing the spark dance across the ring, Zane realized his throat was tight, and he had to swallow twice to rid himself of the feeling as he blinked hard against prickling in his eyes. His chest felt like it had a lead weight on it, and Zane squeezed his eyes shut. It hurt, that feeling, that weight and tension, and he couldn't deal with it right now. He didn't want to hurt like that when he looked at Ty.

Reopening his eyes, Zane reached up with one hand to touch Ty's cheek. "Okay?" he rasped.

Ty groaned softly in response. "Remind me not to provoke you often," he joked wryly.

Zane chuckled, letting his hand splay over Ty's pec. "I suppose you do need to walk occasionally."

Ty moved his hand to rest it over Zane's, his fingers curling around Zane's palm. He hadn't opened his eyes yet. He seemed content to lie there with Zane and hold his hand. Zane had been about to pull away long enough to get rid of the condom, but he was loath to let go when Ty was so amenable. He felt their rings lightly knock together. At that moment it made him want things he knew he couldn't have and shouldn't want, but Zane squeezed Ty's fingers gently anyway.

"Zane," Ty finally said in a low voice. He hadn't moved, but his eyes were open, staring at the ceiling. Zane hummed softly in question. Ty remained silent for a moment, apparently mulling it over before he finally asked, "Any reason why we couldn't just ditch the condoms from now on?"

Surprise streaked through Zane so quickly that he caught his breath, and he had to force himself to resume breathing normally. He would never have guessed that question would come out of Ty's mouth at this moment, especially considering how closely it resembled Zane's half-formed desires. "No," he answered, his voice low and quieter than he expected to hear. "No reason we couldn't," he clarified.

He felt more than saw the movement beside him as Ty turned his head to look at him. Ty didn't say anything else. He just seemed to be either examining Zane for further reaction or pondering what to say next. With Ty he just never knew.

The silence around them seemed to roar in Zane's ears, but it might have been the waves outside. He pulled his hand free of Ty's and gently pressed his fingertips to Ty's lips. Zane knew full well he'd committed himself to Ty months and months ago, even when Ty was still carrying on with barmaids in Baltimore. He'd never faced such an obvious statement of that commitment from Ty, though, even after Ty had flat out told him he wanted to be with him. It made Zane wonder what exactly Ty was thinking. His eyes were hard to read, and he didn't try to speak with Zane's fingers over his mouth. But Zane could see the corners of his lips twitching into the beginnings of a crooked smile.

Zane lifted his fingers and laid his palm against Ty's cheek as he mentally skimmed through several responses, discarding some as too intimate to bear, others too much of a joke. "You ask because . . . ?"

Ty tilted his head slightly, his eyes not leaving Zane's as he considered the question. "Because there hasn't been anyone but you in a long time. And I don't think there will be," he answered bluntly.

There wasn't any reason to play around, not when Ty was being so blatantly honest. "Good," Zane whispered, his thumb brushing Ty's bottom lip. "I've . . . felt that way . . . for a while now," he admitted haltingly.

Ty's crooked smile grew, and he nodded. "I know."

Zane wrinkled his nose and lowered his eyes, a little bit of embarrassment tickling at him. He hadn't thought he was that easy to read. Ty's fingers brushed over his wrist, sliding up his arm slowly, but Ty remained conspicuously silent. Zane looked up again, trying to let the nerves go. If there was anyone he should be comfortable with, truly be himself with, it was Ty. As their eyes met, he nodded, acknowledging that Ty knew him pretty damn well. He knew the good and the bad.

Ty was still smiling at him, but it was a gentle smile that was unusual for his partner. There was no trace of a tease, no joke in his eyes. He was as serious as Zane had ever imagined him being, but there was also a softness to him right then, a gentle tenderness that, combined with his sincerity, made Zane's pulse pick up a little. He moved his hand back to cover Ty's on Ty's chest. Zane couldn't think of anything to say, anything that wouldn't ruin the mood. So instead he leaned in to press his lips gently to Ty's.

Ty slid his hand up Zane's shoulder and hugged him close as they kissed. When it ended, he was still smiling warmly, his hand on the back of Zane's neck. "Go clean up," he ordered gruffly, a smirk curling his lips as his hazel eyes shined with renewed mischief.

Zane kissed him again quickly before he sat up and moved to the precariously curved edge of the bed with a groan. He rubbed his hands over his face as his head whirled. That kiss was so damn . . . much. Zane sighed and stood, slowly stretching his arms up in the air and bowing his back before he let his arms flop back down. He pulled off the condom and padded toward the bathroom, glancing toward Ty as he crossed the room.

Ty had pushed himself up to sit in the bed. He was sitting cross-legged, his eyes closed and his head bowed as he ran a single finger across his eyebrow. His forehead was creased with worry lines, and he was almost imperceptibly rocking. Zane knew the signs of something weighing heavily on Ty's mind. It made Zane's stomach plummet as he entered the bathroom. He chucked the condom at the wastebasket and turned to head back to the bed, climbing onto the mattress and reaching out to touch.

Ty looked up at him critically. "That was not cleaning off," he said with a laugh.

"What?" Zane said with a wave to his own body.

"You didn't even bring me a towel! What kind of Romeo are you, huh?" Ty teased easily.

Zane frowned slightly, his hand pausing just short of Ty's chest. He wasn't able to reconcile Ty's quick shift of hidden emotions, and it bothered him. That frown he'd seen on Ty's face bothered him. But he offered Ty a half a smile, pushed himself off the bed, and padded into the bathroom, where he turned on the light and looked at himself in the mirror as he rubbed his chest, trying to banish that tightness that was making it difficult to breathe. The worry lines on Ty's forehead when he didn't know Zane could see scared him. He was terrified that Ty would pull away from him if he knew how the possessiveness Zane felt was growing into a serious addiction. Zane knew how Ty felt about addictions.

If Zane let himself feel more, if he let this want grow, it would drive Ty away. And it would hurt like hell when he lost him.

CHAPTER TEN

Smuggling the spare scuba tank to the platforms where the boats were moored was not as easy as it had been to sneak in the ceramic knife he had used on his last attempt. He'd had to disembark at the last port and hire his way to this island to get ahead of the cruise ship, then track down the service that would be used for the scuba excursion. But he was quite good at his job, and he managed to slip past the attendants in the little shop and get to the staging area unmolested.

He had failed to kill or maim the blond man on the rock wall, and he had been shocked when he'd learned the man hadn't even fallen when his rope broke, much less been injured. Before taking the assignment, he'd been informed his target might be easily underestimated, but he had fallen into the trap anyway. This time he did not intend to fail. He did not have to kill the man to succeed, merely put him out of commission.

The scuba gear lay lined up on the pier alongside the small boat that would be used to take the group to sea later today. The gear had been conveniently labeled with the names of the users, according to size and skill level. He scuttled along the bundles until he found the one for Del Porter. He hefted the tank he'd brought with him, checking its weight. It was filled with the correct amount of oxygen: approximately twenty-one percent. But the rest of the gases were a dangerous mixture of carbon dioxide and nitrous oxide. Maybe it wasn't lethal, but breathing it would induce a certain lethargy, courtesy of the poisonous carbon dioxide, and combined with the euphoric effect of the nitrous oxide, that certainly would be lethal when a person was underwater.

If the target realized his air was bad once he got down there, he might not care enough to try to surface before he drowned.

"How long has it been since you went diving?" Zane asked as he struggled to pull the skintight suit up his legs. The damn thing was rubber and kept sticking to him. He should have brought some baby powder.

"I get my certification re-upped every year," Ty answered, the fake British accent in full force again today. He wasn't struggling with the neoprene suit. There seemed to be a technique that Zane didn't know. Ty looked up at Zane and smiled. He hadn't shaved that morning, and the dark stubble contrasted alarmingly with his white-blond hair. The aviator glasses he'd snuck off and purchased, the ones almost exactly like the pair he'd left at home, gave him a slightly rakish air as he grinned crookedly and zipped up the suit. "Why?"

"Wondering if you'll be bored while they give us refresher lessons," Zane said of their "mixed experience" diving excursion. He huffed and finally worked the suit up over his thighs and hips. Now he just had to pull it up over his chest to squeeze his arms through the short sleeves. Getting into this thing was more work than the diving would be.

Ty shook his head and picked up his tank. "Instructor told us the experienced divers can go off on their own, farther down the shelf. Do you need help?" he asked bemusedly as he watched Zane struggle.

"An extra hand or three would be appreciated," Zane said, although it seemed silly to ask. "It's not like we're going to get cold in Caribbean waters," he groused about the heavy, insulating suit.

"At least it's a three-quarter and not a steamer," Ty said in a warm voice. He still wore the sunglasses, but Zane somehow knew that Ty was looking up at him instead of down as he rolled the wetsuit up Zane's torso.

Zane let his smile grow a little shark-like. "I think it's steamy enough for a public venue," he agreed, his voice a low purr.

Ty inclined his chin, reaching to take his aviators off and peer at Zane studiously. He looked at home in the body-hugging wetsuit. His skin was a healthy brown in the sunshine, and the salty breeze playfully lifted his unnaturally colored hair off his brow. His eyes were a deep green in the sunlight. And Zane had no desire whatsoever to look away. Ty leaned closer and kissed Zane briefly, a simple brush of their lips. "Next time we should do this for real."

"For real?" Zane repeated, slightly breathless.

"Time off," Ty clarified, his voice dropping to a mere whisper. "In a tropical place where we have no jurisdiction and won't be bothered by murderers or thieves."

Zane felt warmth flush through him, and it wasn't because of being sealed into a wetsuit. He set his hands on Ty's hips and pulled gently so their chests bumped. "I like that idea."

Ty laughed softly and took Zane by both wrists, pulling his hands away. "A little decorum, please," he said primly. He reached down and sealed Zane's wetsuit up slowly, taking care not to catch his skin with the zipper.

"Decorum," Zane muttered. "Sure." He had to look away from Ty and out over the water to keep that concept in mind. Luckily, the instructor spoke up and gave him something else to focus on.

The man presented a basic review of technique and equipment, as well as more in-depth information about the man-made reef below for the more experienced divers, but Zane was only listening with half an ear. Ty checked over Zane's tank, hoses, and gauges to make sure everything was in working order, then did the same to his own. He murmured to himself as he did this, explaining to Zane what he was doing, and that was much more interesting to listen to.

Once the instructor was done, Ty hefted his tank up and slung it over his shoulders, securing it with a level of familiarity and competence even a novice would have recognized.

"Ready to go?" he asked Zane brightly as he pulled his face mask over his head.

"Let's go, hotshot," Zane answered with an indulgent smile as they moved to sit on the edge of the dive boat with the other twenty or so people. He pulled his mask on and settled the breathing apparatus. He figured the worst would be remembering he couldn't breathe through his nose, and that wouldn't be tough. This was kind of exciting, really, in a good way, for a change. He turned to look at

Ty just as his partner fell back into the water and disappeared. After a deep breath, Zane followed.

It was suddenly quiet and calm around him, and all he had to focus on was his breathing. It was soothing. Zane sank slowly through layers of blue and green for what seemed like a long time, letting the weight on the belts he wore pull him down as he got used to the silence roaring in his ears and watched the water mute the glittering light above the surface. He drifted down past several divers who were staying closer to the surface, and one of the dive instructors wearing a bright yellow neoprene suit waved at him. Zane gave her a thumbs-up before righting himself and turning to peer through the shifting water.

When he looked down, Ty—Zane would recognize that body shape anywhere—was several yards below him, arms and legs spread out as if floating on the surface. It was a pose of utter relaxation and pleasure. He gave Zane a little wave, then straightened his body out, gave a strong kick of his legs, and dove backward, relative to Zane, deeper into the clear blue. He reminded Zane of a porpoise, with how easily he wiggled through the water.

Zane saw some divers nearby checking out the coral reef the sea had made its own, but he was content to simply float slowly deeper and keep an eye on where Ty the Super Dolphin swam.

It was easy for Zane to lose himself under water, surrounded by the warmth and silence, schools of fish flitting about, brilliant colors set off by the never-ending aqua. All that marred the view was the black blobs of the other divers, and there were fewer of those the deeper he sank along the shelf.

As he turned lazily in the water, one of those black blobs rushed toward him at alarming speed, swooping down on him from above. Before Zane could react, strong hands grabbed his biceps, and the "attacking" diver hung suspended upside down above him. A faceplate pressed against Zane's, and Ty's hazel eyes sparkled merrily as he looked at him and winked. Zane laughed and had to reach out to set his mouthpiece back between his teeth before he could swipe at Ty, who was already reeling away. Zane was a decent swimmer, but there was no way in hell he could catch Ty. It would be fun to try, though, and Zane grabbed at an arm, his fingers catching on the skin of Ty's wrist, before his partner swished just out of reach.

Ty twisted and turned to circle back around and behind Zane, and from the smile Zane could see even behind the mouthpiece, he could tell Ty was enjoying the cat-and-mouse game just as much as he was. He used Zane's backside to kick off and darted away from him. Zane's longer arms weren't an advantage; the water slowed him down enough that all he ever got was his fingertips on suit or skin. After rolling completely over in the water while chasing a flipper, Zane watched Ty literally cavort away, teasing and waving. It struck Zane that he didn't get to see Ty like this often: playful and relaxed. Zane really liked it. He was very much like a seal, gleefully flitting around a killer whale and daring it to catch him. Zane tried to snort at the comparison but couldn't because of the face mask. If Ty's offer to take off to a tropical island for their next stretch of time off was serious, it was an extremely enticing offer, especially if this was the side of Ty he'd get to see every day.

Ty glided along the sandy ocean floor as Zane watched. The shadows were deeper there, but visibility was still good. The waves above were a world away, and the peace and joy of the moment stole over the scene, lulling Zane into just enjoying it.

He should have known it wouldn't last.

Ty stopped his leisurely swim and sank to his knees in the sand on the ocean floor. A cloud of sediment and disturbed sand billowed in slow motion around him. He seemed to be checking one of the gauges of his air tank. After several breaths, Zane righted himself and kicked his legs a couple times to send him in that direction to see what was going on.

Ty looked up as Zane approached. The murky clouds around him had begun to settle, and Zane could see his chest and shoulders clearly again. He gestured for Zane to come closer, and when Zane got within reach, Ty reached out and took hold of his shoulder, peering at his air gauge closely. He then leaned back and tapped his own, gesturing for Zane to look at it.

It read that the tank was half empty. Plenty of air left. Zane shrugged. Why was Ty looking at it? Zane held out both hands, palms up, and lifted them in a "what's up?" motion.

Ty shook his head and pointed to his mouthpiece. He then made a quit motion across his throat and pointed at the gauge again. He wanted Zane to turn off the air? That couldn't be right. Zane shook his head, shrugged, and peered at Ty, waiting for him to elaborate.

Ty threw his head to the side, rolling his eyes behind the mask in frustration. Then, to Zane's growing surprise, he pulled the mouthpiece out of his mouth and shrugged out of the tank, leaving him with no air at all. Zane called out a garbled "What the hell?" through his mouthpiece and grabbed at Ty's arm as he looked around for one of the yellow suits. If Ty was jerking him around, Zane didn't want the instructor to see it. But another look told Zane that Ty wasn't having fun anymore.

Ty pointed at Zane, then himself, and then jerked his finger upward. Ty wanted them both to surface. Ty waved at the air tank and swiped his fingers across his throat again, Zane glanced down at the discarded tank, and it clicked. Despite what the gauge said, the tank was out of air . . . just as Ty had been for some time now.

Zane nodded, but he caught Ty's arm and tapped his own mouthpiece and then Ty's chest. Zane just had to pull the strap off his equipment, and they could share the mouthpiece and the air.

It had worked in that James Bond movie. Why not now?

Ty nodded jerkily. He wasn't flailing or panicking. Much like his reaction to dangling over the rock wall platform, he was maddeningly sedate. But he had probably been holding his breath for a while, and if the air tank hadn't been full, there was no telling how much air he'd been able to get in that last gasp. When Zane got the mouthpiece free, Ty took it and hastily put it to his own mouth, breathing in deeply before handing it back and nodding.

He reached for the discarded tank and slung it back over his shoulders, his motions clumsy in the water. Then he pointed upward, touching his watch with several slow, exaggerated taps. Zane nodded as he resettled his mouthpiece without fastening the strap and started swimming up toward the light. They had a long way to go.

But Ty wrapped an arm around Zane's neck, pulling on him forcefully and shaking his head. His eyes were almost an aqua color behind the mask, the color of the sea and sun far above reflecting to play tricks with the light. He looked Zane in the eye worriedly as he stopped their progress, and they hung in the water together in the silence, an oddly peaceful moment in the midst of an emergency.

Zane knew Ty was trying to tell him something important, but he just wasn't getting it, and that worried him almost as much as his desire for them to get to the surface quickly.

Then Ty shook his head and tapped his watch again, each tap slower and more deliberate than the last before pointing upward again. Zane frowned and shook his head as he clenched his fist in the water. He knew getting frustrated wouldn't help, but he hated not being able to understand.

Ty seemed to sense what he was feeling, and he patted Zane's hand with one hand as he reached with the other to Zane's belt and loosened one of the weights, letting it fall away. They began to float upward lazily. Ty took hold of the mouthpiece, giving Zane a moment to take one last deep breath before he pulled it out of Zane's mouth. But instead of putting it to his own, he held it out to the side and leaned in to kiss Zane as passionately as the dive masks and the water allowed. The strength in it surprised Zane, and he clutched at Ty, trying not to let the kiss distract him from their problem. Not the best of ideas when they didn't know what had happened to Ty's tank.

They didn't know what had happened to Ty's guide rope on the climbing wall, either.

Zane pulled back, eyes wide as he looked at Ty, then up to the surface and back. There could very well be danger up there.

Ty was shaking his head, as if telling Zane not to think about it. He took a deep breath from the mouthpiece and then popped it back into Zane's mouth. They were rising very slowly, clutching each other close and being pushed around one another by the current in a leisurely dance that would have been wildly romantic and fun in any other scenario. Schools of tiny, colorful fish darted around them playfully. Bubbles chased them upward.

Ty seemed determined to make them go slowly, and Zane slowly calmed. Ty would have been more concerned and active if they were in any imminent danger. So he shifted his arms to hold Ty closer and evened out his breathing as they gently ascended.

They were making progress, though it was hard to judge how much more time it would take to get there. Zane knew one thing; Ty never would have made it to the surface if he'd been down there without help, especially not if Ty believed he had to ascend this slowly.

When Ty took the mouthpiece once more, he drew a deep breath from it, then nudged his nose against Zane's and kissed him again. This was a gentler kiss, a languid indulgence that could almost make Zane forget someone could be trying to drown them.

When Ty broke it off, he looked up and took one more deep breath from the mouthpiece, and then he placed it carefully back in Zane's mouth and dropped a few more of their weights. They rose faster, picking up speed as Ty began to kick toward the surface.

When their heads broke the surface of the water, it was loud, the splash of the water against them and itself nearly deafening Zane for a moment. Ty gasped deep for air and yanked his mask off. He appeared just as relieved as Zane felt as he blinked away the water that streamed into his eyes. Zane jerked his mouthpiece out and looked around. They were about thirty yards from the dive boat, where one of the crew was waving at them. He turned to Ty and reached to take the empty tank off his shoulder.

Ty batted at his pawing hands. "You can't swim and hold onto it too," he said in a harsh voice. Instead he reached out and yanked Zane's mask off his head, both of them treading water with difficulty as the waves lapped at them. Ty didn't say another word. He just pulled Zane closer and kissed him a third time as they bobbed in each other's arms. Zane let Ty control it—and him—as they gasped for breath through the kiss, not letting go.

When Ty finally pulled back, he lifted his chin out of the water and looked at Zane seriously over the gentle roll of the waves. "That's for the air," he gasped out, still slightly out of breath.

"What the hell happened?" Zane asked.

"I felt funny. Giddy. Not supposed to feel like that underwater. Come on," he grunted, and he turned and began swimming with sure, powerful strokes toward the boat.

After that kiss, Zane was about as out of breath as Ty had been. But he gamely started swimming after him.

The crew had already helped Ty aboard the flat end of the craft when Zane reached it, and several strong hands gripped him and pulled him out of the water as well. He knelt beside Ty, who was taking in deep, grateful breaths of the warm Caribbean air.

"I'm sorry," he said to Zane as he reached out and patted his shoulder. He was speaking with the British accent, and after all that happened below the surface, it seemed wildly inappropriate. "I couldn't let us surface too quickly. I was afraid we might be deep enough to risk the bends."

"So that's what you were trying to say." Zane shrugged out of the tank as one of the dive instructors took the weight from his shoulders.

Ty shrugged in embarrassment, his cheeks reddening under his tan as another instructor knelt next to him to take his pulse. Worried, Zane reached out partway but stopped, then remembered he could touch his fake husband without looking odd. So he did reach out to touch the top of Ty's thigh, then his cheek. "You okay?"

"I'm fine," Ty answered with a vigorous nod. He looked up and met Zane's eyes for a moment, then turned his gaze to the woman kneeling beside him. "Brushed against the bottom down there. Suppose I knocked something loose," he told the girl with a carefree laugh and an elegant shrug of his shoulders. It was enough to fool a stranger, and the woman smiled at him worriedly and helped him out of the useless tank.

"It happens to the best of us," she offered kindly. "At least you didn't panic and had someone close enough to help you."

Zane ran his hands through his hair to slick it back and kept watch over Ty carefully. "We'll just have to take it easy this evening," he said, letting his hand drop lightly onto Ty's knee. He knew he was venturing into touchy-feely territory, but damn it, what had just happened was scarier now, thinking about it, than it had been under the water holding Ty in his arms. He knew why Ty was keeping a lid on it, but he wanted to scream from the rooftops that someone had just tried to murder his lover. Again.

Ty smiled at him but remained silent. They didn't want the staff getting wind of yet another attempt on their lives. The news would spread like wildfire on the ship, and they'd already had more attention than they wanted.

After a few more moments to make certain they were both well, the two instructors left them sitting alone near the bow of the little boat. Ty waited until no one was within earshot before he leaned against the back of the padded seat and muttered, "I'm beginning to dislike this case."

Zane groaned and rubbed his eyes. "I hadn't really anticipated murder attempts," he muttered.

Ty's hand slid onto his knee, resting there in a familiar gesture that would have felt so odd just a week ago. "We'll figure it out tonight. I'm tired of sitting around and waiting for someone to kill me."

Zane moved his hand to cover Ty's as he silently agreed, watching his partner instead of the blue Caribbean tossing gently behind him.

After a long, hot shower, Zane simply pulled on one of the plush bathrobes in the bathroom and joined Ty in the main room. He was hungry after their excursion. "Hey, want some sandwiches or something?" he asked before flopping on the couch and putting his feet up on the low table in front of him. It would be six hours before dinnertime, according to the itinerary that ruled their lives.

"Anything but fish," was Ty's disgruntled reply. He was pacing, having foregone the robe after his shower in favor of the soft, tattered jeans he was probably going to end up stealing from Del Porter. He had his head lowered as he worked toward making a groove in the floor in front of the balcony, striding slowly back and forth.

Zane decided to suggest the short walk to a nearby counter-service shop that served burgers and fries. Comfort food sounded like a brilliant idea, and he was sure Ty could use something normal. But for this moment, he sat silently and watched his partner. He could almost literally see the smoke rising above Ty's head.

"Okay, here's what we know," Ty blurted as he turned on Zane and pointed a finger at him almost accusingly. "Vartan Armen hired Del to spy on Corbin Porter. When he saw us playing the happy couple, he decided his plan had backfired, right?"

Zane blinked at the outburst and answered with a drawn-out, careful, "Yeah." Something about that idea bothered him, but he wasn't quite sure what. But Zane was somewhat surprised to discover that the idea of him and Ty described as a "happy couple" engendered both laughter and longing.

"And then we have the Italians in the mix, and if Dolce and Gabbana were legit Guardia di Finanza agents, I will eat my shoes," Ty went on with a careless wave of his hand as he turned and paced away from Zane in agitation. "So we make the logical leap that the Italians are crooked or working off the books. Agreed?" He turned back to look at Zane with raised eyebrows.

"I guess it's possible they could be Guardia di Finanza tailing Bianchi, but it's not really likely that they would be sanctioned to operate on a ship under another country's flag. So, yeah, they're not legit," Zane agreed.

"Okay," Ty said, almost to himself. He abruptly stopped pacing and crossed his arms, lowering his head and closing his eyes. He covered his eyes with one hand and stood there, motionless. "Okay," he repeated, his voice a soft, almost intimate murmur.

The low purr of Ty's voice never failed to get Zane's attention. It didn't matter when he used it: at work, at home, out shopping, while eating . . . and now, thinking more about what Armen must have seen to deem him and Ty a "happy couple," it made Zane wonder about what exactly other people saw.

"Let's say I'm Armen," Ty said, obviously not expecting Zane to comment. "And I have two business partners I want gone. Is it because the Italian authorities are onto them? Is it because I'm a greedy bastard and I want all the business proceeds to myself? If that's the case, then I'd need their information as well, since the business has been compartmentalized. So I'd be after their laptops, cell phones, anything with business records."

Once Zane figured out that Ty was mostly rambling, the majority of his thought processing returned to chew on the "happy couple" idea. Zane knew people at the office saw them as partners who didn't always get along. That was true enough. What about strangers who met them together while on the clock but not undercover?

A change in the tenor of Ty's voice interrupted his thoughts, drawing him back. "I've planted Del with Corbin in order to get what I need from him, but I don't trust him and I plan to eliminate him, too, when I'm done. Bianchi's harder because he's married, so I bribed someone in the Italian authorities to stake him out and then take him down."

Ty was talking faster, warming to his train of thought. It was slightly disturbing to see him shift so easily into Evil Mastermind, and sometimes it made Zane wonder about how differently Ty's brain must be wired. Ty made crazy, intuitive jumps that were more often than not correct. Zane was much more analytical, picking out patterns to connect the dots. So watching Ty like this was sort of awe-inspiring.

And freaky.

And sometimes hot.

Ty continued, undaunted by the lack of supporting evidence or the need to breathe. "So a year or so after planting Del, I've got all their info from him and the dirty Italians, and I suggest this cruise and a special meeting, dangle something as bait that they can't resist. Found treasure? Something from a shipwreck around one of the islands? Something they'll want to be able to get their hands on and sell. But that's irrelevant," he said with a violent wave of his hand. "I set up the meet in the market and make sure it'll go bad for Porter and Bianchi. There doesn't actually have to be anything to sell if I kill them before the end of the cruise."

The word kill diverted Zane's attention from wondering if he and Ty looked like a couple in social situations—dinner at a local restaurant, the occasional shopping trip, even working out in the gym. Ty was still talking. "Even if the planned meet fails, I know their itineraries, I have men on board the ship, and they have nowhere to run."

"But they're only trying to kill you. So far. Not me. Not Corbin," Zane pointed out.

Ty stopped short and stared at him, then narrowed his eyes. "Del may be a problem because I'm beginning to suspect he really does love Corbin," he responded. "So we get rid of him first."

"That would certainly upset Corbin," Zane said. It was upsetting him, and Zane already knew what it was like to deal with losing a loved one. He turned his gaze to lock on Ty. "Depending on how attached they are, Corbin could be seriously out of commission if he lost Del."

Ty's gaze went distant, and he shook his head slowly. "Both attempts were sloppy. Not at all a guaranteed kill. The fall from the wall would have broken bones, done a lot of damage, not to mention the fact there was no way of knowing I'd go first. And there was no way to know if I'd react to the screwy air or if it would kill me. Yeah, there's drowning, but more than likely you're looking at a case of decompression sickness or some hysteria-induced respiratory distress." He shook his head. "Maiming him is just as good as killing him as far as they're concerned. Why? How does that help them get to Corbin?"

"My mind certainly wouldn't be on business," Zane murmured, thinking of the sense of possessiveness and the need to protect that gripped him when Ty was in trouble. His mind definitely wasn't focused on the business at hand.

"No," Ty agreed. His eyes brightened suddenly, and he looked at Zane. "Unless they intend to take you by force. Armen knows Del is a hired thug but suspects his motives now. He thinks Del would protect Corbin because he loves him. But with Del out of the way, they're free to take Corbin. That must mean they need him for something, something physical."

"Something that Del couldn't steal," Zane said as he nodded. "With dirty businessmen, who knows? It could be names, account numbers, passwords. Hell, it could be a voice print or retinal scan, for all we know. So Armen would have to have Corbin in person, under his thumb." He leaned his head back against the wall. "If he thinks they're in love," he mused, "why not just take Del hostage?"

Ty's intent eyes focused on Zane for a long moment, his face unreadable. "Maybe he knows you're not in love," he posed evenly.

Zane tried to hold Ty's eyes, but he was quickly forced to look away. The intensity of the gaze made him more uncomfortable than he would have expected, because he felt something behind it. Something to do with Ty not being Del and Zane not being Corbin. Something about what would happen to either of them if the other were gone and how that made Zane's chest hurt even without throwing the word love around, which truly scared the shit out of him.

That was what bugged Zane about Ty's claim that Armen had come to a conclusion while looking at the Porters. He hadn't been looking at Del and Corbin. He'd been looking at Ty and Zane. And Ty had looked like he was in love . . .

Zane shook his head and drew a settling breath, because he was on edge now, and he wasn't quite sure how to fix it. "So Del has outlived his usefulness."

Ty thumped down heavily beside him with his shoulders slumped and a dejected feel about him. "I'm not worried about Del. He's safely in jail," he murmured. He glanced at Zane, one eyebrow raised. "But the Bianchis?"

Zane lifted one shoulder in a shrug. "He doesn't seem too hardcore. More like a European high roller who dabbles in crime on the side."

Ty sat forward and turned so he could look at Zane more closely.

"Zane," he said impatiently. "I meant what if they've outlived their usefulness too? They're mixed up with bad people, but they don't deserve to die for it."

"No, they don't." It was obvious, seeing Lorenzo and Norina together, how very much in love they were. Either that or they both deserved Oscars—or whatever the Italian equivalent was. "So you think Armen wants the entire ring," Zane posed. "And he's orchestrated this trip tomorrow to clean out his partners and meet the buyers at the same time."

"I do." Ty was silent, continuing to peer at Zane with a thoughtful frown. "Where's your head right now?" he finally asked. It wasn't the caustic tone he would usually have used when he suspected Zane's mind wasn't where he wanted it to be. It was a gentle inquiry, which in itself was odd enough to make Zane answer honestly.

"I was . . . thinking about what Armen must have seen," Zane said somewhat reluctantly, plucking at the belt of his robe.

"Seen where?" Ty asked in earnest confusion.

"Watching us."

Ty snorted. Neither his face nor his normally expressive eyes betrayed a thing before he looked away and stood up. "Well, clearly, he saw that I'm a better actor than you are," he said haughtily as he stepped away.

Zane didn't know how to interpret that response. It wasn't often that Ty stonewalled him anymore, which meant his partner was hiding something. "I thought you said you didn't think you were acting anymore."

"That was in reference to being flamingly gay," Ty answered wryly. His back was still turned to Zane. His hands were on his hips, and his head was cocked just a bit as he looked out the balcony doors.

Zane pushed himself off the couch to his feet and walked up behind Ty. He knew Ty could hear him moving, so he didn't worry about getting smacked. He also knew that Ty was deflecting like crazy. And Zane thought he might know why. He slid his arms around Ty's waist and loosely clasped his hands. "No, it wasn't."

Ty tensed ever so slightly, and he turned his head toward Zane. He seemed surprised that, for once, Zane had called him on his smoke and mirrors act. "What was it, then?" he asked evenly.

"You want me," Zane murmured, feeling remarkably secure about it. That was the reason Ty had looked so convincing to Armen. This wasn't want as in wanting to fuck explosively every half hour, although that was certainly part of it. And it wasn't quite want as in being lonely in the evenings. It was more. Zane smiled slightly as he pressed a tiny kiss to Ty's ear.

Ty snorted loudly and turned his head away, and Zane knew instinctively that Ty was rolling his eyes and probably trying not to smile. "And what is that, a crime now?" Ty asked in a low voice.

Zane chuckled. "I couldn't care less if it is." He tightened his arms, not wanting Ty to move away. "It's more than just fucking around now," he said. "Isn't it?" He made sure the tone of his voice emphasized that it wasn't really a question.

Ty was motionless in response. He didn't even seem to be breathing. The silence stretched on, edging toward tension. Finally, he let out his breath quietly and lowered his head. "No," he lied blithely, just as he'd done in a hotel in New York City over a year ago.

Zane chuckled. A classic Grady response, and definitely the one he preferred to hear. A yes just might have given him a heart attack. He held Ty close. "You owe me."

"Owe you?" Ty repeated in a rough, questioning voice as Zane felt his heartbeat begin to speed up.

"Mm-hmm. How I've wanted you," Zane breathed. "It scares the hell out of me."

"I know," Ty murmured as he turned in place and nuzzled against Zane's neck.

Zane's hands trembled as he cupped Ty's face and kissed him softly, over and over. He didn't know where he'd found the guts to say what he just did. But it had been worth it. Ty wrapped his arms around Zane and pulled him closer. Zane could feel the desire starting to build, quivering like a live wire between them, and he moaned hungrily, fingers clenching at the waistband of the worn jeans hanging on Ty's hips. He was torn between this scary tender side to their relationship that he was seeing more and more and the long-standing desire to tackle Ty to the carpet and fuck him senseless. "Ty," he breathed.

"Come on," Ty urged softly. He tugged at him and started pulling him toward the bed.

Zane's gaze focused on Ty's, which made his heart pound even harder. It was almost too much, letting himself think about what more this could mean: he wanted Ty, Ty wanted him, and . . . and to avoid thinking about it anymore, Zane took two long strides to catch Ty around the waist and claim another kiss.

Ty pushed at the robe on Zane's shoulders. The heavy material slid and caught on Zane's elbows until he straightened his arms to let it fall to the floor, leaving him nude and aroused. Ty unfastened his jeans and pushed them down. As soon as they were undressed, Ty dug his fingers into Zane's hips and shoved him toward the bed.

Zane stumbled the two steps, and his knees hit the side of the round mattress, throwing him off-balance enough that he had to catch himself with both hands to avoid a face-plant in the duvet. Ty took advantage of the precarious position by placing a hand in the center of Zane's back and pushing slightly as he stepped up behind him. His other hand glided over Zane's skin, up the side of his ribs and back down hard muscles.

Zane could feel the head of Ty's bare cock rubbing against him. He pushed back against Ty's thighs, moving his ass to rub close as he arched and practically purred under Ty's hands. Goddamn, it had been too long since he'd been fucked, and now he needed it.

Ty gasped, following the sound with a low groan and a slow thrust of his hips against Zane. "You want it like this?" he asked roughly.

"Yes!" Zane bit out.

Ty ran his hands across the skin of Zane's back again, his fingers tracing the line of the tattoo. "Stay," he ordered in a low voice before moving away to the bedside table.

Zane obeyed, mostly. He reached out and caught Ty's arm. "Just the lube," he said hoarsely. They'd already sort of talked about it. They were both tested with such regularity there was no question as to safety. And he wanted to have Ty inside him with nothing between them.

Ty looked back at him. "You sure?" he asked seriously.

Zane met his eyes and nodded. "Just you."

The sound Ty made in response was more of a growl than anything else. He whirled and began rummaging through the drawer where they had stowed their supplies. While listening to the bottle snap open, Zane pawed at the duvet and pulled it down until it crumpled in a pile against his chest. "Ty," he said urgently, leaning his weight on one hand so he could stroke himself.

"God!" Ty huffed incredulously. He moved back over in one long stride. "Be patient!" he ordered in exasperation as he reached around Zane and stilled his hand, kissing his back as he bent over him. His cock nudged at Zane as he moved.

Zane growled low in his throat but let go of himself as he shuddered under Ty's lips.

"Patience," Ty reminded as he shoved the duvet away and pressed Zane fully onto the mattress and down into the sheets.

Zane let Ty move him around, wanting nothing more right now than to be under him. To have Ty want him. To have Ty show him how much he wanted him. Zane's breaths broke as his knees spread, his cock brushing the sheets. Ty pushed him to his chest as he bit at Zane's shoulder and slid one finger into him. Breath catching, Zane stilled as his chest rubbed the soft sheets and Ty seemed to attack him from two sides at once. He gasped at the tiny bite and shifted back against Ty's finger, making a deeply needy noise. Ty murmured nonsense into his ear and then scraped his teeth over the skin of his shoulder again as he twisted the finger inside him. He pushed at him from behind, using his whole body, and forced Zane's hips to thrust down against the mattress.

Crying out sharply, Zane dug in, rutting his hips against the sheets to stimulate his hardened cock. If he had to hump the mattress in order to get Ty to fuck him, he'd gladly do it.

Ty added another slick finger impatiently and twisted them wickedly.

"Jesus! Ty!" Zane hissed as his ass clenched around Ty's long digits. Ty hummed in response and dug the fingers of his free hand into Zane's hip. He pushed against him demandingly and bent over him to bite into the tender skin under Zane's shoulder blade. Ty knew what kind of response he'd get. Zane yelled again and drove his hips back and then down against the bed. Ty pressed against him and murmured to him again, asking him if he was ready.

"Fuck, yes! Please!" Zane answered mournfully, trying to get more friction against his cock, but the angle was wrong. "Please, baby," he begged hoarsely.

Ty hastily removed his fingers, fumbled with the small bottle next to Zane's knee, and then liberally applied the lubricant to himself. His hand slid over Zane's lower back appreciatively, and the slow slide just made Zane quiver as he felt fingers stroking over the skin. He breathed Ty's name again, trying to hold as still as possible as he gripped the sheets. Ty seemed to be holding his breath as he pressed against Zane. As he felt Ty brush against him, Zane wondered if Ty had ever done this without a condom—he hadn't himself—but Ty's cock pushed into him before he could think about it more.

Ty gave a wanton groan as he rocked slowly in. Zane tried to relax as Ty pushed, but the desire gripping him made him tense up all over. He bit his lip against a gasp and tried to wiggle a little to get Ty to move.

"Stop moving or I'm just gonna come all over your ass right here," Ty growled to him as he dragged his fingers down Zane's back.

Zane hung his head and tried to take in even breaths as his body adjusted to let Ty slide in. Then he moaned aloud and pushed back his hips in encouragement.

"That's it," Ty groaned with difficulty. He reached around Zane and stroked him slowly, his hand practically trapped between Zane's body and the bed. He pushed in further, moaning again as he did so, and he laid himself out on top of Zane and flexed his hips.

Zane cried out wordlessly before burying his face against the sheets. Ty's weight on him changed the whole experience, and he couldn't think at all now. He could only react. "Please," he whispered over and over as Ty moved slowly inside him. He could feel the rock of Ty's hips against his ass, feel the push of his bare cock deeper and deeper, feel his breaths on the back of his neck. Just knowing that Ty would be literally emptying himself inside him made Zane's body tingle—he was so very aware of it.

Ty groaned, a plaintive moan as he began to rock his hips rhythmically, pulling almost all the way out and then sliding back in slowly. He gripped Zane's hip beneath him and trapped Zane under him, and he pressed his open mouth against the back of Zane's shoulder and whispered his name. Moaning constantly, Zane tensed again as the climax started to threaten, and his muscles clamped around Ty as he began to twitch, trying to shift and get just a little more stimulation on his cock.

Ty raised his hips and pulled at Zane, lifting him just enough that with each thrust Zane was pushed into his hand. "Come on, Zane," he coaxed in a low voice. "I promise I'll keep fucking you after you come."

Once he was thrusting into Ty's hand, Zane started writhing, gasping Ty's name with each push. But it had to be faster, harder, deeper. Ty knew, though, just as he always did. He picked up his own rhythm, driving into Zane harder and harder, erratically hitting his prostate, forcing Zane's cock into his slicked hand as he fucked him. Zane bit off a loud yell as he hit orgasm, his hot come stringing over Ty's fingers to drip to the sheets as he pushed back on Ty's cock over and over.

Ty called out in a hoarse voice as Zane's movements became wilder, but he managed to keep thrusting even as Zane clenched and spasmed around his cock. He slid his hand up and over Zane's hip, smearing come on his skin. He gripped him hard and began truly thrusting into him, rocking Zane's body and slapping their damp skin together.

Zane finally moaned out a long, aching wail as his body clutched around Ty. If Ty kept going, Zane was going to come again. He could feel pleasure building again deep in his gut and his balls, and he moved with the pummeling, leaning forward to press his forehead to the sheets. Ty had promised to keep fucking him, and God, was he ever.

Ty stretched out over him, slowing his hips as he whispered, "Okay?"

Drawing in a shaky breath, Zane opened dazed eyes to stare at the tangled sheets. "Don't stop," he breathed. He wanted to come again with Ty's cock deep inside him. He wanted to hear Ty. He wanted to feel Ty empty himself into him at that moment. Oh fucking hell, he wanted it, to feel Ty so fucking close . . .

Ty lowered his head and pressed his forehead against Zane's back, whimpering and then growling plaintively as he complied. He pushed back up, gripping one of Zane's hips and his shoulder to use as leverage. He gasped with the pounding thrusts, and Zane groaned between harsh breaths as he reveled in the way Ty was using his body. He was half-hard again, pleasure radiating from his groin with every move. He reached under himself to palm himself again, reaching far between his legs to massage Ty as well.

Ty simply moaned in response and clutched at Zane hard as he finally found his release. He panted against Zane's skin as his hips continued to rock, his body jerking with the stimulation. Zane gripped himself as Ty came and pumped hard to a smaller but sharper climax, his body tensing around Ty's pulsing cock.

After an eternity of almost painful pleasure, Ty stilled and pressed his forehead against Zane's back, breathing harshly. Then he pulled out quickly, maybe enjoying the fact that he didn't have to worry about a condom. Zane shuddered as he felt a hot trail of come slide along the inside of his thigh, and it was on the tip of his tongue to tell Ty to do it all over again.

Once Ty shifted back, Zane's arms finally gave out, and he sank to his belly, his knees spread wide, before he curled to his side, still flinching as shocks of sensation coursed through him. He watched through barely open eyes as Ty crawled up onto the bed like a man who'd just run a marathon and collapsed beside him.

Ty scooted closer and slid his knee between Zane's legs, pulling himself over and nuzzling against Zane's cheek before kissing him. "You okay?" he asked again softly.

Zane slid his arm over Ty's waist to help them remain close. "Yeah," he whispered, giving in to the urge to shift his hips and feel more of Ty's come sliding between his cheeks and thighs. "You?"

"Maybe," Ty murmured in answer. "We'll see in the morning," he added with a small smile.

Zane was solemn, though. "You gonna wake up in the morning and think better of this?"

Ty kissed him again languidly, sliding his cleaner hand into Zane's hair and breathing in deeply through his nose so he could kiss Zane harder and longer. "No," he assured him once he finally pulled away.

Zane rolled to his back long enough to free his other arm so he could wrap both around Ty possessively. "Okay," he whispered as he managed a breath. He moved just enough to press their foreheads together. "Never saw this kind of thing coming."

"Damn," Ty responded wryly. "Then I could have said it was all your fault."

Zane jabbed at Ty's ribs. Ty oomphed and jerked, snickering.

"You know what I mean," Zane muttered.

Ty quieted and nudged himself closer. "Maybe," he admitted slyly.

Narrowing his eyes, Zane pulled his head back to look at his partner. "Maybe?"

Ty's entire body shivered with a pleasurable ripple as the cool air began to touch him. "You know you wanted me," he teased gently, a smirk in his voice.

Zane snorted quietly. "Certainly wasn't your pleasant disposition that caught my attention," he muttered as he lightly kissed Ty's jaw.

"Sure it was," Ty huffed. "It's my best feature."

"Your ass is your best feature," Zane corrected. Ty gave another insulted huff and began to roll away from him. Zane laughed and flexed his arms, not letting him move. "What? You want me to say something else? Something poetic? Like your flashing eyes? Or your full, pouty lips?"

"My sparkling personality," Ty provided cheekily.

"Your insatiable sex drive," Zane drawled, splaying his hands on Ty's back to anchor him in place as he tangled his lower legs with Ty's.

"That's partly your fault," Ty accused.

Zane grinned. "I'll take the blame," he said. "If you tell me my best feature."

"That's easy," Ty answered. "Your partner," he said cheekily, managing to maintain a straight face.

Zane's smile softened, and slowly he nodded. "I'd say you're right."

"Oh, don't do that," Ty groaned with a little jab to Zane's ribs. "Joke," he murmured. "It was a joke."

Zane just chuckled and shook his head slightly, stealing a kiss just like Ty's. "No joke," he disagreed, though still smiling. "I am no kind of prize."

"Tell me about it," Ty groaned.

Zane laughed and buried his face in the juncture of Ty's neck and shoulder, inhaling deeply.

Ty hummed quietly and rolled onto his back, taking Zane with him. "We should think about getting cleaned up," he muttered. "You made a mess."

"I made a mess?" Zane asked pointedly.

Ty growled deep in his chest as he pulled Zane closer, preventing Zane from fondling him like he was about to. "I enjoyed it," he said with a leer.

Zane turned his head to nip at Ty's neck. "Shower, then?"

"Mm-hmm," Ty responded, though he seemed to have no plan for moving.

"Sounds promising," Zane mumbled, smiling against Ty's collarbone.

"If we stay here all sticky, I may have to fuck you again," Ty warned.

"Oh, the agony," Zane drawled, pulling Ty closer to kiss him soundly.

Ty rolled him suddenly, putting himself on top of Zane with clearly every intention of continuing on in the same vein. But they were closer to the precarious edge of the round mattress than either of them realized, and when Ty put all his weight into Zane, both went tumbling off the edge of the round bed in an ungraceful heap of limbs, curses, and peals of laughter.

CHAPTER ELEVEN

T here were twenty high rollers on board the Queen of the Mediterranean, give or take, and Zane had played poker with them all.

Most of them were above average players. They wouldn't be in the private room of this exclusive pay-to-play lounge if they weren't. A few were excellent players, whether by virtue of skill, intuition, or the ephemeral Lady Luck, it didn't matter. And then there were the experts.

Zane hadn't yet decided if he'd count himself one of those, simply because Vartan Armen and Lorenzo Bianchi weren't, so Zane hadn't pushed himself against the pros he knew well enough to be wary of.

Two of those Zane considered experts sat at the table now with him, Bianchi, and Armen, making a flexible table of five. Luckily, he was here to relax and schmooze, not to win. Considering what a roller coaster his day had been so far, he could use an uneventful night at the table. Zane shifted slightly, trying to ease the mild discomfort from his rather active afternoon. Thinking about leaving Ty all warm and soft and sated in their bed made Zane smile.

"Are you enjoying your evening, Mr. Porter?" Bianchi asked.

"Definitely, Signor Bianchi, definitely," Zane drawled as the dealer approached the table with several new packs of cards.

Seeing the ship's crew actually involved in the high-stakes gambling operation surprised Zane the first night. But it turned out the dealers were paid above and beyond their normal salary to work on their off hours for the players funding their own games in this private lounge. The ship kindly donated use of cards and chips of much higher denominations than any "normal" passenger would see in the game room proper.

Money really could buy more money.

Here in the private game, it was player's choice as they went around the table. They played the old classics five-card draw and seven-card stud, the popular stars Texas Hold'em and Omaha Hi Lo, and occasionally variations like Crazy Pineapple and Follow the Bitch.

Crunching the numbers and figuring the percentages was in a way soothing for Zane. It was easy, it wasn't life-threatening, and he didn't even have to stress about the money. Granted, it was rather appalling to play $5,000 antes or $6,000 big blinds, but after a while the amount of money didn't mean anything anymore.

It all came down to the chips.

Zane looked lazily around the table, cataloging what he knew about his opponents. Expert Numero Uno played aggressively and liked to bet big and bet often, but he bowed out early if he didn't have the cards. He preferred seven-card stud. The lobes of his ears flushed red when he got excited. Expert Numero Dos played evenly, always stayed in to see the bulk of the cards, and ran a decent bluff. She liked Texas Hold'em. But she had a bad habit of tapping one of her manicured fingernails on something when she had good cards. Armen was stoned-faced—big surprise—but just as stuck-up a card player as Zane figured him a businessman. He always chose five-card stud to force the other players to ante. Armen didn't stay in long or risk much unless percentages were on his side. And Bianchi, he was as amenable a poker player as he was a person, laughing and smiling and talking, which was nearly as impossible to see through as Zane's own emotionless mask. Bianchi enjoyed the poker variations, something different every time. But, as Ty had pointed out, he rubbed his cuff links when he was on to something.

Ty's observation had really made Zane pause and think about what he was doing. Drinking aside, he knew he could outplay anyone here, if he put his mind to it. He knew the numbers, he was patient, and he literally had nothing to lose.

For the first hour and a half or so, Zane played conservatively, stuck to Evian over ice with a lemon twist, and kept an eye on the other players, confirming tells and, even more importantly, confirming mood. Even the best player was more likely to betray himself if he was excited or upset or angry rather than content with the world. The cards didn't matter, because a player brought mood with him to the table.

Zane also used the time to begin establishing a fake tell. It was a risk, but one that had paid off in the past, and it didn't hurt anything to use it as long as he stayed consistent. Being the slick, confident Corbin Porter, Zane was sure the man would have a tell. He had too much of an ego not to. Zane chose something subtle: a brief caress for cards he was happy with. Otherwise his hands stayed on the table in clear view.

Then Zane got serious.

Fold if you don't have a pair or better by the third card in five-card stud. In seven-card stud, more hands are won by the highest two pair— or even single pair—than by straights, flushes, or bigger displays. Five-card draw is all about percentages and aces. Play to scoop the pot in Omaha Hi Lo; getting half barely keeps you in the game. Play strong, high hands very aggressively in Texas Hold'em or go ahead and fold 'em. It's all about the numbers.

It's all about the chips.

And Zane started raking them in.

Numero Uno got frustrated early by watching his chip stacks dwindle and let his emotions get the better of him. Zane put him out with a jack-high straight after a round of Texas Hold'em, and the man left. Bianchi started folding out more than he stayed in, content to drink his whiskey and play commentator after losing the bulk of his chips to Numero Dos's nines over sevens in a particularly brutal round of seven-card stud.

Zane's chip stacks grew. Numero Dos held her own until Armen duped her out of a couple hundred thousand dollars in chips by— in Zane's opinion—bluffing her into folding. So that left Armen and Zane with the bulk of the chips between them, and it was Zane's turn to choose the game. Just what he had been waiting for. The prodigious chip stacks meant Armen would be more willing to play, if Zane's profile of him was correct. What Zane didn't know about the hard-to-read Mr. Armen was if the man would be goaded into action.

"Five-card draw. For it all."

Armen raised one brow as Numero Dos let out a harsh breath and fanned herself while Bianchi started counting chip stacks. "Do you know how much money is on the table, Mr. Porter?" Bianchi asked, no small amount of warning in his voice.

"I am aware," Zane said easily, his eyes still locked on Armen's.

"What you propose takes no skill, Mr. Porter, only dumb luck," Armen observed.

"Oh, I'm feeling lucky tonight, Mr. Armen," Zane assured him, despite the spike of annoyance the implication caused. Armen was stalling, and Zane could see the wrinkles forming at the corners of the man's eyes. Then Zane deliberately smirked, throwing Armen an all-out dare.

Armen sniffed. "Very well."

They both pushed their chips into the center of the table, and then Zane sat back with his glass of Evian and nodded to the dealer.

"Will a fold be a redeal, gentlemen?" the dealer asked.

Zane looked to Armen with one of Corbin's full-of-it smiles.

"No redeal," Armen said shortly.

"Just short of a $500,000 pot," the dealer announced without a blink, and he shuffled the deck expertly before beginning to deal. It really wasn't fair, Zane reflected as he picked up his cards. Armen didn't know that Zane had no stake in the money.

The numbers whizzed through his mind as the action went down.

Odds are one in two to receive one pair or higher.

He watched Armen riffle his cards before glancing at his own. Zane didn't bother to sort them.

Odds on being dealt a pair of jacks or higher are one in five.

There was no bidding to be done. Armen had first draw and took two new cards.

The odds against making three of a kind when drawing two cards to a pair and a kicker are twelve to one.

Zane dropped three cards face down for the dealer to replace, picked up the new ones, gave them a look, then set the small stack on the table face down. He focused the entire weight of his attention on Armen.

When drawing three cards to one pair, the odds against making a full house are ninety-seven to one.

Over the chips, Armen watched him closely for any sign, any hint that would help. He broke eye contact to briefly glance at Zane's cards, and his lips compressed hard in a subtle display of pique.

Abruptly Armen stood, gave Zane a death glare, dropped his cards face down on the table, straightened his tie, and walked away.

Zane watched him go, inwardly amazed, and then he realized what Armen had seen: he was stroking his cards ever so slightly with his thumb.

Numero Dos leaned to flip over Armen's cards: three tens with an ace kicker. Nice.

Zane just smiled at her innocently and laid his palm down over his lonely pair of queens.

After trading several trays of chips in for credit on his account, Zane left the casino and game room, admittedly flying a little high. It wasn't every day a man won $500,000 on a sort-of-unintentional poker bluff. Bianchi had tried to entice him into a congratulatory round of that very fine whiskey, and though Zane had been supremely tempted, he had made his excuses, claiming an all-too-true desire to return to his lover for a not-so-small celebration of their own.

Still, after Bianchi's offer, the cravings kicked in, and Zane decided to wander the promenade and window shop a little on his way back to the stateroom.

He passed by the kitschy yet pricey tourist shops and lingered at the leather store, not that he needed another jacket. Zane wouldn't part with his, rips and tears and all. He'd kept it since Ty tossed it at him in New York City during the serial murder case that had almost killed them both.

As he moved on, a small newsstand with a stock of books caught his attention, but Zane resisted the lure of the paperbacks with a sigh, although he did look at a crossword puzzle book and think of getting it for Ty, just to laugh over. He turned a corner on his way to the stairs and was halfway past the big-ticket jewelry store when a dull shine caught Zane's eye. He stopped and idly glanced over the various jewelry cases, and his eyes settled on one understated display.

The details of the piece came into focus as he neared the case, and one of the ubiquitous crew members was there to pull it out and present it without him even asking.

An elegant, polished silver slide pendant hung on a cord of tightly wound black leather, set off by the gray velvet of the display stand. The hand-tooled pendant was roughly the size and shape of a nickel, and the inset boasted a two-tone compass rose. Each of the eight points terminated in a tiny diamond chip set into the round seal.

It was bought, paid for, and wrapped up before Zane gave a thought to what he was doing. If he were feeling particularly romantic, he might have admitted he sometimes thought of Ty as his compass. But those words weren't passing his lips. Not today, anyway. Not until he knew why he thought that. Not until it stopped scaring him.

After experiencing a moment of panic over the impulse rather than the actual purchase, Zane decided on qualifying it as a Christmas present. He could get his partner—his lover—a nice Christmas present, right? It might not be Ty's style, but Zane didn't care. After settling on that, all he saw as he walked back to the stateroom with the small package in his pocket was the compass rose nestled against the hollow of Ty's throat.

Ty hadn't realized he'd fallen asleep until he heard the door click. He jerked awake and reached to the side of the bed, where normally a gun would have been nestled between the mattress and box springs.

Instead, he found the rounded edge of the circular bed he would never grow accustomed to, and he went toppling over the side to the floor.

Zane's "Corbin" voice came floating into the cabin. "Honey, I'm home."

"Christ," Ty muttered as he pushed himself up and peered over the edge of the bed to look at Zane.

Zane sauntered—and there was no other word for it but sauntered—across the room, one hand in his pants pocket, his suit jacket casually unbuttoned. "And how was your afternoon, doll?" he asked with a wink.

"I was enjoying a nap, I think," Ty muttered as he climbed to his feet. "God, you're smug. What have you done?"

Zane grinned. "I had a good day at the tables."

"Oh yeah?" Ty asked, cutting off the words with a yawn as he stretched his arms high above his head.

"Oh yeah," Zane drew out. He moved to stand in front of Ty. "Tell me, baby. What would you do with $500,000?"

Ty raised one eyebrow. "I'd . . . probably put it into savings with all the other money I never spend. Why?"

"There isn't anything you want to splurge on?" Zane asked as he sat down on the edge of the bed. "Maybe if we spend some of it now, the Bureau won't find out about it." That smile was still in place, and he was clearly holding back laughter.

Ty blinked rapidly at him, shocked by his words. Zane had brought him a $10,000 poker chip a couple of nights ago, just to watch Ty goggle. But this? "Are you saying you actually won half a million dollars?" he asked incredulously. Zane nodded and shrugged one shoulder. Ty sat down hard beside him. "Are you shitting me?" he asked with a laugh. "Jesus, Zane. Let's go to Vegas when this is over."

Zane laughed aloud. "Told you I was good at poker." He shook his head and stood again, starting to pull off his jacket. "I'll warn you, though. Armen's going to be cranky for a while."

Ty groaned and flopped to his back. "He's probably going to order Del to kill you now. I hope you bought yourself something nice."

"I've got your back," Zane said as he advanced on the bed and knelt on the mattress, one knee on each side of Ty's thighs, and he leaned over him. "And your front," he drawled. "C'mon, doll. It wouldn't be right if we didn't go out and celebrate tonight."

Ty snorted and shook his head as he looked up into Zane's eyes. "Or," he said slowly, "we could stay in and celebrate. Spend your ill-gotten gains on room service, not have to worry about being killed, and I could drop the accent for the night."

Zane's gaze turned hungry and intense as he focused on Ty. Ty loved that look in his eyes. "I could be easily swayed to that idea."

Ty bit his lip and raised his chin just slightly, shifting his shoulders in invitation. He and Zane both knew he didn't have to actually say anything to sway Zane. And Zane didn't disappoint; he leaned down to kiss Ty rather sweetly. "It's not very often I could say, 'You can have anything you want, baby,'" Zane practically purred. "But now is one of those times."

Ty smiled serenely, trying to keep the hint of melancholy out of it. He knew Zane meant what he said. The Bureau had no way of knowing he'd just won all that money. They could go out and blow it all, and no one would be the wiser. But Ty had never been a very materialistic man.

"Only thing I want is you," he whispered.

After the scuba diving scare the day before, they agreed to skip the WaveRunner rides and snorkeling in favor of trying to figure out how to break something—anything—in this seriously fucked-up case. Ty had known going in that they wouldn't see much action. They were on the periphery of a larger investigation; they knew that. But he and Zane weren't likely candidates to sit around and do nothing for long.

There was a meal tonight with everyone in attendance. But while they were sure to learn about the coming "meeting" that was planned at that dinner, Ty preferred to be a step ahead. It was driving him crazy that they couldn't even take baby steps. So he was scouring the books Del Porter had used to make notes, trying to glean anything of use from them.

So far he'd been unsuccessful.

He had proposed a search of Armen's suite, but Zane had vetoed the idea. Ty was still of the opinion that they would find the information they were after in Armen's stateroom, but he couldn't make the search alone. Zane wasn't in the mood to hear him out, and probably for good reason, considering the very real possibility that Armen was trying to kill one or both of them. And Ty would find no help from their support team. He and Zane had tried yet again to hunt down one of the FBI team members, to no avail. Some support team. When Ty ran into any of those yahoos, he was going to give them an earful. Earful of pencil tip, preferably.

He couldn't make heads or tails of the gibberish written in the books, and trying was starting to give him a headache. Finally, he tossed the book onto the table and leaned his elbows on his knees, rubbing his temples with his fingertips. When that didn't help, he took one hand and searched for the pressure point between his thumb and forefinger, squeezing hard. Warm hands settled on his shoulders and began to knead at the base of his skull, working at the stiff, sore muscles in his neck. Ty groaned softly, continuing to squeeze at the pressure point until that and the fingers at his neck began to force the headache back.

"Thanks," he murmured.

"You're stressing," Zane said. "More than usual. Not that it's unwarranted."

Ty sighed heavily. He put his hand near his head, searching for an analogy that Zane could identify with. "I'm just . . . getting too much input," he tried in a frustrated voice.

"Too many details, not enough context," Zane said.

"Yes," Ty said in relief. He leaned more into Zane's hands. "Normally I'd be profiling the criminal, but we don't even have a real crime. We can't look too close at the rock wall or scuba incidents or we blow our cover. And without any concrete information, anything we can glean from all this is just . . . educated guesses."

"Not even all that educated, for all we're in the dark and cut off from resources." Zane continued to massage the knots in Ty's neck, and his fingers were warm, catching on Ty's skin. Ty craned his neck to look up at him, resting the top of his head against Zane's belly.

Zane stopped the rubbing and looked down to meet Ty's eyes. "Too hard?" He gently pressed his fingers against one of the recalcitrant knots.

"I'm not as sore as I was," Ty murmured. "It just feels good. Are you still opposed to searching Armen's suite?"

Zane kept up the petting, the fingers applying more pressure. "I think the chance of finding something useful is less than the chance of getting hurt," he murmured. It wasn't really an answer to the question. But it wasn't the flat no he'd given Ty earlier.

Ty raised one eyebrow in the mischievous smirk that Zane was probably all too familiar with. It probably looked odd upside down. "That's a solid maybe."

"There are a hell of a lot of questions we don't have answers for to try a search like that. We don't even know if we can get into the room without the key card. Do you plan to pick Armen's pocket?"

"I'm actually quite good at that," Ty told him frankly. He moved, sliding away from Zane's hands regretfully. He stood and turned to face Zane, and he winced as he said, "I kind of had a different idea."

Zane's brow furrowed. "What?"

"Well . . ." Ty glanced to the balcony and clucked his tongue. "Let me show you." He waved for Zane to follow him. He stepped out onto the balcony and pointed at the thick partition that divided the balconies from their neighbors. "Armen's suite is right next to ours, right?"

"That's the suite we see him going in and out of, anyway," Zane allowed as he moved to look at the balconies.

"And the one he told us he was in. So I figure maybe I can just . . . swing over onto his balcony."

Zane glanced over the edge of the railing and looked away with a roll of his eyes and a grimace. The ocean was quite a distance below. The fall would likely be . . . painful.

"Okay," Zane hedged. "Getting in isn't much of a challenge. But getting Armen out might be. As far as I can tell, he goes to dinner and poker games, and that's it."

Ty shrugged. "So go to a poker game. Make sure I have at least thirty minutes to get in and get out."

"There's not another scheduled tournament until the end of the cruise," Zane said. "He's made it clear he's not interested in socializing." He huffed and walked back into the cabin, hands on his hips.

"So . . . ask him to meet you to talk business. Hell, maybe you'll learn something."

Zane didn't look too happy, but he didn't stomp on the idea. "I still think it's a bad idea. We don't know who else could be in there, and they've tried to kill you twice already."

"Okay," Ty agreed with a thoughtful nod. He glanced at the partition and stepped back into the suite, closing the door behind him. "So we wait until dinner. Every time I've seen him at dinner, he has his bodyguards with him. I doubt they leave a man behind alone.

Armen doesn't seem the type to trust anyone that much. I'll leave dinner early for some reason, and you make sure he stays there for at least half an hour."

Zane nodded, and when he spoke, his voice was reluctant. "All right. I guess that's about as good a setup as we're going to get."

Ty gave him a pleased smile. "Thank you."

"I won't be able to back you up if I'm playing nice with Armen at the table," Zane pointed out.

"I can handle it," Ty assured him. He stepped closer and clapped him on the shoulder. "I got along pretty well before you came along, remember?"

"I'm thinking about a few days ago," Zane murmured.

Dolce and Gabbana. Ty cocked his head and smiled warmly. He stepped closer and pulled Zane near to him by his belt loops, then pressed his nose and lips to Zane's cheek. Zane sighed quietly and slid his arms around Ty's waist as he turned his face to catch a kiss on his lips instead.

"You look good today, Zane," Ty commented in a low voice, smiling. "You look like bait."

"Excuse me?" Zane's voice rose at the end, and he leaned back to look at him.

Ty just looked at him, a small smile curling his lips.

"What are you planning now?" Zane asked, looking at Ty through narrowed eyes. "And what do you mean I look good today?" he tacked on.

Ty laughed lightly and kissed Zane again, just because he could. Then he stepped away. "We need to try again to find our backup before dinner," he told Zane as he turned away. "That should frustrate us both."

The crystal lowball glasses held the finest in Scotch whiskey. Distilled on the Isle of Skye eighteen years ago, with additional spices introduced to produce a distinctive flavor that was often described as fiery, the liquor had a dark color and singular nose, not to be mistaken for any other whiskey.

The bartender set the glasses on a tray atop two navy blue napkins to match the ship's flags. The other drinks intended for the table stood on green and gold napkins to match, and he signaled to the waitress that the tray was ready.

The bartender moved on to the next order. A man seated at the bar turned to look at the drinks, then carefully peered over his shoulder to check the waitress's progress. She was nowhere near, and he furtively moved to open the hidden packet he slid out of his sleeve and hastily dribbled the contents into each of the lowball glasses.

The poison had no smell and very little taste. The salty Talisker the extravagant Italian had ordered for the two gay men would mask it nicely.

He took out another packet, preparing to seed the drinks of the Italians next, but movement caught his eye, and he was forced to move away as the waitress made her way toward the bar.

She lifted the tray of drinks expertly into the air, whisking it above the heads of the other diners toward the round table near the corner of the dining room. A somewhat sedate round of thanks greeted her arrival with the libations.

She placed the blue napkins and their glasses in front of their intended recipients, the dark whiskey concealing the deadly contents.

They sat at the elegant table near the dance floor, Ty with one hand on the white linen in front of him and the other in Zane's lap, his fingers laced among Zane's. Zane hoped that holding onto each other would give them some measure of composure from which to draw patience. They had looked yet again for any of the other team members, even pretending to stumble into some service areas, and finding no one had just added to their frustration. Either they were doing a better job of being discreet than Ty had given them credit for, or something had gone wrong.

Even a team relegated to invisible emergency backup had to be more available than this.

Zane had called an abrupt halt to the search so they could get ready for dinner, and they had arrived just after Lorenzo and Norina

Bianchi. Now they were making small talk over the live band playing old, romantic torch songs, waiting for Vartan Armen and the show Zane was sure to come. Finally, after eight days, a real lead to the smuggling ring's business would have to present itself. As undercover operations went, eight days was nothing. It was the environs and the whole "married couple" situation with Ty that made it so surreal.

Norina leaned slightly toward Ty after the waitress set a champagne flute on a green napkin in front of her. "Are you enjoying the cruise, Del? Can you believe it is already halfway over?" she asked in a pleasant tone. Her husband looked on tolerantly from her other side.

Ty smiled at her and nodded, leaning back a bit to make room for the server. "It's been quite pleasant," he answered stiffly. He couldn't seem to muster the energy to be effusive with her anymore. He had done an admirable job before tonight, though. He'd lasted longer than Zane would have predicted.

"Oh, my poor Del," Norina said sympathetically as she patted his cheek with her hand. "You have had a stressful time, no? It is settled, then. Tomorrow while they play with their toys, perhaps you and I, we will have fun somewhere else? Perhaps some time with the masseuse?"

"Del enjoys anything that makes him more beautiful," Zane drawled as he listened in.

Ty looked sideways at Zane, giving him a brief, hateful look. But he chose to ignore the comment and looked back at Norina with a weak smile. "As long as the fun doesn't involve climbing," he said to her.

She laughed lightly. "My fun has nothing to do with climbing."

"I'm sure you'll have a great time," Zane said, trying to keep the atmosphere pleasant. "I'll be happy knowing Del is entertained while I'm working."

"If they have money to spend, they will be happy," Bianchi predicted as he leaned sideways in his chair.

Norina lightly slapped his hand. "It will keep my lonely thoughts from you."

Ty sniffed at them both, obviously insulted but holding his tongue as Armen strolled up to the table.

"Apologies for my tardiness," the man murmured as he pulled out the seat next to Zane and sat down. He didn't offer an excuse.

Zane smiled politely. "Not at all. We were just passing the time."

"I ordered drinks for us all, Signor Armen," Bianchi declared.

"Very well," Armen murmured as he glanced toward the bar.

"I think I would like the seafood tonight, Lorenzo," Norina said as she perused the menu.

"After fish the last three meals, I am not surprised, my gioia. Order whatever you like," Bianchi said.

Ty looked down and rubbed at his forehead uncomfortably. Zane knew he wished the two Italians would ease up on the lovey-dovey stuff a little. It was getting on his nerves, so Zane knew it had to be aggravating Ty, who reached for his glass of Scotch. Apparently he was figuring he might as well make the best of it if the criminals were footing the bill.

Watching as Ty picked up the heavy crystal lowball glass and raised it to his lips, Zane could almost feel the spicy liquid burning its way to the back of his throat, and the thought was enough to raise the hairs on his arms even before Ty took a swallow.

He'd be able to taste it on Ty's tongue.

"I see Del is anxious for a toast, no?" Bianchi said with a hearty laugh.

Ty cleared his throat before ever taking a sip, and he put the glass down with an apologetic smile.

"We're just pleased to be here," Zane said. He glanced to his own glass and decided he wasn't even going to pick it up. He'd toast with the water glass, bad luck and cover identity be damned.

"Then let us toast to pleasure," Bianchi started, raising his glass. Armen and Ty both held their glasses out, and Zane reached for his water glass. Norina delicately touched her champagne glass to her husband's, and Zane couldn't help but watch as Ty put his glass to his lips again.

Ty had been right: putting two of the things Zane was addicted to together like this was sort of cruel.

The band struck the opening chord on a new song, and Norina clapped and bounced excitedly as she grabbed at Ty's arm. The whiskey in his glass sloshed, and he pulled it away from his face before it could spill across his lap.

"A tango! Del, you must dance with me! Please, tesoro, let us dance while you do your boring things," Norina said as she turned to her husband.

"Ah, the whims of a woman," Bianchi said fondly. "If you must."

Norina turned to Ty, one graceful hand outstretched. "You promised me a tango while at sea."

Ty stared at her, eyes slightly wide. "I did?" he asked, obviously caught off guard. "I did," he repeated more confidently, trying to cover his initial reaction as he took her hand gingerly. He glanced at Zane as if seeking rescue.

Zane raised both brows and shrugged, though he felt a wash of anxiety. He had no idea if Ty knew how to tango. On a dance floor, anyway. It wasn't exactly the type of thing one learned in a bar. "Go ahead, doll. I'm sure there will be more songs for us to dance to this evening."

Ty gave him the most evil glare Zane thought he had ever seen, but he stood and held Norina's hand as she rose. The others stood as she did, and Ty escorted her away from the table like a perfect gentleman, leading her out onto the open dance floor in the middle of the dining room.

"Ah, our loved ones are such delights, are they not?" Bianchi said as he swirled the liquor in his glass.

"Delights. Right," Zane murmured as he kept his eyes on the couple. There weren't many brave enough to dance the tango, which made Ty and Norina all the more conspicuous. Zane would bet his recent windfall that Ty wouldn't have walked out there without at least some idea of how to tango, but he was still worried. There was nowhere for Ty to hide.

The melody restarted.

When they started dancing, it was a slow, almost tentative start. More stop and go than a smooth flow of steps. But Zane knew that was how most tangos started. They didn't miss any steps, and Norina was smiling as they turned in a half-circle. Then the music picked up, becoming more robust, and Ty whirled Norina around in time with the music and dipped her grandly as she laughed. That was when they truly began dancing.

Zane almost broke cover and showed his surprise as he watched. Ty could tango. And pretty damn well. Surprise, surprise.

The diners at the tables nearest the dance floor were watching the four couples dancing. All of them were quite good, but Ty and Norina were the only ones who were truly fun to watch. Two attractive people with shining personalities who knew what they were doing and enjoyed doing it—they were hard not to watch.

"Ah, he makes my gioia smile," Bianchi remarked, his voice full of pride. "She is so beautiful," he added, almost to himself. A man truly in love.

That thought shakily in mind, Zane spoke. "They both are," he agreed with no doubt at all.

"What about you, Mr. Armen? Why did you not bring someone with you? Perhaps someone as stunning as my Norina . . . or as handsome as Mr. Porter?" Bianchi asked.

"Beautiful people are in general a distraction," Armen said stiffly. "And more trouble than they are worth." He made no effort to qualify the statement or excuse their spouses from the broad generalization. He glanced out at them, now dancing a more vigorous version of the tango as each grew familiar with how the other moved.

If Lorenzo Bianchi had known the fake Del Porter on the dance floor was actually bisexual and had the reputation Ty did at home, there was no way he'd sit passively by while his wife danced with him like that. Zane found himself swallowing on no small amount of jealousy as well, especially upon seeing the real enjoyment on Ty's face. Ty and Norina grinned widely at each other as they moved in graceful box steps and the occasional twirl or dip.

"A distraction, perhaps," Zane started before forcing himself to turn back to the table. "But also motivation to conduct a successful business."

"Leave it to the American to skip the small talk and move right on to the business," Bianchi remarked bemusedly. He picked up his glass, holding it up to Zane. "I salute your ability to ignore beautiful things in favor of business."

Zane nodded once and leveled an expectant look at Armen. "While they're otherwise occupied, no time like the present."

"To business, then," Armen murmured as he raised his own glass. He and Bianchi touched their glasses together.

After a moment's hesitation under Bianchi's expectant eye, Zane went against his earlier decision and lifted the lowball glass in front of him from the dark blue napkin. "To successful business."

The music hit a crescendo, and there was a smattering of applause from the people watching as one or two of the couples attempted some difficult dips or spins. A glance back saw Norina almost parallel to the ground, one dainty hand trailing the shining wood surface as the other gripped Ty's elbow. Her feet were between Ty's legs, sliding easily as Ty pulled her up and into an impressive spinning turn that required some fancy footwork on both their parts.

Zane's curiosity was in overdrive: Where the hell had Ty learned to dance like that? They would be having a talk about this. Zane lifted the glass halfway to his lips but stopped as he continued to watch, wanting . . . no, aching to be . . . After a long moment's feeling, he shook his head and turned back to the table, letting the lowball glass thump gently to the table as the music faded back into the slow strand of the last vestiges of the tango. He sure did have his occasional flights of fantasy, Zane reflected with no small amount of regret. Dancing a tango with Ty definitely qualified.

"I have arranged for a meeting tomorrow, during the shore excursions," Armen told them as the music finally ended. He spoke quickly, as if to get it out of the way before the other two returned to the table. "We are to be taken to the objects, allowed to examine them, and then we will negotiate a price for any we deem worthy."

He had just finished with this curt explanation when Ty and Norina came gliding back to the table.

"Oh, how wonderful!" Norina was exclaiming, hanging onto Ty's arm and practically dragging him. "I have not danced in such a fashion in too long! We must do it again!"

Zane stood once again with the other men, observing the formalities, and waited for Ty to seat Norina and rejoin him. "Did you enjoy yourself, doll?" he asked, a little more seriously than he'd actually planned.

Ty's face was flushed, though whether from the exertion or from embarrassment Zane couldn't be sure. "Yes," Ty answered curtly. The tone was enough to let Zane know he was blushing and not merely overheated.

Zane slid his arm around Ty's waist and pulled him in close for a moment. "You looked incredible," he said honestly. It was good luck that it was in character.

Ty shivered violently. He turned his head and exposed his neck to Zane's lips as he spoke. "Shut up," he whispered, flustered yet slightly amused. Zane chuckled and decided to let up. Otherwise he'd pay for it later. So he pulled Ty's chair out for him instead, but his hands still itched to touch.

"Well done, my lovelies," Bianchi said as Ty seated himself and Norina beamed at her husband. "Del, I thank you for sparing my poor feet."

"My pleasure," Ty responded with a weak attempt at a smile. Norina turned her charming smile on Ty and began speaking rapidly in Italian to him, obviously too excited to remain in English.

Ty was merely nodding in apparent agreement to whatever she said as he reached for his whiskey. But Zane didn't want to wait, and he knew getting Ty out on the dance floor wasn't really a viable option. So he caught Ty's hand and lifted it to his lips for a soft kiss along Ty's knuckles. He leaned very close, brushing his lips against Ty's cheekbone as he whispered. "How about another blush so they don't suspect I'm telling you about the meet."

Ty glanced down slightly and then turned just enough that his breath was warm against Zane's cheek. He put his drink back down, so distracted that he almost missed the blue napkin. "Is it soon?" he asked softly.

"Tomorrow," Zane breathed. "On shore." He leaned a little closer, draping his arm over the back of Ty's chair. "Maybe you can go shopping," he murmured.

Ty made a strangled noise in the back of his throat before pulling back and looking away from Zane with a sharp shake of his head. He followed it by stamping hard on Zane's foot. Zane stifled a pained gasp and a grimace. Bastard. Ty wanted to be in the market when the deal went down, didn't he? Zane jabbed Ty in the ribs with two fingers and kicked his shin in return while starting to settle back in his chair.

Ty jerked and sat forward too hard, jostling the table and the glass he'd again been reaching for. The hundreds of dollars' worth of Scotch in his glass splattered everywhere, soaking the linen tablecloth and the majority of it flowing over the edge onto Ty's chest and lap.

He stood quickly with a curse under his breath. Norina exclaimed loudly and reached with her napkin to help him. Zane sat back quickly, managing to avoid all but a small splatter across one pants leg, and he had to stifle a laugh. He hadn't expected Ty to react so violently, but maybe he was in a worse mood than Zane suspected.

Ty convinced Norina not to help him dry off, instead taking her napkin with thanks and then turning narrowed eyes on Zane, as if it had been his fault. "Excuse me, won't you?" he said to the rest of the table through gritted teeth. "Order me fish, darling. I'll be back," he snapped at Zane as he turned and made his way out of the dining room quickly.

Only after he was out of sight did Zane realize Ty had probably taken advantage of the heavy tuxedo to hide a weapon on himself for the first time all week. He couldn't take the jacket off—they'd see his gun.

Ty wouldn't let this go without payback, and Zane resigned himself to his fate with a small smirk. It had been worth it.

CHAPTER TWELVE

Ty didn't bother changing once he got to their cabin. He did take off his coat and toss it on the couch as he moved past it. After a moment's thought, he also regretfully pulled their one gun out of his waistband and set it down on a side table. He didn't have a holster to carry it safely, and if he had the bad luck to get caught in Armen's room, having a weapon would only increase his chances of being shot.

Muttering, he dug into their luggage and found the portable scanner Knight had outfitted them with before they'd left Baltimore. He shoved it into one of the deep pockets of his satin-lined tuxedo trousers and headed for the balcony. He tried not to think about just how badly it would hurt to smack into the water so many stories below as he hoisted himself up onto the slippery railing. His knuckles were white as he gripped the thick partition that he would need to swing around to reach Armen's balcony.

He was beginning to wish Zane had objected to this plan.

Ty took a deep breath, dug his fingers under the slight lip at the edge of the partition, and swung his foot out over open air. He threw the weight of his body with it, knowing the railing on that side would be just as slippery and damp as his side was and hoping to propel himself over it rather than bouncing off of it and toppling into the sea.

The strategy worked, sort of.

It wasn't nearly as difficult as he'd imagined it would be, and he went sailing over the balcony and landed in an ungraceful heap on the deck.

He popped to his feet and looked around, straightening his shirt and nodding. "I'm okay," he said to the deck chairs. He cleared his throat and tried not to laugh at himself, glad that this was a solo mission. Zane would never have let him live it down if he'd seen that nimble bit of action.

He headed for the glass doors of the balcony, confident that they'd be unlocked. No one ever locked their balcony doors, trusting in gravity to keep intruders out. So he was nonplussed when he found the glass sliding door not only locked but barred with a piece of wood.

"Son of a . . ." He looked around for something to counter the low-tech obstacle. He didn't want to leave evidence of his being here, so throwing a piece of furniture through the door was not a good idea. He slipped out his knife and knelt in front of the door, sliding it through the crack and easily tripping the lock. He was able to get the door open an inch or so, but then the piece of wood stopped it. It appeared to be a thick cord of balsa wood, most likely taken from a piece of decorative furniture in the suite. Ty slipped his hand through the crack and pushed with all his strength, levering himself against the wall. Nothing budged for a moment, save for perhaps a tendon or two in his elbow that wasn't supposed to stretch that way, but then the wood gave in to the pressure. It didn't so much snap as it imploded, bursting into little shreds and causing the door to fly open. Ty pitched forward as soon as the door was no longer there to take his weight and fell face-first into the deck. Again.

He pushed himself up with a grumbled "I hate this case" and crawled into the stateroom.

Zane settled back into his seat after a small smile at Norina and reached for his water glass. Bianchi waved down a waiter, who promised to bring more drinks immediately, as well as their salads. Zane wondered if he'd have to come up with any sort of ploy to keep Armen here, since they were literally starting dinner.

"Mr. Porter, could I trouble you a moment?" Armen's voice broke into Bianchi's ongoing monologue about the relative benefits of wine and a middle-aged man's health.

Zane glanced at Armen, curious. "Sure."

"If you're not going to enjoy that Scotch, it's a shame for it to go to waste," Armen said. He sounded a little harried.

With a small shrug, Zane waved a hand at it. "Be my guest."

Armen nodded his thanks and picked up the lowball glass from in front of Zane, immediately taking a strong slug out of the glass. Zane watched, somewhat intrigued. He didn't remember ever seeing Armen drink, even during the poker games.

When he set the glass down, he actually smiled wanly at Zane. "Such business often causes me undue stress," he explained, almost embarrassed to admit it. Zane blinked at him but offered him a benign smile.

Their salads arrived a few minutes later; ten minutes had passed since Ty left. Zane joined in a new conversation as Norina talked about upcoming dance classes on board, but he kept an eye on Armen, who started fidgeting slightly. And it had to be a trick of the subtle lighting in the restaurant, because when Armen abruptly dropped his salad fork, Zane would have sworn the man was pale and sweating.

"Mr. Armen, are you all right?" Zane asked with a frown.

Armen cleared his throat twice before pushing back from the table. "I'm afraid I'm not feeling well. Please . . . excuse me," he said softly, and even as Zane said, "Wait," he was up and moving woodenly out of the restaurant.

"I hope he is not seasick," Norina said.

Zane shook his head. It had only been about twenty minutes. Not enough time. Now Armen and his two trailing bodyguards were on their way back to his cabin, and Zane had no way to warn Ty.

"I think I'm going to go check on Del before the entrées arrive," Zane murmured, placing his napkin next to his nearly untouched salad as he stood.

"Hurry back. You do not want your dinner to get cold. And bring my Del back with you!" Norina bid him. Zane nodded as he walked away, hoping he could catch up enough to follow Armen back to his stateroom—Zane could shoulder his way in past the bodyguards if he had to.

If Ty needed him, he would be there.

Ty sat behind the large desk in one part of the suite, flipping through documents and reading over them quickly. He was using the portable scanner to make copies of some of the papers, but he knew he didn't have time to copy every one. He was trying to glean critical information and determine which ones might be pertinent while keeping an ear toward the front of the suite.

His head jerked up when he heard a scratching at the door, then the distinctive sound of the key card being swiped. He glanced around the stateroom furtively, looking for a place to hide. There was no way he'd get out the door and around the balcony partition in time without being seen.

He ducked behind the desk and cursed inwardly when he realized there was no back to the damn thing. He saw a pair of legs enter the stateroom and several more in the hallway. Armen and his bodyguards.

Ty turned and put his back to the side of the desk, momentarily out of sight. But as they moved around the room, they would quickly catch sight of him. He peered around the corner and counted three men. Armen was yanking at his tie in obvious displeasure. Maybe he hated wearing tuxedos as much as Ty did.

"It is stuffy," Armen muttered to one of his bodyguards, and the man went over to the thermostat to adjust the temperature accordingly.

"You seem ill," one of the men commented, but his accent was so thick Ty wasn't quite sure if that was what he said or not. The thug began to walk around the sofa, bringing him alarmingly close to Ty's hiding place. Ty ducked away, commando crawling behind the desk and peering around the other side. Armen sat on the side of his round bed, the side that didn't look like the end of the bed, anyway, and he was facing away from Ty. One of the bodyguards had disappeared into the bathroom, and the other was facing away as well, apparently giving his boss some modicum of privacy. Ty took the chance and crawled across the floor to the bed, intending to slide under it before he remembered that the damn thing was on a solid pedestal. He resisted the urge to curse and hugged to the expensive carpet, rolling as close as he could to the side of the bed as he heard one of the three men begin to move around the stateroom.

The comforter almost covered him, but he was still just some dude sprawled on the floor if any of the men decided to walk around to that side of the bed.

He held his breath, waiting.

"I am overtired. Perhaps the expensive Scotch Mr. Porter shared does not agree with me," Armen muttered finally. "All is well. Please leave me," he ordered in the same monotone voice he'd always spoken in.

Ty frowned. Mr. Porter was Zane. He had shared his Scotch with Armen? Ty didn't even try to ponder that one. He listened as the two men muttered obediently, and Ty counted to ten before he heard the door shut behind them.

He remained where he was, frowning heavily and breathing shallowly, straining his ears so he could hear Armen's movements.

But the man wasn't moving. He wasn't even shifting around on the bed. Ty made a slow count of ten again; then he pushed himself up and raised his head over the bed. Armen was still sitting where he'd been, shoulders slumped, head down. As Ty watched, he raised his head and took in a deep, seemingly painful breath.

What the hell was wrong with him?

His breathing became more labored, and he pressed a hand to his chest just before his body seemed to collapse inward and he toppled forward to the floor. Ty shot up and slid over the bed before he thought better of it, landing next to Armen's prone form on the other side of the bed.

"Armen?" Ty whispered as he put a hand to Armen's neck. The man merely gurgled in response.

Ty quickly rolled him over and stretched his arms above his head, taking note of how wrong his body felt. He was completely limp, devoid of any muscular control. Ty gripped his hand, and his fingers were icy cold to the touch. He blinked rapidly up at Ty, but then even the blinking stopped. There were no facial tics or movements, nothing to indicate the man was still alive. His eyes were so dilated that the normally coffee-colored irises were completely black. His entire body was soaked in sweat. Ty bent his head to listen and could hear faltering, rasping breaths. The pulse at his neck was thready, and even as he checked for it, Armen's body began to twitch all over, the muscles jumping.

Ty certainly wasn't an expert, but he knew poison when he saw it. Syncope and paralysis, respiratory distress, dilation of the pupils, profuse perspiration. And one last stuttering breath before the body went completely still.

Ty winced and shook his head as he sat down hard and looked down at Armen's body helplessly. Ty was familiar with poisons and silent ways of killing. He was almost certain he'd used this one himself a time or two. The culprit was probably a Calabar bean, a native of Africa. Half a bean would be lethal, but to act so quickly it had to have been several, ground up and slipped into something to hide the subtle taste.

Fear gripped him suddenly, so strong it nearly made him sick. Armen had shared a glass of Scotch with Zane.

Ty left Armen where he'd fallen, knowing the man was past help. He shot out the balcony door, barely thinking to close it behind him, and he didn't take as much care as he probably should have as he stood on the railing of the balcony to Armen's stateroom and swung himself around the partition. But he couldn't afford to be careful when Zane might already be dying from the same poison that had killed Vartan Armen. It could be treated with atropine with varying success, but the best thing to do was vomit it up. Violently. He had to get to Zane now if he'd had as big a dose as Armen.

He might already be too late.

He landed on the floor of the balcony with a heavy thump, and he barged in through the balcony doors. Luckily they weren't latched, or he would have merely gone through the glass to get inside.

"Ty!"

There was Zane, striding toward him, looking intent and upset, but breathing and not yet paralyzed. Ty didn't think, he merely pounced on Zane and hugged him tightly as his heart pounded from fear and adrenaline. He closed his eyes and let himself just soak in the warmth and the scent of Zane's body next to his. He'd been so panicked he'd almost unconsciously convinced himself he'd never be able to do this again. Zane's arms were just as tight around him, and after a long moment, he realized Zane was actually talking to him.

"—was no way I could let you know to get out of there," Zane was saying, lips moving against Ty's ear and hair.

Ty pulled his head back and looked at Zane almost frantically.

"What? No, shut up—stop talking. Did you drink anything?"

"What? Drink anything? We all had drinks with dinner," Zane said as he clasped Ty's upper arms. "Why? You're practically freaking out."

"Did you drink your drink, Zane?" Ty nearly shouted, grabbing Zane in the same manner and shaking him violently.

"Jesus! No! What the fuck? I told you I wouldn't drink anymore if I didn't absolutely have to!" Zane exclaimed, hurt clear in his voice.

Ty took Zane's face in his hands and shook his head, struck speechless with relief. He allowed a moment to calm himself before trying to explain, and finally he just came out with, "Armen's dead."

Zane's confusion was clear, but he didn't snap at Ty about it. "How?" He stepped back enough to look Ty up and down. "You're okay?"

Ty shook his head. "I didn't kill him! He came back from dinner before I got out, talking about not feeling well and having shared your Scotch. Then he dropped dead in his room. Classic poisoning. I thought . . . Are you sure you're okay? You didn't even have a sip?"

Zane cupped one of Ty's cheeks in his palm. "Not even a sip. Came close, but there was a very distracting attraction out on the dance floor." Ty hugged him again in relief. Zane huffed quietly but pulled him close for several deep breaths before starting to relax. "As great as this is, we've got problems, baby."

"Big problems," Ty agreed without letting Zane go. "Armen's dead because he drank your drink. So not only was he not the one trying to kill us, but someone's still fucking trying to kill us!" He pulled back and looked Zane over yet again to assure himself that he was fine. He nodded grimly. Zane was right: they had work to do. "And the Bianchis are either guilty, or they're in danger too."

"Or dead on the goddamn dining room floor," Zane said, his voice rough. "Bianchi drinks like a fucking fish." Then he crossed his arms. "Wait. If Armen drank my drink, and it was the one that was poisoned, then Bianchi would already be down," he said, looking at his watch. "We had those drinks almost from the time we sat down, and Armen didn't take mine until a good ten minutes after you left. But he took off really quickly after you. Call it . . . five minutes onset, maybe fifteen minutes to death?"

Ty closed his eyes and waved his hands through the air. "Stop doing math!" he shouted as he grabbed his jacket and moved around Zane to head for the door. "Come on, we have to find them."

"I left them in the dining room waiting on the entrées," Zane said as they practically ran out of the stateroom.

Zane didn't even think to slow down as he and Ty ran through the promenade, skidding around Christmas trees and dodging through groups of people. He knew Ty was beside him, and they both knew what had to be done: find the Bianchis. As he swung around the last corner before the restaurant, Zane found himself hoping Lorenzo and Norina were both breathing and innocent. For criminals, they were pleasant company, rather unusual in Zane's hardcore Miami drug scene experience.

Neither he nor Ty stopped moving when they entered the restaurant. After noting the absence of screaming, EMTs, or any other unusual excitement, Zane immediately scoped out the left side of the restaurant from where he stood inside the door, spotted Bianchi at the bar without any trouble, and cut past the hostess. Zane sensed Ty heading off in the other direction; he knew without asking that he was going after Norina.

Zane reached the bar and set a hand on Bianchi's shoulder.

"Signor Bianchi?"

Bianchi turned, a wide smile on his face. "Ah, Mr. Porter, you must have hurried to return to us so quickly from checking on your Del. Scotch?" he asked, holding up a bottle.

"Not yet, thank you," Zane said smoothly as he reached out to take the proffered flask. He watched Bianchi carefully, looking for a tell. Was the man trying to poison him? "I'll wait for dessert, I think."

"A sound idea," Bianchi said, sounding approving. "Bring it to the table, and we'll all finish the bottle off."

Zane nodded slowly, and movement over Bianchi's shoulder caught his attention. He glanced up to see two men in ill-fitted suits walking along the bar toward them. The men were totally focused on him and Bianchi, and Zane's instincts went on alert. He'd have to take a risk.

"Listen to me. Armen is dead."

Bianchi's eyes instantly went comically wide—it was about as natural a reaction as Zane had ever seen. "Dead?" he asked, aghast.

"Yes. Poisoned," Zane said, nodding to the bottle.

Bianchi yanked his hand back from it like it had burned him. "But . . . but we ordered our drinks from the bar, all of us!" Then Bianchi flinched. "What about my Norina?" he said urgently, sliding off the bar stool and standing. "She had drinks as well!"

Zane took his arm to keep him from hurrying off. "To your right, do you know those men?"

"Men? What men? What do I care about men? My Norina!" Bianchi babbled. It was pretty damn clear to Zane that the man wasn't involved in any poisoning.

"Del is with her. Lorenzo," Zane said, trying to hold the man's attention as the two men drew closer. To Zane's eye, they looked like some kind of law enforcement. "The men behind you."

Bianchi glanced over his shoulder and shook his head. "No. No, I don't know."

Zane gripped Bianchi's arm to hold him in place. "Stand up," he ordered.

Bianchi glanced at him, looking wild around the eyes, but he obeyed just as the two men stopped in front of them. Their smiles weren't particularly pleasant looking.

"Signor Bianchi?" the blue suit asked with an obvious Italian accent.

Bianchi cleared his throat nervously and glanced to Zane, who nodded slightly. "Si, sono il signor Bianchi."

"Deve venire con noi," the blue suit said flatly.

"Cosa? Perchè? Chi siete?" Bianchi asked. Zane wasn't sure what they were saying, but he knew what con noi was: come with us.

"Ci sarà tempo dopo per le domande. Ora venga con noi," the beige suit said as he slid his hand into his jacket.

Zane didn't hesitate. He surged forward to grab the man's arm and elbowed him in the throat, sending the man to the floor choking and gasping, too focused on trying to breathe to attempt to draw a weapon. The blue suit grabbed Bianchi, but a harsh kick to the back of the suit's knee and a left cross shoved him off as people around them gasped and jerked away from their tables, starting a commotion. Zane pulled at Bianchi's arm to get him moving away from the bar as the beige suit started to climb to his feet.

"That's what you get for hanging me over a railing, you dick!" Ty called out in triumph over the chaos of the gawking diners.

Hearing that crow, Zane located his partner in the bustling crowd and steered Bianchi in that direction. Bianchi hurried to Norina— Ty was dragging her along with him—and swept her into a hug with a spate of worried Italian. Zane turned to look around them. The milling patrons blocked the way to the door, and he cast around for another exit they could use before the threat or the crew closed in.

"Kitchen," he said to Ty as he pulled at Bianchi again. "Time to go before the suits get froggy again."

"Froggy?" Bianchi said blankly.

"Just go!" Zane urged as he pushed the man and his wife ahead of him.

Ty wrapped an arm around Zane and hugged him excitedly. "You knocked that bastard on his ass," he said gleefully. "God, that was great!"

"What happened to your accent?" Norina demanded of him as she was shuffled along.

"That's what you're worried about right now?" Ty asked her incredulously.

"Where's our gun?" Zane asked.

"You don't have it?" Ty asked blankly, and Zane swore under his breath as shouts and angry screams from behind them signified that the men who must be Ty's Dolce and Gabbana were in pursuit.

They pushed through the double doors into the industrial kitchen, garnering odd looks from employees inside as they hurried through the walkways, dodging wait staff, trays, and carts of dirty dishes. They'd reached a service door in the back when Zane glanced back across the kitchen to see Dolce and Gabbana thump through the doors and run straight into a passing busboy. All three of them crashed to the floor in a comic display.

Ty shouldered open the employee entrance and tumbled out into the corridor, only to put on the brakes and throw his arms out wide to prevent the rest of them from following. "Back, back!" he cried, right before a gunshot pinged off the top of the metal doorway. Norina let out a shrill yelp as she fell back against Zane, and he pulled her back into the kitchen. Ty and Bianchi were with them as Zane turned them down an aisle running along the back of the large kitchen, keeping the bulk of the cabinets, stoves, and prep area between them and Dolce and Gabbana. They didn't have much time, though. Whoever was out in the hall would be behind them, and fast.

Zane almost ran past the elevator but caught the edge of the door to stop himself. He motioned to Bianchi and Norina. "Move!" he ordered, pushing them when they stopped just inside the threshold.

"There is not room!" Bianchi huffed as he tried to wedge himself between two large laundry carts. He pulled Norina as close as he could, barely getting her inside. Zane was able to edge just inside the wall next to the controls, but the rest of the service elevator was full.

Zane glanced out at Ty. "Get in here," he urged as he reached up to grab the strap that would close the metal gate and heavy doors.

Ty reached up, grabbed the solid metal bar above the gate, and swung himself up over the service cart to drop into one of the laundry trolleys with an oomph. As soon as he let go of the bar, Zane had the gate shut and slammed his fist against the button, sending the elevator creaking slowly upward.

For a long minute, the only sound was the metal gears grinding as the elevator worked, and Zane craned his neck to look back at Ty. He had to snort; Ty had his feet kicked out, crossed at the ankles, and his hands laced casually behind his head as he lounged on top of the mess of laundry.

"You are not Corbin and Del Porter," Bianchi said with an obvious certainty.

"Turns out that's good for you, so don't knock it," Zane said shortly as he looked up through the grating above them into the dark elevator shaft. It wasn't likely any of their pursuers would know where the elevator went, so he and Ty would have a legitimate chance to get the Bianchis to something resembling safety before tracking down ship's security.

"You are not my good friend Del?" Norina said in a small voice. "But you tango so well!"

"Yes, you tango so well," Zane parroted, looking back at his partner. "How is that, by the way?"

"Don't start with me, Garrett," Ty mumbled. He turned a sincerely apologetic look on Norina. "It's a long story. I'm sorry."

She bit her lip, obviously upset, and then turned in what little room she had and whacked him in the head with her designer purse. Zane laughed aloud, drawing a glare from his partner and a sniff from Norina.

The elevator creaked to a stop, and the lurch caused Ty to flail and lose his balance. He fell between the piles of dirty linens he'd been perched atop. As he cussed and struggled to climb out of the laundry bin, the doors cranked open noisily.

Zane grinned at Ty for a moment before carefully peering out of the elevator, checking both sides. The hallway was empty, and he didn't hear any running footsteps. "Looks clear. Let's go. We need to find security and get you two somewhere safe."

"But what is going on?" Norina started demanding as they hurried down the passageway to a set of fire doors.

"A little help back here!" Ty called after them just as a crash sounded from within the elevator and Ty crawled out from between the doors, covered in towels and pillowcases. "I'm okay," he muttered as he struggled to his feet and jogged to catch up with them. When he reached them, Norina rewarded him with another smack, just for good measure.

"Who are those men?" she demanded of them all.

"Two of them are Italian police, my gioia," Bianchi said apologetically.

"Oh, Lorenzo, how did they find us?" Norina asked.

"I'm betting on Armen," Zane said as they reached the doors. "Not that we can ask, now, considering."

"Why not?" Norina asked. She looked around at the three men who stood silently around her, and she paled.

Zane shook his head and opened one of the doors carefully. It opened into one of the smaller lobbies off the gaily decorated promenade. He didn't see anyone but passengers, and he gestured for the others to follow him out. "Stay close," he warned them. "We don't know where those guys will pop up, and we have no idea who the second set of shooters is."

"I would rather deal with Dolce and Gabbana than the guys with guns," Ty claimed.

"It is not Dolce and Gabbana!" Norina cried as she waved her purse threateningly. "White ostrich leather Hobo, it is the only one of its kind, and look! Ruined because of your face!"

"I'm sorry!" Ty cried helplessly, holding up his hands to ward off more attacks.

"Not helping!" Zane hissed at them, and Bianchi managed to calm Norina enough to save Ty another whack over the head with the ostrich leather.

They filed out, trying to act casual. Zane led the way back into the promenade, though they stayed to the far side against the wall, moving toward the main staircase and elevator that would take them up toward the bridge. That was the only place Zane could think of where they'd be sure to find real security with firearms. They couldn't just grab any random crewmember to get effective help, and a frantic phone call wouldn't help either.

By the time they made it to the central entry to the promenade, Zane had calmed enough to be able to start thinking further ahead. They'd have to get on a satellite phone to call in. They'd need to get jurisdictional approval, and as much as he hated it, what passed for the local officials would have to be involved, at least to shut down their attackers.

As they stopped at the foot of the staircase, Zane glanced around them and turned to look right at a man raising his arm to point a gun at him.

"Down!" Zane exclaimed, grabbing Bianchi's and Norina's heads and dropping to the floor just as the gunshot rang out and ricocheted behind them. Screams rang out through the gallery, and Zane chanced a look at their attacker, only to have to duck immediately as the man shot at him again. This time the bullet clanged off the metal embedded in the staircase wall.

"Out, out, out!" Zane urged, pushing Bianchi toward the door that would let them out onto the open-air deck.

Zane could hear Ty complaining as he brought up the rear. "If that bastard shoots at me one more time I'm gonna shove that gun up his—"

"Right!" Bianchi called out as he grabbed Norina's arm and pulled her in the direction Zane pointed, heading for the bridge just as Zane wanted. What Zane didn't want was for the man to barrel right into a group of vacationers who squawked and hollered, slowing their progress as Norina tried to apologize and help people up.

"Take her and go," Zane said as Ty stopped at his side. Ty grabbed Norina by the hand and began jogging on ahead. As they hurried off, Zane yanked a profusely apologetic Bianchi away from the women now laughing the accident off. "Not the time!" he insisted, pushing the Italian ahead of him. Bianchi followed Ty and Norina around the corner to a deck walkway that ran along the length of the ship, and Zane paused to look behind them. He saw three men run out of the promenade and start searching the crowd, and Zane let out a slow breath. They might have dodged a bullet again . . . until the group of ladies Bianchi had steamrollered pointed in his direction. One of the men yelled at him, but Zane turned on his heel and ran after the others.

After a half minute's hard run, he was close on Bianchi's heels and chanced a glance over his shoulder as they ran along the deck on the port side of the ship, still in the public areas. The thugs chasing them hadn't pulled their guns and shot at them again, probably because of the mass of people enjoying the music and nighttime activities along the open decks. But every time Zane checked, they were losing ground, and he wasn't sure just how far they'd be able to run.

Norina yelled something in Italian, and Zane turned his attention back to where he was going: inside and up a flight of stairs, rather than the wide, open-air staircase that would skyline them by the large swimming pool, now open to the moon in the warmer Caribbean weather. Good thinking on Ty's part, leading them into some kind of shelter. Zane just hoped it didn't dead-end them.

They pounded up the stairs, climbing two decks before the next exit. When Zane skidded through the fire door, Ty, Bianchi, and Norina were waiting for him.

"Block it," Ty ordered, winded but not gasping for breath like the poor Italians. He was already moving to a heavy teak lounge chair to try and block the door, but he cursed creatively when he discovered the chairs were bolted to the deck. Zane checked the door and heard the thuds of heavy treads on the stairs. "We've got to move now," he said as he tried to recall the layout of the ship's decks. "Go left and outside, we should be able to cut through a passenger deck to get back to the promenade and up to the bridge."

Ty reached for him and pushed him on to take the lead. Then he turned to the woman. "Norina, give me your shoes," he demanded.

"They are not your size!" Norina protested as she stepped away from Ty.

"I'm not going to wear them!" Ty shouted at her in frustration.

"They are alligator skin Manolo—"

"Give him your shoes!" Bianchi urged as he reached down to yank them off her feet.

Ty took them and shoved one of them under his jacket. Zane knew his partner was dying for a weapon, but he'd have to settle for alligator skin stilettos and taking up the rear guard. Zane took off for the door and ran back out into the night and took the left turn, cutting through the open-air sitting area of a closed coffee shop, heading for another door set into the bulkhead. He stopped in front of this, catching his momentum and weight on one hand, and pulled at the door handle.

Locked.

"Oh come on," Zane growled. He starting digging in his pockets for his key card. Norina and Bianchi stopped beside him.

"That is a fire hazard," Bianchi commented after pulling on the handle himself.

Zane snorted, found his card, and skimmed it through the reader next to the door. The little box blinked red.

A series of crashes and bangs followed them, accompanied by the odd melody of off-tune Christmas carols being played by a mechanical decoration. Soon Ty rounded the corner, skidding in his expensive Italian leather dress shoes. He had managed to keep his tuxedo shirt tucked in, but it was no longer buttoned. Zane snorted. Just like Ty to find a way to show off his chest as they were being chased by armed men across a cruise ship. He glanced over his shoulder, laughing under his breath at whatever blockade he had managed to devise.

"Did you buy us a little time?" Zane asked. "We need it. Can't get in the door. Come on," he said, taking Norina's elbow and turning her back to the deck. "We need to find another way in."

"I am wishing I joined the aerobics class now, my gioia," Bianchi huffed as they took off again. Norina's tinkling laughter was lighter than Zane expected to hear, considering they were pretty much running for their lives.

They came upon a maintenance door, which was also locked, but before Zane could try the key card, Ty barked at him to move aside. Zane had barely managed to sidestep out of the way before Ty threw himself, shoulder first, against the edge of the door. The door was heavy, solid metal, but the doorjamb was not. Norina screamed and clapped her hands over her mouth, and Bianchi shouted wordlessly in surprise as the doorjamb splintered under the assault. Ty gave the door a hard kick, but it wasn't quite enough. He took a step back and then kicked the door again.

It fell open with a groan of protest.

"Go," Zane said, pushing Bianchi and Norina toward the doorway. "It's got to lead to an inner hallway." As they moved, he looked Ty over quickly. "Okay?"

Ty grunted at him, rubbing at his upper arm as he followed the Bianchis upward. Zane pushed the door shut behind them, but it wouldn't latch. They were in some sort of mechanical room. Lights blinked all over the walls, and wires threaded everywhere.

Norina was already at the far end of the room, opening a door that led back out onto the deck.

"No, we want to be inside. We have to get to the bridge," Zane called out, turning in a circle, looking for another door. But there wasn't one.

"Out's better than trapped," Ty argued, pointing at the door and moving toward it. He scanned the room as he went. "Anybody know enough about electronics to do damage with any of this stuff?"

Zane shook his head. There wasn't time. Bianchi shrugged and looked around the room.

"Let us go!" Norina whispered urgently, and she opened the door to peer out. Bianchi and Ty were close on her heels.

They exited back on deck, now a little farther down the side of the ship. They weren't but fifty yards from the stern now, and doors were getting scarce.

"You ever watch horror movies and bitch at the girl for running upstairs instead of out?" Ty was saying to no one in particular as they edged cautiously along the outer deck. Zane knew what he meant, because they were doing the equivalent: heading up where they'd be easily trapped if they couldn't find another way down.

Looking down at the ocean far below was a dizzying experience from this height. Zane swallowed hard, turned his back to the water, and glanced back the way they came. Hopefully the pursuers would follow through the mechanical room and lose time instead of staying on deck and closing in fast. When he heard loud footfalls, he turned to chase after the others.

When he made the next turn, Zane skidded to a stop. Bianchi, Norina, and Ty all stood in the middle of an open sitting area sheltered under an overhang, and there was no other exit except the way they had come, the way their pursuers were blocking.

Bianchi and Norina were holding close to one another, backing toward the railing as Ty stood in front of them holding two alligator skin stilettos, as if he could protect the two people behind them when they were attacked. Zane wouldn't put it past Ty Grady to be lethal with a pair of high heels in close quarters. But the men chasing them weren't interested in sparring. They'd shoot first.

Ty met Zane's eyes, and it was obvious even before he said anything that they'd finally hit the end of the line. There was nowhere to run.

Behind him, Zane could hear the men chasing them, shouting and banging around inside the mechanical compartment. They'd blocked the door as best they could, but it wouldn't hold them long. He hurried over to his partner.

Ty looked up at the awning, then behind them at the railing. He shook his head. "Only way out is down," he said breathlessly. He looked at Zane. "We have to jump."

"Jump to where?" Zane asked in disbelief.

Ty gripped his arm hard and pulled him toward the railing. "The pool is down there. We're lucky—they have the roof retracted for the warm weather," he said as he peered over. When Ty spoke again he was yelling, giving orders to Norina and Bianchi. "Gather the cushions off these loungers, toss them over. Try to hit the water," he barked as he tossed the shoes aside and began doing the very thing he'd told them to.

Zane watched as Ty yanked the first thick cushion off one of the loungers and tossed it like an over-sized discus over the railing. He didn't wait to see where it landed but hurried to the next chair. Bianchi soon moved into action to help him, his frightened wife following at his heels.

"But I do not understand!" she said as she struggled with one of the heavy cushions. "Why must we do this?"

"You've got to disperse the weight when you hit water from this high up, or you'll go straight to the bottom just as if you were hitting concrete," Ty answered as he tossed another of the cushions over the railing. He turned to Norina and grabbed her hand, pulling her toward the railing.

"Wait!" she cried, and she yanked away from him and gathered her heels and her ruined purse. She slid the shoes on and straightened her shoulders. "I will go as a lady should," she claimed bravely. "In patent leather heels."

Ty actually cracked a smile as he pulled her to the railing. "When you jump, make sure you aim for a cushion."

She looked over the railing and immediately turned her head and put her fingers over her mouth, closing her eyes. Zane thought his heart might stop. They'd be falling three decks or so down to the pool.

"Come, Norina. Just think of the cliff diving," Bianchi said in a shaky voice as he helped her climb up to sit on the railing. He kissed her hard and fast, and as she started to speak rapidly in Italian, he threw her off the side. Ty and Bianchi both watched her fall, making certain she hit the cushions like she was supposed to. Listening to her thin wail and the distant splash that followed, Zane flinched as Bianchi thumped Ty's shoulder and then leaped off the railing as well.

Zane heard the next splash and hurried back across the deck to check the walkway. He was just in time to see men bust out of a door and slide into the railing of the side of the ship, almost pitching over. But then they righted themselves and got to moving.

"Fifty yards and closing," Zane said, his pulse pounding as he slowly walked backward, watching the hunters approach.

"Come on, Garrett," Ty urged in a low, tense voice. When Zane finally looked to him, Ty was straddling the railing, holding his hand out. But Zane couldn't make himself move. He could already feel himself falling as he looked at Ty, and he distantly admitted to himself that he was scared out of his mind.

Ty waited a few heartbeats; then he slid off the railing, crossed the ten feet between them, and took Zane's hand. He didn't pull at him, though. "Come on, Zane. There's no other way. Please."

Zane had to force the words out as he gripped Ty's hand like the lifeline it was and stared at his lover. "I can't," he breathed. He would have backed away like he had at the cliffs, but he could hear the pounding footsteps approaching.

Ty's eyes darted to look over Zane's shoulder, and Zane knew what he was seeing without having to turn. They didn't have much time. Those hazel eyes he was so familiar with turned back to him, pleading and anxious. "Please, baby. I don't want to die up here with you," he said with a weak laugh.

"No," Zane said painfully. The thought of him being the cause of Ty's death was too much to handle, and he balked. He pried his shaking hand loose from Ty's and pushed at him gently. "Go jump. Now."

"Fuck you, Garrett. I'm not leaving you up here," Ty growled as he took Zane's hand again. This time he did pull at him. Despite Zane's size, Ty's strength was hard to fight, and Ty got him to move three jerky steps to the railing. "If I have to push you over I will, but then you won't be able to aim and you'll break a leg and I'll never hear the end of it," Ty grumbled at him almost under his breath as he looked behind them at the three-story drop.

Zane wrapped his free hand around the railing in a death grip. "I'm sorry, Ty," he whispered as he met Ty's worried gaze. Visions of falling warred with the sight of Ty nearly begging him to jump, and for a moment Zane thought he might be sick right then and there.

The first ill-advised shot sent through a decorative grating rang out, pinging off the awning above their heads. Ty ducked instinctively, but he didn't take his eyes off Zane. Ty's eyes had always been easy for Zane to read, and now Ty was desperate and scared and not trying to hide it. He put one hand on Zane's cheek, squeezing Zane's fingers with the other. "Zane," he whispered brokenly. He hesitated, his mouth working but no sound coming out. Another shot, this one closer and slightly more accurate, had them ducking together as sparks from the metal railing showered them. Their pursuers were moving cautiously in case their quarry was armed, but time was running out.

"Zane," Ty repeated desperately as he stood and pulled Zane closer to the edge before climbing over the rail again. "I love you," he blurted, grip tightening on Zane's hand in case he tried to pull away. "Please trust me."

Zane didn't think it was possible to be shocked out of mind-numbing fear. But Ty's words shook him enough that he allowed Ty to pull and guide him, and Zane found himself climbing up to throw one leg over and straddle the railing next to his partner in a sort of fog. "I trust you," he said in a shaking voice that revealed all too much of his fear.

Ty's fingers were like a vise grip on Zane's hand. "On three," he said softly.

Behind them the men finally rounded the corner, came out into the open, and fired several quick, poorly aimed shots—though one pinged off the railing between them, causing Zane to flinch and wobble enough that he grabbed at the railing desperately, the fright blooming in his chest and blanking his mind.

"Three!" Ty shouted. He wrapped his arm around Zane's shoulder and leaned sideways, kicking off the railing at the last minute and sending them both plummeting over the edge.

The fall passed much more quickly than Zane expected. Dazed by Ty's declaration, he barely got in two breaths before suddenly the cushions were there and he slammed into the water, plunging below the surface. Despite the cushions helping to break his fall, Zane felt like all the air was knocked out of him. He gasped before he could stop himself and took in a mouthful of saline water as the momentum took him to the bottom of the pool.

He instinctively launched himself right back up, gasping and coughing as he surfaced, and he flailed helplessly for several seconds. Trying to breathe and tread water and open his eyes all at the same time was too much to accomplish when his pulse was racing and his heart was practically pounding out of his chest.

A firm grip tugged on his shoulder then just as quickly released him, and he could hear coughing and sputtering nearby as someone else struggled in the water. Screaming and shouting mingled with the rushing sound of adrenaline in Zane's ears and someone barking orders nearby.

Free of the fear that had frozen him but now literally shaking, Zane finally managed to right himself and wipe his stinging eyes so he could see Ty next to him. "Did you say that to get me to jump?" he choked out.

Ty was struggling through the water toward the edge of the pool. He looked more like a drowning puppy than the graceful swimmer Zane had seen in the ocean and pool several days ago. Ty didn't respond; he merely spit out a mouthful of water and shook his head. He threw both arms over the edge of the wall, pulling himself just enough out of the water to be able to gasp in several deep breaths. Zane got to the side of the pool as well, still trying to wrap his brain around Ty's manipulation and the obvious fact that it had been successful.

Zane was ill, angry, aghast, still scared out of his mind, desperately relieved . . . a mishmash of flaring emotions he couldn't sort out. He kept his eyes on his partner, wondering if Ty was going to respond. But Ty just stared at the deck of the pool as he rested his elbows on it, looking a little dazed.

As Zane watched, a heavy black boot stepped in front of his partner's face, causing Ty to look up at its owner. One of the ship's security officers stood above him, looking down at them with his arms crossed disapprovingly. Behind him, the Bianchis were wrapped in towels and handcuffed, two other security officers flanking them.

Ty looked up at the man for a few moments longer, then thumped his head down to his forearms in surrender.

CHAPTER THIRTEEN

Ty sat with one foot pulled up on the hard berth, his elbow resting on his knee as he stared at the sterile white walls of the holding cells. There were three of them, each separated by thick wire fencing. Ty leaned his shoulder against the wire of his cell and exhaled slowly.

"At least we're not being shot at anymore," he drawled to Zane, maintaining the British accent just because it annoyed the Italian agents and the ship's security, who were still trying to figure out who the hell they really were. And because he fucking could.

"True," Zane agreed, shifting tiredly on the small bench in the next cell. He still looked tense. "They'll clear it up soon enough and let us out of here."

Once the ship's security had gotten their shit together, the situation had settled down fast. Mostly because everyone was locked up somewhere or another, according to the various and sundry visitors they'd received to fill them in or taunt them.

Dolce and Gabbana had come by to berate them for sticking their American (maybe) noses where they didn't belong. The two goons turned out to really be Italian Guardia di Finanza, presumably assigned to shut down the Bianchis. Ty and Zane could only assume Vartan Armen really had been trying for a coup; he'd supplied the Guardia with the information they needed to bust the Italian couple. Ty was fairly sure these two wouldn't be long for their jobs after all the reports got filed.

It was possible Armen actually hadn't resorted to attempted murder, but they would never know for sure, since he was now in the ship's morgue and couldn't tell anyone what had happened. While Armen may or may not have been the guilty party where the attempts on Ty's life were concerned, the perpetrators of the scuba-diving and rock-climbing incidents might not be found, according to the captain.

Ty suspected the same men who'd been doing the shooting and chasing; it was probable they had planned to cheat the entire smuggling ring and kill them all. They weren't talking either, which left a whole lot up to conjecture about who the hell they really were and what had truly happened. They'd been locked up in the jail on Tortola, and they were being held on charges of attempted murder. They might even face charges for attempting to hijack the cruise ship, if prosecutors were feeling particularly vindictive. Ty thought for sure there would be other charges coming along as well, including smuggling, money laundering, and weapons charges pending extradition.

The captain had politely informed them that the Bianchis were on house arrest in their cabin until Dolce and Gabbana could claim jurisdiction.

Ty wondered how the hell he and Zane got stuck in the damn holding cell instead of in their luxurious stateroom with a guard at the door. When Ty had voiced that objection, the captain had politely informed them that they would remain right where they were . . . until they made port in Maryland.

They might as well get comfortable.

Ty turned his head to peer through the wire at Zane, his mouth twitching into a smirk. "McCoy specifically told me if I ended up in the brig not to call him," he said with wry amusement. "I'm not sure what annoys me more, the fact that he assumed I'd end up here, or that he was right."

Zane grimaced, but he still laughed. "But we met the challenge," he said. "He owes us—you—for that one."

"Us," Ty corrected. He nodded, looking at Zane closely. He shifted and turned, putting his fingers through the wire as he pressed his nose against it. "I know this wasn't all fun and games for you."

Zane huffed out a pained laugh. "You could say that." He glanced at Ty, disbelief clear on this face. "I still can't believe you said that to me."

Ty tapped his finger against the thick wire, the wedding band making a small clinking sound next to his ear. He smiled weakly. He had to agree, but probably not for the same reasons Zane couldn't believe it. He didn't say anything in response, hoping the smile would suffice. Zane just shook his head and looked away.

Ty released the wire partition and sat back, lounging back on the hard bed with his arm propped on his knee again. His shoulder hurt where he'd rammed the door and then hit the bottom of the pool a little harder than expected. But it was nothing compared to the tightness in his chest. His finger hurt too, but he was loath to ask someone to cut the ring off. He would miss it when it was gone. And he'd probably never wear another one that meant anything to him.

He watched the light play off the scuffed silver band.

There was nowhere to go, and they had all the time in the world to get there. It was an oddly freeing thought, one that made that tightness in his chest ease a little. He licked his lips as his thumb grazed the ring. I love you was not something he had ever really planned on telling Zane, especially not in a situation when neither of them could hide from the other. But it had come out so naturally up there on that railing he hadn't been able to stop himself. Now, he could either lie right to Zane's face and let Zane believe it had been a mere ploy to get him to jump, or he could tell him the truth. Again.

Ty was tired of hiding it.

"I have a problem, Zane," he admitted, sounding slightly surprised that he was saying it out loud, especially now, when everything seemed to be going well for their odd relationship.

Zane raised one brow. "Besides sitting soaking wet in a jail cell in the middle of the Caribbean?"

"I have to say, it's not a first for me," Ty muttered. He smiled and looked up at the ceiling, almost talking himself out of saying it. He waited a moment to make sure he truly wanted to say it, and when he spoke he had finally dropped the fake accent. "No, this is a different kind of problem."

Despite the expressed surprise from a moment ago, this time Zane's voice was more serious, with a shade of audible concern. "What is it?"

Ty bit the inside of his lip as he looked down at his hands and turned them over. They had begun to shake slightly. He could feel the nerves coursing through his body. If he told Zane, nothing would be the same. Their entire partnership would change, for better or for worse. And he knew he would get nothing out of it except the relief of coming clean.

He took a deep breath and looked up at Zane, meeting his eyes through the painted wire. Zane frowned slightly and moved closer to the fence, flattening one palm against it as though trying to get to Ty to help him.

Ty didn't reach out to touch him, knowing it would make it too hard for him to get the words out. He knew what Zane's response would be. He hadn't really thought this through—the repercussions, the ripple effects—but he rarely thought anything through before doing it. It was sort of like the first jump out of a plane. Close your eyes and take a step and hope the ground doesn't hit you too fast. Either way, you knew wind was going up your nose at two hundred miles per hour.

Falling in love or just plain falling: they were both terrifying at any speed.

He sighed heavily and lifted his chin stubbornly, meeting Zane's eyes without flinching. "I didn't say it just to get you to jump. I'm in love with you, Zane," he admitted in a calm, clear voice. "I have been for a while."

Zane's eyes widened, and the shock was clear in them. He didn't try to hide it. That, at least, was telling of the trust they'd built between them. He didn't hide his emotions from Ty much anymore. No more than Ty did from him. Zane's lips parted like he was about to say something, but nothing came out as he tipped his head slightly to one side.

"You don't have to say anything," Ty said quickly. He'd known how Zane would respond, and he'd come to terms with it. He still didn't want to hear the words, though. He couldn't meet Zane's eyes any longer, and he could feel his face warming. He looked down at his hand and turned it over. "I know you don't . . ." He shook his head and glanced up at the stark white wall across the way from his cell, starting over. "I know you care about me. That's all I need. I just figured . . . we have enough secrets between us," he continued as he looked back up at Zane and smiled nervously. "Now it's just one less."

The cascade of emotions across Zane's face surprised him; Ty didn't think he'd ever seen Zane look so startled. Zane's fingers curled into the fencing, and he nodded just slightly. "One less," he echoed softly, though his lips moved like he was starting to say something else and stopped. Then he restarted. "Why tell me that way?"

Ty shrugged one sore shoulder. "Seemed like a good idea at the time," he answered, embarrassed.

"I was pretty much blind, deaf, and scared out of my mind." Zane admitted. "But I . . . heard you."

Ty nodded uncomfortably. It was harder than he thought, knowing an admission of love in return wouldn't be coming. He was glad to have told Zane, but he sort of wanted to change the subject now.

"I guess that explains why you've not minded me being so possessive," Zane added abruptly a minute later.

Ty raised one eyebrow and shook his head. He was almost relieved that Zane hadn't tried to deny any of it and seemed to be going for a lighter, less meaningful response. He smiled gratefully. "Try that shit on land, and we'll see how I react."

Zane rolled his eyes. "I wondered how much of it was Del and how much of it was you. After a while I wasn't sure I could tell anymore."

Ty wasn't certain what to say to that, and anything else coming to mind just took them back into that territory that might end up being painful if they weren't careful. He found he was disappointed that Zane's most natural response to learning Ty loved him was to talk about their case. He watched Zane for a moment longer before turning to rest his shoulders against the wall behind him and looking down at his fingers again. In his peripheral vision, he saw Zane do the same. They sat in a somewhat tense silence until Zane spoke.

"I'm thinking I'll take my chances."

"On what?" Ty asked as he looked over at Zane with a frown.

A smile slowly pulled at Zane's lips. "Trying that shit on land."

Ty leaned away from him and turned his head to be able to see him better. He hadn't expected to hear an I love you from Zane. If he had gotten one, he probably wouldn't have believed it. But he supposed trying that shit on land—and the implication behind it that Zane wanted Ty to himself—was about as close as he'd get. The realization made him smile slowly.

"You're so easy," he told Zane in satisfaction as he looked at the plain white wall again.

"Only for you, doll," Zane drawled in his Corbin voice.

Ty sighed and ran a hand through his blond hair. "Don't ever call me that again," he warned in a tired voice. "Asshole."

Zane chuckled, visibly releasing the tension he'd been carrying in his shoulders, and he laid his head back against the wall. He didn't look at all worried. Ty watched him from the corner of his eye. All Ty had to do was keep that look on Zane's face, that one right there, relaxed and content and slightly amused. Then they'd be just fine.

"Oh, by the way," Ty murmured. "Merry Christmas, Zane."

Zane looked at him in some surprise, then glanced to the plastic clock on the opposite wall. It was just past midnight. He snorted softly. "Merry Christmas, Ty."

Ty had anticipated a barrage of questions when they reached dry land, but he had also expected a trip home, a nice shower, and some new clothing first. But there hadn't been any detours from the waterfront to the Bureau office. They were to be debriefed ASAP.

Ty sat at one of the interrogation tables—on the wrong side. They were bringing in someone to cut the ring off his finger while he wrote up his report, but they also wanted an agent to speak to him, which was unusual. He was a little nervous that he and Zane had missed something or fucked up somewhere, especially since Zane had been conducted to another room for a separate debriefing.

He tried to tamp down the nerves as he finished up his brief synopsis of what had happened on the ship. He signed the bottom of the report and pushed it away, taking a deep breath to calm himself.

The door opened, and he exhaled slowly as three men entered. SAIC Dan McCoy smiled at him and held the door open for one of the lab techs and Special Agent Scott Alston, who trailed behind him.

"Grady. Good to have you back," McCoy greeted as he seated himself across from Ty.

The lab tech rolled out a piece of gauze and extracted a pair of sharp utensils that looked like a cross between scissors and a prop from Hellraiser. Ty swallowed on an uncomfortable sense of déjà vu. The last set of utensils he'd seen rolled out in an interrogation hadn't been used to cut metal. He cleared his throat and looked away quickly, giving the tech his left hand so the man could cut the silver ring off his swollen finger.

He met McCoy's eyes as the tech began trying to work one side of the wicked scissors under the ring.

"Turned into a real shitstorm, huh?" McCoy said with a sympathetic smile.

Ty snorted. "You could say that. What the hell happened, anyway? There were people trying to kill us left and right!"

"Yes," McCoy replied slowly, nodding. "We stepped in it. Sorry."

Ty stared at him incredulously. "Sorry?"

McCoy shrugged. "It looks like you two never really got into the eye of the storm. You were more like . . . the cows who got tossed around on the outskirts."

Alston snorted and tried to cover it with a cough and a hand to his mouth.

Ty glanced between them with a frown, unamused. "I'm feeling more like a goat on this one, Mac," he growled.

McCoy held up his hands in surrender. He had a small dossier in one. "We had no way of knowing all this was going on." He slid the file across the desk to Ty. "There were four different groups at play. The feds, the Guardia di Finanza, Vartan Armen's hired thugs, and a fourth group that appears to be antiquities dealers from Dubai. Where they came from, we have no clue, but they're the ones who were trying to kill you. I mean Del."

"Why?" Ty asked dubiously as he opened up the folder.

"There is a tenuous connection between them and Armen's end of the business, and also between them and Del Porter, whose real name is not Del Porter," Alston told him. "Apparently the thieves planned to take over the smuggling ring by force. Having all three members of the ring—Vartan Armen, Corbin Porter, and Lorenzo Bianchi—in one place made staging a coup pretty easy."

"From what we're getting in interrogations, it appears their intention was to put each of the men out of commission somehow and then take their places at the final meeting on Tortola. Targeting

Del—I mean you—was intended to keep Corbin on board the cruise ship with his injured husband. They were going to let the Guardia di Finanza take care of the Bianchis. And it's anyone's guess what their original plan was for Armen.

"When they realized they weren't going to maim you so easily, they went for hardcore and tried to kill all of you."

"Awesome," Ty said sarcastically as he looked down at the typed documents. Everything Alston and McCoy had just told him was in there, and there was more.

Those men would be locked up for a long time as authorities kept adding to their laundry list of crimes.

Vartan Armen's body had been claimed by Turkish nationals, and they had departed on a flight to Istanbul. The Bureau was working with the Turkish government to investigate Armen's business, but it was slow going.

The day after the final chase, a maintenance man had found the FBI backup team locked up in a grocery storage room in the hold. They were tired, supremely annoyed, and seriously wired on pastries and sodas, but otherwise unharmed. That explained where those fuckers had been the entire time. They'd been ferreted out by Dolce and Gabbana, who had thought they were after Corbin and Del when they'd spotted the members of the team sticking too close to Ty and Zane. How they'd expected to keep their jobs, stay out of jail, and avoid an international incident by abducting and illegally detaining American federal agents, Ty didn't know.

Cruises in international waters did weird shit to people.

The Bianchis had returned to Italy with the Guardia di Finanza. Bianchi was reportedly cooperating with the Guardia to recover antiquities in exchange for leniency and immunity for Norina, who really hadn't been involved in the business except on the periphery.

Ty did regret how that had ended. He'd liked the Italian woman and had felt almost guilty for lying to her.

For her part, Norina hadn't forgiven Ty for destroying her shoes and her handbag, but she had requested a message be sent to Ty and Zane, one that thanked them for saving her and her husband's lives. The note was in the dossier, written in English so Ty could actually read it.

He snorted and smiled slightly.

"So," Alston said, interrupting his line of thought. Ty looked up at him. "Was it a king-size bed?"

"It was round," Ty answered drolly. "And if the cat jokes are going to be replaced with gay jokes, just let it be known that I don't find those funny," he added seriously.

Alston's smirk faded, and he nodded, recognizing that Ty wasn't messing around.

The sound of metal grating on metal had accompanied his words, and Ty glanced over to see the silver band finally being pulled off his aching finger. The sight of the sliced ring and the impression it left on his skin was more painful than he'd anticipated.

"Thank you," he muttered to the tech. The man nodded and handed him the wedding band. Ty palmed it and slid it into his pocket, glad McCoy didn't demand he give it back.

The interview went on for another hour or so, the questions mundane and steering far clear of anything that could have been embarrassing or damaging. Ty's attention was only half there, though. The other half was on Zane and the ring burning a hole through Ty's pocket.

Zane forced himself to pay attention to the congested holiday traffic. He was behind schedule, but at this point all he could do was drive. He drummed his thumb on the steering wheel and glanced in the rearview mirror.

He looked like himself again. His trimmed brown hair lay naturally without gel, and the earring was gone, though Zane had caught himself looking for the ruby stone a few times during the past week. Not his style, though. He wore his own tailored gray suit, a crisp white dress shirt, and a red and silver silk tie. All nice, but not pricey like Corbin Porter's extravagant wardrobe. Under the suit, the tattoo was now fading. Zane had considered having it actually inked, but then he'd thought about what Ty would say and abandoned the idea. It wasn't really his style either.

Zane had removed the last vestige of his fake persona four days after they returned from the cruise—this afternoon, actually. He was so accustomed to wearing a wedding ring that he simply hadn't thought about removing the silver one provided for the case until he'd been washing spaghetti sauce off his fingers after lunch and noticed the ring was the wrong color.

He had stood there at the sink looking at the ring for several minutes, the water running, memories of the cruise cascading through his mind. But it wasn't the casework and danger Zane remembered. It was the quiet time he and Ty had spent sitting together, relaxing. The heady, sultry sexual tension thrumming between them that they both not only allowed but fed. The laughter and the dancing and the banter and just being together.

With all that on his mind, it had felt odd—wrong, somehow—to remove the ring that connected him to Ty.

After drying his hands, he took the ring to the bedroom and the wooden keepsake box on his dresser. He opened the top with a soft snap of the magnetic clasp and saw his gold wedding ring inside, with all its dings and scratches. Zane slowly set the nearly pristine silver ring next to it before sliding his fingertips over the gold ring.

When he thought about Becky, it was more difficult to call her face to mind, and when he did, it was dim and fuzzy around the edges, faded with time. It had been more than six years since his wife had died, and though he still missed her, it didn't hurt like it used to.

Zane had closed the box, leaving both rings inside.

Then he'd looked at the small ribbon-wrapped box next to it and huffed slightly. He'd bought the compass rose pendant for Ty on a whim, and he still wanted to give it to him. He just wasn't sure . . . why. Zane's chest got tight when he thought about Ty's declaration of love, and compared to that? The pendant seemed pedestrian. Plus they'd missed Christmas while stuck in that damn holding cell, and now just handing the necklace to Ty felt silly.

Zane had left it behind as well when he grabbed his suit jacket and walked out of the apartment.

So a little over three hours later he was here, navigating through traffic into a small parking lot. Zane squeezed the truck into a space meant for a smaller vehicle, wishing that he could have ridden the

Valkyrie despite the cold but dry weather that would have nearly frozen him on the ride through town. Not only was the motorcycle more maneuverable, but it was much easier to park between cars that hogged a space and a third of stingy parking at full restaurants in Baltimore.

He hadn't ridden it because it was hard to keep a suit and tie tidy while doing so.

The popular privately owned steakhouse that was located in two old renovated row houses near Fell's Point was always jammed; New Year's Eve made it even worse. He was glad he'd thought to call and get reservations as soon as they'd gotten home.

He got in the door fifteen minutes late—not the best of ideas for a dinner reservation on a regular night, much less a holiday, but he was sure Ty would have been on time. It was one of Ty's favorite restaurants. After all the fish on the cruise ship, Zane figured a high-grade piece of beef would endear him to his carnivorous partner.

In a couple minutes one of the hostesses led him toward the back of the narrow restaurant; along the side wall ran a whole line of booths for two to four, and as he expected, Ty was facing the restaurant proper. Zane had given up the fight over who would sit with their back to a full room some time ago. Ty always proffered the argument that more people wanted to kill him, and he was right.

Ty sat diligently tearing a piece of paper into thin shreds, his knee bouncing under the table as he tried to keep himself occupied while he waited. He glanced up when he saw the hostess leading Zane toward him, and he straightened slightly, gathering the pieces of paper and crumpling them into a ball in his fist.

"Hey," Zane greeted, handing the hostess his heavy, waist-length wool coat, unbuttoning his suit jacket, and sliding into the booth across from him.

Sitting in the booth straight and tall, well-fitted suit actually pressed and his stylishly narrow tie straight, the bleached-blond hair shaved almost completely off in what was practically a scalp trim, Ty looked more like a Jarhead than Zane had ever seen him. Damn the man, he even made a shaved head look good. And he looked much more like himself. Zane was pretty sure Ty had gone somewhere and rolled around in the mud for several hours once they had gotten home from the cruise ship. That would have made him feel better.

Now Ty seemed nervous, which wasn't like him. While apart the past few days, back to their normal routine of sometimes together, sometimes apart—as wrong as it felt—Zane had worried Ty's confession of love and his conspicuous lack of response would make things awkward between them the first time they got back together. So Zane drew a settling breath as he sat on the bench and offered Ty a smile.

"I'm sorry I'm late," Zane started.

Ty nodded and leaned forward, resting his elbows on the table. "You all right?" he asked with a frown.

"Yeah," Zane said, trying not to wince. "I didn't think I'd be this late or I would have called."

"It's okay," Ty told him easily as his eyes traveled carefully over Zane, as if checking him for injuries or any undue wear and tear. Ty didn't trust Zane's motorcycle any further than he could throw it, and he knew Zane usually rode it. With that look, Zane felt a lot warmer, inside and out, than from just walking into a heated building from the cold weather outside. He tried to catch Ty's eyes. It was a little weird, this new dynamic to their partnership. Maybe he should call it an actual relationship now. Yeah. Weird. But Zane really liked it, and he smiled slowly.

"What?" Ty asked him suspiciously as he met Zane's eyes and saw the smile forming. He groaned. "What have you done now?"

Zane shook his head, just looking at his lover across the table. "I didn't do anything," he protested, amused by Ty's reaction. Now Ty knew how he felt every day when he woke up or came to work to see Ty smirking.

Ty narrowed his eyes and pointed a warning finger at Zane, obviously not believing that he wasn't up to something. Zane instantly noticed what was missing from Ty's hand, and he found himself oddly disconcerted to see the ring gone. The finger was still noticeably swollen, and Zane could guess what had happened. "They had to cut it off, huh?"

"Cut what off?" Ty asked, shoulders squaring as he sat back, almost offended.

Zane had to laugh. "Your ring."

Ty looked down at his hand. "Oh." He nodded. "Yeah, no way was it coming off without taking my finger with it."

"You sound disappointed."

Ty shrugged, and Zane could tell he was uncomfortable. "I miss it," he admitted, making Zane's stomach flip-flop. "It gave me something to do with my hands," Ty continued, holding his hand up and moving his thumb as if he were playing with a ring on his finger.

Zane snorted. Yeah, that sounded more like Ty than being emotionally attached to a piece of jewelry. Now he was kind of glad he'd left the necklace at home.

They glanced up as a server arrived with bread and the drinks Ty had already ordered.

Once the server was gone with their appetizer and entrée orders, Ty picked up his glass, which was full of soda instead of beer or champagne, and raised it to Zane with a smirk. "Here's to being us again."

Zane chuckled and lifted his goblet of iced tea to clink it against Ty's. "Hear, hear," he said. "Bon voyage, Corbin and Del Porter."

"I can't say it was fun," Ty muttered wryly as he set his glass down. He glanced up at Zane almost carefully. "Did you hear what ended up coming out of the interrogations?"

Zane knew that Corbin and Del Porter were now in New York under long-term investigation by the FBI for Corbin's extended criminal activities. He hadn't heard anything more about them, though. "No. Anything interesting?"

Ty shrugged uncomfortably, as if he wasn't sure the news was interesting or not. "Well, Del admitted he'd been hired by Armen to weasel his way into Corbin's life, seduce him and spy on him, and send out information. But in the end, he actually fell for him. He said he was told about Armen's plan to take over during the cruise, and he claims he deliberately orchestrated having himself and Corbin caught before the ship sailed to save Corbin's life." He looked up at Zane as he said the last, watching his reaction.

Zane blinked in surprise, raising both brows. "That's pretty impressive. Del didn't seem to have much of a backbone, and that would certainly take one."

"I think he fooled a lot of people. Us included," Ty said softly. "He had to have known he risked losing Corbin either way. He sacrificed himself." Ty paused, letting that sink in. What he left unspoken was clear. Del had sacrificed his freedom and his heart just to keep the man he loved safe.

Zane couldn't escape the meaning in Ty's words. "Takes a special person to do that," he said quietly.

Ty nodded and looked away. The knowledge put Del and Corbin in a different light than Zane had originally perceived. It reminded him that he shouldn't make assumptions, especially when it came to matters of the heart.

"I did finish and submit my report," Zane finally said. "Took a while to figure out what to include and what to ... edit."

"I hope you didn't edit out the copious amounts of sex," Ty said dryly. He lifted his glass to his lips as he spoke, trying to hide his smirk. "Because I took detailed notes."

Zane chuckled as he picked up his water glass. "Wouldn't that give McCoy a thrill," he said deadpan.

Ty was smiling when he set his glass down, his eyes on Zane with that same intensity Zane had been noticing more and more often. The kind that usually came right before clothing started being ripped off. It made Zane shiver even though he flushed with warmth. He tried to hold back the grin, propping one elbow on the table as he rubbed his fingers over his chin in a bid to hide some of the giddiness that threatened.

Ty looked up at Zane critically. "You're too pleased with yourself," he observed, still suspicious. "I don't like it. Stop it."

Zane blinked. He didn't think he was projecting anything. But it was getting more difficult to hide things from Ty, even if he wanted to. As for now ... damn it. Zane cleared his throat. Leave it to Ty to ferret out something before he was ready to share it.

Ty reached across the table and took his hand suddenly, squeezing it gently. Instead of letting go immediately like he usually did, though, he held on, not seeming to care who saw them in the crowded restaurant. He slid his hand up to Zane's wrist and gave it another squeeze before he let go and reached for his glass again. "It's okay," he assured Zane as he lifted the glass to his lips. "You're kind of cute when you're scheming."

Zane's stomach flipped, and he wet his bottom lip, nerves fluttering. It wasn't the gesture, or even the venue. It was the trust. "I, ah, made a New Year's resolution," he said, embarrassed that it came out a little shaky.

"Oh yeah?" Ty asked in amusement. "My last one was not to shoot anyone for a year," he told Zane ruefully as he looked down at his glass and swirled the ice around. "I'm not very good at them," he observed with a faint frown. He looked back up at Zane. "What did you resolve?"

Zane huffed out a little laugh at Ty's self-deprecating comment, but it didn't dispel the nerves. He was annoyed with himself for a moment and drummed his fingers on the tablecloth. "I resolved to take better care of myself."

Ty's eyebrows climbed slowly. "Good. Less work for me," he said, winking at Zane to ease the truth in the words.

It helped Zane relax a little, knowing Ty was in a good enough mood to tease. He reminded himself that Ty had really taken a hell of a plunge with announcing that I love you with no warning; surely a smaller admission like this wasn't that difficult. He swallowed hard. "That's why I was late," he said before adding in a little bit of a rush, "The AA meeting ran over."

Ty looked at him in true surprise, his hazel eyes wide, struck speechless for a long moment. Finally, he nodded slowly, his expression entirely serious. "That's good, Zane," he whispered. He nodded again, smiling slowly. "That's really good."

Relief flushed through Zane, and he wondered when Ty's approval had come to mean so much. He relaxed and let out a slow breath. He wanted Ty to know that he could trust his partner and that Zane cared enough about him to make an effort he hadn't made before to earn that trust. If Ty was going to love him, Zane wanted to at least be worthy of it. "Good," he repeated quietly, drumming his fingers again to loosen some of the remaining tension, inexplicably happy to have made Ty smile.

Ty looked down at Zane's right hand briefly before taking it back up with both hands and pulling it toward him. He leaned forward and kissed Zane's fingers, as if thanking him for the effort. Then he looked back up at Zane and smiled widely. For perhaps the first time Zane could remember, Ty wasn't blushing after such a display of affection in public, and his eyes weren't seeking out anyone who might be watching them. All his attention was focused on Zane.

The smile was catching. They probably looked like idiots, sitting there grinning at each other, but Zane couldn't have cared less.

Ty didn't say anything, just took his napkin and put it in his lap as he continued to watch Zane affectionately. Zane reflected upon the fact that if Ty looked at him like that more often, he'd be putty in the man's hands. That was more than a little scary, especially because it hinted at emotions within himself Zane hadn't yet found the courage to consider. He cleared his throat and thought that with Ty at his side, he might find that strength sooner rather than later.

"Happy New Year," Zane offered, lifting his glass for a toast.

Ty touched his glass to Zane's. "Happy New Year."

Looking at his partner sitting across from him, Zane thought it might just be his best year yet. He was looking forward to it.

Explore more of the *Cut & Run* series at:
riptidepublishing.com/collections/cut-run

CUT & RUN

THE SERIES

ABIGAIL ROUX

ACKNOWLEDGMENTS

Thanks must go out to Ginerva, Rae Isha, and Laura Iskra for their invaluable help and advice regarding the Italian language. Ty is not the only one who doesn't speak Italian!

And to Polly West for keeping an eye out for details when she took her well-deserved cruise and then relaying them to those of us still on land.

Dear Reader,

Thank you for reading Abigail Roux's *Fish & Chips*!

We know your time is precious and you have many, many entertainment options, so it means a lot that you've chosen to spend your time reading. We really hope you enjoyed it.

We'd be honored if you'd consider posting a review—good or bad—on sites like **Amazon, Barnes & Noble, Kobo, Goodreads, Twitter, Facebook, Tumblr,** and your blog or website. We'd also be honored if you told your friends and family about this book. Word of mouth is a book's lifeblood!

For more information on upcoming releases, author interviews, blog tours, contests, giveaways, and more, please sign up for our weekly, spam-free newsletter and visit us around the web:

Newsletter: riptidepublishing.com/newsletter
Twitter: twitter.com/RiptideBooks
Facebook: facebook.com/RiptidePublishing
Goodreads: tinyurl.com/RiptideOnGoodreads
Tumblr: riptidepublishing.tumblr.com

Thank you so much for Reading the Rainbow!

RiptidePublishing.com

ALSO BY ABIGAIL ROUX

ABOUT
THE AUTHOR

Abigail Roux was born and raised in North Carolina. A past volleyball star who specializes in sarcasm and painful historical accuracy, she currently spends her time coaching high school volleyball and investigating the mysteries of single motherhood. Any spare time is spent living and dying with every Atlanta Braves and Carolina Panthers game of the year. Abigail has a daughter, Little Roux, who is the light of her life, a boxer, four rescued cats who play an ongoing live-action variation of Call of Duty throughout the house, one evil Ragdoll, a certifiable extended family down the road, and a cast of thousands in her head.

Enjoy more stories like
Fish & Chips
at RiptidePublishing.com!

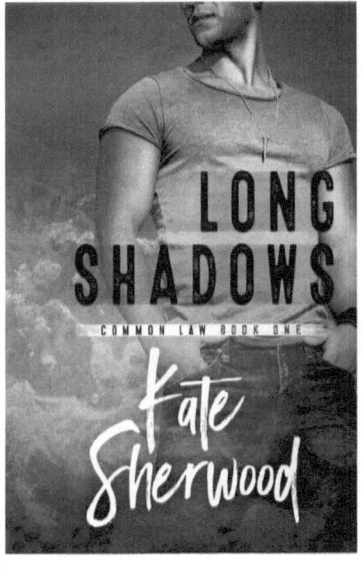

Long Shadows

Sometimes a bad decision is so much better than a good one.

ISBN: 978-1-62649-526-5

Anyone But You

Murder is one hell of a drag.

ISBN: 978-1-62649-891-4

www.ingramcontent.com/pod-product-compliance
Lightning Source LLC
Chambersburg PA
CBHW031338020726
47499CB00005B/1319